BLACK SHIP

Also by Carola Dunn

THE DAISY DALRYMPLE MYSTERIES

BLACK SHIP

A Daisy Dalrymple

Mystery

CAROLA DUNN

ST. MARTIN'S MINOTAUR

NEW YORK

BLACK SHIP. Copyright © 2008 by Carola Dunn. All rights reserved. Printed in the United States of America. For information, address St. Martin's Press, 175 Fifth Avenue, New York, N.Y. 10010.

www.minotaurbooks.com

Library of Congress Cataloging-in-Publication Data

Dunn, Carola.
    Black ship : a Daisy Dalrymple mystery / Carola Dunn. — 1st ed.
        p. cm.
    ISBN-13: 978-0-312-36307-9
    ISBN-10: 0-312-36307-9
    1. Dalrymple, Daisy (Fictitious character)—Fiction. 2. Women journalists—Fiction. 3. Police spouses—Fiction. 4. Americans—England—Fiction. 5. Liquor industry—Great Britain—Fiction.
6. Smuggling—England—Fiction. 7. Criminals—England—Fiction.
8. Nineteen twenties—Fiction. 9. London (England)—Fiction. I. Title.
    PR6054.U537B53   2008
    823'.914—dc22

                                                           2008020345

First Edition: September 2008

10 9 8 7 6 5 4 3 2 1

To my "full-service" agent,
Alice Volpe of Northwest Literary Agency, Inc.,
and to Alan (and Slick), with thanks

ACKNOWLEDGMENTS

My thanks to Scott T. Price, historian, of the U.S. Coast Guard, for the book *Rum War at Sea*, by Commander Malcolm F. Willoughby, which, with *The Black Ships* by Everett S. Allen, provided a great deal of invaluable information about rum-runners and their opponents. Thanks also to Drs. Larry Karp and D. P. Lyle for medical information; Lynne Connolly for help with Manchester speech and Kate Dunn for New England speech; Norma and Dick Huss for nautical tips; and my brother Tony for rugger and cricket details.

BLACK SHIP

ONE

A last teeth-rattling sneeze escaped Daisy as she stepped out to the front porch. The tall, spare solicitor, locking the door behind them, gave her a worried look. That is, she thought she detected anxiety, though the layer of dust on his pince-nez obscured his expression.

Having dusted off his hat, Mr. Irwin carefully settled it on his thinning hair, then took out a large white linen handkerchief to polish the pince-nez. "Oh dear, I expect I ought to have had cleaners in before I showed you the house."

Being too well brought up to voice her hearty agreement, Daisy said politely, "It wouldn't have been so bad if I hadn't taken the dust sheet off that rocking chair and wafted it about a bit." Glad she'd worn grey gloves, she brushed down her lovat green costume.

"I'm afraid the late Mr. Walsall's staff let things slide. The butler and housekeeper were as aged as he himself, having been with him for a great many years. The unfortunate condition of the interior may deter you from taking up your abode in the house; perfectly understandable."

"You said the electrical system is quite new."

"It was installed in 1910, I believe. I should not describe fifteen years as precisely new. There have been great improvements in such things in the past fifteen years."

"New enough. The building itself seems sound. No damp patches in the attics, no creaking floorboards, no smell of drains."

"Structurally," he said with obvious reluctance, "I believe the house is comparatively sound."

"I'm glad to hear it."

"Though there's no knowing what defects a surveyor might find. Dry rot, perhaps? If you decide to sell the property, I shall, of course, be happy to handle the conveyancing for you."

"But, if I understand you correctly, the way my husband's great-uncle left things, we don't inherit his money unless we live in the house. It goes to the Home for Aged Donkeys."

"Superannuated and Superfluous Carriage Horses."

"I suppose there must be a great many about, what with motor-cars and all."

"I dare say," Irwin grunted. He didn't seem any happier at the prospect of the horses getting the money than at the prospect of the Fletchers moving into his late client's house. "It is only one of several worthy causes to be benefited according to the instructions in Mr. Walsall's last will and testament, should you decline to reside in the house."

"Does that include the proceeds of the sale of the house?"

He cheered up. "No. The proceeds would be yours—your husband's—free and clear. Apart from any taxes due, naturally. So you'll be able to purchase a more suitable residence elsewhere."

More suitable? Daisy gazed across the cobbled street at the communal garden in the middle of the ring of houses. In central London, it would have been a square, but one couldn't very well call it a square, because it was round.

In the slanting sun of the late September afternoon, it was bright with neat beds of chrysanthemums and the red and gold leaves of bushes and the ring of trees that enclosed the whole.

Directly opposite her, a paved path sloped down across the lawn, levelling off to circle the marble-rimmed pool in the centre, with park benches on either side. The pool had a fountain, a marble maiden in vaguely Greek draperies holding an urn on her shoulder from which water spilled. ·

Three small children toddled about under the watchful eyes of a pair of uniformed nannies. In next to no time, Miranda and Oliver would be old enough to play with them.

"Mrs. Fletcher?" the lawyer ventured tentatively.

"Sorry, Mr. Irwin, I was thinking. Is that an alley I see between those houses down there, on the other side of the communal garden?"

"Not exactly an alley. It might better be described as a foot passage, leading down to Well Walk."

"How convenient! And where is the Heath?"

"The Heath?"

"Hampstead Heath. It can't be too far away?"

"Oh, the Heath. Just around the corner—literally. If you would care to descend the steps and walk to the corner . . ."

Running up the side of the house and garden was a cobbled alley leading to a block of carriage houses now used as garages for motors. Beyond these, the way narrowed to another foot passage ending with a gate onto a lane, and on the other side of the lane was the Heath. It couldn't be more perfect for Belinda and her friends, and for the twins when they were old enough. They'd have many of the advantages of both town and country life.

Not to mention being able to give the dog a good run without the dreary trudge through the streets to Primrose Hill. Daisy would walk Nana much more often when it was so easy, and perhaps at last she'd take off a few of those extra pounds.

"Ahem!"

Once again, Daisy apologised for her abstraction. As she pondered, she had strolled back to the foot of the steps up to the front door of number 6, Constable Circle. Now she stepped backwards to the edge of the pavement and looked up at the façade. It was an attractive place, a detached house built in the last decade of the nineteenth century of red brick, the first floor hung with matching tile in alternating bands of plain and patterned. The front porch was set back between protruding wings, and the paired gables in the tile roof had a dormer between. Four stories from semibasement to attics, it was considerably larger than their semidetached in St. John's Wood.

Now that the twins were mobile, Nurse Gilpin really had to have a nursery maid whether they moved or not. Their present house would be terribly crowded when Belinda came home from school for the holidays. Besides, poor Bel deserved more than the tiny box of a room she had nobly put up with over the summer. For Alec, the journey to Westminster would actually be easier from Hampstead when he went in by tube, not having to change at Baker Street, and by car it was very little farther. Nor would Daisy and Belinda be far from their St. John's Wood friends.

The rates were bound to be higher, plus their share of the upkeep of the garden, and Mrs. Dobson would need the help of a house-parlour maid as well as a full-time daily woman. But if they kept the house, they'd keep old Mr. Walsall's fortune, as well.

Logic told her to jump at the prospect. Then why did it make her so uneasy?

Perhaps her reluctance was just sentimental, an atavistic—was that the word she wanted?—attachment to family land, bred in the blood by her aristocratic ancestors. But, Daisy's brother having been killed in the War, the Dalrymple estate now belonged to a distant cousin. The suburban semi bought two or three decades ago by Alec's father was scarcely in the same category as Fairacres.

More likely, Daisy decided with cynical honesty, she just didn't want to face the disruption of the move. Yet if they sold, the sensible thing to do with the money would be to buy a bigger house elsewhere, which would involve hunting for one, as well as the horrors of moving.

"We'll keep it!"

"But Mr. Fletcher hasn't even seen it yet."

"He said it's for me to decide." Though Daisy might wish Alec had not left the decision to her—it was *his* great-uncle's legacy, after all—she wasn't going to acknowledge that to the solicitor.

"But . . . but—"

"I'm the one who'll be spending most of my time here, with the babies and working."

"Working!"

"Yes, Mr. Irwin, working. I'm a journalist."

"Oh. How . . . how enterprising," he said weakly. Then he rallied. "Mr. Fletcher will have to sign all the documents, of course."

"Naturally. Mr. Walsall was his relative. I'm afraid he's out of town at present, though, and I don't know when he'll be back."

"I suppose in his . . . er . . . his occupation, he is often away."

Daisy was inured to the way even the most law-abiding people looked askance at a Scotland Yard detective, not to mention his wife. The average suburban solicitor rarely, if ever, came into contact with a criminal investigation.

Mr. Irwin must have carried out his own investigation into Alec's life before approaching him about his great-uncle's will, if only to make sure he was really the heir. Old Mr. Walsall seemed to have cut off all connection with his sister's family long ago. Alec had only the vaguest memory of his mother once mentioning a rich uncle.

Naturally, Daisy was dying to know the reason for the breach.

She wouldn't dream of asking her mother-in-law, though. The elder Mrs. Fletcher would not only undoubtedly refuse to tell her, she'd make snubbing remarks about people prying into other people's business and curiosity killing cats. Which was most unfair, as what was Alec's business was surely his wife's business, and if one didn't ask questions, how was one ever to find out anything?

Daisy resolved on the spot that nothing should be allowed to suppress her own children's sense of curiosity. Besides, Alec's mother had obviously failed with him, or he wouldn't have become a detective.

"Yes, his work often takes him away. But I know he'll love the house." She looked up at it again, already with a proprietorial pride.

It was altogether a substantial house, the sort of house even her own mother could not possibly object to. The Dowager Lady Dalrymple might even consider it worthy of her spending the odd night in the spare bedroom.

Now there was a prospect that failed to please. "Oh dear!" said Daisy.

"Are you having second thoughts, Mrs. Fletcher?" the solicitor enquired hopefully. "You have time to consider, and to consult Mr. Fletcher. Mr. Walsall set a time limit for the decision, to ensure the funds reaching his chosen charities without excessive delay should you decline to live here, but he was not unreasonable. You have two months from the date Mr. Fletcher received my communication with regard to the will. I'm sure he ought to visit the house. He may take it in dislike."

"I'll ask him, but I'm sure he's much too busy. I expect Tommy—Mr. Pearson, that is, our solicitor—will want to go over the figures with you to make sure we won't be biting off more than we can chew. But assuming, as you say, that we'll have enough funds to cover increased expenses, we'll move in as soon as possible."

Mr. Irwin sighed heavily. He seemed less than thrilled by her decision. In fact, thinking back over the past hour, she suspected he had done his best to present the house in the worst-possible light, without going so far as to claim an infestation of deathwatch beetle. She could only suppose that he had hoped to profit from the conveyancing fees if they sold it.

"In that case," he said gloomily, "perhaps you would not be averse to meeting your future next-door neighbours?"

"The neighbours?" Daisy asked in astonishment. Though she had never been in precisely this situation before, she couldn't believe the duties of a solicitor included introducing neighbours to one another.

"My daughter, Mrs. Aidan Jessup, resides at number five. She and her mother-in-law expressed a wish to make your acquaintance should this situation arise, if you would be so kind as to step in for afternoon tea."

Had he told his daughter that Daisy's father had been Viscount Dalrymple? He must have found out while investigating Alec. She gave him a frosty look with eyebrows raised, one of the Dowager Lady Dalrymple's armoury of pretension-depressing weapons. Much as Daisy abhorred the possibility of becoming in any way similar to her mother, she was fed up with people whose only interest in her was the accident of her aristocratic birth.

It was even worse than their shying away on learning her husband was a detective. That, at least, had been her own choice.

The solicitor responded to her chilliness with stiff rectitude. "I've told Audrey and Mrs. Jessup only that you and Mr. Fletcher may move in next door. Any other information I may have gathered is, of course, confidential."

"Of course," Daisy said apologetically. This was the third or fourth time she'd had to apologise to him. However perfect the house, did she really want to live next door to a relative of someone who kept putting her in the wrong? "I'll be happy to make their acquaintance."

What else could she say?

The house next door was similar in style to number 6 but lacked the pleasing symmetry. A neat young parlour maid answered Mr. Irwin's ring.

"Good afternoon, Enid. Tell your mistress I've brought Mrs. Fletcher to meet her."

"Oh, yes, sir, madam told me you might." The maid admitted them to the hall, trotted off, and returned a moment later to usher them to the back of the house and into a vast, glittering room.

After a startled moment, Daisy realised that the room was actually quite small. A multitude of mirrors created an illusion of illimitable space, reflecting one another and themselves and the windows in endless reduplication. Practically everything that wasn't mirror was gilt, she observed, dazzled. Even the rococo plasterwork of the ceiling (not mirrored, thank heaven) was picked out in gilt. In the centre hung a ballroom-size chandelier. Countless crystal drops sparkled in the glow of its electric bulbs.

From the midst of this outré magnificence came forth a petite silver-haired lady with bright, shrewd blue eyes. Her milky skin was beautifully made up, with a discreet touch of rouge, and she wore a well-cut navy silk tea frock. In contrast to the flamboyance around her, her only jewellery was a triple strand of superb pearls and a large diamond on her ring finger.

"Mrs. Fletcher, I'm Mrs. Jessup." Her voice was unexpectedly resonant for such a small frame, and had an intriguing hint, the merest flavour, of an accent. "How do you do? It's very kind of you to accept our unconventional invitation."

"Not at all. It's kind of you to invite me." Daisy smiled at the younger woman who came up behind her hostess.

Mrs. Jessup introduced her daughter-in-law. Mrs. Aidan Jessup's peaches and cream complexion would never need powder or rouge, nor develop freckles, Daisy thought enviously. She was thin as her solicitor father; the still-current straight up and down style with hip-level waistline suited her boyish figure. However, she had considerably more hair than Mr. Irwin—a smooth flaxen bob—and less twitchiness.

"We ought to have waited for you to move in and then left our cards," she said placidly, returning Daisy's smile. "We hoped you might be encouraged to know you have friendly neighbours. Father seemed to doubt that you'd want to come to live here."

Mr. Irwin shot her an irritated glance. "Not at all," he muttered. "But the house has been standing empty, and there's no knowing what condition—"

"That's just it, Father," Audrey Jessup broke in, her tranquillity undiminished; "we don't care for living next door to an empty house."

"As for the condition," said Mrs. Jessup robustly, "it's only a couple of months since Mr. Walsall went to his reward, and Maurice—my husband, Mrs. Fletcher—visited him twice a week right up to the end for a game of chess. These past few years, he was the only person the poor old fellow would see. He was nervous of burglars, so Maurice always checked upstairs and down before he left to make sure all was secure. He'd surely have noticed if anything was seriously amiss."

So much for Mr. Irwin's excuse for trying to put Daisy off the house.

She was intrigued by these first hints of Alec's great-uncle's personality. All she'd known of him before was that he had cut off all communication with his sister, but mightn't that have been the sister's fault as much as his? Judging by her offspring, Alec's mother, she could well have been an extremely difficult person to get along with.

"You will stay for tea, won't you, Mrs. Fletcher? And Jonathan? Audrey, ring the bell, please."

"You must excuse me, ladies," said Mr. Irwin. "I have another appointment. The taxicab should be at the door any minute. Mrs. Fletcher, you'll let me know when your husband returns to town?"

"Of course. In the meantime, please arrange for a surveyor to inspect the house."

"When Mr. Fletcher—"

"I see no need to wait." Daisy was growing impatient with his incomprehensible delaying tactics. "You said yourself that it would have to be surveyed anyway if we decide to sell. I should like to have a report to show Alec when he gets home."

"I'll see what I can do," he promised glumly. "These things

take time. Audrey, you'd better telephone for a taxicab when Mrs. Fletcher is ready to leave."

"Thank you for the thought, Mr. Irwin, but I don't need one. I left my car in Well Walk."

"Your car!" Shaking his head at the shocking state of the modern world, the solicitor departed.

"I'm afraid Father is frightfully old-fashioned," said Audrey Jessup as they all sat down on chairs upholstered in gold brocade. "What kind of car is it?"

"An Austin Chummy. Alec didn't need it today, and I was in a bit of a rush. I don't usually drive in town, but it's nice for a ride in the country, just big enough to squeeze in my twelve-year-old stepdaughter, two babies and their nurse, and a picnic."

"Good heavens!" the elder Mrs. Jessup exclaimed, laughing.

"You have little ones?" her daughter-in-law asked. "You absolutely must come to live here. How old are they?"

"Seven months."

"And the other?"

"Both seven months. They're twins, boy and girl."

"Double trouble," said the elder Mrs. Jessup with a smile. Daisy had heard the comment often enough to be mildly irritated without feeling any need to retort.

"Double joy, Mama Moira! Marilyn, my five-year-old, will be thrilled to death. She adores babies. Percy's getting too old to appreciate being smothered in kisses."

The parlour maid brought in the tea trolley. As Mrs. Jessup poured, Daisy and Audrey Jessup compared notes on their children.

"They change so fast," said the elder Mrs. Jessup with a sigh. "Aidan, my eldest, was such a staid, sensible child. Then he went away to school. Next thing we knew, we were being congratulated on his becoming a positive demon on the Rugby football field!"

Daisy believed her. Her friend Lucy had married a quiet,

mild-mannered man who turned into a ravening beast on the rugger field.

"But Aidan's very staid and sensible now," Audrey observed with a touch of wistfulness.

"I should hope so, with a growing family of his own. My youngest, on the other hand, was a rough-and-tumble boy, always looking for trouble." A shadow of anxiety crossed Mrs. Jessup's face, and Daisy wondered if her youngest was still looking for trouble. "Yet he took up cricket, which has always seemed to me a rather sedate affair."

"Compared to rugger, positively placid!" Daisy agreed.

"And my daughter, Deirdre, wasn't at all like Audrey's little Marilyn. She never cared much about dolls or babies. All she ever wanted was a horse, and though we couldn't manage that, she took riding lessons for years. Somewhat to my surprise, she's turned into a devoted mother."

"How many grandchildren have you?"

"Five. Just wait until you're a grandmother, Mrs. Fletcher. The pleasures of motherhood are nothing to it."

Daisy wished her mother and Alec's could bring themselves to enjoy Belinda, Miranda, and Oliver instead of always finding fault. She also envied the easy relationship between the two Mrs. Jessups, so different from her own with her exacting mother-in-law.

She finished her second cup of tea and was about to say regretfully that it was time she was going, when the maid came in.

"There's someone to see the master, madam. A foreigner. On business, he says. I told him Mr. Jessup don't do business at home, but he said the master wouldn't take kindly to him turning up at the shop, and it's not my place, 'm, to tell him the master's gone abroad. So!"

Mrs. Jessup looked dismayed, even alarmed. "Didn't he give his name, Enid?"

"No'm. I ast for his card, but he didn't have one. He's a foreigner." In the maid's eyes, this fact clearly explained any and all peculiarities of conduct.

"I suppose I'd better speak to him. Please excuse me, Mrs. Fletcher." She stood up.

Daisy also rose. Her curiosity aroused, she had to force herself to obey the dictates of manners. "I really must be off," she said. "Thank you so much for tea. I'm looking forward to our being neighbours."

Mrs. Jessup went out. Daisy stayed chatting to Audrey for a few minutes before going into the hall, where the maid waited to usher her out.

A door towards the front of the hall was slightly ajar. Stopping at the looking glass hanging over the hall table to straighten her hat and powder her nose, Daisy heard a man's voice. He spoke too low to make out his words, but something about the intonation sounded to her distinctly American, rather than any more exotic incarnation of English. On the other hand, Mrs. Jessup's voice, when she spoke, was unmistakably Irish. That brogue was what she had caught a hint of earlier, Daisy realised.

"As it happens," Mrs. Jessup said coldly, "my husband is travelling on the Continent. He moves about a great deal from country to country—France, Spain, Italy, Portugal, even Germany. I have no way to get in touch."

The visitor's voice rose. "Aw, don't give me that, lady! You must know when you're expecting him home at least."

"I don't. His plans often change, so he sends a telegram when he's on his way home."

"OK, if you say so." He sounded disgruntled, almost threatening. "But you better tell him I came looking for him, and tell him I'll be back."

The door swung open. A short, wiry man in a blue suit strode out into the hall. In passing, his dark eyes gave Daisy a sidelong glance. Something about it made her shiver. She glimpsed black slicked-back hair before he clapped a grey-blue fedora on his head, pulling it well down over his swarthy face. A black-avised devil—the phrase surfaced from somewhere in the depths of Daisy's memory.

He reached the front door before the maid could open it for him. Letting himself out, he failed to shut it behind him. He ran down the steps and walked quickly away around Constable Circle.

"Well, I never!" the maid exclaimed. "Manners!"

"Born in a barn," Daisy agreed with a friendly smile. "I take it he's not a frequent visitor?"

"Never set eyes on him before, madam, and I'm sure I hope I never do again. We get plenty of foreign visitors, the family being in the importing business, but most of 'em are polite as you please, in their foreign sort of way. Begging your pardon, 'm, but is it right what I heard, that you're taking the house next door? If you was to be wanting a parlour maid, my sister's looking for a new situation. . . ."

Daisy promised to let her know as soon as their plans were certain. Down the steps she went and started across the street, intending to cross the garden by the path.

"Excuse me, madam!" A man came towards her, hurrying up the path. Well dressed in an unobtrusive dark grey suit and carrying a tightly rolled umbrella, he looked very respectable, a banker perhaps, in no way an alarming figure.

Daisy paused. The man came closer, raising his hat politely. He was quite young, early thirties at a guess, though his dark hair was already greying a little at the temples.

"I beg your pardon for accosting you, ma'am. I saw you come out of my house. I'm Aidan Jessup."

The staid, sensible older son? Lucy's Gerald would have let himself be boiled in oil before he'd have accosted in the street a lady to whom he had not been introduced, even having observed her departure from his house. Unless the house was going up in flames . . . But a quick backward glance showed Daisy such was not the case. However, she was not the sort to cut off a possible source of information just because of a certain disregard of etiquette.

"Afternoon tea," she explained, and added encouragingly, "Can I help you?"

"You noticed the fellow who came out just before you? Who dashed off at such a pace?" He stared frowning after the American, now out of sight. "I don't suppose you know who he was?"

"I'm afraid not. I didn't meet him. I imagine Mrs. Jessup—your mother—can tell you."

"Mother spoke to him?"

"I believe so. I did hear his voice, and he sounded as if he came from America."

His already-pale face blanched. "Oh Hades!" he groaned. "I knew it was a terrible idea. Thank you, madam, and once more, my apologies." He raised his hat again and made for the Jessup house at a hasty pace.

Interesting! Daisy thought, making her way back to the car.

There seemed to be enough secrets and mysteries at number 5 to furnish a half-ruined Gothic mansion. They ought to have an old crone for a housekeeper, instead of a smart young parlour maid.

She had liked both the Jessup ladies, though. If they were aware of her aristocratic background, they had showed no signs of toadying. In fact, their unaffected manners were very much at odds with the flamboyance of their interior decorating. Could it be Mr. Jessup's taste that ruled?

If anything, the mysteries associated with the Jessups made Daisy keener to get to know them better. Who was the intrusive, aggressive American whose arrival so alarmed Aidan Jessup? What was the "terrible idea" that had apparently led to his arrival? Was the younger brother in trouble with the law?

Could that explain Mr. Irwin's reluctance to have a CID detective move in next door to his daughter?

FIRST SEA INTERLUDE

There was three men came out of the west,
Their fortunes for to try,

And those three made a solemn vow,
John Barleycorn should die.
They ploughed, they sowed, they harrowed him in,
Throwed clods upon his head,
And these three men made a solemn vow,
John Barleycorn was dead.

—OLD ENGLISH BALLAD

" 'It was a dark and stormy night . . . ' "

Clinging to the rail, sleet streaming down his neck, Patrick muttered the words to himself. He'd have had to shout to be heard above the howl of the wind in the rigging, and in any case, he doubted his present companions would appreciate the literary allusion.

At the best of times, the seamen had little regard for the supercargo.

Bulwer-Lytton's London couldn't possibly have been as dark and stormy as the North Atlantic in a September gale, at night, on board a ship with all lights extinguished. The best that could be said for the situation was that the U.S. Coast Guard was not likely to find the *Iphigenia*. If they had any sense, they wouldn't even be afloat tonight.

On the other hand, nor would *Iffie*'s customers find her.

Captain Watkins had insisted that the supercargo must be on deck, ready to keep tally of the merchandise handed over when the inshore boats arrived. Teeth chattering, Patrick suspected— to the point of near certainty—that Watkins had been having him on. Surely on a night like this the captain couldn't even guarantee that the black ship was in the vicinity of Rum Row. If she was, one could only hope that a dozen—or a score or more—unlighted ships were not circling blindly in the area, waiting for the storm to ease.

At least they were not likely to be blown ashore, Patrick was glad to realise. Last year, in May 1924 to be precise, the old three-mile limit had changed to twelve, so Rum Row was now some fifteen miles from the coast.

A song ran through his head:

Oh, 'twas in the broad Atlantic,
Mid the equinoctial gales,
That a young fellow fell overboard . . .

His frozen hands gripped the rail tighter. Not that he was afraid. He had, after all, chosen to come, in search of adventure. But he was so cold, he hardly felt the touch on his arm until the bo'sun's voice bellowed in his ear, "You'd best come below, lad. The runners won't be out tonight."

Turning, he was grateful for the man's steadying hand on his elbow. Thank heaven he wasn't seasick. That would have been the ultimate humiliation.

A faint light glimmering through the downpour showed the position of the open deckhouse door. Finding his feet on the heaving deck, he made for it, the bo'sun a step behind.

Once sheltered from the storm's savagery, Patrick felt the steady, reassuring thump of the engines. His breath caught in his throat as he stepped into the cabin. After the bracing air outside, the fug seemed thick enough to scoop with a ladle. On the outward voyage, everyone but the captain slept, ate, smoked, and drank in the narrow space, to allow room for more bottles and barrels of their precious cargo—of which one cask had been broached since he went on deck. The watch below greeted him with a steaming tankard.

"Not to worry, mate," said one bewhiskered mariner, grinning. "'T ain't the ten-year-old Haig and Haig."

He reached for the toddy eagerly. "Th-thank you." His teeth were still not quite under control. He took a swig and started to warm up inside. "I'll put it d-down as lost overboard."

"That's the spirit." The bo'sun's witticism raised a laugh.

One of the men threw Patrick a towel. "Better get out o' them wet duds."

The ordeal outside seemed to have been some sort of test. Apparently, he had passed. The son of the cargo's owner could never really be one of the crew, though someone made room on the steam pipes for him to hang his dripping clothes among theirs.

But he remembered the story of the Norwegian black ship *Sagatind:* The crew had broken into the cargo, drunk their fill, quarrelled and fought, and, when the Coast Guard seized the ship, were found blotto and bloody belowdecks.

TWO

"*What I* want to know," said Daisy, "is why Alec's great-uncle's solicitor is nervous about having a policeman move into that house."

Alec and Tommy Pearson had just joined her and Madge in the sitting room. It was a pleasant, comfortable room, half the size of Mr. Walsall's drawing room and without a scrap of the Jessups' flamboyance.

Tommy liked his glass of port after dinner, but Alec had promised Daisy they wouldn't discuss Mr. Walsall's will in her absence. They hadn't kept the ladies waiting more than a quarter of an hour.

Daisy's demand brought a frown to the face of the stocky, bespectacled solicitor. "That, I can't tell you," he said, accepting a cup of coffee. He helped himself to a lump of sugar. Tongs poised to take a second, he glanced at his wife and regretfully forbore.

Madge's blond curls nodded approval, but as he sat down beside her, she said tartly, "He *won't* tell you, more likely. Tommy's refused to say a word to me about why you invited us to dinner tonight."

"For the pleasure of your company, of course, darling," said Daisy.

"Well, of course! But I know he has business to discuss with Alec, too. Do you want me to go and powder my nose while you talk? Or I could go up and admire the babies. They're always so angelic when they're asleep."

"As far as I'm concerned, you're welcome to stay, Madge," Daisy assured her. "Only it's really Alec's business. . . ."

"There's no reason you shouldn't stay," said Alec, "but it's not particularly interesting business, unless Pearson's going to drag some hitherto unsuspected family skeleton out of the cupboard?"

"Good Lord, no!" Tommy was shocked. "Nothing like that."

Daisy was always somewhat taken aback by evidence of Tommy's earnest outlook on life. She had heard tales of his derring-do during the War, in the course of which he had been badly shot up. In fact, he had met Madge—then Lady Margaret Allinston—in the military hospital where she had been a VAD nurse and Daisy had worked in the office. Since returning to the long-established law firm of Pearson, Pearson, Watts & Pearson, Tommy had reverted to the conventions with a vengeance.

Although he *had* been extremely helpful in that extremely unconventional business in Worcestershire, Daisy reminded herself.

Doubtless his retreat into stolidity was his way of coping with the horrors he had lived through. People had different ways of dealing with the memories, some more efficacious, some less so. Tommy and Madge and their little boy were a happy family, and he was doing well in his profession. A certain degree of gravity was required of solicitors, as well as of policemen.

Alec wasn't being a policeman this evening, though, just a hopeful heir.

Tommy took some papers out of an attaché case. "Let me say right away," he stated, "that William Walsall was a very wealthy man. He left considerable sums to various charities—"

"Buying his place in heaven," said the irrepressible Madge.

Her husband gave her an affectionately exasperated look. "There's no reason to suppose so. He made generous provision for his butler and housekeeper, a married couple, though given their advanced ages, the annuities could not have been expensive. Be that as it may, I can assure you, Fletcher, your income from investments will be quite sufficient to cover the increased cost of a larger household, without—"

"That's what Mr. Irwin told me," said Daisy, "but with the utmost reluctance, which I don't understand at all."

"Perhaps he's been misappropriating funds," Madge suggested.

"My dear, you mustn't say such things, even in jest," Tommy remonstrated. "Phelps, Irwin, and Apsley is a highly regarded firm. Besides, the sale of the property would be equally likely to bring to light any discrepancy in the accounts."

"We might not have delved deep, as we'd be happy to get the funds from the sale," Daisy pointed out. "It would have been the horses he cheated, and they'd not likely complain."

Madge had to be told about the Home for Superannuated and Superfluous Carriage Horses. "No," she agreed, laughing, "they'd never look a gift horse in the mouth."

"Probably not," said Alec. "Whereas if he'd left us skint, or without sufficient funds to keep up the house—"

"Either way, I shall have everything checked by an accountant, though I'm sure Madge is quite mistaken. Still, it is odd that Irwin appeared not to want you to move in."

"Entirely Daisy's rampant imagination, I expect," said Alec.

"It was not! Don't be beastly, darling."

He grinned at her. "You were saying, Pearson, 'without' . . . ?"

"Without? Oh yes, without considering the leases."

"Leases? Mr. Irwin didn't mention leases, only investments. I told you he was holding out on us, Alec."

"Land is an investment," Tommy said patiently. "Assuming you keep the house, you appear to own the freehold of the whole of Constable Circle."

"Constable Circle!" Madge burst out laughing. "You'll have to change it to Chief Inspector Circle."

"I must admit the name was something of a shock," said Alec with a smile. "It's called after the painter, of course."

"John Constable lived in Hampstead," Daisy confirmed. "In Well Walk, actually, just around the corner. There's a Gainsborough Gardens nearby, too."

"As I was about to say," Tommy continued, "the ground rents don't amount to much in modern terms, as the ninety-nine-year leases were signed in the mid-1890s, when prices were much lower than since the War. Under certain circumstances, you can raise them, of course."

"What circs?" Daisy enquired.

"It's a complicated subject, as leases are all different. I'll have to have time to study them before I can explain properly. But if you were ever in need of capital, you could sell the freehold. It must be worth a pretty penny. Not that I'd recommend such a course unless you found yourselves in desperate straits. Land is an excellent investment."

"How clever of your great-uncle to buy it up," Madge congratulated Alec.

"He didn't actually buy it," said Tommy.

"Aha, the skeleton in the cupboard!" Madge crowed. "He was a gambler and won it in a game of cards."

"Stuff and nonsense. No one could have been more respectable. Jonathan Irwin's father was Walsall's solicitor back then, and knew him quite well. Irwin told me his history—in confidence, of course."

"Tell all," Daisy commanded. "Do you know what caused the breach with Alec's grandmother?"

Tommy looked at Alec, who shrugged. "Surely you can tell me, and Daisy will find out one way or another. I gather the next-door neighbour—"

"The one with the Versailles sitting room?" Madge interrupted. She exchanged a glance with Daisy, who had described the Jessups' sitting room to her as a miniature Galerie des Glaces.

Not that Daisy had ever seen the original, but she'd read descriptions. "That's the one," she said. "Mrs. Jessup told me her husband used to visit the old man regularly."

"So it's quite likely Mr. Jessup and perhaps his wife know all there is to know about my forebears, in which case Daisy'll have it out of them in no time. You may reveal the worst, Pearson."

"It's not so bad. More old-fashioned, really, though I have plenty of clients who still have the old attitudes. Mr. Walsall acquired the land that became Constable Circle in payment of a debt. He owned the majority of shares in a bank, which he sold when he retired, to one of the bigger banks. Barclay's, if I remember correctly."

"Never mind that," Daisy said impatiently. "What about Alec's grandmother?"

"It's all tied together. His sister—your grandmother, Alec—married his chief clerk, against his bitter opposition."

"I suppose he gave my grandfather the sack," Alec guessed. Tommy nodded.

"That's disgraceful!" Daisy burst out. "Even my mother didn't behave as badly as that when I married Alec. Darling, we ought to reject his house and his blasted money!"

Aghast, Tommy was speechless. Madge intervened. "Daisy, don't you think Mr. Walsall was trying to make amends when he left everything to Alec?"

"Ha! When he was already dead and it didn't cost him anything!"

"Calm down, love. My grandparents did all right, and my mother ended up as a bank manager's wife. You could call that a revenge of sorts."

"Besides," said Madge, "it would be cutting off the twins' and Belinda's noses to spite their great-great-uncle's face, and he won't even know about it."

Daisy laughed ruefully. "True. As a gesture, it wouldn't give the same satisfaction as throwing a bag of gold in his face. But what—" She stopped and listened. "That's the doorbell. Who on earth, at this time of night . . . ? Darling, you promised—"

"I told them we'd be out. Anyway, the Yard would telephone, not send someone to my doorstep. Mrs. Dobson's getting it."

The heavy footsteps of the cook-housekeeper were heard in the hall. Called from the washing up, she was probably wiping her hands on her damp apron as she went and tucking wisps of hair behind her ears. Soon, perhaps, they'd have a neatly uniformed house-parlour maid. . . . Still, Mrs. Dobson was more than capable of getting rid of unwanted visitors.

They heard the rattle of the chain, the murmur of voices, a door closing with a decided thud, then Mrs. Dobson's footsteps again, coming to the sitting room.

The door opened. "It's an American with a carpetbag, madam. He says you know him, you and the master. 'Mr. and Mrs. Fletcher,' he said. It's pouring cats and dogs, it is," added Mrs. Dobson, "and he's ever so wet. Sopping wet."

Another mysterious American visitor? "Didn't he give his name?" Daisy demanded.

"No, madam. I ast him, and he looked behind him, sort of shifty like, and said he better not tell. So I shut the door on him."

"Very wise," said Tommy.

"Shall I tell him to go away, madam?"

"Heavens no!" Daisy started to get up. "I'll go and see who it is."

Alec put out his hand to stop her. "Stay here. I'll go. You made friends with some pretty strange people over there."

"So did you," she retorted as he went out, followed by Tommy.

Alec had told her some rather odd stories about the director of the new Federal Bureau of Investigation, J. Edgar Hoover, with whom he'd briefly worked. Judging by the peculiar behaviour of the man on the doorstep, he could well be one of Hoover's agents. He had claimed to know both of them, though, and events had prevented her joining Alec in Washington, D.C.

So much had happened in her life since the American trip that it seemed like aeons ago. But come to think of it, she had met one FBI man, and he, of all people, might conceivably turn up on their doorstep without notice, sopping wet, and refuse to give his name.

"Wait, Alec! I shan't be a minute," she excused herself to Madge.

"I'm coming, too. You don't think I'd miss the excitement, do you?"

They went after the men.

Alec had his hand on the chain, about to unhook it and open the door, when he hesitated.

"What is it?" Pearson asked.

"Probably nothing. You may have read reports from America about the rise of large criminal gangs, fuelled by the vast sums to be made by evading Prohibition. It's been in the *Times*, I think."

"Small-time hoodlums—mostly Italian, Irish, and Jewish, aren't they?—joining together into well-organised groups, leading to a rising level of violence. There were some pretty virulent letters about the idiocy of the Volstead Act. It's unenforceable over here, though, nothing to do with Scotland Yard."

"Bootlegging, no, but the violent crimes are extraditable offences. Not long ago, the FBI asked us to collar an Irish fugitive, an American with family in Dublin, and I got landed with the job."

"Because of your American expertise? So you think someone's out for blood because you arrested—"

"Actually, we didn't arrest him. He got away to the Irish Free State. But—"

"Oh come on, darling," said Daisy, reaching past him to open the door. "I bet I know who it is." She peered through the three-inch gap allowed by the chain. The electric light was on in the porch. She saw a huddled, dripping figure of misery, who raised his head hopefully, revealing spattered horn-rimmed glasses, and lifted his trilby. "I knew it, it's Mr. Lambert. Just a minute, Mr. Lambert!" She closed the door and unfastened the chain.

"Lambert? Who . . . ? Oh, your watch-sheep." Alec had not held a high opinion of Lambert even before the youthful agent had abandoned them somewhere in the middle of the United States. "I suppose we'd better take him in." Sighing, he opened the door.

"Darling," Madge said to Daisy, "I'm simply dying to hear all about it!"

Half an hour later, Lambert was ensconced in a chair by the fire, the damp change of clothes from his bag steaming gently, as was the glass of whisky toddy in his hand. Judging by the rate at which the latter was disappearing, he was no great devotee of Prohibition.

Daisy decided to offer coffee rather than a refill.

While the American was changing, she had told Madge a bit about their mutual adventures in the States. Subsequently, Tommy had tried, without success, to persuade his wife it was time they went home. She gazed in fascination at the American.

Alec stood leaning against the mantelpiece, tamping tobacco in his pipe, frowning down at Lambert. "All right," he said, "now let's hear just what exactly you're doing here."

"Here?" Lambert bleated. Since their last meeting, two years ago, his face had not lost its youthful ingenuousness.

"Here in London. Here in my house. Here—"

"Oh, *here*! My pocket was picked—on the boat train. Luckily,

Mrs. Fletcher's letter was in a different pocket, so I still had your address."

"Her letter?" Alec threw an accusatory glare at Daisy.

"Don't you remember, sir? After . . . after what happened, I wrote you in care of the Bureau to apologise, and I enclosed an apology addressed to Mrs. Fletcher. She kindly wrote back."

"So you came here because you have no money for a hotel?"

Lambert blushed. "It's worse than that, I'm afraid, sir. The thief took my passport as well as my money, and my credentials, too."

"You're still with the FBI?"

The blush deepened, even his ears reddening as he sheepishly put down his now-empty glass and pushed it away. "No, sir. I'm with the Treasury Department, Bureau of Internal Revenue, Prohibition Division."

"Then what the deuce are you doing in England?" Tommy gave the empty glass a pointed look. "Alcohol is not illegal here."

"I know that, sir." Turning to Alec, the hapless Prohibition agent asked, "Sir, who is this guy . . . er, gentleman?"

"Mr. Pearson is a solicitor—that is, a lawyer. You may place absolute trust in his discretion. Mrs. Pearson's also, I believe."

"Oh yes, I shan't breathe a word." Madge was entranced.

Lambert stood up, bowed to Madge, shook Tommy's hand, and said solemnly, "Pleased to meet you, ma'am, sir. If Mr. Fletcher vouches for you, I guess that's good enough for me. The thing is, I know we can't enforce the Volstead Act here, not even for American citizens, but what we can do is find out who's shipping the stuff to our bootleggers. Your British government says there's no law stops us doing that."

"Outrageous!" sputtered Tommy. "Spying on our citizens? I shall speak to my MP."

"Member of Parliament," Daisy explained to the American.

"Kind of like a congressman? Well, I guess that's your right, sir."

"But how do you do it, Mr. Lambert?" asked Madge. "Surely you can't keep watch on every wine merchant in the country?"

"Gee whiz, no, ma'am. We're kind of shorthanded at best. I guess it's OK to tell you. See, the Coast Guard's gotten itself some new ships, fast ones, and they're keeping the black ships on the move—"

"Black ships?" Daisy queried.

"That's what they call the rumrunners, ma'am. There're the freighters from Europe and Canada—they're wholesalers—and the inshore boats that pick up the liquor out at sea, on Rum Row. But the Coast Guard's disrupting business now, forcing the ships to keep moving so they can't meet up. The rumrunners have started using radio to arrange new meeting places, but we're listening in, so they have to transmit in code. Some of these bootleggers, the big guys, are sending contact men over here to arrange codes. Also to figure out how to pay without the risk of the cash being confiscated if they get caught."

"And your job is to follow the contact men?" Alec suggested.

"That's right, sir. They're real tough guys, though," he added despondently, "and your Customs took away my gun."

"I should hope so!" Tommy exclaimed. "This isn't the Wild West, you know. Even the police are rarely armed."

Lambert came very close to pouting. "OK I guess, if that's the way you do things."

"How do you propose to find these tough guys?" Alec asked.

"The embassy's supposed to help, but the public desk was closed when I got there and I didn't have my credentials, so they told me to come back in the morning."

"Did you report your loss to the police?"

"Yes, sir, I walked on over to Scotland Yard and asked for you, but I didn't have—"

"Your credentials, yes, I realise that."

"And I guess you're too important to disturb for a pick-pocket. A bobby took a report and said they'd get in touch if my passport was found, but I couldn't tell them where I'd be at because I didn't have—"

"Money for a hotel," Daisy put in.

"You got it, ma'am. So seeing I had your address, I asked the way to your home. He gave me directions and a dime—a shilling?—for the bus ride, and here I am. I'm mighty sorry to intrude like this, Mrs. Fletcher, but I didn't know what else to do."

He was so disconsolate, Daisy hadn't the heart to say anything but that he was more than welcome and she'd have Mrs. Dobson make up a bed. "I expect you haven't eaten," she said kindly. "If you wouldn't mind coming to the kitchen, I'm sure Mrs. Dobson will find you something."

Lambert followed her docilely, and she left him in the cook-housekeeper's competent hands.

Returning to the sitting room, she sank into a chair. "Well! Still singularly lacking in eptness."

"*Eptness,* darling?" said Madge.

"Should it be *eptitude,* do you think, like *aptitude?*"

"He's not merely inept," Alec snorted, "he's incompetent. I can't imagine how he got another government job after leaving the FBI, except that I've heard that Prohibition agents are exempted from the usual civil service requirements."

"It sounds," Tommy remarked, "as if someone didn't want them to be too efficient! Come along, Madge, we really must be going." The Pearsons left.

"Two unexpected American visitors within just a few days," Daisy mused.

Surprised, Alec asked, "Have we had a visitor you haven't mentioned?"

"No, darling, the Jessups, remember? Our neighbours-to-be. I told you."

"None of our business."

"Don't you think it's an odd coincidence?"

"Coincidences happen. Perhaps Lambert called on them, too."

"No, it wasn't him. I caught a glimpse of the man's face. You don't doubt Lambert's story, do you?"

"Great Scott no. If I were a pickpocket, he's just the sort of feckless-looking mark I'd head straight for. Besides, I don't believe he has the wits to invent it."

"True. He'll have to have Bel's room tonight."

Alec sighed. "I suppose you expect me to take him with me tomorrow and sort him out."

"After all, he did *try* to protect me in New York," said Daisy.

SECOND SEA INTERLUDE

Then they let him lie for a very long time
Till the rain from heaven did fall,
Then little Sir John sprung up his head,
And soon amazed them all.
They let him stand till midsummer
Till he looked both pale and wan,
And little Sir John he growed a long beard
And so became a man.

The dark of the moon, and not a lamp showed on either vessel, yet Patrick could see the motor launch bobbing alongside *Iphigenia* as clearly as if they were sailing the Solent on a sunny Sunday afternoon. By the starlight reflected off the inky, satin-smooth swells, he watched the last sack lowered to the deck of the inshore boat and hastily stowed by the men below. She was considerably lower in the water than when she had arrived at Rum Row.

"Your turn, lad, if you're up for it."

"I'm ready, Captain." Patrick slung his kit over his shoulder.

"Just sign my copy of the manifest here—the true manifest, not the one we show the Yanks if they stop us." White teeth glinted in a grin. "So there's no trouble when we get back to Blighty."

Shading the torch beam with his hand, he pointed to the spot on the top sheet of his sheaf of papers. Patrick scribbled his name.

"Thanks, Captain. You may be sure I'll tell my father he can rely on you in any future business of this kind."

"You've not done too badly yourself. Watch your back when you get among those cutthroat bootleggers. They owe you plenty, and who knows how keen they are to pay. Right, over you go."

The bo'sun himself took charge of the sling to which Patrick now entrusted himself. Dangling from the side of the black ship, he looked down at the strip of inky water between the freighter and the launch and prayed he wouldn't get a dunking. He was concerned less about an icy soaking than the humiliation involved.

With a thud, he dropped safely to the deck. A waiting seaman disentangled him from the sling and tugged twice on the rope. As Patrick waved good-bye at the darkness above, the idling engines of both vessels took on a more urgent note and they began to move apart.

He hadn't paid much attention to the captain's warning. His father had been doing business with the same people—at least, the top man—since before Prohibition. A Boston Irishman whose father owned a bar, he had a ready market for good stuff, the best wines and Champagnes and, in particular, Haig & Haig and Gordon's gin, both for some reason especially popular with the smart set.

In view of all the tales of piracy on Rum Row, they had arranged a code between them, so that no cash need change hands at sea. In a belt pouch sewn by Patrick's mother were the playing cards, torn in half, used as identification by the inshore boats as they arrived at the *Iphigenia* to pick up their loads. Now matched with the halves Patrick had brought with him, they would prove to the agent ashore that business had been properly transacted as planned. No cash to be seized by pirates, Coast Guard, or Treasury men—the agent would transfer payment to a New York bank to be transmitted to the firm's London account.

But first, Patrick must reach the Irishman's agent. *Iffie*'s bo'sun had warned him that the Coast Guard, rather than merely firing warning shots at suspected boats, had actually killed several seamen.

He had chosen adventure, yet he watched *Iffie*'s shadowy shape disappear into the night with a shiver of apprehension. Behind her spread her wake, pointing at her as plainly as a white arrow painted on tarmac.

THREE

The day after Lambert's arrival, having gone into town with Alec in the morning, he turned up in St. John's Wood again in the middle of the afternoon. When Mrs. Dobson showed him into the small office Daisy shared with Alec, he stood before her desk, more sheepish than ever.

"Mr. Fletcher told me to come back," he mumbled miserably.

"Still no money for a hotel?" Daisy enquired with resignation, lowering her hands from the typewriter.

"No, ma'am. The guy at the embassy took the chief inspector's word that I'm Absalom Lambert, but—"

"You are?" Trying to hide her incredulity, she wondered what sort of person could saddle a child with such a name. It was tempting Fate to kill him by way of a nasty accident. Of course, he wore his hair cut too short to get entangled in a tree, but still . . . "I don't believe I ever heard your Christian name before."

Lambert blushed. "I guess you never asked me to show my credentials back home, but I did show Mr. Fletcher in New York. So today he told them I used to be a federal agent, but he

couldn't vouch that I still am, though with a different department. They wired Washington."

"With any luck, then, they'll hear back tomorrow."

"Gee whiz, don't I wish! The trouble is, the embassy wants
a photograph, so it'll take at least a week, maybe more."

"Good gracious! I'd have thought they'd be more cooperative, more helpful to a citizen in distress."

"I expect they are, normally. See, they don't like the Prohibition Division. No one—well, hardly anyone—does. They
don't understand over here how bad things are getting in the
big cities, what with the bootleggers, like I was telling you.
They'll have to help, though, soon as they get my credentials."

"In a week or so. Did Alec invite you to stay here in the
meantime?" Daisy enquired dangerously, ready to be furious.

"Oh no, Mrs. Fletcher! He said it's entirely up to you."

Pipped at the post. With Lambert standing in front of her,
unhappily studying the toes of his shoes, how could she not
offer to put him up?

"I suppose I'd better drive you to the station to retrieve your
bags from left luggage," she said with a sigh. "Or was your luggage ticket pinched, too?"

Lambert perked up. "No, I stuck it in my hat band. It got
soaked, but Mrs. Dobson kindly dried it out for me, and I think
it's OK. Here," he said, handing it to her, "don't you?"

The man at left luggage gave Lambert an extremely dubious
look. He examined both sides of the wrinkled scrap of card-
board carefully, while Daisy held her breath. But a glance at
Daisy, who was wearing her most respectable coat, reassured
him and he handed over Lambert's belongings.

Lambert fitted himself into the household with remarkable
ease. He had a good appetite, which endeared him to Mrs.
Dobson. The helpless quality, which sometimes made Daisy

want to scream, appealed to Nurse Gilpin. He was always welcome in the nursery, where he soon made himself popular with the twins. Daisy would feel quite jealous when she went upstairs and found Miranda sitting on his lap, studying a picture book, or Oliver shrieking with laughter as he climbed over the American's recumbent form.

Not that there was much room to recline, what with all the babies' stuff as well as Mrs. Gilpin's bed and chest of drawers. The Hampstead nursery was going to be a great improvement.

Daisy's pangs of jealousy abated when Miranda held out her chubby arms to her mama to be picked up for a kiss and Oliver raced across the floor with his spiderlike crawl to pull himself up by her leg to a wobbly standing position. Daisy's stockings might suffer, but she reaffirmed her determination to be a modern mother, not the sort who left her children's upbringing to a nurse, however capable. Besides, the older the babies grew, the more fun they were.

Lambert was popular with the dog, too. He was always ready to take Nana for a walk, whatever the weather. What was more, on returning, he washed her down if she was muddy and dried her off when she was wet.

In fact, such were his domestic virtues that Daisy thought it a great pity he was so determined to make a go of it in the cloak-and-dagger world. He ought to go home to a safe if dull job in his father's business—insurance, she recalled him mentioning—marry a nice girl, and have a family.

Whatever his failings as an agent of the law, however, he was an excellent guest. It was just as well. Ten days passed and still the American embassy had not received any response to their wire.

"Perhaps they never will," Alec said morosely at bedtime, wrenching off his tie. "Is one evening alone, just the two of us, too much to ask?"

"I could give him money for the cinema," Daisy proposed, "though it seems a bit inhospitable when he's so helpful during the day. Darling, you don't think he actually did make up the whole story, do you?"

"Not really. Why would he choose to foist himself indefinitely on *us*?"

"I expect it's just that his department has lost his photo. On purpose, I shouldn't be surprised. Or they haven't got one. Oh dear, I hope they don't have to get in touch with his family to ask for one. Goodness knows how long that might take."

"More likely they're happy to have lost him and hope he'll disappear for good."

Daisy giggled as she helped him undo his collar stud. Though they didn't usually change for dinner, he'd had a meeting that afternoon with the Assistant Commissioner (Crime), who didn't approve of soft collars.

"Now that we *are* alone," she said, "don't let's waste time talking about Lambert."

So they didn't.

The very next day, Tommy Pearson telephoned to say the Fletchers could move into the Hampstead house as soon as they wanted. Daisy was startled. With memories of Jarndyce and Jarndyce, she had anticipated a *Bleak House*–like sluggishness in the windings of the law. Certainly she hadn't expected to be able to leave St. John's Wood before the new year.

"Did you just say what I think you said?"

"What do you think I said?" Tommy asked patiently.

"I can start putting the Hampstead house in order?"

"That's not precisely what I said, but that's what it amounts to. There are a few *i*'s to be dotted and *t*'s to be crossed, and Alec'll have to sign more papers. However, I've managed to convince Irwin that given Walsall's explicit instructions, the sooner you take possession, the less likely the will is to be contested."

"He really doesn't want us there, does he."

"So it would appear," said Tommy with lawyerly caution. "At least, he's unenthusiastic. I dare say he was had up for pinching a bobby's helmet in his salad days and has developed an inhibition about the police."

"A complex, I think, not an inhibition. Is one allowed to become a lawyer after pinching a bobby's helmet?"

"Yes, as a matter of fact."

"Oh Tommy, you, too? What is the fascination of bobbies' helmets for young men?"

"Daisy, I do have other clients—"

"Sorry, but you raised the subject. To return to Mr. Irwin, complex or no, he could have refused the Jessup ladies' request to introduce me to them, or vice versa, but he didn't. They were friendly and welcoming. I should think they'll be good neighbours, and the house is perfect, except for a lot of cleaning and a lick of paint. I wonder whether we'll be able to move in before Bel comes home for half term."

"Is that odd Yankee still hanging about? Have him give you a hand with packing up and so on. He must be good for something. Tell Alec to give me a ring, will you?"

"Right-oh."

"Speaking of which, you'll want to get the house wired for telephone service. The old man electrified, but he didn't believe in the infernal apparatus."

"Oh bother! Thanks, Tommy. Love to Madge and Robin." Daisy rang off.

Lambert came down the stairs and found her sitting in the hall, feeling rather stunned.

"Gee whiz, Mrs. Fletcher, are you OK? I hope you haven't had bad news?"

"No, good news. At least, it's what I was hoping for. The trouble is, I just don't know where to start!"

Alec was called away to the outer reaches of the kingdom, whether by good (from his point of view) luck or good management. Lambert, still without papers or money, offered to accompany Daisy to the new house to go over it thoroughly

36

and see what needed to be done before the Fletchers could move in.

After touring the house in increasing consternation, they stood in a sitting room at the rear, peering out into the dusk—made duskier by the grimy French windows—over the paved terrace and the weed-grown terraced garden to the leafless trees at the top. Though Mr. Irwin had had the furniture uncovered and dusted, Daisy was dismayed anew by how dismally dingy the old man had let his home become.

"It's a nice room," Lambert said doubtfully.

"It could be. Before, I was concentrating on the size and number of the rooms," she explained. "But after a proper cleaning, the whole place is going to have to be painted and wallpapered from top to bottom. Bother! Choosing colours and patterns could take ages, and then Alec might not like my choices. I wish he hadn't gone away just now. I'd hoped to have it ready for Belinda's half-term holiday."

His ears turned red. "It looks like Miss Belinda will need her old room. Don't worry about me, Mrs. Fletcher. I'll find somewhere to stay."

"I wasn't exactly worrying." Daisy couldn't keep a note of asperity from her voice, and his flush deepened. "All the same, I would have liked to move before she comes home."

"How about you just paint everything white? That way, it'd look nice and fresh, and it wouldn't be too hard to paint or paper over if you wanted to change."

"Light and bright." Perhaps even a judicious use of looking glasses here and there at strategic points, avoiding the excesses of the house next door! "Yes, that might work. I'll think about it. Thank heaven Mr. Walsall preferred good-quality, comfortable furniture rather than the latest fashion. Much of it is perfectly all right."

"And so little used, it's hardly worn."

"The cleaners are going to be here for the next couple of days and I can't— Isn't that the doorbell? Someone at the front door? Who on earth . . . ?"

"Must be a Fuller Brush man."

"A what?"

"Don't you have them here? A door-to-door salesman. Shall I get rid of him?"

"Yes, please."

As he went out, Daisy turned away from the window. The room was larger than their only sitting room in St. John's Wood, and there was the drawing room at the front, as well. The furniture really wasn't bad, though she might use the St. John's Wood stuff in here. White paint and new curtains—yes, she could see the possibilities. Once the electricity was turned on, and the boiler stoked and lighted to run the radiators—

"It's a maid from next door, Mrs. Fletcher," Lambert announced buoyantly. "We're invited for cocktails."

"Oh dear! I can't possibly go. I'm covered in dust and cobwebs."

The maid had followed him in. "It don't show, ma'am," she said.

"That's because I wore brown tweed, on purpose."

"I'll fetch you a clothes brush."

"Thank you. But no amount of brushing will transform a coat and skirt into a cocktail dress."

"Not to worry, 'm. It'll just be family. Mrs. Jessup said to tell you it's just so's the master can meet the new neighbours, seeing he came home yesterday from foreign parts. Mr. Aidan's back from the shop, too."

As usual with Daisy, curiosity overcame any reluctance to appear incorrectly dressed. With the gentlemen present, perhaps she'd get the answers to some of her questions about the Jessups.

A few minutes later, the maid preceded them into a large drawing room at the front of the Jessups' house. It was furnished—to Daisy's disappointment—in a thoroughly conventional manner.

"Mr. and Mrs. Fletcher, madam," the maid announced.

"Who, me?" bleated Lambert, at his most inane.

"Oh, this gentleman isn't my husband," Daisy said at the same time. "This is Mr. Lambert. He's visiting from America."

Mrs. Jessup, rising to greet them, sank back into her chair as if her legs had suddenly lost their strength. Already on their feet, the two men froze. After a moment, they exchanged a silent glance of consternation.

Audrey Jessup stepped into the breach. "How do you do, Mr. Lambert? Mrs. Fletcher, Father says you've definitely decided to move in. I'm thrilled!"

By the time she had made all necessary introductions, the others had recovered their sangfroid. Her husband made no mention of his previous meeting with Daisy in the garden, so she followed his lead, despite wondering about the reason for his reticence.

His father, Maurice Jessup, a portly man, was wearing a well-cut suit designed to disguise that fact. His jowls hung over the knot of his tie, and his forehead was receding towards the crown of his head. His present worried frown looked out of place on a face that seemed essentially genial. He offered drinks: "Anything you fancy," he said, gesturing at a cabinet standing open to display bottles of every conceivable shape, size, and colour. "Aidan, you do the honours, will you?"

While his son poured and mixed, he turned to Lambert and asked warily, "Are you over here on business?"

"Not really, sir. Well, kind of."

This response—to Daisy's ears, typical of Lambert's vagueness—appeared to hold some sinister significance to the Jessups. She was tempted to tell them he was on government business, just to see what their reactions would be. She resisted temptation, remembering how chary he'd been of revealing his "business" to the Pearsons. It was quite conceivable that he was being obfuscatory on purpose.

"Which part of America are you from?" asked Audrey, the only one not disturbed by Lambert's presence.

"Arizona, ma'am."

"Is that in the South?"

"Southwest. It's mostly desert and mountains, no real big cities. The population of the whole state's not much above three hundred thousand. My father owns the biggest insurance company in the state. Both our senators are customers. That's how he got me a job in . . . er, hmm, on the East Coast."

Daisy came to the rescue. "We met in New York a couple of years ago. I was over there on a writing assignment."

"Oh yes, Father mentioned that you're a writer. How marvellous!" Audrey exclaimed. "What do you write? Do you use a pen name?"

"Magazine articles, under my maiden name, Daisy Dalrymple."

"In *Town and Country?*" asked Mrs. Jessup. "I've read several. You always have such fascinating snippets of the history of the places you write about."

Everyone seized on this new topic and worried it to death. Then they moved on to the house next door and Daisy's plans for it.

Mr. Jessup was given to colourful notions, such as enclosing the front porch and turning it into a conservatory for hothouse orchids. Recalling his Continental travels, Daisy decided the miniature Galerie des Glaces must be blamed on him rather than on his wife. She, in contrast, made several helpful suggestions about the kitchens and servants' rooms. Aidan took after his mother in practicality, offering the name of a housepainter whose work and charges they had found satisfactory. His wife seconded everyone's proposals with enthusiasm, but her chief interest was in the nursery, which she was longing to see.

"As soon as it's been cleaned and painted," Daisy promised. "I'm sure you'll be able to give me some ideas."

When Daisy started making "time we were getting home" noises, Mr. Jessup said, "If by any chance you're thinking of having a housewarming party, I'll be glad to let you have any wines and spirits you want at wholesale."

Daisy must have looked as blank as she felt, because Aidan

added, "We're in the business, you know, Mrs. Fletcher. Jessup and Sons of New Bond Street, since 1837."

"Oh, I didn't realise." That would explain Mr. Jessup's travels, visiting wine growers, no doubt. About to comment, she recalled just in time that she had been eavesdropping when she overheard Mrs. Jessup's mention of his whereabouts. "That's awfully kind of you."

"Just a gesture to welcome new neighbours," said Aidan, perhaps with an eye to depressing future expectations.

"I'm afraid," Daisy went on regretfully, "my husband's job precludes our accepting favours."

"Civil service?" he asked.

"Yes, sort of."

"No one need know," said his father.

"Thank you, but it's just not on." The inevitable moment had come when Mr. Irwin's discretion went for nothing and all must be revealed. "Alec's a policeman, you see. Scotland Yard. He's a detective."

"Too thrilling!" Audrey exclaimed.

The rest of the Jessups appeared more dismayed than thrilled.

"Of course he can't accept a gift, then," said Mr. Jessup with a jovial laugh that didn't quite come off. "Are you a policeman, too, Mr. Lambert?"

"Who, me?" Lambert said blankly.

"Lambert's usual idiotic response to any question about himself," Daisy told Alec later that evening when he rang up, "but it averted further interrogation and they dropped the subject."

"They were alarmed, though, to hear I'm a copper?"

Daisy considered. "*Perturbed* is the word. They didn't seem as worried as Mr. Irwin was."

"Perhaps Irwin, as a lawyer, is more aware of the legal ramifications of whatever they're doing. You say the Jessups run an off-licence?"

"I should think they call themselves 'Purveyors of Fine Wines and Spirits to the Aristocracy.' Premises in New Bond Street, and the elder Jessup trots around the Continent, presumably visiting vineyards."

"Most likely they're evading duty somewhere. Not my headache, thank heaven. I don't feel obliged to tip off Customs and Excise, especially as the whole thing may exist only in your imagination."

"It's not!" said Daisy indignantly. "You don't think it could have something to do with their unwanted Yankee visitor?"

"Great Scott, Daisy, it's not against the law to have visitors from America, even unwanted ones, or we'd be in trouble ourselves! It's probably just the shiftiness the law-abiding public so often display when coming face-to-face with the police. Are you having second thoughts about moving in next door?"

"Oh no, darling. I like them. Mrs. Jessup's read my articles—"

"A sure way to a writer's heart."

"And she didn't tell the others about my writing as 'the Hon.,' which was jolly decent of her. It would have been frightfully embarrassing! Of course, maybe she didn't notice or had forgotten."

"I wish you could persuade your editors to leave it off."

"Believe me, so do I. At least in England. I don't care if—"

"Your time is up, caller," the exchange operator announced. "Do you want another three minutes?"

"Let me see if I have change. Daisy, I'll be home tomorrow late, but I have to leave again early the next—"

Click click bzzzz. They were cut off. With a sigh, Daisy hung up the receiver.

"Gee whiz!" Lambert stood on the stairs, staring at Daisy. "Are you telling me some guy from the States called on the Jessups?"

"No."

"They didn't have an American—?"

"I wasn't telling you anything."

Lambert looked confused. "You mean there *was*—?"

"I mean it's not really any of your business. Or mine, come to that."

"Aw, gee, come on, Mrs. Fletcher! I'm here to do a job for the government—"

"Not my government. As it happens, I can't tell you anything for certain anyway. I overheard what sounded to me like an American accent, but I could well have been mistaken."

"And old Jessup's a wine merchant. What a stroke of luck! It gives me somewhere to start looking. As soon as my papers arrive," he added sheepishly.

"Let's hope it's soon," said Daisy in heartfelt tones.

THIRD SEA INTERLUDE

They hired men with the scythes so sharp
To cut him off at the knee.
They rolled him and tied him by the waist,
And served him most barbarously.
They hired men with the sharp pitchforks,
Who pricked him to the heart,
And the loader he served him worse than that,
For he bound him to the cart.

"Welcome aboard *Barleycorn*," grunted the seaman who had helped Patrick to descend from *Iffie*. A couple of others were busy stowing sacks and crates. "Skipper's in the wheelhouse."

Taking this as an invitation—or perhaps an order—Patrick made his way cautiously forward by starlight, making for the blacker black rectangle in the bow. The wheelhouse was much lower than he would have expected. He couldn't imagine how a man might stand upright inside.

Beneath his feet, the deck surged as the *Barleycorn* put on speed, her engines running smooth and quiet. Having found his sea legs weeks ago aboard *Iphigenia*, Patrick adjusted easily to the motion.

"And these three men made a solemn vow, John Barleycorn was dead . . . ," he sang silently to himself.

"Then little Sir John sprung up his head, and soon amazed them all."

Whoever had christened the bootleggers' boat had a sense of humour, though somewhat lacking in common sense. Her name would surely arouse suspicion in anyone who knew the old ballad.

He was quite close to the wheelhouse before he could make out the windows, faintly illuminated by the binnacle lamp within. But glancing back, he saw the wide white curve of the wake. If Coast Guard vessels were about, they could hardly miss that signal. Then, the very absence of required lights would be cause enough to stop her.

The wheelhouse roof was just above his waist level. Stooping, he peered through the side window and saw the silhouette of a mariner in a peaked cap. He knocked.

The man at the wheel gestured to him to enter. He had to crouch to enter and climb down a short ladder to reach the deck inside.

"Sir, I'm Patrick—"

"No names," growled the skipper.

"Right-oh. I mean, aye, sir. But I'm supposed to be meeting a man. . . ."

"The Irishman."

"Is he aboard?"

"Nope. Waiting ashore."

"Oh." While not exactly gushing, the skipper didn't seem actually hostile. Patrick ventured a question. "May I ask why the wheelhouse is lower than the main deck?"

"So there's somewhere to duck down when the bullets start flying."

"Gosh, I'd hoped the stories I've heard were exaggerated. The Coast Guard actually shoot to kill?"

"Ayup. Leastways, I don't say they mean to kill, but when you turn a machine gun on a manned ship, accidents happen."

"I suppose so."

"Even with bulletproof glass and armour plating."

"Which she has?"

"Purpose-built."

Patrick was silent for a moment, contemplating the degree of adventure he was encountering. "Are you . . . er . . . are we expecting to meet any Coast Guard ships?"

"Regular patrol cutter hereabouts is paid off. Shore station likewise. But there's no knowing where they'll pop up. We can outrun 'em, given half a chance, even their new cutters."

"I thought your engines sounded sweet. Where do you intend to land the stuff?"

"No names. We'll get you where you're bound. You don't need to know how."

"Sorry!"

Patrick expected to be dismissed ignominiously to join the crew. However, the nameless captain ignored him henceforth. After waiting for a few minutes, he found a stool and sat down, leaning back against the rear window. He even managed to sink into an uneasy doze without falling off the stool.

He dreamt he was standing in the middle of Piccadilly Circus, with motor-car horns blaring all around him. The noise woke him.

A brilliant white light flooded the small cabin. The moon? No, much too bright, and it moved with a disconcerting unsteadiness. "What . . . ?" he asked, confused.

"Get down! Last thing we need is them to find a limey aboard. Go nap on those sacks." The captain pointed at a pile in the corner. "Pull one over you. If you're questioned, you're my sister's deaf-mute boy."

"Aye, sir." As Patrick ducked below window level and scuttled over to the sacks, a Klaxon horn bellowed again, followed by a loud-hailer.

"Ahoy, *Barleycorn*! U.S. Coast Guard. Stand by to be boarded."

The beam of the searchlight remained on the wheelhouse. "Damn their eyes!" the captain swore. "It's illegal to throw a searchlight on the bridge of a ship! Pity I'm in no position to report them, though if it comes to trial. . . ." He let roll a slew of oaths but throttled back the engine. He hauled himself up the short ladder to the main deck.

Huddled among the sacks, which smelled of a curious mixture of fish, spirits, and tar, Patrick heard only fragments of the ensuing conversation.

". . . Double-crossing whoreson skunk . . ."

"Hey, take it easy. Me and the boys just figured . . ."

". . . Had a deal . . ."

". . . Spare a coupla crates . . ."

Concluding that he was not going to be arrested in the immediate future, Patrick stopped cowering and made himself as comfortable as possible on his odiferous bed. He was half-asleep again by the time the captain returned with another man.

"Greedy bastard's made us run late," the captain growled. He resumed his post at the wheel and the purr of the engines swelled. "It'll be daylight before we're in signalling distance."

"What we need's one of those radio transmitters," said the other in the dogmatic tone of one who was repeating oft-unheeded advice.

"That's what the limey's here for." Without turning his head, the captain asked, "You awake, son?"

"Yes, sir." Patrick scrambled to his feet.

"You're here to set up radio codes, that right?"

"That's right, sir. We've heard your Coast Guard is intercepting uncoded messages from ship to shore, so my father hired a top-notch cryptographer—a chap who worked for the War Office during the War—to set up a code for us. It's not hard to use, and it can be changed at irregular, prearranged intervals, so they won't get a chance to work it out. I'm going to set it up with Mr. . . . uh . . . ." He recalled the warning against naming names. "With our buyer's agent."

"What did I say, skipper? These days, you gotta have radio."

The captain gave an unenthusiastic grunt. When nothing more was forthcoming, the seaman went out and Patrick subsided on his pile of sacks again.

When next he roused, day was breaking. A light mist swirled over the sea. The captain still stood at the wheel, steady as a rock. Feeling chilly, Patrick yawned and stretched. He was dying for a cuppa, but he knew one didn't ask New Englanders for tea.

"Good morning, sir."

The captain, now revealed as a tall, lean man with a long, seamed face fringed with grizzled whiskers, hooked a laconic thumb over his shoulder. "Bread and cheese in the locker."

"Thanks. Will you have some?"

"Ayup."

With the half loaf and hunk of cheese in the locker, Patrick found a thermos flask of coffee and a couple of battered tin mugs. Having acquired a seaman's knife aboard the *Iphigenia* (for which he now felt a nostalgic affection), he cut a doorstep of bread and a slab of the cheese. The coffee smelled very strong. He poured a cup and carried the makeshift meal to the captain.

When Patrick tasted the coffee, he discovered the aroma disguised a healthy slug of whisky. It wasn't the breakfast he'd have chosen, but it warmed him through. Evidently, the captain of the *Barleycorn* believed in his work, unlike the Boston Irishman, who, according to Patrick's father, was a teetotaller.

An Irishman, a *Catholic* Irishman, who didn't drink was oddity enough. A teetotaller who broke the law to import booze for his fellow citizens boggled the mind, Patrick mused, gnawing on his bread and cheese. Love of money was the root of all evil, they said. Not, of course, that he considered dealing in high-quality alcoholic beverages to be an evil.

A young seaman burst into the wheelhouse. "Skipper, Jed spotted a destroyer astern!"

Startled, Patrick choked on a crumb.

The captain swore a brief but pungent oath. "He's sure?"

"Just a glimpse, but he's using the spyglass."

"Did they see us?"

"She ain't hailed us. Nor shot at us . . . yet."

"Which way's she heading?"

"Dunno, skipper. He couldn't tell."

"This fog's going to burn off soon as the sun rises. So much for the weather forecast! Tell the boys to hold on to their hats. We'll run for it."

By the time Patrick got over his choking fit, the heavy-laden *Barleycorn* was ploughing through the swells at her top speed. The mist turned to gold as the sun's first rays touched it, and soon its wraithlike wisps dissipated.

The young seaman returned, bursting with excitement. "She's turning, skipper. She's spotted us for sure. A mile and a half astern, Jed says. D'you want us to chuck the stuff overboard?"

"Send a hundred thousand bucks' worth of good liquor to Davy Jones's locker? Not danged likely," said the captain grimly. "We'll give her a run for her money."

FOUR

A smell of paint still hovered in the hallways when Belinda came home for her half-term holiday. That the Fletchers had managed to move from St. John's Wood by then was in no small part due to Lambert.

Though he still spent every weekday morning haunting the American embassy, an unhappy ghost who had lost his obol for Charon, he would then go to the Hampstead house to "ginger up" cleaners and workmen, as he put it. Daisy didn't tell Alec that when she dropped in to see how things were going, Lambert was generally standing at a window with borrowed binoculars, watching the doings of the next-door neighbours.

Daisy wasn't sure what he was looking for, but she was pretty sure he hadn't seen it. He couldn't have hidden his subsequent excitement from her.

Be that as it might, the refurbishment was completed in record time. The house was light and bright. Bel loved her new bedroom, three times the size of the one she had occupied since the twins' arrival.

The very morning after she came home, Lambert returned

from the embassy with his passport and papers, and took his leave.

His gratitude for the Fletchers' hospitality was so heartfelt that Daisy began to feel quite mean for having scoffed at him and resented his intrusion into their lives.

"You've been a great help," she said. "I hope you'll come back to say good-bye before you leave England."

He cast a furtive look behind him and whispered, "You may see me around, Mrs. Fletcher. If you do, please pretend you don't know me. Don't speak to me, and don't tell anyone. Except Mr. Fletcher, of course."

She bit her lip to hold back a laugh. He was so keen to be a hero out of Anthony Hope's romances, or John Buchan's, or the American equivalent, and he just wasn't cut out for the role. "I won't," she promised.

He stood on the threshold for a moment, scanning his surroundings before he ventured forth. As he went down the steps, Daisy saw him turn up his coat collar and pull down his hat.

She told Alec when he turned up in the middle of the afternoon and announced that he was taking three days off while Belinda was at home. To her surprise, her news made his dark brows lower in a frown.

"What's the matter, darling? Aren't you glad he's gone at last?"

"Naturally. I just hope he's not going to cause any trouble."

"What kind of trouble?"

"The Americans are pushing us to help them enforce their stupid law. It started last year with extending territorial waters from three to twelve miles. Well, the government approved that treaty for our own reasons, and a lot of grief it's caused already. They've seized a number of British-registered ships, some actually outside the new limit, when they've caught them off-loading alcohol, or even just with alcohol aboard. Now they're sending agents over here to investigate the shippers. The last thing we need is trigger-happy idiots like Lambert wandering about."

"Customs took away his gun, remember?"

"Thank heaven for small mercies! Let's forget about him, for the present at least. No doubt he'll turn up again sooner or later, like a bad penny. Where's Bel?"

"She went with Mrs. Gilpin and Bertha. . . . Don't look blank, darling. Bertha's our new nursery maid. They've taken the babies and Nana for a walk on the Heath. It's such a beautiful day, let's go to meet them."

"Right-oh. Just let me get changed."

A two-minute walk took them to the edge of the Heath, eight hundred acres of woodland and meadow practically on their doorstep. From their high position, on this clear October afternoon, they could see the glint of the sun's slanting rays on the Crystal Palace, far off beyond St. Paul's. At the foot of the hill, a large pond gleamed between leafless trees.

Quite a number of people were taking advantage of the weather: boys kicking balls, well-wrapped pensioners chatting on benches, dog walkers, pram pushers, and, combining the last two, a small group coming up the slope towards Daisy and Alec.

Nana was first to spot them. Off her lead, she came bounding up to them, tail gyrating wildly. Behind her, at a snail's pace, came Belinda, bent double with Oliver clutching her forefingers and staggering along on his own two feet. Next was Bertha, a plump, toothy girl with a soft West Country voice, carrying Miranda. Keeping an eye on her charges, Nurse Gilpin brought up the rear with the empty pushchair, a newfangled contraption she had fought tooth and nail until it was made plain to her that Daisy's brother-in-law, *Lord* John, had had it specially designed and built for the twins. Nurse Gilpin was a snob.

Belinda looked up to see where Nana had gone. Of course, Oliver promptly sat down. He opened his mouth to yell but stopped when Bel picked him up, the burden making her look skinnier than ever. She had been a thin child as long as Daisy had known her, and since going back to boarding school after the summer hols, she seemed to have grown an inch without putting on an ounce. Daisy hoped she was getting enough to eat. She didn't seem to have any trouble carrying the baby, though, and gave him up reluctantly to Daisy when they met.

Alec relieved the nursemaid of Miranda and sat her on his shoulders, wincing as she buried her little hands in his dark, springy hair.

"Hold on tight, Daddy. She doesn't understand she mustn't let go."

"Da-da," Miranda observed with satisfaction.

With a smug smile at Daisy, Alec said, "Da-da before Ma-ma."

"It's just babbling at this age, isn't it, Mrs. Gilpin?"

"I'm sure I can't say, madam. In the old days, I'd've said so, but what with all these modern notions, who can tell?" The nurse had reluctantly given in to Daisy's "modern notions" about parents actually being allowed free access to their children, but she didn't pretend to approve. Now and then, she managed to get in a dig on the subject.

An elderly man came down the hill towards them. He walked stiffly, with the aid of a stick, and was dressed in tweed knickerbockers, like a country squire out to view his estate. He had a pair of binoculars dangling on a cord around his neck and a pair of fat spaniels waddling at his heels. Nana rushed to meet the dogs.

"You'd better put her on the lead, Bel," said Alec.

The man heard him. "It's all right, they know one another. Nana, isn't it? They met in the garden when your maid let her out one morning." Pale, washed-out eyes scrutinized them from under bushy eyebrows. "You'll be the new people at number six. My sister and I are at number ten. Bennett's the name, two *t*'s. Settling in all right, eh?"

"Yes, thank you," said Daisy. "I'm Mrs. Fletcher. My husband. Our daughter Belinda."

"And who was the young fellow I saw leaving this morning with bag and baggage, eh?"

"A guest," Alec said repressively.

"A guest, eh? We thought he might be a relative, the way he's been popping in and out the last couple of weeks, before you moved in. Or a decorator. You've spent a fortune having the place done up nicely, I expect?"

"Nothing terribly exciting," said Daisy. "We've kept it quite simple."

"Haven't you even bought new furniture? We haven't seen a furniture van pull up, only Pickford's moving van."

"We've kept it simple," Daisy repeated. Feeling Alec seething beside her—he was more accustomed to interrogating than to being interrogated—she went on: "I hope you'll excuse us, Mr. Bennett. We must get on home before the little ones catch a chill."

Mr. Bennett peered at the babies. "Twins, eh? Not identical, though!" he said disagreeably.

Oliver's face crumpled, preparatory to a yell, but as the old man stumped off, he decided to blow a raspberry instead, a skill he had recently mastered.

"Why did he ask so many questions, Daddy?" Belinda whispered.

Alec grunted.

Daisy said diplomatically, "It's natural to be interested when new people move in nearby."

"Which doesn't mean you have to answer any questions he may ask you, Bel," said her father.

"Certainly not," Daisy agreed. "But try not to be rude."

"Like you, Mummy. You didn't really tell him anything, but you were perfectly polite. I don't expect I can do it so well."

"Practice makes perfect," said Alec with a grin.

"I expect he's grumpy because he's feeling rheumaticky," Daisy said forgivingly.

As they reached the top of the hill, Alec started to swing Miranda down. She refused to let go of his hair.

"Bel, you're quite wrong. She understands about hanging on. What she doesn't understand is that Da-da doesn't care for a damp collar."

"Oh, Daddy!" Belinda giggled, and a muffled snort came from Bertha. "Bend down and I'll make her let go. There you are. Mirrie, darling, I'm not carrying you wet. You'll have to go back in the pushchair."

Daisy deposited Oliver, too, who was beginning to smell less than fragrant. It was Mrs. Gilpin's turn to look smug. "They should have gone on the pot half an hour ago," she announced, "but Miss Belinda *would* walk on." Stately as a dowager duchess, she sailed ahead with the pushchair, Bertha trotting at her side, receiving low-voiced instruction.

Belinda skipped along between Daisy and Alec, arms linked through theirs. "I'm glad I don't have to change nappies," she said.

"You'd better learn how, darling," said Daisy. "I have the best of both worlds, playing with the twins as much as I want but not having to do the dirty work. When I was little, Nanny ruled supreme, and we hardly ever saw my parents. Of course," she mused, "I'm not at all sure Mother ever had the least desire to challenge Nanny's rule. But by the time you have children, who knows how the world will be?"

Bel wrinkled her nose. "All right, Mummy, I'll ask Bertha to show me how. I'll even do it myself. Practice makes perfect! I do like helping to give them baths, though. It's such fun watching them splash."

When they reached the house, the parlour maid met them with a folded note. Daisy opened it.

"From next door. An invitation to drinks before dinner tomorrow, to meet the neighbours."

Alec groaned. "Must we?"

"I'm afraid so, darling." She checked that the parlour maid had returned downstairs. "Unless you want to hide behind closed curtains with all the lights off. But we'd never get away with it anyway. Remember, Elsie's sister is parlour maid next door."

"And a rotten idea that will probably prove to be! I bet that's how the Jessups know I'm home for a few days. We could try for theatre or concert tickets?"

"We could, but we'll have to take the plunge sooner or later. After all, we're not only neighbours, we're their landlords. We don't want to behave as if we're high-and-mighty, and turn them against us. Besides, the Jessups are nice people. Mr. Jessup did offer to provide drink at cost for a housewarming party."

"Trying to worm his way into my good graces. We don't have to have a party, do we?"

"I thought the best thing would be to wait till Christmas and hold an open house for everyone, your friends, my friends, relatives—"

"Mothers?" Alec asked with deep foreboding.

"We'll have to sometime, darling. This way, they'll be sort of diluted."

"You have a point." He sighed. "All right, drinks next door tomorrow. I suppose that nosy old man from the Heath will be there."

"Diluted," Daisy said hopefully.

"She was on the stage, you know," said Miss Bennett in an insinuating tone. A pudgy woman with pepper-and-salt hair, confined in a net, and a round, pale, doughy face, she had cornered Daisy.

"Our hostess?" Chorus girl? Music hall turn? Though dying to know, she wouldn't have asked for the world. To do so would only encourage the beastly woman's tattling, and she didn't need any encouragement. Obviously, the Bennetts were going to be the flies in the ointment. One ought to be able to interview one's prospective neighbours before moving.

"We all know about actresses. And Irish, into the bargain!" said Miss Bennett darkly.

"Such charming people, I've always found."

Miss Bennett looked at her as if she were mad. "Charming? Always blowing up policemen—"

"I don't suppose Mrs. Jessup's career left her any time for blowing up policemen. Mine certainly doesn't."

"Your career?" Her nose positively twitched. "You have a job?"

"I write. Oh, excuse me, Miss Bennett, I believe my husband wants to speak to me."

"Write? Write what?" Her nose twitched eagerly, but Daisy was already moving away with an insincere smile. "*Novels,* no doubt," came a mutter behind her, the inflexion leaving no doubt about the kind of novels Miss Bennett was imagining.

Aidan Jessup, bottle in hand, intercepted Daisy on her way across the room towards Alec. "Now what has that dreadful woman been saying to put you in such a pucker?" he asked with a wry look. "Let me fill up your glass. Dubonnet, wasn't it?"

"Yes, thanks. No doubt you'll soon be hearing that I write blue novels."

"But you write magazine articles, don't you? I'm afraid I don't read much besides the trade journals, but Mother enjoys your work. Good Lord, you didn't tell Miss Bennett—?"

"Not I. It's what she prefers to assume."

"Oh yes, Always Assume the Worst is their motto. I suppose they've told you Mother was a chorus girl."

Daisy willed herself not to blush. "Just that she was on the stage."

"As a matter of fact," he said a trifle belligerently, "she started as a soubrette in the provinces and was playing decent roles in London—Celia and Nerissa and that sort of thing—when she met Father. She might have gone on to Rosalind and Portia if she hadn't retired when they married."

"Not the Lady Macbeth type, I take it."

That made him laugh. "No, Mother's not made for tragedy. She doesn't even take the Bennetts' mischief making too seriously. If you ask me, it's a great pity my revered papa-in-law didn't put a spoke in the Bennetts' wheel when they decided to buy here." He nodded towards Mr. Irwin, who stood staring gloomily into his glass, his expression suggesting that the stout, prosperous-looking citizen holding forth at his side might be asking for free legal advice.

"Could a reputable lawyer do that?"

"There must be a way, don't you think? As it is, unfortunately, one can't easily exclude them from a gathering of Constable Circle residents. It doesn't do to be at odds with one's neighbours."

"No, of course not. Their tales would only grow the wilder. Otherwise, everyone seems to be very pleasant."

"Not a bad lot. Is there anyone you haven't met yet?"

"I've talked to all the neighbours, I think. Your brother and sister aren't here? Your sister's married, I understand, but I didn't gather where she lives. I had the impression that your brother lives here, though."

Aidan looked disconcerted. "Deirdre lives in Birmingham," he said. "My brother often goes on buying trips with our father, to learn that side of the business. I've never been much of a one for travel. I prefer to stay home, and one of the family has to be here to mind things at this end. There's Audrey and the children to be considered, too. Have you travelled much on the Continent?"

"Just one flying visit, a few days last summer. If it hadn't been for the War, I'd undoubtedly have been shipped off to finishing school, like my sister Violet. I'm glad to have avoided that—I don't think it would have suited me at all—but I'd like to see some of the rest of the world. Besides America, that is."

"Ah, yes, I'd forgotten you were in America." He turned with obvious relief to Alec, who came up just then. "May I get you another drink, Mr. Fletcher?"

"Thank you, no. We ought to be making our adieus, ought we not, Daisy?"

People were beginning to drift away, and the Fletchers had to run the gauntlet of new acquaintances saying "So glad to have met you." A few last good nights were exchanged on the pavement before they attained their own front steps.

57

Daisy tucked her hand into Alec's arm as they went up.

"Did you talk to the Bennetts?" he asked, delving into his pocket for the door key. "He asked me if it's true I'm a peeler—a peeler! I thought the word went out of use decades ago. And then he had the nerve to say he hoped not, because many respectable people don't care to associate with the police."

"Don't worry, at least Miss Bennett seems to disapprove of blowing up policemen. She told me in the most horridly insinuating way that Moira Jessup is Irish and pointed out that the Irish have a habit of blowing up policemen. They're in luck, as I have no intention of associating with them any more than absolutely unavoidable."

Small wonder if Daisy forgot Aidan's odd reactions and patent attempt to change the subject of his brother's whereabouts. She did remember next morning but decided against telling Alec. He'd only say she was imagining things.

FOURTH SEA INTERLUDE

They wheeled him round and round the field
Till they came unto a barn,
And there they made a solemn mow
Of poor John Barleycorn.
They hired men with the crab-tree sticks
To cut him skin from bones,
And the miller he served him worse than that,
For he ground him between two stones.

The moment the Coast Guard destroyer was sighted, *Barleycorn*'s skipper had changed course. Now, though he knew they were on his tail, he held steady.

"Can we outrun them?" Patrick asked.

"Not with this load. But they're slow to turn. Just watch. Go out on deck if you want."

Two considerations weighed against Patrick's reluctance to leave whatever cover the wheelhouse offered: He didn't want to appear a coward, and surely the skipper wouldn't let him go out if they were in range of the destroyer's guns. Would he?

He climbed the short ladder to the low door. Two deck-hands had opened several of the lockers lining the port and starboard rails and were spreading fish from a large crate over the illegal contents.

Glancing around, Patrick saw the lookout standing on the railed roof of the wheelhouse, gazing astern with his spyglass to his eye. Now and then he would swing round to scan the horizon. Near him, smoke poured from the smokestack as the *Barleycorn*'s engines put forth their utmost effort. Though the smoke quickly dissipated in the wind created by their speed, it must appear as a banner to the pursuing destroyer. Staring sternward into the glare of sea and sky, Patrick could just make out the distant banner of smoke from the Coast Guard ship's four funnels.

He was about to ask the lookout man for a turn with the spyglass when one of the others called to him. "Bear a hand here," he requested, holding out a bucket.

"What are you doing?"

"Can't hurt to tell 'em we're innocent fishermen," the other drawled. "Not that they'll believe it, 'less they're looking for an excuse to let us go."

Patrick took the bucket and scooped up a mess of fish. They were very dead, with dull eyes, and beginning to smell. Fresh fish might have better helped the deception, he thought, crossing to an open locker to slosh the contents of his bucket across the bulging sacks within. Perhaps the bootleggers hoped the smell would deter the Coast Guard from further investigation.

Perhaps they were right. Holding his nose, he returned for another bucketful. No wonder they didn't want to attempt this ruse unnecessarily. When time came to unload, not only would the fish have to be disposed of but the burlap swathing the bottles would have absorbed the stench. Patrick could only hope he would not be expected to help with that, too.

As he worked, he kept an eye on the destroyer. At first, the four smoke trails grew more indistinct. The distance between her and *Barleycorn* must be increasing, Patrick realised. Gradually, the four appeared to merge into one as she came around to chase the rumrunner. And then the intervening distance began to shrink.

Patrick started to wonder what American gaols were like. It was a happier alternative to wondering what it felt like to be shot.

The lookout on the roof shouted to his shipmates, "OK, go ahead!"

One of the men put down his bucket and moved aft, where he crouched to fiddle with three cylindrical canisters. Puzzled, Patrick stopped mucking about with fish and moved closer to watch. The man delved into the pockets of his pea jacket, came up empty-handed, and called to Patrick, "Matches?"

Patrick threw him a box, his aim sure despite the motion of the boat.

The seaman caught it. Cupping his hands, he struck a match and applied it to the top of one of the canisters. He paused to study the result. No effect was visible to Patrick, but the man nodded in satisfaction and proceeded to light the other two canisters.

The third failed to ignite on the first try. By the time he got it going, smoke billowed from the first and streamed out behind the *Barleycorn*.

"Tell the skipper to give it a couple of minutes," he directed Patrick.

Grinning, Patrick hurried forward. The destroyer was already invisible. Therefore, he presumed, *Barleycorn* was invisible to the destroyer.

Leaning down, he passed on the message. The skipper glanced back through the rear window at the thickening, spreading screen, then gestured to him to enter.

He obeyed. "They'll never catch us now," he said with enthusiasm.

"*They* won't."

"Oh." Patrick pondered. Of course, the destroyer would have a radio transmitter. At this moment, they were doubtless sending out wireless messages to all Coast Guard ships within reach, with details of *Barleycorn*'s course. "Oh," he said again, crestfallen. Given the hint, the conclusion was obvious, and he should have worked it out for himself right away.

The skipper glanced back again at the smoke screen, then changed course.

Since the skipper didn't dismiss him, Patrick stayed below, dropping onto the stool. This time, the result of his subsequent cogitations was still less cheering: The skipper expected shooting, and since the codes Patrick carried were important to the success of the lucrative business, he was to be protected.

He didn't exactly want to be on deck, dodging flying bullets, yet he felt like a coward, hiding out of sight while the others risked their lives on deck. If he had fought in the War, would he have been one of those who did his duty, even a hero, perhaps, or would he have funked it? He couldn't help wondering, though it was a futile question. He had been too young to bear arms for king and country.

Not that his present business was in any way comparable. He was doing nothing illegal by English law, but he was deliberately flouting American law. In American terms, he was a criminal.

Too late to worry about that. He had a job to do for his family, and he'd do it unless prevented by force majeure.

The approach of force majeure was announced just a few minutes later.

"Cutter on the starboard bow." The man relaying the sighting from Jed on the wheelhouse roof stayed by the open door.

Patrick stared through the windscreen, or whatever it was called on a boat. He couldn't see the cutter, but what had been a shadow on the horizon was now unmistakably land, green and grey and growing clearer by the moment.

"He's spotted us. Changing course to intercept, and there's another on the port bow."

The skipper's mouth took on a grimmer set, but he held steady on their course.

"Jed reckons they'll fall astern afore they're in range."

That sounded like good news to Patrick. However, this time he paused before voicing his relief. The cutters would be behind *Barleycorn*, but within firing range nonetheless. One on each side, they could rake the launch from stem to stern if she refused to stop—or they could hold their fire, follow her to her landing place, and make their arrests on shore.

Now there were low headlands on either side as *Barleycorn* entered a bay.

A Klaxon horn blared, followed by a loud-hailer: "U.S. Coast Guard. *Barleycorn*, stand by to be boarded."

The skipper's response was to shout to the man at the door, "Get Jed off the roof, and all of you lie flat!"

"But skipper—"

"Get your heads down!"

The man disappeared.

Another hail was followed by a warning shot screaming overhead. A fountain of water and mud arose where it landed in the shallows. The *Barleycorn* veered left, then right, then left again. Patrick assumed they were dodging further shots, until he realised the banks were closing in as they sped up a narrowing, winding inlet.

And ahead loomed a low drawbridge—a *very* low bridge.

"Skipper—"

"Duck!"

Patrick flung himself to the floor, arms covering his head. Above him, the roof splintered and disappeared, the smokestack crumpled, and windows shattered as they struck the bridge.

The skipper bobbed up and resumed steering, his gaze fixed on the river ahead. His cap had been knocked off and shards of glass glittered in his hair and whiskers. He spared a quick glance back at Patrick, prone amid the wreckage, and a manic grin bared his teeth.

"Too shallow for the cutters," he explained, "and they can't fire in case there's people around."

"Geez, skipper!" came a choking protest from the deck to the rear.

Half-hidden by smoke billowing from the truncated smoke-stack, three wobbly figures were picking themselves up from the backswept rubble of the roof. *Barleycorn* was now moving too slowly in the narrow channel to disperse the pungent fumes. Coughing, the men stumbled forward, one of them dabbing at a trickle of blood running down his cheek.

"Geez, skipper, there ain't much of that drawbridge left. The township's not gonna be too happy."

"We'll tell 'em a Coast Guard shell demolished it. They can try for compensation. Jed, get forward and watch for shoals. The rest of you, watch for the shore signal."

Patrick said hesitantly, "There's a chap over there who seems to be trying to attract our attention." He pointed at a couple of men on the wooded bank, one waving both arms, the other launching a dory.

Throttling back, the skipper kept just enough way on the launch to hold her in place against the current in the middle of the stream. The dory pulled alongside and the oarsman hung on to a fender. On his face, a naturally dour expression seemed to be warring with inward amusement.

"You're to unload in town," he said laconically.

"In town?" Turning his head, the skipper stared at him.

"Ayup."

"What's going on?" Patrick asked uneasily in a low voice. "Has something gone wrong?"

"Looks that way."

"Is it safe to go into the town? Won't the police be waiting for us?"

"We'll find out."

"You trust the man who told us—?"

"My brother."

Patrick didn't like to point out that history was full of brothers betraying brothers, starting with Cain and Abel. After all, he trusted his own brother, the old stick-in-the-mud!

Meantime, the oarsman had briefly conferred with his passenger. He hoicked a thumb at Patrick and asked his brother, "That the fella you picked up out there?" The thumb hoicked seaward.

"Ayup."

The thumb indicated his companion. "This fella's come to pick him up."

In contrast to the overall-clad boatman, the other was wearing a yellowish brown suit, of a colour and cut that would have raised eyebrows in London—but Patrick had no way of knowing whether it was proper business dress in America. The passenger started to stand up, subsiding abruptly as the dory rocked but raising his brown fedora enough to show reddish hair and bright blue eyes in a pale face scattered with pale, blotchy freckles.

An Irishman, if ever Patrick had seen one.

"Now?" asked the skipper.

"Ayup."

Patrick retrieved his kit bag from under a heap of debris and clambered out of the remains of the wheelhouse. He turned to thank the skipper, receiving a silent nod in response. With a wave to the deckhands, he went over the side and landed nimbly enough in the dory to preserve his self-respect. His natural inclination was to introduce himself, but he recalled the ban on naming names and refrained, uttering merely, "How do you do?"

"Uh, howdy."

"What went wrong, sir?" Patrick asked the local man as he rowed them towards the riverbank. "Why is the *Barleycorn* going into the town?"

"Farmer called the feds."

"After taking our money for the use of his barn!" the Irishman exclaimed. He sounded more American than Irish, and very angry.

"Changed his mind," the skipper's brother said mildly. "It's a free country. Man's allowed to change his mind."

"Not after taking our money. He's going to regret it, I can tell you."

"Not too badly, if you want folks hereabouts to cooperate in future."

"He called the feds."

"And his boy called us. So what happens? The feds rope in the local cops and every last one of 'em heads out to the farm to set an ambush. So 'stead of a dozen men tramping to and fro through the mud from river to farm with their arms full, *Barleycorn* sails into town and unloads at the dock, straight onto the trucks. Sounds like a good deal to me."

He shipped his oars as the dory nosed into the bank. Patrick jumped ashore with a painter. He tied up securely to a stake he found there, then turned to take the oars and boat hook from the boatman.

"Thanks." The man joined him, handed him his kit bag, and took the oars.

"Thank *you*, for ferrying me from *Barleycorn*."

Patrick used the boat hook to bring the dory close and then gave the Irishman a hand up onto the bank. The air was so thick with animosity, he felt a nervous desire to chatter but managed to keep his mouth shut. The local man led the way into the woods, along a barely visible path. Birds fell silent as they passed.

In the rear, the city man, wearing utterly inappropriate shoes, picked his way with care through the damp leaf mould. Patrick paused to let him catch up.

"Where are we going?" he ventured to ask.

"To see a man. You don't need to know his name, but he works for the Eyetie who works for the big boss, your customer. That is, you are Patrick Jessup, I presume?"

"Yes. And you?"

The man considered a moment. "I guess you'll have to know sooner or later, seeing I'm going to England with you."

"You are?" Patrick exclaimed.

"Yeah, so they tell me. Someone's gotta make sure our competitors don't get at you. But don't let's talk about that here. It's none of the hick's business." He nodded towards the man trudging ahead. In a low voice he added, "You can call me Mickie Callaghan. Pleased to meetcha."

"Callaghan! That's my mother's maiden name."

"No kidding. Well, is that a coincidence or what?"

The local man was waiting for them beside an unpaved road. He had stowed the oars in a farm cart pulled off onto the verge. The cart horse was looking back at him with patient hope.

A little farther along, a large Packard was parked; half-concealed by bushes, it faced in the opposite direction from the cart. Callaghan pointed. "That's us." He looked Patrick up and down. "Mary Mother of God, you're a mess altogether. You brush yourself down before you get into my auto. I guess I better pay this guy off, or he'll be calling the feds on us."

Patrick handed the boat hook to the boatman and went on to the car. As he took off his jacket and shook the wood and glass debris out of it, he watched Callaghan hand over a wad of banknotes. Both he and the recipient looked grim.

Patrick was glad he was not the object of their anger. His energy was beginning to flag. He hoped he wouldn't be expected to crank the Packard. When Callaghan came over and curtly gestured to him to get in, he realised with relief that the car had a self-starter. Callaghan climbed in behind the wheel.

He stuck his hand inside his jacket, pulled out a pistol from a shoulder holster, and chucked it onto the backseat.

The Packard failed to start on the first attempt. Before Callaghan could press the button again, the local man came up from behind. Boat hook in hand, he loomed over Callaghan.

"I'm telling you," he said, and his voice carried no less conviction for being calm and quiet, "you and your buddies better not be seen in these parts ever again if any harm comes to that family."

The motor caught and they spurted away in a cloud of dust. Like it or not, Patrick was committed to travelling with the aggressive, vengeful, and armed Irishman.

FIVE

Daisy wanted to reciprocate for the Jessups' drinks party, but with Alec's schedule so erratic, a similar evening do was impossible. Besides, the Fletchers simply could not compete in variety or quality with the wine merchant's vast selection. Worse, she'd have to choose between inviting the Bennetts, who would ruin the affair, or offending them by not asking them.

She decided afternoon tea for the Jessup ladies would be the proper response, especially if she included an invitation to the children for nursery tea. Her St. John's Wood friends, Melanie and Sakari, would round out the party.

Sakari couldn't come because of a prior engagement at India House, where her husband was something important. Daisy rang up Madge.

"The people with the Versailles room? Darling, I'd love to meet them."

"Here, not at their house."

"Of course. Just watch me wangle an invitation. Will Lucy be there?"

"Lucy? Gosh no. Afternoon tea in suburbia is definitely not Lucy's . . . well, cup of tea."

Madge laughed. "True. I'm not so choosy. I'll be there. Shall I be Lady Margaret, do you think? Are they that sort of people?"

"I don't think so," Daisy said doubtfully. "I suspect they'd be *less* likely to invite you. But I don't know them very well yet."

"Then Mrs. Pearson it is."

"Bring Robin, too, if you like. There's to be nursery tea, as well."

"Heavens, darling, you are becoming positively domesticated."

"It's all right, we don't have to watch feeding time at the zoo. There will be nurses aplenty to scrub their jammy faces. But the little Jessup girl adores the twins, and Mrs. Jessup—Mrs. Aidan Jessup—is very motherly, so I thought it would please her."

"You want to please Mrs. Aidan Jessup? What are you up to, Daisy?"

"Nothing!"

"Aidan? Isn't that Irish?"

"I believe so. The elder Mrs. Jessup was Moira Callaghan when she was on the stage."

"A chorus girl?" Madge sounded amused.

"Shakespearean," Daisy said severely.

"And Irish. Have you moved in next door to a nest of Republicans?"

"Not at all! Aidan is frightfully English, in spite of his name. So is his father, in spite of all his travels on the Continent. It's the younger son . . . Irish Republican—I hadn't even considered that possibility. I think he's in America, not Ireland."

"I'll come early and you can tell me all about it."

"Right-oh. Yes, I'd better ring off now or Alec's going to be asking nasty questions about the telephone bill. Cheerio, darling."

Hanging up, Daisy went down to the kitchen to discuss the tea party with Mrs. Dobson. The cook-housekeeper was delighted at the prospect of showing off her baking skills. Daisy left her to make out a shopping list, and went up to the nursery to tell Oliver and Miranda about their coming treat—and to warn Nurse Gilpin.

Oh dear, she thought, realising she ought to have consulted Nurse first. Mrs. Gilpin would be offended, but then, she was offended with Daisy most of the time anyway.

The new nursery was light and bright, with plenty of room for two cribs, dressers, toy chests, a rocking horse, and all the other necessary accoutrements. The walls were hung with paintings by Belinda of bunnies, kittens, squirrels, and puppies, some more recognisable than others. A small room connected to it was Mrs. Gilpin's bedroom, so that she had some privacy but, with the door open, could hear the slightest sound from the babies at night. She had grudgingly approved the arrangement. It meant Alec could go into the nursery with good-night kisses even when he got home very late.

Nana, the subject of one of Belinda's paintings, lay sprawled on the floor. She had been allowed into the nursery occasionally on sufferance for several months. Then Daisy thought to mention to Mrs. Gilpin that, during her own childhood, a couple of dogs were always to be found in the nurseries at Fairacres. After that, Nana was made welcome. Oliver and Miranda crawled over her, cooing with delight, the way they had over Lambert.

Watching them, Daisy found it impossible to believe in a nest of Irish Republicans next door. Did they still go around blowing up English policemen, now that they had their own country? She hadn't heard of any such incidents recently, but she'd never been much of a newspaper reader.

When she was growing up, any young lady taking an interest in politics was assumed to be a suffragette—horror of horrors! Men still had a tendency to go into a female-excluding huddle when the subject arose. But the suffragettes had won, and there were already several women MPs. Daisy was twenty-eight years old. In two years, she'd be thirty (more horrors!) and able to vote in national elections, and she hadn't the foggiest what it was all about. She decided she had better start reading Alec's morning paper.

In the meantime, with Miranda crawling towards her crying "Ma-ma"—indubitably "Ma-ma"!—Daisy couldn't put off much longer broaching the delicate subject of nursery tea.

Oliver raced after his sister, shouting "Ga-ga-gak."

Daisy sat down and the babies climbed onto her lap. Inhaling the sweet milk and talcum smell of them, she gave each a kiss and said over their heads, "I've invited the children next door to tea, Mrs. Gilpin."

"Indeed, madam!" said Nurse with a sniff. "I hardly think Master Oliver and Miss Miranda are old enough to entertain guests."

"Their nanny will come, too, of course."

"Indeed, madam."

"Besides, I expect Miss Marilyn will entertain the twins. You know how she dotes on them when they meet in the gardens. And there will be another two-year-old to play with Percy Jessup—Mrs. Pearson's Robin."

"Lady . . . Mrs. Pearson's little boy? How nice for our little ones to make his acquaintance."

What a change of tune! Daisy assumed Mrs. Dobson must have told her that Madge was Lady Margaret. If Nurse knew, then the nursery maid surely knew, and what Bertha knew the parlour maid knew, and what Elsie knew, her sister next door was bound to know. So no doubt the Jessups would also find out within a short time. It would be interesting to see whether they were more impressed by someone with the genuine title of "Lady" than by someone with a mere "Honourable" before her name.

Alec came home early for once. He had obtained tickets for that night's concert at Queen's Hall, a rare occasion, given his erratic schedule. Daisy didn't want to spoil the evening, so she postponed asking him whether the Irish Republicans were still in the habit of blowing up policemen. Perhaps she'd learn enough about the Jessups at the tea party not to have to ask him at all.

It was quite late when they got home. As it was drizzling, Alec stopped the Austin right in front of the house to let Daisy out, then went to put the car in the garage in the alley. As Daisy started up the steps, the Jessups' front door opened, silhouetting a man against the lighted hall. Then the door slammed shut and the figure hurried down the next-door steps. Daisy couldn't see his face, but something about the way he moved seemed familiar.

She was in the house and taking off her coat before she made the connection: Surely he was the American visitor who had so upset Mrs. Jessup. Judging by his hasty retreat, his reception hadn't been any better today.

When Alec came in, rain dripping from his hat, Daisy almost told him. But he had other plans for what was left of the evening.

"Time for bed," he said firmly, and with his arm snug about her waist, she wasn't going to argue.

The next afternoon, Madge arrived in good time for a chat, as she had promised. They went straight up to the nursery, however, and by the time Robin, Oliver, and Miranda had been introduced and induced to play more or less nicely with one another, it was too late for Daisy to tell Madge any details of the mysteries surrounding the Jessups. She did warn her, though, that her title was no secret.

When they went downstairs, Elsie was just opening the door to Melanie. Madge had met Mel a couple of times but didn't know her at all well. Besides, Melanie, the very proper wife of a bank manager, was rendered acutely uncomfortable by gossip that involved speaking ill of anyone. Though Daisy had no intention of maligning the Jessups, discussing the possible involvement of one or more members with the Irish Republicans was bound to distress Mel.

The Jessup ladies, children, and nanny arrived a few moments later. After greetings and introductions and the despatching of the nursery party upstairs, Daisy poured tea. Elsie passed it around, along with watercress sandwiches (Mrs. Dobson was a genius at cutting bread practically paper-thin) and a variety of homemade biscuits (including Daisy's favourite macaroons, which she allowed herself only on special occasions).

Once everyone was served, Daisy dismissed Elsie. Madge and Audrey Jessup, both cheerful, practical women with two-year-old boys, were already getting on like a house on fire. Mel and Mrs. Jessup, on the other hand, were making polite conversation, so Daisy joined in.

It wasn't difficult to introduce the subject of foreign travel. The Germonds had taken the whole family to Brittany in the summer. Daisy asked Melanie about the difficulties of travelling with children, and went on to mention quite naturally that Mr. Jessup took his younger son with him on his business trips to the Continent.

"How old was he the first time he went abroad with your husband?" she asked Mrs. Jessup.

"Fifteen or sixteen," Mrs. Jessup did not elaborate.

"And now he goes himself," said Daisy.

"You must worry about him," said Mel.

Since Mrs. Jessup didn't respond, Daisy pointed out, "Surely if he's old enough to do business on his own, he's old enough not to worry about."

"Oh Daisy, I don't think one ever stops worrying about one's children. Wouldn't you agree, Mrs. Jessup?"

"Absolutely," she agreed with an amused smile. "Even into one's dotage, I dare say, when the 'children' themselves are growing elderly."

Daisy thought that behind the calm façade, the smile was forced, stagy even, but perhaps she was influenced by knowing Mrs. Jessup had been an actress. She ventured another probe. "He isn't in Germany, is he? As far as I can recall, most German wines come from the Rhine and Moselle, and that part of Germany has been pretty unsettled recently, even more so than the rest."

"There are some vineyards farther east, but yes, most are in the Rhineland. Maurice doesn't handle many German wines, though, because there's still a lot of prejudice against them. But I don't want to bore you with business talk, Mrs. Germond. Are you an aficionado of the theatre?"

"I should be happy to go more often than I do."

"Perhaps Mrs. Fletcher has told you that I was on the stage. It's an odd world." She proceeded to entertain them with stories of theatre life. Madge, who was a great playgoer, joined in, while Audrey Jessup prompted her mother-in-law, suggesting particularly interesting incidents. Once again, Daisy envied their easy relationship.

Mrs. Jessup was very amusing, but when everyone departed, a frustrated Daisy was no wiser about the whereabouts of her younger son.

Madge was last to leave. "I wish I could stay and talk," she said. "I must say, they seem like nice people. Not a single 'your ladyship' to be heard, thank heaven! Mrs. Aidan has invited me to go and see the Galerie des Glaces one of these days."

"Madge! How did you manage it?"

"I just mentioned that you'd mentioned it," Madge said airily, "and that it sounded interesting. She told me her father-in-law had it made as a compliment to her mother-in-law, because she was so beautiful, he wanted to see her everywhere he looked. Mr. Jessup must have been quite a romantic, though nowadays apparently he uses it mostly to entertain foreign businessmen and their wives."

"And there I've been tiptoeing around the subject for weeks!"

"I even found out that the ladies entertained you in there that first time because the children had been playing in the drawing room earlier and little Percy threw a wooden train through a windowpane."

"Well, that's one little mystery cleared up. I trust they don't let him play in the Galerie?"

"Catastrophe! But Mrs. Jessup sounds like a very affectionate, not to say indulgent, grandmother. I can't believe she's involved in any dastardly plots. Here's my taxi, so we'll have to talk about that another time. Bye, darling."

They kissed cheeks, and Daisy waved as Madge stepped into the cab. As it pulled away, her eye was caught by a movement in the garden opposite. Many of the bushes were leafless now, but there was a clump of laurels and rhododendrons. The evergreen leaves were waving in an unnatural manner, even considering the slight breeze that was chasing clouds across the sky.

Daisy watched. Someone was lurking there.

She was as certain as certain could be without actually confronting him that it was Lambert. She had glimpsed him once or twice in the streets of Hampstead but had obeyed his instructions to pretend she hadn't. Could anyone else who made a practice of lurking possibly be so inefficient at it?

"Alec?"

"Mmm-hmm?" He looked up from the *Daily Chronicle*.

"Do the Irish still go around blowing up policemen?"

"I can't promise they've given up the practice, love, but at the moment they seem more intent on blowing up one another."

"Oh. I suppose that's a good thing, in its way. Sort of."

Alec grinned. "Sort of. They'd probably give it up if they didn't get endless support, guns and money, from their fellow countrymen who have emigrated to America. But it's not my problem at the moment, thank heaven."

"Leave me the paper, will you, darling? Do you realise I'm going to be old enough to vote soon? I ought to know what's going on in the world."

"You mean you're not going to vote as your husband directs you?"

"Alec!"

"Ah well. As long as you don't start writing political diatribes." He folded the newspaper and passed it over. "Here you go. Have fun."

Daisy wrinkled her nose at him. "I don't suppose it'll actually be fun, but I'm sure it must be my duty to king and country, so I'll give it a try."

He drained his coffee and left for work. Daisy spread the *Chronicle* on the table in front of her, but instead of reading the headlines, she found herself considering what he had said.

The bellicose Irish Republicans obtained arms and money from their compatriots in America. So the younger Jessup son—she realised she still didn't know his name—might be in America raising funds. Why were the Irish fighting among themselves? It was all very muddling. Perhaps something in the newspaper would help her sort it out.

The first headline that caught her eye informed her that the French were bombing Damascus. Fighting in Ireland was bad enough, she decided; she simply didn't want to know why the French were bombing Damascus. Thankfully, she remembered that she had to get started on an article about Hampstead Heath, and of course she had to go and see the babies first.

It was a couple of days later that Daisy came out of the High Street stationer's with a packet of carbon paper and a heavy sigh. She nearly bumped into Audrey Jessup.

"Oh, Mrs. Fletcher, good morning. Whatever is the matter?"

"Mrs. Jessup! I beg your pardon. I wasn't looking where I was going. It's nothing, just a minor irritation, but . . . irritating."

"I know just what you mean. I expect Mr. Knowles can't find what you need."

"A typewriter ribbon, for the commonest make of machine available, an old one that everyone has. I suppose I'll just have to go back to the stationer in St. John's Wood. He always has the right one."

"Knowles is the most disorganised person, and if he can't lay hands on something immediately, he gets flustered and denies the possibility of ever being able to get it. But one just has to be patient and firm."

"Is that all? Then if you'll excuse me, I'll just go back in and be firm."

"He's probably standing there now with the ribbon in his hands, wondering what to do with it." Audrey smiled. "If you're not in a great hurry to get back to work, would you like to meet for coffee after you sort him out? There's a Kardomah just down the street, opposite the bank."

Daisy was only too glad to agree. It was the first opportunity she'd had to talk to Audrey alone. Perhaps, on her own, Mrs. Aidan Jessup would be more forthcoming about her husband's family.

Her mother-in-law always evaded talk about the younger son's whereabouts. Why, if he were simply visiting vineyards in Europe, or even relatives in Ireland? Daisy was practically convinced he was in America. Whether he was rumrunning or gunrunning, she couldn't be sure, but he must be up to something fishy, or his mother wouldn't be so worried. Further questions also remained to be answered. Who, for instance, was the angry American? Might he be another agent, unknown to Lambert? After all, no one could expect poor Lambert to actually accomplish anything.

These reflections were no hindrance to dealing firmly with Mr. Knowles. Daisy reemerged into Hampstead High Street with a typewriter ribbon nestling alongside the carbon paper in her basket.

As arranged, Audrey had gone into the Kardomah to bag a table before the morning rush hit. When Daisy entered, she was standing next to a table for four, talking to a pair of seated women. Daisy hoped she wouldn't want to join them.

Seeing her, Audrey waved. Daisy went over and was introduced as the mother of adorable twins. The two ladies invited her and Audrey to sit down, but Audrey said she had already taken possession of a table for two by the window. They stood for a couple of minutes, chatting about their various offspring.

Quite the most annoying thing about having children, Daisy decided, was being forced to listen politely while other people talked about theirs.

Mrs. Vane's and Mrs. Darby's coffees arrived, accompanied by toasted tea cakes. Daisy had resolved to be good, but the spicy, buttery aroma of one of her favourite treats undermined her resolve. She and Audrey repaired to their table, saved by a scarf flung over one chair and a basket on the other.

"My treat," said Audrey as they sat down. "You will have something to eat, won't you? Otherwise, I can't, and I'm simply starving." She lowered her voice. "I'm pretty sure we'll be having an addition to the family in the spring."

"Congratulations!" More baby talk, Daisy thought, but perhaps she'd be able to lead it round to Mrs. Jessup's missing offspring.

A waitress, neat in black, with a frilly white apron and cap, came to take their order—two coffees, a tea cake, and a Bath bun.

As she left, Daisy added, "No wonder you're blooming."

Audrey beamed. "I'm so happy. We're all happy. Not just about the baby. My father-in-law has heard from Patrick at last—my brother-in-law, you know. Mama Moira's been dreadfully anxious about him. Being an actress, she doesn't show it, but I always know. Now Patrick's on his way home, we can all be comfortable again."

Before Daisy could think of a polite way to enquire where Patrick was coming home from and what he'd been doing there, the waitress arrived with a tray. And then it was too late. Audrey revealed that she had read Daisy's latest article in *Town and Country*, because "Mama Moira said I ought, with you living next door. I'm not much of a reader," she confessed, laughing. "I just don't seem to have time. But I really enjoyed your article."

She had lots of questions, and Daisy never managed to steer the conversation back to Patrick Jessup. At least she now knew his name!

HOME SWEET HOME

Here's little Sir John in a nut-brown bowl,
And brandy in a glass;
And little Sir John in the nut-brown bowl
Proved the stronger man at last.
And the huntsman he can't hunt the fox,
Nor so loudly blow his horn,
And the tinker he can't mend kettles or pots
Without a little of Barleycorn.

As a child, Patrick had found the long lift ride at Hampstead tube station spooky, though he'd have died rather than admit it to his brother or his friends. Once he was old enough, he preferred to climb the three hundred steps to the surface from the deepest platforms in the whole Underground network. Though the staircase was pretty grim and gloomy, at least he wasn't shut up in a cage. He used to say it was to keep himself fit for cricket.

Arriving in London on a rainy afternoon with Mickie Callaghan in tow, he assumed they would take a taxi from the boat train to Constable Circle.

"Nix," said Callaghan. "Cabs can be traced. We take the subway, or whatever you ride in in this burg."

The implications did not make Patrick happy. He was already unhappy about taking the Irish American home to his family. They had crossed the Atlantic together, Callaghan hiding in their cabin most of the way in a most unsettling manner. Patrick still wasn't sure what the man was after, but it seemed impossible to get rid of him.

His father had set up this whole affair. Patrick had carried out his part successfully. His father would have to deal with Callaghan.

They reached Hampstead station just early enough not to

have to stand in line for the lift, but Callaghan took one look at the lift attendant and said, "We take the stairs."

"He takes thousands of people up and down every day. He won't remember you."

"We take the stairs."

Maliciously, Patrick failed to inform him that they were not much less than two hundred feet below ground level. Callaghan, silent in his rubber-soled shoes, set off at a fast pace that would have taken him quickly to the top of a four-story building. Patrick didn't attempt to keep up. He was not at all surprised when he caught up with Callaghan plodding upward, looking disgruntled. Knowing from experience that taking the climb too slowly was as exhausting as attempting to take it too fast, Patrick kept going, giving the disgruntled American a wave as he passed.

"See you at the top."

Callaghan scowled.

The last step behind him, Patrick was pleased to find that he was less out of shape than he had feared. He was breathing hard but by no means winded. Leaning against a poster advertising *The Lost World*, starring Bessie Love, he waited for Callaghan, who appeared at last, after a considerable interval. He came up the final flight breathing easily. Patrick was sure he had stopped to rest on the last landing. If he had learnt anything about Mickie Callaghan, it was that he'd go to considerable trouble to avoid being caught at a disadvantage.

As always, it was a relief to exit into the open air. The rain had stopped, but dark clouds hung overhead, bringing an early twilight. Patrick turned left and left again, into Flask Walk. Callaghan, silent and morose, kept pace with him along the narrow paved lane, past the Flask public house. It was just opening.

"Let's stop in for a pint," Patrick suggested, trying to postpone the moment when he'd have to introduce his companion to the family.

"Nix. I bet you're known in there. They'd remember me."

The two-story workmen's cottages opening directly onto

the pavement gave way to larger houses and big trees as they crossed into Well Walk. At the old Chalybeate Well monument, they left the street and took a passage uphill between two large redbrick houses. They came out on the south side of Constable Circle.

"We'll cut across the garden," said Patrick, turning his head to speak to Callaghan, who had fallen a step or two behind.

"Nice place. Which is your house?"

"To the left of the one at the top." He pointed. Someone was coming down the steps. "I think that's my brother." In the dusk, he couldn't be sure.

The man crossed the street and started down the path. It *was* Aidan. Good old Aidan! Patrick had never in his life been so glad to see the old sobersides. He waved. Aidan waved back and they both walked faster. Callaghan fell behind Patrick.

A man stepped out of the bushes and accosted Aidan. He spoke too softly for Patrick to hear at that distance, but his gestures were forceful. Aidan brushed him off and kept going. The man persisted, striding along at Aidan's side, gesticulating. He seemed to be angry.

They all converged on the fountain.

The stranger's rant cut off abruptly, as if he had suddenly noticed he and Aidan were not alone. He stared towards Patrick.

"You!" he exclaimed, his tone venomous. Thrusting his hand inside his coat, he took a couple of quick paces forward. His hand reappeared gripping a pistol.

SIX

"*Madam!*" *Elsie* burst into the dining room in a manner most unlike her usual parlour-maidenly propriety. "Oh madam!"

"What's the matter?" Daisy sloshed tea over the *Chronicle* as she jumped up in alarm. "Not the twins—?"

"Oh no, 'm, not the babies."

Flooded with relief, Daisy took a closer look at the maid. "You're white as a sheet, Elsie. Here, sit down. What's wrong?"

"It's the little dog, 'm. I let her out same as usual to go over to the garden—"

"Don't tell me she's been run over!"

"Oh no, madam. Nothing drives that fast round the Circle. But usually she's that good about coming right away when I call her, and this morning I called and called and she didn't come—"

"She's run away?" Daisy asked incredulously.

"Oh no, 'm. I went up the area steps to the pavement to look if I could see her, and there she was in the garden, over by them bushes, the evergreen ones? And she was barking and whining fit to bust, and she just wouldn't come away, so I went to fetch her. And I grabbed her collar and she kept on

whining and I was scolding her like anything when I saw it."
The maid fell silent, her eyes and mouth round with remembered shock.

Daisy mustered all her patience. "What did you see, Elsie?"

"A glove, madam. Someone dropped it, I thought, and I went to pick it up—a good leather glove, someone'd be looking for it—but it had a hand in it, and I thought, 'Oh it's one of them nasty drunkards. What cheek sleeping in our garden!' And I moved the branches, like, to give him a piece of my mind, but he wasn't drunk, madam. He's dead! As a doornail."

"Good gracious! Oh dear, I suppose he must have died of exposure. It was cold and wet last night."

"I must say, 'm, he didn't look like a common drunk." Elsie was regaining her sangfroid. "Good-quality clothes he has on. He looked sort of familiar, but I can't quite place . . . Has the master gone already?"

"I don't think so. He went up to say good-bye to the twins." Daisy had got up early to have breakfast with Alec, who had to leave for Scotland Yard earlier than usual to finish writing a report before a meeting with Superintendent Crane and the AC (Crime). "You're right, Elsie. He'll have to be told."

What, after all, was the point of being married to a policeman if one had to cope oneself with dead bodies carelessly strewn around? It was no use, however, expecting him to be pleased.

Daisy went upstairs. She met Alec on the landing, as he came down.

"I'm off, love. I shouldn't be too late tonight."

"Darling, I'm afraid you're going to be late this morning. There's a tramp lying under the bushes in the garden, and it looks as if he's dead."

"Daisy, if you *must* fall over bodies wherever you go, could you not at least wait until I've left for work?"

"It wasn't me! Elsie found him."

"Not me, 'm!" Elsie, who had come up the stairs behind Daisy, was equally anxious to disclaim responsibility. "It was the little dog, sir."

"Where is she?" Daisy asked. "Where's Nana?"

"Oh madam, I must've forgot her, what with the shock and all. She'll be out there guarding him still, I 'spect. And I don't think he's a tramp, sir, not by his clothes."

Alec groaned. "Couldn't we just pretend you found him when I was already gone?" When Elsie looked almost as shocked as she had in reporting the body, he went on quickly: "No, of course we couldn't. Daisy, you'd better ring up the local station, but I suppose I'll have to take a look."

"Elsie, go with Mr. Fletcher and fetch Nana in."

"Oh madam, not me. I'm not going anywhere near that body again, not for nobody, not if you was to tell me to pack my box this instant."

Daisy looked at Alec. Alec looked at Daisy.

He sighed. "Right-oh, you'll have to come and get the dog. I can't cope with her as well as a corpse. Telephone the locals first. Elsie, I suppose you're quite sure he really is dead?"

"I saw bodies in the War, sir, when they bombed the East End. He looked to me about as dead as a jellied eel." She paused to consider. "No, not a jellied eel, not really. Dead as—"

"Never mind," Alec said hastily, "I'll take your word for it." He looked at his wristwatch. "I'm not going to make it to that meeting. Daisy, after you've spoken to the locals, you're going to have to ring up the Yard and tell the Super what's going on."

"Darling, he's bound to blame me!"

"Can't be helped." His grin was infuriating. Daisy wondered whether on the whole it might be preferable to have a husband who was *not* a policeman if one had to cope with a body. "If he carries on at you, say you have to secure the dog. In the meantime, no doubt she'll show me where to look."

With that, he bounded down the stairs and disappeared through the front door.

Before she followed, Daisy fixed the parlour maid with a stern eye. "This is police business now, Elsie. You mustn't talk about it to anyone. Not a soul, not even your sister, or you'll be in serious trouble. Did you talk to anyone outside?"

"No one was about, 'm. Leastways, I didn't see anyone, but then after I saw it, I wasn't looking. There could've been someone I didn't notice."

"When you talk to the police, just tell them exactly what you saw, not what or who might have been there."

Her eyes went round again. "Ooh, madam, will I have to talk to the police?"

"Very likely not, but if so, it's nothing to be afraid of. You speak to Mr. Fletcher every day, don't you?"

"Yes'm, but he's the master. It's not the same."

Daisy wished she had never embarked upon the subject. "Well, I dare say they won't want to see you, with the master to explain what happened. I must go and telephone."

The desk sergeant at Hampstead police station sounded bored. She gave him her name.

"Mrs. Fletcher, what can I— Mrs. Fletcher?" The voice perked up. "Mrs. DCI Fletcher, by any chance?"

"Yes, actually."

"What can we do for you, ma'am?"

"I'm ringing for my husband. Could I speak to a detective, please?"

"Of course, Mrs. Fletcher. DS Mackinnon is on duty."

"Oh good, I know him." And she liked him. Alec approved of him, too. "At least I think I do. Was he in St. John's Wood?"

"Moved here a few months ago, ma'am. Half a jiffy. I'll get him right on the line."

There were advantages to being notorious, Daisy thought with a sigh.

A moment later: "Mrs. Fletcher?" The rolling Scottish *r*'s were unmistakable, as was—she hoped—the pleasure in his voice as he continued. "Good morning, ma'am. What can I do for you?"

"Good morning, Mr. Mackinnon. I'm afraid it's a body."

"You've found a body?" he asked cautiously.

Silently, Daisy blessed him for not saying "*another* body." "Not exactly. That is, my maid found it. Or rather, the dog."

"Your dog found a body. Where, exactly?"

"In the garden—it's a sort of park, actually, or circular square, if you see what I mean." Daisy discovered she was more upset than she had supposed. "I'm explaining it very badly."

"Not at all. Chust take your time, Mrs. Fletcher. It isna the private garden of your own house, then?"

"No, not exactly. It's communal, for all the residents of Constable Circle. In Hampstead. Did you know we moved to Hampstead? Constable Circle, number six."

"Got it. You've seen this body, ma'am?"

"No, but my husband has gone to take a look. He told me to telephone."

"DCI Fletcher is on the scene? Excellent," Mackinnon said soothingly. "Nae doot it'll be best if I wait for his confirmation, sin ye've only the maid's word for it. What do you think?"

"No . . . Yes . . . Yes, perhaps. Right-oh, I'll tell him. You'll be standing by?"

"Of course, Mrs. Fletcher. I'll be ready."

"Thank you." Reluctantly, Daisy depressed the hook and asked the operator for Whitehall 1212. She did not want to speak to Superintendent Crane. She wasn't responsible for the body in the bushes; she hadn't even been the one to find the body in the bushes; but she knew perfectly well that, because of certain unfortunate incidents in her past, Crane would find some way to persuade himself it was all her fault.

A glance at old Mr. Walsall's grandfather clock suggested a ray of hope. Surely it was much too early for so exalted a person as the Super to be in his office. She would have to leave a message.

"I would like to leave a message for Superintendent Crane, please," she told the Scotland Yard operator.

"Who is calling, please?" came the inevitable question.

"This is Mrs. Fletcher, with a message from DCI Fletcher."

"Oh, Mrs. Fletcher, I'm sure the superintendent will want to speak to you directly. One moment while I connect you."

Daisy managed to suppress a howl of "NO," though a click told her it was too late anyway.

"Superintendent Crane's office. May I help you?"

"This is Mrs. Fletcher." She went on quickly: "My husband asked me to let Mr. Crane know he's been unavoidably delayed and won't—"

"Just a minute, Mrs. Fletcher. You can tell him yourself."

"But I don't want—"

"Good morning, Mrs. Fletcher." Crane sounded irritable, though she hadn't told him yet about the body. "What's up? Has he forgotten we have an important meeting this morning?"

"No, Mr. Crane, he's well aware of it. But he simply can't get away in time." She absolutely could not think of an easy way to break the news. "I'm afraid our dog found a body. Alec has to wait for the local police to come."

There was dead silence on the line. Then Crane asked with a sort of incredulous resignation, "Did I hear you correctly, Mrs. Fletcher? You've found another murder victim?"

"No! *I* didn't find him, and I don't know if he was *murdered* or not. I haven't even *seen* him yet."

"Yet!" exploded from the much-tried superintendent. "I dare say he's a particular friend of yours?"

"I don't know who he is. Believe me, I sincerely hope I shan't have to look at him. However," Daisy said firmly, "I told Alec I'd go and get the dog out of his way, so I'm afraid I shall have to hang up." And she did. Shockingly bad manners, but he was already annoyed with her. She might as well be hanged for a sheep as a lamb.

"Oh madam!" Elsie hovered anxiously by the green baize door to the stairs down to the kitchen. "I'm sure I wish I'd never gone after the little dog."

"Nonsense. It was your job, and if you hadn't found the man, someone else would have." As she spoke, Daisy took her coat from the coat tree. She started to put it on before she realised she was still wearing her dressing gown. "Bother! Oh well, it's perfectly decent, and Alec can't wait." She buttoned the coat to the neck and tied a scarf over her head.

For once, Nana's lead was hanging in its proper place on the coatrack. Daisy reached for it.

"Madam, your slippers!" Elsie pushed through the swing door and returned immediately with a pair of galoshes, ancient enough to have belonged to Mr. Walsall.

Daisy put them on over her slippers and at last went outside.

Descending the steps—with care, because the galoshes were not hers and were too big—she called to Nana. She could see the little dog's rear end sticking out of the bushes, tail wagging now that Alec had joined in the excitement.

Nana backed out and came to meet Daisy, whining. She submitted docilely to having the lead clipped to her collar, but she had no intention of tamely returning to the house. With a couple of sharp barks—*Come and see what I found*—she pulled towards the bushes. In the oversized galoshes, Daisy had no traction to resist. She slip-slopped across the grass after the dog, losing one galosh halfway there.

Squish. "Oh blast!"

"Daisy! For pity's sake, you're going to muck up any footprints."

"It's murder?"

"It doesn't look good," Alec admitted, backing out of the bushes.

"Not someone we know?" Daisy removed a twig from his hair. "Not one of the neighbours?"

"No one I've met."

"Alec, it couldn't be . . . The Jessups are expecting the younger son home."

"I don't think so. This poor chap looks about the same age as Aidan Jessup, or a year or two older, though it's hard to tell once they're dead. Are the locals on their way?"

"It's DS Mackinnon. Remember him? He said he'd wait till

he had confirmation from you that there really is a corpse, but he's ready to get moving."

"Good. Go and get him moving. And in the meantime, I need someone stationed at each end of the path until Mackinnon arrives, to keep people out of the garden. I've done all I can here. I'll take the top end. People are more likely to come that way at this time of day."

"Oh for a good, solid, authoritative butler! I suppose I'd better take the bottom." Glancing down the slope, Daisy saw the local beat constable about to start up the path.

"Stop!" she and Alec cried in unison.

PC Norris hesitated.

"He'll do. Daisy, give Mackinnon the word," Alec ordered. "I'll deal with this."

Just as well, Daisy thought, remembering she hadn't dressed before coming out. She looked down at her feet, abandoned the second galosh, and tugged Nana back across the lawn, careful to place her ruined slippers in the marks she had already made. She didn't want to be accused of messing up the evidence.

SEVEN

The beat bobby had recognised Alec and was staying put, as instructed. Alec picked his way towards him by the route he thought least likely to disturb any traces of the night's doings. It was pure guesswork at this stage, so he examined the ground ahead intently before he took each step.

The grass was lush, having been too wet for mowing for a couple of weeks. So far, October had brought lots of rain and little frost. When Alec looked back, his trail was clearly visible, but blurred, unlikely to convey any useful information except direction. No, not even that; just where he had walked.

And if he wasn't mistaken— He held out his hand, palm up. Yes, it was starting to rain again.

PC Norris looked up at the lowering grey overcast. "More to come, sir," he opined. "Came down heavy in the night, it did. What's happened, sir? Anything I can do to help?"

He was a burly middle-aged man. Talking to him when the Fletchers first moved to his district, Alec had found him intelligent but unambitious, with no desire for promotion. He enjoyed patrolling his beat, one of the pleasantest in the metropolitan area, and he knew all the residents by sight, most by name.

"Yes," Alec said grimly. "We have a suspicious death. Right now, I want you to stay exactly where you are and make sure no one enters the garden from this end. Later, I'll have you take a look at the deceased."

"Right you are, sir. Will I blow my whistle for help?"

"No. It would bring every servant in the Circle running, and half their masters and mistresses." Alec eyed the nearest house, number 10, where the nosy Bennetts lived. He was happy to see all the blinds still closed. "We don't want to alarm people more than we must. The chaps from your division HQ should be here shortly."

"Right, sir, but there'll be them that see me here and come to ask. What do I tell 'em?"

"Tell them you have no idea what's going on."

Norris grinned. "No more I don't," he said.

"True." Alec left him, treading on the edge of the paving on the side of the path closest to where the body lay. He had considered going around the outside of the garden to see if there were any signs of the body having been deposited from that direction, but that would have made it impossible to see or prevent people walking down the path. He kept a close watch on the edge of the lawn and was rewarded, just before he reached the fountain, with clear evidence of something heavy having been dragged across the wet grass.

He was about to stoop to examine the traces, when a loud voice hailed him. "I say, Fletcher! What's up?" His neighbour from number 7, George Whitcomb, was on his way to whatever he did for a living.

"Stop! Not another step!" Alec yelled, and hurried up the slope.

Though Whitcomb obeyed, he looked affronted and indignant. Alec had met him at the Jessups' party and had exchanged cordial greetings when their paths happened to cross thereafter. The man knew he was a police officer—but that was theory; this was practice. Apparently, Whitcomb either had not expected to encounter Alec in his official capacity or didn't like being ordered about by the police—or both.

At that moment, Alec realised he could not take on this case. All his neighbours would have to be questioned, as possible witnesses, if not as suspects. He was not only a fellow resident of Constable Circle, he was their leaseholder.

He could hold the fort until DS Mackinnon arrived, and then he'd have to bow out.

Yet Daisy, who knew the neighbours considerably better than Alec did, was sure to be an important source of information. However peripherally she was involved, Superintendent Crane and the Assistant Commissioner would expect Alec to keep her from meddling. Unless, he thought hopefully, they had at long last realised that nothing and nobody was capable of keeping Daisy from meddling.

It was all in the lap of the gods, alias the AC and the Super. Right now, Alec's job was to keep Whitcomb from marching down the garden path.

Whitcomb was armoured for the day's battle in pinstriped trousers, a fur-collared overcoat, and a bowler hat, and his chosen weapon was a tightly furled black umbrella. He was respectability personified and respectability outraged.

"I say, what the deuce . . . ," he spluttered. "You're not thinking of closing off the garden to the rest of us, are you, Fletcher?"

"Great Scott no! I wouldn't dream of it. The thing is, there's been a spot of bother down there and I'm just lending a hand while the local chaps gather their forces."

"Forces? Ah, the police, eh? Splendid chaps. Anything I can do?"

Civil servant, not businessman, Alec guessed. "Not at present, thank you," he said. "I expect the detective in charge will be in touch. You won't mind walking round instead of across the garden, I hope."

"No, no, of course not. Don't suppose you can give me a hint? No," he said hastily as Alec shook his head, "of course not." And off he went.

Alec didn't foresee objections from the Jessups, who were amiable types. For the rest of the inhabitants of the Circle, going around by the street was actually a more direct route than crossing the garden.

His thoughts turned to Detective Sergeant Mackinnon. The young Scot was competent and cooperative, if a little too inclined to believe Daisy walked on water. Still, Alec had worked with him once or twice since the case in which she had been involved, and his own feet seemed firmly grounded. He had matured, but he was still on the young side to lead a murder investigation.

And pending the doctor's report, Alec was pretty certain this was going to be a murder investigation.

The local police surgeon, Ridgeway, was also a good man. With luck, he was available and on his way. Not that it really mattered to Alec, as this wasn't going to be his case, but if people were going to get themselves bumped off not a hundred yards from his front door, he wanted the murderer under arrest. The sooner the better.

In fact, for once, when it was out of the question, Alec really wanted to be in charge. He wanted to be on his knees in the leaf mould beneath the bushes, rain dripping down the back of his neck, looking for clues anyone else just might miss.

The rain was belting down, blurring still further the already-indistinct traces of activity on the lawn. Daisy came down the steps towards him, fully dressed at last under her red umbrella, bringing him his conventional black one.

"Darling, you'll be soaked. Mackinnon's on his way, and so's that nice Dr. Ridgeway. And Mr. Crane rang back. He was a bit grumpy, but he said he'll try to soothe the AC's savage breast. No, that's not what he actually said, but that's what it amounted to. I've been thinking—"

"Please don't, Daisy! Besides, there's no point in passing on your speculations to me. I can't take the case. You must see that."

"Because of the neighbours? I wondered if interrogating

them was going to be a problem. But you have to find a way to do it, or we won't have any servants left."

"*What?*"

"The only reason they aren't quitting en masse is that they trust you to bag the murderer quickly. Yes, they all know. I made Elsie promise not to tell a soul, but one can't expect something like this to remain a secret from the rest, not when they can see out of the windows that something's going on. She swore, cross her heart and hope to die, that she wouldn't talk to her sister about it."

Alec snorted. "Fat chance!"

"There is a chance. She likes working next door to her sister, and I told her she wouldn't be any longer if she breathed a word about police business."

"It sounds as if, one way or another, we're doomed to lose all our servants."

"It's no laughing matter, you wretch! Mrs. Dobson won't desert us, come what may, but Mrs. Gilpin says if you aren't put in charge, she's not staying to see her babies murdered in their beds. *Her* babies, forsooth!"

"Did I just hear you say 'forsooth'?" Alec queried.

"Yes, and it just goes to show how upset I am. If she really thought of them as her babies, she wouldn't threaten to desert them. But I can tell you, if you're not busy solving the murder, you're going to be busy changing nappies!"

"Calm down, love. Such things have happened before in your vicinity without your getting in such a state."

"It's never happened right on my front doorstep before," she wailed. "So close to the twins!"

Alec would have put an arm around her to comfort her, but the umbrellas got in the way. "You know it's up to the Super whether I get the case," he pointed out. "But if Crane should be so ill-advised as to give it to me, we might have to move. The neighbours wouldn't take kindly to being interrogated by a fellow resident of the Circle."

"Couldn't you direct the investigation without actually seeing people yourself? You could stay at the Yard, or the local station, and tell your men what questions to ask. Mackinnon, Tom, Ernie Piper, and DC Ross, they're all good detectives, I've heard you say so."

With a sigh, Alec conceded. "If Crane doesn't absolutely forbid my having anything to do with it, I'll pass on your suggestion."

"For pity's sake, don't tell him it's mine."

"I shan't. But if it works and I get stuck behind a desk for the rest of my natural, I'll know whom to blame!"

To his relief, she smiled. "I expect you'll soon find out it was nothing to do with anyone in the Circle, so you'll be able to take a more active part. You did say you didn't recognise him, so it's not one of the neighbours."

"Are you sure we met all of them at that party?"

"No, not absolutely. Mrs. Jessup told me they had invited everyone, but I don't suppose she'd have mentioned it if some sent their regrets. I'm glad the victim is too old to be her younger son."

"Daisy, I can't swear to it. Death changes appearances. Don't go telling them it's not young Jessup, when one of them may have to identify the body."

"I shan't, don't worry. Here come your reinforcements."

She pointed down the hill and Alec turned, to see a cluster of men around PC Norris, some in uniform with waterproof capes, some in plainclothes macs. In turn, Norris pointed up the slope.

"I'd better go down to them," Alec said hastily, "before the whole troop troops up and destroys any clues there may be. Would you stay here just for a moment, till I can send a man around, just in case someone else tries to walk down this way?"

"Of course, darling," Daisy said to his retreating back.

Shivering, she hoped he meant "just for a moment." The rain was coming down harder than ever, with sideways gusts that splashed her legs, though the umbrella kept her upper half dry. Trousers! she thought longingly. Why couldn't one of those fashion tyrants who dictated what women should wear design warm tweed trousers instead of slinky evening frocks that made most figures look terrible?

She couldn't even distract herself by watching what the men were up to, as she was supposed to look out for encroaching pedestrians.

She turned her back on the garden just in time to see a man come out of the Jessups' front door. Swathed in an overcoat, umbrella held low, he was unrecognisable, but presumably one of the Jessup men. Daisy wondered how to bar his way down the path without telling him more than she ought about what had happened.

The problem didn't arise. Somewhat to her surprise, he didn't approach her, but hurried away down the pavement on the other side of the street. Perhaps he was late for work—no, she rather thought that as proprietors they usually didn't go to the shop till half past nine or so, and it couldn't be that yet. Of course, the weather was not exactly suitable for chatting outdoors. One of the household had no doubt observed from a window that no one was being allowed to cross the garden.

Yet Daisy couldn't help recalling the man she had twice before seen hurrying down those same steps, the American visitor. It couldn't be him. Surely he would not have been invited to spend the night at the Jessups'? The very night when someone was murdered in the garden?

EIGHT

"*Mr. Fletcher!*" DS Mackinnon greeted Alec thankfully, raising his hat to reveal short-cropped red hair. "Good morning, sir. Ye've a body in the bushes, Mrs. Fletcher said. Those evergreens up there, it'd be?"

"That's right." Alec curbed his irritation at Daisy's immediate intrusion into the case. "You'd better have one of your uniform chaps go up to the top to take over from my wife and keep people out. I suggest you send him round by the street."

Mackinnon duly nodded to one of the men, who set off up the hill as directed, but his dismay was apparent. "*Suggest*, sir?"

"This is your case, Sergeant. At least for the present." Drawing the Scotsman off to one side, Alec explained the situation.

"I see, sir. But I've never handled a murder case before. Not on my own."

"Your superintendent will probably put one of his DIs in charge."

"Yes, sir. But in the meantime, you're here, sir, and you know what's happened and what needs to be done. Can ye no stay and make *suggestions*?" he pleaded. "Or at least warn me if I'm missing something, or going wrong."

"Damn it, man, I should have been at the Yard half an hour ago!" But it was impossible now to have that report finished for the meeting with the AC, and Crane wasn't expecting him. And he did want to know what had happened practically on his doorstep while he slept. And Mackinnon was regarding him hopefully, like a persistent Scottish terrier—a dripping-wet terrier. Clues were washing away. "All right, let's get on with it."

"Thank you, sir! Dr. Ridgeway should be here any moment."

"I see you've brought photographic equipment."

"Yes, sir." He turned back to the group. "This is DC Ardmore, sir. He's pretty good with it."

"Going to be tricky under them bushes in the rain," said Ardmore dispassionately.

"Do what you can," said Mackinnon. "But keep your big boots out of there till we've seen what else there may be to see."

Alec listened to his instructions to his men, giving a slight nod now and then when Mackinnon glanced at him for approval. The young Scot had the theory down pat. Whether he had that indefinable other sense, the ability to see beneath surface appearances, to spot the detail that didn't quite fit, and to weave apparently unrelated facts into a coherent story, remained to be seen. Part of it could be developed with experience, but part was sheer instinct.

He had shown definite promise on the previous occasions when he had worked with Alec. Running an investigation was another kettle of fish.

He knew PC Norris's name. That was a good sign, whether he was already acquainted or had checked to see who was the copper on the beat before coming out. Alec was not one of those detectives who considered the humble beat bobby a lesser breed. Without those flat-footed plodders to prevent countless crimes, the CID would be even more overworked than it already was.

The second uniformed man Mackinnon had brought with him was sent to complete Norris's round, so that Norris would be on the spot when the body was available for viewing. There was always the chance the local man might have noticed the victim earlier, alive, and be able to give some hint of a reason for his presence.

Before starting up the path, Mackinnon turned to Alec and said, "I don't suppose you could have taken a proper look without leaving traces, sir. You'll point them out when we come to them?"

"Of course." He was pretty sure the circuitous routes he had taken had not obliterated anything of significance. The effects of the maid's movements were less certain.

The signs of something having been hauled across the grass were still visible, and Mackinnon spotted them at once.

"You can see the troughs where his heels dragged," he said. "They caught on some blades of grass and uprooted them. And these indentations could be the footprints of someone heavy, or pulling a heavy load, moving backwards, with *his* heels digging in. They're nowhere near clear enough for identification, though, and there's not much point looking for footprints on the paving in this weather."

"I'm afraid not," Alec agreed. "It rained heavily during the night and everything was mushy by the time I came out this morning."

"Better take some snaps anyway, Ardmore. Warren, give him a hand."

As DC Ardmore started to erect his tripod and DC Warren put up the enormous umbrella he had been carrying over his arm, Mackinnon set off across the grass on one side of the trail. Alec went with him. They studied the marks as they walked. Alec agreed with Mackinnon's analysis.

"And look over there. The rain's just about washed them out, but you can just about see several more sets of tracks converging on the spot—mine, my wife's, the maid's, and the dog's. These are much clearer, fortunately."

They reached the shrubbery. A leather glove was visible, and a few inches of the sodden sleeve of a dark blue sharkskin jacket.

"You won't see much more under there without a torch," said Alec.

Mackinnon took an electric torch from the pocket of his mackintosh and switched it on. The light gleamed on the wet leaves framing the scene. "Looks as if a couple of branches have been hacked off with a pocketknife. Probably broke them getting him in and removed them so as not to draw attention. What do you think, sir?"

"That was my conclusion. The branches are lying beside the body."

"But in the dark, he didn't realise the hand was showing."

"He?"

Grasping Alec's meaning at once, Mackinnon looked back along the trail and said, "I hae my doots a woman could have carried anything so heavy."

"Possibly that's why it was dragged. In these days of sportswomen, it doesn't do to jump to conclusions. Even pre-War, there were plenty of farm women and market women capable of moving quite a weight, though neither is very likely in Hampstead."

"But sporting ladies are quite likely, tennis players and such. I'll keep yon in mind, sir."

"I must apologise for any footprints I left beyond the edge of the grass, by the body. I stood—or rather, crouched—as far back as possible, but there's not much room, I couldn't see very well, and I had to make sure he was dead. I hope I haven't mucked anything up."

Without comment, Mackinnon directed the beam at Alec's wet, muddy shoes, then crouched and shone it into the bushes. "He looks pretty dead to me." He prodded the hand with the torch. "Rigor well established. Dr. Ridgeway should be here by now."

Alec looked back. No doctor, but Ardmore was diligently photographing the lawn while Warren held the umbrella over him and his camera.

Mackinnon inserted his upper body beneath the leaves,

which released their burden of raindrops in a cascade onto his back. "One or two prints I'd say are yours, sir. The rest seems to have been deliberately smoothed. A hardened villain, would you say, sir?"

"Or anyone who's ever read detective fiction."

"Och, aye, nae doot." He hesitated. "If I squeeze in to take a closer look at the deceased, sir, I'm bound to leave more foot-prints. I shan't see anything you haven't already found out, not to mention what the doctor will tell us. Could ye no tell me—"

"I could, but how much are you going to learn if I spoon-feed you? I understand your reluctance, believe me. However, you chose to become a detective, and if you want to rise—"

"I'll go." Mackinnon visibly braced himself and ducked into the shrubbery.

His body blocked Alec's view of what he was doing. Leaves rustled and a twig snapped underfoot.

"Mud on the heels," he observed. "Feels as if his clothes are pretty dry underneath him, for what that's worth."

A voice came from behind Alec. "Done what I could, sir." It was the photographer, tripod and attached camera in his hands, Warren at his heels with the umbrella held high and a flashpan under his arm. "The prints aren't going to be any too clear, though."

"The impressions aren't any too clear." Alec eyed the pair. "I hope you're going to be able to get your stuff in there."

"Not till the sergeant comes out, any road," said Warren. "Then we'll just have to see. It'll be pretty close quarters."

Mackinnon backed out. He had taken off one glove and was eyeing his fingertips with distaste. "I couldn't see anything amiss, sir," he said, "but it feels as if the hair on the top of his head is matted with blood from a wound. That's aboot all I can tell. Enough, with the removal of the body, to make it murder."

"To make it, at the very least, distinctly fishy," said Alec.

They stood back to let Ardmore and his assistant scuffle

their way into the bushes. Entering last, the huge black umbrella completely blocked their view of what was going on.

Minute examination of his finger having apparently revealed no bloodstains, Mackinnon put his glove back on. "I didn't search his pockets, sir," he said a trifle defensively. "It seemed best to leave everything undisturbed until it's been photographed, since there's no hurry over identifying the deceased."

"What makes you think that, Sergeant?"

Mackinnon flushed. "Well, sir, if it was urgent, you'd have—"

A muffled thump interrupted him, coincident with the brilliant flash of magnesium powder igniting, visible in spite of the umbrella.

The umbrella went up in flames. Alec and Mackinnon stepped back as, along with the usual cloud of white powder, black, glowing fragments floated down.

"I take it, Fletcher," said the police surgeon, arriving at this inopportune moment, "that you won't want a report in the autopsy on any superficial burns."

A fit of coughing overtook Alec as he breathed in the acrid fumes of burning silk. Before either he or Mackinnon had a chance to respond to Dr. Ridgeway's quip, Ardmore's voice issued from the bushes: "Said it was close, didn't I? Good job everything's wet, or the whole bloody lot'd've gone up in flames."

Still clutching the skeleton of the umbrella, Warren backed out, muttering, "Cor, strike me pink! If it wasn't wet, we wouldn't've needed the bloody brolly, would we."

He turned, revealing a powder-whitened face with black crescents above his eyes.

"Better take off your hat, laddie," said Ridgeway, "the brim's smouldering. I'll put some ointment on your eyebrows. Where they were, that is."

Warren raised his hand towards his face and almost put out an eye with a spoke of the denuded umbrella frame. Mackinnon removed it from his shaking hand.

"Sarge, I feel kind of funny."

"You look kind of funny," said DC Ardmore unhelpfully. He, too, was coated in white powder, but his eyebrows appeared to be intact.

"Shock," Ridgeway diagnosed. "Sit down and put your head between your knees."

Warren dropped to the wet grass and the doctor took his pulse. "Not too bad. Does your face feel hot?"

"Yes, Doc, like I got sunburn."

"Scorched. I'll want to take a look at it, but you'll have to wait till I've had a gander at our dead chum. Fletcher, can we get him out of this rain?"

"He could take my umbrella and sit on one of those benches." Seeing Ridgeway's frown, he sighed and went on: "But I expect he'd better go up to my house, number six." He pointed. "My housekeeper will take care of him." Which Daisy would regard as a heaven-sent invitation to meddle, he thought gloomily.

"Strewth, I think I'm going to be sick," Warren mumbled.

"Keep your head down till the feeling goes away," advised Ridgeway. "Anything you want to tell me about the corpse, Fletcher?"

"He's not mine, Doctor; he's the sergeant's."

"Oh? Mackinnon, isn't it?"

"Yes, sir."

"Well?"

"I . . . uh . . ." He looked to Alec, who gave a slight shrug. "I don't think so, sir. Go ahead. Would you like my torch?"

"Hmm, yes, thanks." Without further ado, Ridgeway dived into the shrubbery. For a few minutes, the only sound was the rustle of leaves; then his voice emerged. "He was bashed on the head, but I rather doubt that was the cause of death. Probably occurred very shortly before death, judging by the amount of blood. Are you getting this down, Mackinnon?"

Mackinnon whipped out his notebook. "Yes, sir."

"Rigor is fully established. He died at least twelve hours ago, not more than twenty-four, probably of deliberate compression of the carotid arteries, though I'll have to get him on the table to be certain. Not something he could do to himself. It looks as if you've got a murder on your hands, Sergeant."

NINE

Left to guard the northern approaches, Daisy frowned as she looked up at the Jessups' house. The more she thought about it, the odder it seemed that the man who had come out of their front door and hurried off down the street had not at least waved a greeting. Furthermore, though not all the world matched her own inquisitive nature, surely he must have wondered what was going on in the garden.

Unless he already knew, perhaps because Elsie had disobeyed orders and told her sister, Enid, what she had seen, which Daisy considered unlikely. But even if she had, and Enid had relayed the news to her employers, wouldn't they want to know more and from a more reliable source than a parlour maid?

That was assuming the man hurrying away had, in fact, been one of the Jessups. Daisy couldn't put out of her mind the unwelcome visitor who had pushed past her in the Jessups' front hall and torn off down the steps, nor that she was fairly certain she had seen him again later. He was an American. She suspected Patrick Jessup had been in America, and she knew he was expected home. There *must* be some connection.

Suppose the man she had just seen was the American. Had he met Patrick in America and come to look for him, and if so, as a friend or an enemy?

She recalled Aidan's remark when she told him about the American's first visit: "I knew it was a terrible idea." Perhaps "the idea" seemed terrible to him, the stay-at-home member of the family, only because it was unconventional. As she didn't know what it was, she couldn't tell.

At any rate, his words had reinforced her impression that the American was not a desirable acquaintance, as her mother would put it. Friend or enemy to Patrick, he would hardly be invited to spend the night at number 5, Constable Circle.

Not the American, then. But why had Mr. Jessup, or Aidan, not greeted her?

He was in a hurry.

Not even a wave? When hordes of police had just arrived in the garden opposite his house?

Number 5 was awfully quiet. Suppose—

The tramp of heavy boots diverted her attention. Round the bend came a constable, a comfortingly solid figure in his cape and helmet. "Mrs. Fletcher, ma'am, I've been sent to relieve you," he announced, saluting.

"Th-thank you."

He looked at her with concern. "You're half-froze, ma'am. Better get inside quick and get something hot inside you."

"Yes, thanks, I will." She couldn't tell him it wasn't just the cold that made her shiver; she'd scared herself silly with idiotic imaginings.

But once indoors, sitting at the kitchen table in dry stockings and shoes, with her hands wrapped around a mug of hot cocoa, she couldn't shake the thoughts. What if something had happened to the Jessups, and she did nothing? She managed to steer clear of picturing exactly what might have happened.

"You're still pale as ice, madam," said Mrs. Dobson. "Shock as well as cold, I shouldn't wonder. I'll fill a hot bottle you can put on your lap."

As if alerted by the last word, Nana, who had been lying good as gold under the table, sat up and placed a comforting, if still slightly damp, paw on Daisy's lap.

Daisy stroked her head and said absently, "Good girl." The dog had, after all, done her duty, and it was no good wishing she had left it to the Bennetts' horrid fat spaniels to discover the body.

Now Daisy had to decide what was *her* duty. Alec would say it was to go straight to the police with her fears. But she'd feel very silly if the Jessups, except for one bound for Bond Street, were just having a lie-in after a late celebration of the prodigal's return.

Was the prodigal home already? Could it have been he himself who had hurried past without so much as a wave? He didn't know her, after all.

Before she said anything to the police, was there a way to find out whether anything was amiss? Go and knock on the door, and they'd wonder what on earth she wanted so early in the morning. If they were up and about and she was invited in, she could hardly avoid mentioning the body in the garden, which would make Alec furious. She could telephone, but again, she'd need an excuse. Suppose she invited the ladies and children to afternoon tea. No, it would look as if she wanted to gossip about the murder.

The cook-housekeeper presented her with a hot-water bottle, neatly shrouded in a woolly cover. The faint rubbery smell was somehow comforting. "There you go, dearie, that'll help, I hope."

"Lovely. I'm sure it will. Mrs. Dobson, are you on cup-of-sugar borrowing terms with next door?"

"Certainly, madam. Their Mrs. Innes is a very good sort of woman."

"Then could you please think up something you need to borrow right now?"

"Well, I don't know, madam, I'll be popping round to the shops this morning anyway. . . . Well, now, I could say I want to make some biscuits for elevenses before I do the shopping, though there's plenty in the tin, perfectly good."

"Perfect. And who knows, you may have a kitchenful of frozen bobbies to feed by then."

"And a finer body of men I couldn't wish for, though I says it as shouldn't."

Daisy was diverted. "Why shouldn't you, Mrs. Dobson?"

"Because of working for a police detective, madam. Looks like boasting, doesn't it? But I must say, madam, all these years of working for the master, and I never thought something like this'd happen so close to home."

"Nor did any of us," Daisy helplessly. "I know you won't desert us, Mrs. Dobson."

Mrs. Dobson put her hands on her hips and glared. "As though I would, madam! Me that's been with Mr. Fletcher through thick and thin. And if that Mrs. Gilpin says another word, I'll give her the rough side of my tongue, so I will."

"Oh dear, Nurse Gilpin is still threatening to leave?"

"Now don't you fret, madam. She won't leave the babies. You can say what you will of her, and nobody's perfect, but I will say this: She's proper fond of the babies. There now, I never meant to say nothing about that dreadful murder, and you upset already—"

"I started it, talking about frozen bobbies. I know you won't say anything to anyone else."

"That I won't. Now I'll just find Elsie and tell her to go next door and borrow a bit of brown sugar."

"Couldn't you go yourself, Mrs. Dobson?"

"Oh no, madam, it wouldn't be proper, not now we've got a parlour maid. They'd think it ever so queer next door."

"Really? We don't want that. I'll tell her, then. I'm feeling much better, thanks to your cocoa and hot-water bottle. How much brown sugar do you need?"

"None at all, seeing I've a canister full in the larder, but she can ask for a quarter of a pound. Right, madam, I'll just get on with weighing out the ingredients."

Elsie was dusting the drawing room. "I'll go and put my hat on this instant, madam," she said when Daisy asked her to beg, borrow, or steal a quarter of a pound of brown sugar from next door.

"You'll need an umbrella. Elsie, Mr. Fletcher will be quite annoyed that you didn't obey my order not to talk to anyone about what you found in the garden."

"I only told Mrs. Dobson, 'm. That's not the same, is it? Mrs. Dobson isn't just anyone."

Daisy could hardly deny this, having just involved Mrs. Dobson in a somewhat mendacious scheme. Nor did she feel up to getting into a discussion of what she had meant by "anyone." With a sigh, she said, "Well, if you breathe a word to your sister, you'll find it a lot more difficult to chat with her in future, because you won't be working here."

"Oh, I know, 'm. I wouldn't want that. I won't say a word next door, honest."

The moment Elsie left, Daisy had second thoughts. She must be crazy to trust the rattle-tongued girl to be discreet. But on the point of calling her back, she hesitated. She really was desperate to know whether the Jessup household were all right.

She returned to the kitchen to wait, as Elsie would no doubt take the sugar straight there. She watched Mrs. Dobson measure, melt, mix, and stir together butter, golden syrup, rolled oats, and brown sugar.

"Flapjacks," she said. "Quick and easy, 'cause I've got to be off to the shops if lunch isn't to be late." Heaven forbid a mere murder on the doorstep should make lunch late. "The twins like 'em, and they're good and filling if those frozen coppers turn up. I'm making a double batch in case, and I've used the last of the brown sugar, so it's not stretching the truth too much borrowing from Mrs. Innes."

"I'm sorry I made you stretch it at all."

"That's all right, madam. I know you wouldn't without good reason." She scooped the mixture into a couple of baking tins and flattened it with the back of a spoon. Stooping, she listened to the oven. "Still heating up. Wonderful invention, these thermo whatchamacallits, aren't they? No more guesswork. I'm that glad the house had a gas stove. It'd be hard to go back to a coal range."

"We'd have bought you a gas stove if there hadn't been one already installed, Mrs. Dobson."

"I don't know how I'd get on without one, and that's the truth. There, the burners have stopped; that's hot enough now." Mrs. Dobson put the tins in the oven and started clearing up. "And the geyser for the hot water, too, always ready to hand. When I remember all the carrying of coal, with coal dust everywhere, and blacking the range to stop it rusting, and the hot oven too hot and the cool oven too cool . . ." She went on reminiscing about the bad old days.

Daisy half-listened, wondering why Elsie had not yet returned. Surely she should be back by now with the unneeded brown sugar. Suppose she, too, had been attacked. . . . No, much more likely everyone was perfectly all right and she was having a good chin-wag with the Jessups' cook. But what could she have to talk about if not the dead man in the garden?

"Where's that dratted girl got to?" said Mrs. Dobson. "If I'd really needed that sugar, it'd be too late by now. Ah, sounds like her now."

Elsie came in through the kitchen door from the paved area outside. "I didn't see my sister, madam," she announced, crossing the kitchen to deposit her dripping umbrella in the scullery. "Here's your sugar, Mrs. Dobson. I didn't say a word to Mrs. Innes about that out there in the garden, 'm, no matter what she asked me, but she'd a good deal to say on her own account, so I let her talk."

"Oh?" Daisy didn't exactly want to encourage servants' gossip, but how else was she to find out what was going on?

The monosyllable was encouragement enough. "Seems Mr. Patrick came home last night from foreign parts. He's been gone ever such a long time, not but what him and Mr. Jessup don't go off a-travelling for weeks on end every year, but they usually go together. Mr. Patrick's old enough now to do business by himself, seemingly. But Mr. Aidan must've been waiting for him to get back to go off himself. He's already left to visit some customers up north somewheres."

"He left as soon as his brother came home?"

"Yes, 'm."

"Did they have a disagreement? A quarrel?" Horrible possibilities raced through Daisy's mind—but Aidan was the one who had disappeared, and Alec would have recognised his body.

"No, 'm. Leastways, my sister didn't hear nothing like that, she told Mrs. Innes. The only thing is, Mrs. Aidan's ever so upset. Crying her eyes out, poor thing, Mrs. Innes said. Course, Mr. Aidan's the one that usually stays home, but it's not like he's going abroad, is it? And her always cheerful as anything."

Daisy was so relieved to hear the Jessups were still in the land of the living, not, as in her direst imaginings, weltering in their own blood, that some time passed before she began to wonder what had so upset Audrey. She was in the nursery by then, so naturally her thoughts flew to the Jessup children. But Mrs. Innes would know if Marilyn or Percy was hurt or ill.

Could Audrey and Aidan have quarrelled unbeknownst to the servants, leading to his precipitate departure? More likely—if one did not know the couple. Daisy had seldom met a less quarrelsome, more peaceable, even-tempered pair.

Whatever the cause of her woes, Audrey might be glad of a shoulder to weep on other than her mother-in-law's. Daisy just had to come up with an excuse to call next door, one that would satisfy both the Jessups and Alec.

Which left her right where she had started, except that she knew the Jessups were alive, thank heaven.

It was time to stop worrying about them and concentrate on the twins. Seated cross-legged on the nursery floor, she built an umpteenth tower of wooden blocks, which Oliver knocked down with as much delight as he had the first one.

"Gak!" he shouted.

Meanwhile, Miranda, in Daisy's lap, turned the pages of a cloth picture book and chanted in a language of her own invention.

"Going to be a bookworm, that one," said Nurse Gilpin disapprovingly.

"I do hope so," said Daisy. "I was one myself."

Sparring with Mrs. Gilpin, she almost managed to forget what was going on outside. Then Elsie came in.

"Madam, it's that Mr. Crane on the telephone. He wants to speak to Mr. Fletcher. I told him he's not here, but he says if he's not here, why isn't he at Scotland Yard, and I'm sure it's not my place to say, so I thought maybe you'd better talk to him."

For one craven moment, Daisy was on the brink of saying, "Tell him I'm not here, either." Then sanity returned. Getting up from the floor, she straightened her stocking-seams—Lucy always claimed crooked seams sapped one's self-confidence. "I'm on my way," she sighed.

TEN

Stiff as a board, the body had not been easy to move without wrecking the shrubbery. By natural light, however grey, Dr. Ridgeway had confirmed the probable cause of death, so slight as to have escaped Alec's and Mackinnon's notice by torchlight. The obvious injury to the scalp, from a blunt instrument wielded without a great deal of force, had knocked him out and the wound had bled a good deal. Innocent-looking but deadly, there was a small bruise on either side at the base of the neck.

"Thumb marks," said Ridgeway, "though I don't imagine you'll be able to get prints from them. Once the fellow was unconscious, it would have been the easiest thing in the world to apply enough pressure to shut off the arteries. A couple of minutes is all it takes."

"How long after the head bashing d'you reckon, sir?" asked Mackinnon.

"Almost immediately. The scalp bleeds freely, so it wouldn't take long to produce this much blood. But, as I'm sure you're aware, Sergeant, dead men don't bleed, or he'd have lost considerably more before it clotted. Not likely to bleed to death, though."

"What about the rain?" Alec asked, before he recalled that this was not his case. "Is it possible a significant quantity of blood simply washed away?"

"Certainly, for a brief period. Clotting usually starts in three to ten minutes. If that happened, if he bled significantly more than appears here, then the time between the blow and the application of pressure to the arteries might have been longer than a minute or two. Since it seems impossible that he was hit under the bushes, as there's no room to raise a weapon, you'd have to find out where he was killed and exactly when it was raining there, in relation to the time of death. That, I shall endeavour to discover for you, but it's unlikely to be accurate within an hour or two, or more."

"Never is," Warren grumbled. He had recovered enough not to retire to the house.

The doctor grinned. "I'll be able to tell you more, if not enough to satisfy you, when I've had a go at him."

"Will you be able to tell us the shape of the weapon?" Mackinnon asked.

"Possibly. Roughly. I'll do what I can, but now I must get back to my surgery." Ridgeway departed.

Mackinnon told Ardmore to take a few more photos of the body. "And try not to set anything else on fire," he added.

"Don't need the flash in this light, if I can do some long exposures," Ardmore said. He set to work, anxious to atone for the flaming umbrella.

"We'd better start looking for the weapon, don't you reckon, sir?" Mackinnon asked Alec.

"Sounds like a good idea. Where will you start?"

"He—or she—might have thrown it in the bushes, but likely he wouldna carry the weapon while moving the body. The way those drag marks run, I'd no be surprised if it was in the fountain. Warren, take a look."

DC Warren looked gloomily down at his feet. "S'pose I can't get much wetter," he said.

"The water's not too scummy," said Alec. "Take a look first;

then if you need to wade, go up to my house and borrow a pair of rubber boots."

Warren thanked him, looking a trifle happier, and tramped off to circle the fountain.

Lips pursed, Mackinnon watched Ardmore photographing the corpse. "There's something a wee bit odd about his suit," he declared. "Would ye no agree, sir?"

"Not Savile Row, as far as one can tell when it's soaking wet."

"Not English."

"Scottish?" Alec suggested with a grin.

"Foreign, I'm thinking."

"Could be."

"Is it too much to hope that he'll have a passport on him?"

"We can hope. Looks as if Ardmore's finished, so you can go through his pockets."

"Would ye care to—?"

"This is not my case," Alec said firmly.

"Ardmore, ye can start searching the shrubbery for a weapon."

As Mackinnon stooped over the body, Alec saw a black van pull up at the bottom of the garden. PC Norris went over to speak to the driver. Two men got out, opened the back doors, and started pulling out a stretcher.

"The mortuary people are here," Alec told Mackinnon.

The sergeant had folded back the man's jacket and was staring down at his chest. "Will ye look at that, sir! He's wearing a shoulder holster."

"Great Scott! Empty?"

"Yes, sir. Ardmore! Keep your eyes peeled for a gun, as well as yon blunt instrument."

"A gun!" came an astonished voice from the bushes. "You're kidding."

"I am not."

"Right, Sarge. A gun it is."

Mackinnon straightened with an air of triumph.

"Here's his pocket-book. Lots of cash, so it wasna robbery. And look here, sir!" He opened a thin water-stained booklet and read, " 'The United States of America—Passport.' He's a Yank! From New York, it says. And there's a photograph, which will come in handy. The rain hasna damaged it."

"Excellent."

"I canna read the name, though. The signature's a scribble, and where it's written out at the top, by a clerk, likely, the water's seeped in and the ink has run. It looks as if the Christian name might begin with an *M*. And the surname—this could be a *C*, or a *G*. Quite a long name, more than one syllable."

Alec took the passport and examined it. "Yes, *M*, and this blur suggests the dot of an *i*, wouldn't you say? I wouldn't like to swear to your *C* or *G*, but this looks as if it might be a double *l*. You'd think they'd use India ink. Has he a watch?"

"Not in his fob. Ah, a wristwatch. Gold. Looks like an expensive one. Let's see—no inscription on the back."

"It might be worth checking his hands for rings before they cart him off. American men are more apt to wear rings than the English. Or Scots."

"Stiff as he is, I'll have to cut his gloves off," Mackinnon said doubtfully.

"Let's not do that if we can help it. It'd be difficult without marking the skin, which could mislead the doctor. The leather seems to be thin and flexible. Perhaps you can feel whether he has any."

Mackinnon grimaced. Alec agreed with his implied comment: For some reason, feeling the dead man's fingers for rings seemed even more distasteful than anything they had so far put the poor chap through.

But the sergeant obeyed—or rather, followed Alec's suggestion—and reported, "Nothing, sae far as I can tell. He could be wearing a flat band o' some sort, like a wedding ring."

"We'll leave that for Dr. Ridgeway to find out."

The stretcher arrived and Mackinnon told the men they

could remove the body. "Let PC Norris down there take a look at his face."

He and Alec, sheltering under the latter's umbrella, took off their hats as a gesture of respect as the dead man was lifted onto the stretcher, covered with a sheet, and borne off.

Mackinnon offered the passport, pocket-book, and watch to Alec, who was tempted but managed to resist.

"You'd better come up to the house and telephone your super," he said as Mackinnon tucked the objects into his pocket.

"Thank you, sir. Och, here comes Mrs. Fletcher."

The pillar-box red umbrella came down the garden path towards them, in a hurry.

"Alec," she called, "Superintendent Crane just rang up. He wants you to ring back immediately."

"I'm on my way. Daisy, DS Mackinnon needs to use our telephone, too, as soon as I've finished, and can we find a pair of rubber boots for DC Warren?"

"I should think so."

Warren came over. "Can't see anything, sir, but the water's pretty murky. I could do with a rake or summat like that."

"I expect we have one," Daisy said vaguely. "Don't we, darling? Or does the gardener bring his own? We could borrow one from the neighbours."

"On no account are the neighbours to be involved! There's a rake in the shed." Alec was the member of the family who took most interest in the garden, though he rarely had time to work in it.

"Good." Daisy smiled at Warren. "Are you fishing in the fountain for clues?"

"For the weapon, ma'am."

"Was he shot?"

"Daisy!" Alec exclaimed in exasperation.

"Sorry," she said unrepentantly. "Why don't you all come to the kitchen for tea and biscuits before you do anything else. You must be frozen, and Mrs. Dobson has them ready."

Mackinnon and Warren gave Alec hopeful looks, and Ardmore emerged from the bushes to do likewise.

Alec gestured to Mackinnon.

"Thank you, Mrs. Fletcher," he said. "That will be verra welcome. Nobody can interfere with the scene of the crime with the bobbies on duty."

"You can bring them a hot drink when you come back here," Daisy proposed, reminding Alec of why he loved her, however infuriating she was at times.

They all trooped up the path to the house, Daisy leading the three local detectives down the area steps to the kitchen while Alec went straight up to the front hall to ring up the Yard.

The switchboard girl put him through. "What's going on, Fletcher?" barked Superintendent Crane.

"I'm on my way, sir. I should get that report to the AC by noon."

Crane's sigh of relief gusted along the wires. "So it's not a homicide on your front doorstep. Thank heaven for that."

"I'm afraid it is, sir. Well, not quite on my front doorstep, but, in fact, it's almost certainly murder."

"Damn it all, are you sure?"

"The divisional surgeon says so, and he's a good man. And I have to agree with him. But it's not my pigeon."

"Oh yes it is. I've had the S Division super on the line. Claims he's shorthanded, and if it's homicide, he wants you on the case."

"But we're shorthanded, too. It's chronic—"

"You know what the Commissioner said just the other day about cooperation with the divisions, Fletcher. It's your case."

"But sir, it's going to mean questioning all my close neighbours, for a start. I can't—"

"No, I see that. But someone else can do that part while you direct behind the scenes. You can come in and write up that report while you're waiting for them to report to you."

"I suppose so," Alec said reluctantly. He liked to have his finger directly on the pulse of an investigation.

But his neighbours were no lords and ladies, merely wealthy cits, in the idiom of the eighteenth century, which Alec had studied at university. Tom Tring could cope perfectly well with interrogating nobs as long as he wore his best suit, not one of his checked monstrosities.

Could Mackinnon? He didn't know him well enough to count on it. "I'll want DS Tring, sir, and DC Piper. They've worked well before with the S Division detective sergeant on the job."

"Done. And you'll have the report by noon?"

"I said that before you dumped this case in my lap, sir! I need to discuss it with Tring and Mackinnon so that they can get going. And the American embassy will have to be notified."

"What? What?" Crane demanded wildly. "The American embassy?"

"Yes, sir. The victim was a U.S. citizen."

"Are you sure?"

"Passport in his pocket. The photo and description match."

"If the divisional chappie had known that, he'd have handed it over to us anyway." The superintendent sounded slightly mollified.

"No doubt. Come to think of it, sir, I'd like your permission to get in touch with the New York police, and perhaps the FBI."

"FBI?"

"Federal Bureau of Investigation, sir. In Washington."

"Oh yes, those chappies you gave a helping hand to over there. Why? Do you suspect he was a wrong 'un?"

Alec chose his words with care. "Let's just say there are aspects of the case that point to the possibility. Or perhaps it would be more accurate to say that it wouldn't surprise me." It dawned on him that the holster might equally well mean the man was an agent, like Lambert. Like Lambert, he could have had his gun confiscated by Customs—but then he'd have had no reason to wear the holster. Alec didn't have time just now to think it through, what with Crane panting on the other end of the line. "Would you like details?"

"No, no. Go ahead and cable whomever you need to." This time, his sigh expressed long-suffering rather than relief. "I'll try to explain to the AC why he won't be getting the report for a while. If you can *possibly* spare me a moment, you might pop in and tell me what you've learnt so far about your Hampstead murder. By the by, how is Mrs. Fletcher holding up? She sounded pretty chipper when I spoke to her just now, but it must have been a shock to her, finding *yet another* body."

One cannot tell one's superior in the police force that sarcasm does not become him. "She didn't actually find this one, sir," Alec reminded him. "She hasn't actually seen him."

"I dare say, Fletcher, but it is, to my recollection, the first to be found on—I beg your pardon—*practically* on her own doorstep." With that, he rang off, which was just as well, as the retort that sprang to Alec's lips was most improper.

Alec arranged for Ernie Piper to come out to Hampstead to help with the search, and for Tom Tring to meet him and Mackinnon at the Yard. He had to get copies of the passport photo made, and some good photographs of the entire passport to show at the U.S. embassy and to send to the NYPD and FBI. In the meantime, he could cable the passport number to them.

He went down to the kitchen, where Daisy and Mrs. Dobson were presiding over the consumption of tea and flapjacks. "You can go up and ring your station," he said grumpily to Mackinnon, "but I can tell you what your super's going to say: He's talked mine into handing over the case to me."

"Good!" said Mackinnon. "I mean, I'm sorry you're being troubled with it, but I'm glad to be working with you again, sir."

"DC Piper's coming to give your men a hand. You and I will go to the Yard."

"Yes, sir." Mackinnon went off to telephone.

"Ardmore, Warren," said Alec, "off you go to see if you can find that weapon before Piper arrives."

There was some scurrying about while boots and a rake were procured for the fountain-fishing expedition; then the two detective constables departed, carrying a couple of thermos flasks and flapjacks wrapped in wax paper for the uniformed men. Alec sat down at the kitchen table.

"Darling, you're not going to have to interrogate the Jessups, are you?" Daisy poured him a cup of tea. "And the Whitcombs and everyone?"

"I sincerely hope not. Initially at least, the others can do it, but if it turns out any of them are involved, then all bets are off." He helped himself to a flapjack, chewy and still slightly warm from the oven. A large bite effectively stopped his mouth, allowing Daisy to have her say.

"I hope it doesn't come to that. We shan't dare poke our noses outside the door, Mrs. Dobson."

"Not to worry, madam," said the cook-housekeeper, clearing cups and plates and sweeping away crumbs. "You know how it is. There's some as'll blame you no matter what, and others that'll know it's none of it your fault. That's how you tell your true friends."

"Very true. Come to think of it, Alec, you can give the Bennetts the 'third degree' with my goodwill. Do you have any reason to think one of the neighbours may be involved?"

"I can't talk about it here."

Mrs. Dobson drew herself up, her hands on her hips. "If it's because I'm here, sir, I take leave to tell you there's many and many a secret I've known that's never crossed my lips, and I'm sure I never gave you cause—"

"Of course not." Harassed on every side, Alec tried to sound soothing. "I just meant that at present it's a matter to be discussed only with my colleagues in the police."

"Hmm."

"I suppose you won't tell us who he is, either," said Daisy.

"I don't know his name. If I did, you're right, I wouldn't tell you."

Mackinnon came in. "All settled, sir," he said cheerfully. "I'm to take my orders from you, and I don't even have to give my super a report until we've made an arrest."

"Assuming we do. Let's get going. There's one good thing about crime on the doorstep, Daisy, I should be home on time for dinner, if not before."

ELEVEN

"*Will you* look at that, madam! Those policemen haven't left hardly enough flapjacks to be sent up to the nursery."

"I've already eaten more than my share, Mrs. Dobson," Daisy said guiltily.

"Then I'll just put what's left on the tray here for the kiddies and Mrs. Gilpin's morning coffee and be off about the shopping. It's to be hoped that butcher hasn't already sold his best cuts, the master being home for dinner tonight."

She put on her hat and coat, took up her basket and umbrella, and set off, leaving Daisy once again pondering a way to infiltrate the Jessups' house. She still wanted to talk to them, though at least she was no longer worried about their safety.

Another cup of tea failed to inspire her. Perhaps a bath would help. Having dressed in a tearing hurry, she had omitted even a lick and a promise earlier.

On her way up the kitchen stairs, she heard the front doorbell ring. As she pushed open the baize door at the top, Elsie opened the front door. Though she couldn't be seen, Daisy didn't step out into the passage. She held the door ajar and listened.

A man's voice asked for Detective Chief Inspector Fletcher.

"He's left for the Yard," said Elsie. No *sir*, Daisy noted. "You from the papers?"

"That's right. You're a sharp girl, you are."

"Seeing you got a notebook and a cam'ra, and any copper'd be ashamed to go about looking like a ragbag, it weren't too difficult."

"Sharp in mind and sharp in tongue." The reporter sounded disconcerted. "I bet you wouldn't mind making a couple of pounds telling me what's going on in the garden there?"

"Go on, you really think I'd risk losing a place like this for a couple of quid? No, not for ten, not for twenty, no thank you! They treat me proper, and it suits me. So you can just get along with you and—"

"Here, hold on! Don't be so hasty. What about your missus, eh? I bet she'd like to see her name in the paper, and maybe her face, too."

"Not likely! Madam's a real lady, not the sort that'd want to see her picture on every street corner. 'Sides, she's not at home." The parlour maid closed the front door with a brisk thud. "Not at home to the likes of you, anyway!" she added.

Daisy came out of hiding. Elsie turned and saw her.

"Oh, madam, I hope I done right. There was this nasty reporter—"

"I heard every word. You were wonderful, quite perfect. Anyone would think you'd been turning newshounds away from the door for years. I'm afraid you may have to do it again, once word gets around."

"Now I know what they're like, I'll get rid of the next one in half the time. You just watch me!"

Daisy went upstairs and took a bath, which thawed the bits of her still chilled in spite of hot tea and the warmth of the kitchen. She was almost dressed when Elsie tapped on the bedroom door and announced, "Mrs. Jessup's called, madam. I said I'd see if you're at home."

"Yes, I'm at home! Tell her I'll be down in just a minute. Offer her a cup of coffee." *If Mahomet can't think of an adequate reason to go to the mountain*, she thought, *then let him wait until the mountain comes to him!*

She went down a few minutes later, to find Mrs. Maurice Jessup—she had for some reason expected Audrey—standing at the window of the drawing room, gazing out over the garden. It had stopped raining. As Daisy crossed the room, she could see that Ernie Piper had joined Ardmore and Warren. They stood by the fountain, Warren waving the rake like a magic wand, as if he hoped to bring the nymph in the centre to life.

"Good morning, Mrs. Jessup," said Daisy.

Swinging round, Mrs. Jessup said, "Oh, good morning! I didn't hear you come in. You gave me quite a start."

"Isn't it odd how something one is expecting sometimes startles one more than the unexpected?"

"Yes indeed. Especially when you're waiting by the telephone for a particular call, and when at last it rings, you jump out of your skin. At least I do."

"Exactly! Won't you sit down? Elsie's bringing coffee, I hope."

Moving with the studied grace of an actress, Mrs. Jessup sat down on the edge of a chair. After a moment's hesitation, she shifted back and relaxed. "Mrs. Fletcher, as you have no doubt guessed, we are dying of curiosity about the very unexpected goings-on down in the garden. I'm afraid our Enid has taken quite a pet because her sister refused to talk about it."

"I sympathise," Daisy said with a smile. "That's just how I feel when Alec won't tell me what's happening."

"He won't? How very irritating men can be. I suppose Audrey will just have to go away wondering."

"Go away? Where is she off to?"

"Oh, didn't she tell you? Of course, when the two of you are together, you never need any subject of conversation beyond the children. She's taking Marilyn and Percy to her sister's, in Lincolnshire. The visit has been planned for ages, but the exact date was uncertain. You see, Aidan has business in the North, customers to see and so on. He's been post-poning the trip until Patrick's return—my younger son, you know. So when we heard from Patrick that he was on his way home, Aidan made arrangements to take the night train last night."

"And Audrey's going to her sister's while Aidan's away?"

"That's right. Vivien married a country squire, and he and Aidan simply have nothing in common. Besides, Aidan loves his own children, but you know how men are with other people's offspring."

"Better to visit without him."

"Much better. The taxi will be here any minute to take them to Liverpool Street. Patrick's going to see them off, to help Audrey cope with children and Nanny and luggage and all at the station. She's dreading the journey."

"I'm sure it takes a good deal of coping, even if she wasn't expecting."

Mrs. Jessup seized on this remark. "That's another reason to go right away, while she's feeling well and not showing yet."

"I travelled quite a bit while I was pregnant, but I haven't tried it with the twins yet."

"It's a difficult journey anyway, changing trains twice. I just hope they don't miss any connections."

"How nice that your Patrick is home to give her a hand at this end at least. When did he—"

Her question was interrupted as Elsie came in with the cof-fee tray. While dispensing coffee and biscuits—the flapjacks were all gone, but as Mrs. Dobson had said, the biscuits from the tin were perfectly good—Daisy pondered the situation.

Alec would be unhappy to have potential witnesses scatter-ing to all corners of the kingdom, but there wasn't anything Daisy could do about it. In any case, many of the residents of Constable Circle must have departed about their lawful occa-sions before the police got things organised out there.

On the other hand, most of them had probably gone no farther than the City, whereas Audrey was bound for the rural fastnesses of Lincolnshire. Daisy wondered whether she ought to suggest that Audrey wait until she had talked to the police.

Daisy was sure she had only to drop a word in Piper's ear and he'd stop the taxi leaving, but he might get into trouble for it. Also, it would make Audrey's journey even more difficult, if not impossible. Imagine having to start all over again tomorrow, getting the children ready for travelling—it didn't bear thinking of.

If Alec wanted to know why she hadn't attempted to foil their departure, she'd tell him it was his own fault for not giving her more information.

The unknown Patrick was going only to the station and back, so he would be available for questioning. Daisy wondered exactly what time he had arrived. Not that she knew the time of the murder.

"You must be happy to have your son safe at home again," she said.

"Yes, I was a little worried, I confess. He's not been gone so long on his own before, and it's hard to recognise that he's an adult now. He's still my little boy."

"When did he—"

"Listen!" Mrs. Jessup held up one hand. The chimes of the grandfather clock in the hall were heard. She rose. "I didn't realise it was so late. They'll be leaving as soon as the luggage is loaded into the taxicab, and I must be there to say good-bye. Thank you for the coffee, Mrs. Fletcher. It was very bad of me to interrupt your morning just for the sake of vulgar curiosity. I know you write in the mornings."

"Not today."

"No, I dare say not. Well, vulgar or not, my curiosity remains unslaked." She moved towards the window and glanced out. "I hope you'll pass on any account of the police activity out there that you glean from your husband. He surely must give you some sort of explanation!"

"I can't count on it." Daisy laughed. "He's quite capable of leaving me entirely in ignorance if it suits him. I'll pop out with you to say good-bye to Audrey and the children."

"Oh no, don't do that. It looks to me as if it's going to pour with rain again any moment. I'll tell Audrey you sent your best wishes."

"Please do, and bon voyage."

Daisy accompanied Mrs. Jessup to the front door. A taxi was just pulling up next door. As the cabbie climbed out, Mrs. Jessup hurried down the steps to the pavement. Both of them started up the Jessups' steps together.

Daisy would have liked to watch, perhaps to manage a word or two with Audrey. Mrs. Jessup might call it vulgar curiosity, but Daisy had long ago accepted that, like Kipling's Elephant's Child, she was cursed with "satiable curtiosity." She had a hundred questions.

Had her friend really been crying, as the servants reported? If so, what about? Had she quarrelled with Aidan, or was she unhappy because they were to part for an unknown period, or was she merely overtired from preparing for her trip? Pregnancy could be exhausting, too, even right at the beginning. Daisy remembered morning sickness all too clearly.

Where had Patrick been, and exactly what time did he arrive home? Daisy wanted to meet him. What was he like? Adventurous, his mother had said, yet with the patience and coolness to be a good cricketer.

He sounded interesting, more interesting than Aidan. Surely Audrey wasn't in love with him, was she? It would explain his long absence, her distress coincident with his return, Aidan's sudden departure, followed by hers. . . . But Mrs. Jessup would never let Patrick accompany Audrey to Liverpool Street if such were the situation.

What was more, Daisy remembered Audrey saying that once Patrick came home, they could all be comfortable again. That didn't sound like an illicit passion. No, once again, she realised, she was wandering in the realm of pure speculation.

Any moment, the Jessups would come out and see her standing there staring. Besides, it was cold on the doorstep, though no sign of impending rain was apparent.

She went in, pausing on the threshold for one last backward glance. The sun gleamed palely through thinning clouds.

The twins should go out for an airing before it disappeared again. All nannies agreed on the health-giving effects of fresh air on children. Nana ought to go out, too. If Daisy managed to get Mrs. Gilpin to hurry, they could all take a walk before either the rain or Alec returned. In the latter case, she might get a chance to talk to Ernie Piper.

Her timing was perfect. As the group set out towards the path to the Heath, Ernie backed out of the bushes, took off his hat, and shook the drips from it. It was natural for Daisy to wave the others onwards while she stopped to speak to him.

"Good morning, Mr. Piper. Any luck?"

"Morning, Mrs. Fletcher." He paused to respond to Nana's rapturous greeting. They were old friends. "I haven't found anything, and I expect Ardmore or Warren would've shouted if they had."

"What exactly are you looking for? 'A weapon' is a bit vague."

"That's what we don't know, Mrs. Fletcher," said DC Warren, joining them. His face, eyebrowless and scorched red, was gloomy. He had indeed been struck pink, Daisy thought. It was lucky he hadn't had a moustache. He would have got flames up his nose, assuredly a horribly painful experience. "Could be a stick or a stone or some weird African knobkerrie like in the detective stories."

"You read too many of those." Ardmore had arrived. "Dr. Ridgeway should be able to tell us what shape we're looking for."

"Doesn't much matter what shape," Piper pointed out, "seeing none of us has found anything that could be it. Leastways, I don't see either of you carrying a life preserver or a crowbar or even a heavy walking stick."

"Whatever it is," said Warren, "it's not in the pond. No

need to call in divers. It's less'n a foot deep and there's nothing in it bigger'n a twig."

"The children drop toys in regularly," said Daisy, "but the nannies always fish them out. If it's a walking stick, I can't see how you'd ever find it. I mean, the murderer could just have walked off with it and stuck it in an umbrella stand somewhere, or thrown it in the river."

"Prob'ly has done just that," said Warren.

"It's not that bad," Piper insisted. "This here's a private garden, isn't it, Mrs. Fletcher?"

"Yes, sort of. Not belonging to one family, but to all the residents of Constable Circle."

"Not like a public park at any rate. You don't get Tom, Dick, and Harry using it. It's not by way of being a shortcut either, is it? I looked at a map before I came."

"No, not really. There are footpaths to the Heath up here and to Well Walk down there, but they don't really cut corners for anyone not living here."

"Right. So chances are, if the victim wasn't a resident, which he prob'ly wasn't, or the Chief'd've recognised him, then he was somehow connected to a resident. These houses here, they're big houses and you can bet they all have servants. It's not likely he could have called on anyone without being seen by someone else, so it shouldn't be too hard to find out which house he was connected with. And chances are, it was someone in that house that killed him, and chances are, he just went home afterwards and stuck the walking stick in the umbrella stand, like Mrs. Fletcher said," Piper concluded triumphantly.

"Always s'posing it was a walking stick he used," Warren said sourly.

"Whatever it was, he'd have trouble getting rid of it this morning," Ardmore put in. "He'd've looked funny carrying anything but a brolly."

"Whatever it was," said Daisy, "it probably doesn't have nice helpful fingerprints on it. Last night was so cold and wet, no one would have gone out without gloves."

"True." Warren sank still further into gloom.

"Might the weapon have been chucked down into an area?" Daisy proposed. "That would be a quick and easy way to get rid of it without going far."

Piper nodded. "It's a thought. Only thing is, it must have been heavyish, would have made a noise landing. Unless the servants were listening to the wireless or something . . . but still they'd've found it this morning."

"Might not think anything of it," said Ardmore. "Not enough to call it to our attention anyway. It needn't be very big. Dr. Ridgeway was pretty sure it wasn't getting clobbered that killed him."

"Really?" said Daisy. "What killed him?"

All three men looked at her. She realised at once that she had inadvertently stepped over an invisible boundary. She had reminded them, even Ernie Piper, that they ought not to be discussing the case with her, even though she was the chief inspector's wife. On his own, Ernie might have answered her question, but not with the other two as witnesses.

"Gosh," she said, "Nurse and the babies are out of sight! I'd better catch up with them. Come along, Nana. Good luck!"

Hurrying along the footpath, she pondered what she had learnt and found herself impressed by Piper's chain of logic. Unfortunately, it led to the inescapable conclusion that one of her neighbours was a murderer.

TWELVE

"*Mackinnon, you* give Mr. Tring the details, please." Alec started skimming through the papers on his desk, but as he initialled some and put them on a new pile, and set others in a third pile to be read more thoroughly, he was listening intently.

He wanted to know whether the young detective sergeant understood and remembered all the information they had gathered so far and what conclusions—if any—he had drawn. It was also possible that he had picked up something Alec himself had missed.

Tom Tring listened with appropriate gravity, making a note now and then. His amusement every time Daisy's name came up was apparent to Alec, but sufficiently discreet to evade Mackinnon's notice. His moustache, the magnificent hirsuteness compensating for the vast baldness of his head, twitched occasionally as Daisy and her red umbrella wove their way through the narrative.

Tom was very fond of Daisy, and vice versa. In fact, he was Oliver's godfather. But his fondness didn't make him consider her an infallible oracle, as Ernie Piper did.

Mackinnon's view seemed to be somewhere in between. He was a fervent admirer, but he failed to believe she was always right.

His exposition brought out one fact that Alec had failed to enquire after. "Constable Norris didn't recognise the deceased," Mackinnon said. "He was pretty certain he'd never seen him about. As he pointed out, though, he's been on the early-morning beat for several weeks, so unless the Yank was an early riser, he could well have missed him."

"We'll give the local station a copy of the photo," said Tom, "and make sure everyone takes a look at it. You want to circulate it elsewhere, Chief?"

"Not yet. Go on, Mackinnon."

"Well, sir," Mackinnon said tentatively, "Norris did say a different American has been seen aboot the area, a laddie that was known to be staying with you and Mrs. Fletcher, it seems."

"Lambert. He left us some time ago."

"But he's still aboot, sir, according to PC Norris."

"The devil he is! I wonder what bee he has in his bonnet now. Two shady Americans haunting Hampstead—it's not quite beyond the bounds of coincidence, but . . ." Alec sighed in exasperation. "I can't see Lambert as the murderer of his fellow countryman, but he may conceivably have useful information for once. Next time he's spotted, or if they can find out where he's lodging, he'll have to be brought in."

Tom made a note. "You have a picture of him, Chief?"

"No. The embassy does, and may even know where to find him, as he's supposed to be on official business, but for heaven's sake, let's not get them involved yet."

"Mrs. Fletcher'll be able to identify him for us," said Tom with an innocent expression.

Alec scowled at him. "For heaven's sake, let's not get Daisy involved, if we can possibly avoid it."

Tom made no attempt to hide his grin. "We'll do our best, Chief."

Mackinnon continued to brief Tom, laying out the known facts without attempting interpretation.

When he finished, Tom asked, "Mrs. Fletcher didn't actually view the body, then?"

"I believe not, Mr. Tring. Sir . . . ?"

"No." Alec abandoned the papers with relief. He hated desk work. "At most, she saw the outstretched hand, gloved."

"I'm glad to hear it, Chief. It's an odd business, for sure. This empty holster now. I'll be blowed if I can think of any reason he'd go out wearing it without a gun, bloody uncomfortable as they are. So what was he doing walking about London with a gun? And where is it now?"

"They're looking for it in the garden, for a start," said Mackinnon, "along with whatever was used to bash him over the head."

"Ah." Tom ruminated for a moment. "Now that's another odd thing. Just supposing the victim started this whole bit of bother by drawing his gun. Hitting him on the head could have been self-defence. But the business with the pressure on the arteries, that's plain cold-blooded murder."

"That's what it looks like," Alec agreed. "We'll have to wait for the autopsy to be certain of the cause of death."

"Why go so far as murder when the chap's out of it and you could just run away?"

"Because you were afraid he'd come after you?" said Mackinnon, hazarding a guess. "When he came round, I mean."

"Which makes it sound like it's the victim that's the real villain."

"Cold-blooded murder," Alec reminded them. "You can speculate to your hearts' content on your way to Hampstead. I've got this damn report to finish and an irate AC to placate. Tom, between the two of you, can you work out what questions you need to ask my neighbours in this preliminary round?" Alec was being tactful. He knew Tom was perfectly capable of doing the job, but he wasn't sure of Mackinnon. Now, Tom would instruct the young sergeant under the guise of a discussion.

"I reckon so, Chief. Let me just get the times straight. The doctor saw the body about eight o'clock this morning and said he'd been dead twelve to twenty-four hours?"

"That's right."

"So he was killed before eight in the evening. Sounds like the body must have been pretty much out in the open before it was moved, so not before dusk, probably. Say around five o'clock. Between five and eight."

"Close enough, for the present. They should have finished photographing that passport by now, and made a couple of quick prints for you to take with you."

"D'ye want us to drop the passport—the original—off at the American embassy, sir?"

"Ah," Tom said weightily.

Alec grinned at him. "Are we of one mind on this, Tom? As soon as they know an American is involved, or possibly two, they'll want to 'muscle in,' as they themselves would put it. We can't turn over evidence in a murder case at the drop of a hat. It will have to go through the proper channels—as many channels as we can dig."

"We'll give 'em the number and a copy of the photo in a couple of days?"

"Depending on how our enquiries proceed."

"Right, Chief. Any questions you want to ask Mr. Fletcher before we go, Mr. Mackinnon?"

"I canna think of any," Mackinnon said hesitantly.

"If there's anything we can't work out between us, there's always the telephone. Let's be off, then."

Alec had a sudden thought. "Hang on a sec, Tom. Do you happen to recall the name of that chap at the British Museum who was a cryptographer in the War? The one who helped us round up the Gloucester Customs raid gang last year? Poplar, Pollard, something like that."

"Peplow? I couldn't swear to it, Chief, but young Piper will know. Or if there's no hurry, you could always ask Records, but don't hold your breath. Why?"

"His job at the museum is actually deciphering palimpsests."

"And what may a palimpsest be when he's at home?"

"Another useful word to add to your dazzling vocabulary. It's a used parchment that's been scraped clean and written on again. Often the obliterated text is of more interest than the overwriting. This chap—Popkin? Yes, I believe it's Popkin—he's an expert at making out the original writing. Perhaps he can get the victim's name from the passport."

"Worth a try," Tom agreed.

"Will he need the original, sir?" Mackinnon asked. "I doot a photograph will do as well."

"Good point. I'll deal with it when I've dealt with the AC." He turned to his report at last as the two sergeants went out.

By the time Daisy and her entourage returned homeward from the Heath, the sun was shining. The change in the weather, as much as the change of scene and the passage of several hours, made the murder in the garden seem like a bad dream, or at least an event that had taken place aeons ago.

Reality intruded all too soon. From the end of the alley, Daisy saw DS Mackinnon and one of the detective constables coming down the steps of number 8. They turned down the hill, then ascended the steps of number 9.

Number 9, the Ormonds, she thought. Inherited money; four children, all away at school; Mr. Ormond dabbled in painting and had turned up at the Jessups' drinks party with longish hair and a flowing cravat; Mrs. Ormond, very smart, kept busy with the sort of committees that organised charity balls. Disappointed to learn that Daisy didn't play bridge, she had attempted without success to co-opt her onto one of these committees. The lure she held out was the chance to hobnob with the aristocracy.

Unlured, Daisy had been relieved that the Jessups had not revealed her own family background, though doubtless Mrs.

Ormond would find out sooner or later. In the meantime, the Ormonds were pleasant enough neighbours, but she didn't anticipate their becoming great friends.

The same applied to all the residents of Constable Circle apart from the abominable Bennetts at one end of the scale and the Jessups at the other.

Perhaps by now, Mackinnon had talked to the Jessups and they had given him satisfactory answers to all the questions Daisy hoped he had confronted them with. She wished she had had a chance to suggest exactly what questions ought to be posed.

Or perhaps she didn't. If there was something fishy about the Jessups' conduct, she didn't really want to be the one to draw it to the attention of the police. They would soon enough uncover it without her help. Wouldn't they?

Nor could she make up her mind whether she had rather talk to Alec, who would know at once if she prevaricated, or to one of the others, who might not notice.

She wondered whether Mackinnon had already called at number 6 in her absence. She was tempted to wait for him to come out of the Ormonds' house to ask if he had any questions for her. She nobly resisted temptation, the more easily because she was carrying Miranda, who was hanging on to her with a death grip.

A few minutes ago on the Heath, when she had tried to put her daughter in the pushchair to give Oliver a turn in her arms, Miranda had produced an eldritch screech that turned all heads for a hundred yards. The audience included Mr. Bennett and his spaniels. Daisy was certain he would subsequently spread the word that she was cruel to her children. She only hoped he wouldn't go so far as to report her to the NSPCC. Not likely, she thought. He and his wife preferred "insinuendo" to outright accusations that could be disproved.

Thus, despite Nurse Gilpin's protests about spoiling the child so that she would always expect to be carried in future, Daisy had Miranda on her hip when they reached the Circle.

Somewhere in the back of her mind she could hear her mother rebuking her, saying she looked like a gypsy, carrying a baby on her hip, but it was quite the most comfortable way to do it.

What with one thing and another, she simply hadn't much attention to spare for a police investigation just at that moment.

Even with three adults in attendance, steps up to the front door and down to the area door made getting two babies and a pushchair into the house a complicated matter. Daisy kept Miranda until they reached the front hall, by which time she was unhappy even in her mother's arms.

"She's hungry, poor lamb," said Nurse accusingly, taking her.

Daisy felt as guilty as if she had deliberately withheld food from her child, in spite of knowing that was exactly what Mrs. Gilpin intended.

"So's Oliver," said Bertha.

"Well then," snapped Mrs. Gilpin, "hurry and take him upstairs so you can come down for their lunch."

Lunch sounded like a good idea to Daisy, too, but the parlour maid was hovering at the rear of the hall, having obviously kept a lookout for their return.

"Oh madam!" she exclaimed as the nursery party headed up the stairs.

"What is it, Elsie?"

"Oh madam, a policeman came by while you were out!"

"As we expected," Daisy pointed out reassuringly.

"Yes'm." The girl sounded as doubtful as if the possibility had never crossed her mind.

"Come into the sitting room and tell me about it."

To the left of the stairs was a small sitting room that caught the afternoon sun. Daisy had furnished it with the chintzes and cheerful paintings of Paris scenes that Alec's first wife had chosen to brighten the house in St. John's Wood. Daisy and Alec used it far more than the formal drawing room at the front of the house.

Daisy sank into a chair, glad that they were the kind of chairs one could sink into. "Sit down, Elsie."

"Oh madam, I didn't ought!" She twisted the corner of her apron in agitated fingers. "It was the Scottish one, madam. Detective Sergeant Mackinnon, he calls himself. He wanted to know exackly what I saw and what I did, and I told him I already told the master, but he said I had to tell it all over again."

"So you did?"

"Oh yes'm. And the other one, Detective Constable Warren, the one with his eyebrows burnt off—you know?—he wrote it all down. Like as if he thought I might tell it all different next time!"

"Did you happen to think of anything you hadn't already mentioned to me or to Mr. Fletcher?"

"Oh no'm. I told you every single thing, just like it happened."

"Good. I'm sure Mr. Mackinnon didn't mistrust you, Elsie. He was just doing his job, following the rules."

"Well, that's as may be. It's not very nice for a girl to have every word she speaks wrote down."

"No, it's never nice being mixed up in a police case." Not nice, Daisy thought, but always interesting. "Did he ask for me?"

"No'm. I said did he want to see the mistress, because you'd gone for a walk, but he said he was sure you'd told the master all you knew. Like as if I hadn't!"

"I'm sure you did," Daisy assured her, and the girl departed soothed.

Daisy, however, was left quite indignant. She would have liked a chance to go over the whole affair with Mackinnon, or, better still, with Tom Tring. What she really wanted, she realised, was to be reassured that they knew all about the Jessups' comings and goings and were certain they had nothing to do with the stranger's death.

In fact, she was not a little peeved at being ignored. On the other hand, as long as they didn't want her contribution, she didn't have to make up her mind what she really ought to reveal about the Jessups.

Her next aim, she decided, must be to meet Patrick Jessup. Though it was his elder brother who had fled, if the family was somehow caught up in the murder in the garden, could Patrick's return from America that very night have been pure coincidence, or had it set the affair in motion? Only by talking to him could she judge to her own satisfaction—if not that of the police—whether the fatal outcome was inadvertent or the result of malice aforethought.

What was the cause of death? Ernie Piper might have had the decency to tell her!

Mackinnon might be an easier mark. He didn't know her as well, and besides, she would be very careful not to alarm him with a direct question. He must be tired and hungry by now, tramping up and down the hill and all those steps. She would invite him to lunch.

THIRTEEN

As soon as she stepped out of the front door, Daisy saw Tom Tring approaching the Jessups' house. He and Mackinnon must have split the circle between them, she deduced.

What was more, Ernie Piper was at his side. She had forgotten that when she saw Mackinnon, he'd had a DC accompanying him.

She sighed. Tom wasn't in the least likely to reveal any information he didn't intend to, but even if he hadn't been a dear friend, she couldn't possibly invite Mackinnon to lunch without him, and Piper and the other chap. That made four detectives for lunch. She hoped Mrs. Dobson had plenty of eggs, cold meat, bread, and cheese on hand.

Then after eating, she thought, cheering up, she would take Tom up to the nursery to see Oliver. Surely he couldn't be so heartless as to refuse to pass on a tip or two to the mother of his godson.

Piper saw her, waved, and pointed her out to Tom. She gestured to them to come over.

"Tom, Mr. Piper, you must be hungry, and I'm about to sit

down to a lonely meal. Won't you and Sergeant Mackinnon join me? And DC Warren, of course."

"That's very kind of you, Mrs. Fletcher." The twinkle in his eyes told her he was well aware of her ulterior motive. "I was just hoping to catch Mr. Mackinnon and Mr. Warren and suggest we go for a quick bite, rather than disturbing people at their lunches."

"Perfect! There they are now, just leaving number nine."

Mrs. Dobson, warned to expect a guest before Daisy went out to find Mackinnon, had refused adamantly to have her kitchen cluttered again with constabulary. "Once in one morning is enough, madam. I'll never get a thing done today. It'll have to be the dining room."

Leading her horde into the house, Daisy was afraid it would be awkward when they found the table set for two. But Elsie—a veritable paragon of a parlour maid!—had looked out of the window and seen them all arriving, as she told Daisy later. Five place settings welcomed them, and Elsie carried in laden platters, as well as several bottles of beer. Mrs. Dobson had done her proud. Signs of haste might have been apparent to the housewifely eye, but that was something Daisy had never claimed to possess. As far as she could tell, fussing about whether everything was perfect never caused anything but grief.

Soon the sound of contented munching filled the room. Daisy was careful to ask no questions of more significance than "Another slice of bread, Mr. Mackinnon?"

Her forbearance was rewarded when Warren, the first pangs of hunger assuaged, grumbled, "I hope you had better luck than we did, Mr. Tring."

"Not much!" said Piper. "Mostly, there was no one home but the servants, and not a one of them heard or saw anything out of the ordinary, nor recognised the photo."

Photo? No one had shown Daisy a photo. She managed not to voice her outrage, but Tom caught her eye and raised questioning eyebrows. She shook her head very slightly. He answered with an equally infinitesimal nod, perceptible only by the shifting sheen on the reflective dome of his head.

"Same here with the photo," Warren confirmed. "Leastways, there was a housemaid swore she'd seen him peeping in her bedroom window one night, but seeing she sleeps in the attic—"

The others laughed.

"And it was her mistress," Warren continued, apparently forgetting Daisy's presence, "who didn't sleep a wink all night for the screams and groans. Sarge asked why she hadn't reported the disturbance to us, and she said her husband was in such a temper at breakfast because his egg was boiled too long that it put everything else right out of her mind."

Daisy knew exactly whom he was talking about. She ought not to listen to their discussing her neighbours, but it was irresistible. What was more, Tom, who could have put a stop to it anytime, let them continue. Perhaps he hoped their talk might spark a useful idea or two in Daisy's brain. After all, much as it pained Alec to admit it, she had occasionally been helpful in the past.

However, nothing occurred to her. She simply didn't know most of the neighbours well enough to have more than the most superficial impressions of them.

Elsie brought in coffee.

"Tom," said Daisy, "would you like to bring yours up to the nursery to say hello to your godson?"

"I would indeed, Mrs. Fletcher, thank you very much. Mr. Mackinnon, I shan't be long. I'd appreciate a word with you before you finish up down the road. How is the little fellow?" he continued, following Daisy from the room with the light tread that revealed his mountainous bulk as mostly muscle.

She closed the door. "*I'd* appreciate a word with *you*," she echoed. " 'Word' first or babies first?"

His grin made his moustache wiggle. "Let's get the word over with, so that I can enjoy the twins in peace."

"Come into the office." She led the way through a door next to the foot of the stairs.

The room had two desks, as she shared it with Alec. His had little on it besides an inkwell and blotter, since he did most of his paperwork at the Yard. Hers, a massive rosewood creation inherited from Mr. Walsall, was dominated by her aged, secondhand, but trusty Underwood typewriter. Around it were piles of paper and reference books. No one could have called the result tidy, but Daisy could generally find what she needed when she needed it.

More books filled the shelves against the wall backing the stairs. When Belinda was home and young feet had thundered up and down those stairs, the books had muffled the noise. Under the window facing north onto the terraced garden stood the Georgian writing table, one of the few objects Daisy still possessed from her childhood home. She sat there to write personal letters, and sometimes just to think, when she was at the planning stage of future articles. Beside it, a glass-paned door led out onto the paved lowest terrace, where green-painted wrought-iron chairs awaited the return of summer.

Daisy perched on the corner of her desk and waved Tom to a chair by Alec's desk, one he had occupied before, talking police business with Alec.

"Well?" she said severely. "Why haven't I seen the photograph?"

"I understand you were out when Mr. Mackinnon came to speak to your household. And, strictly between ourselves, Mrs. Fletcher, the Chief was most adamant that you shouldn't be involved any more than absolutely necessary. It's possible the lad took his words rather too much to heart. Or he felt the Chief should cope with you himself! Or both."

"So you do concede I ought to have a go at identifying the victim? Not that I exactly want to study a picture of a corpse, mind you, but in the interests of—"

"Not to worry. It's not a picture of a corpse we're showing

around." Tom reached into the breast pocket of his green-and-maroon check jacket. He was wearing one of his more sober outfits today. "The deceased had a passport in his pocket, so we're using the photo from that."

"A passport? British?"

"Ah." Tom pondered as he handed over the photo. "I don't see why you shouldn't know. American."

"Oh!" Dismayed, Daisy took a moment to focus on the face. Then, instantly, she recognised it. "Oh no!"

"You've seen him before. You're quite sure?"

"Yes."

"Do you know who he is?"

She shook her head. "I just saw him in passing."

"Where?"

Slipping down from the desk, she went over to the garden door and stood there staring out at the dank flower beds, tidy now but bleak. She couldn't avoid telling Tom she had seen the American at the Jessups', but need she report that he was dashing away after an acrimonious meeting with Mrs. Jessup? Did she have to reveal Aidan's dismay on hearing of his visit? After all, the former was hearsay, not proper evidence, and the latter just her reading of Aidan's emotion.

She knew what Alec would say to that rationalisation!

Turning, she found Tom regarding her with a steady gaze, part quizzical, part stern. "Where did you see him, Mrs. Fletcher?"

With a sigh, she admitted, "At the Jessups' house, number five, next door. Several weeks ago." She made up her mind. "And I really think that's all I can tell you, at least until you've talked to them yourself."

He nodded. "Fair enough. They're next on my list, the last. You didn't react much to anything the others were saying over lunch. I take it there's nothing to tell about the rest of the residents?"

"Nothing I know of." Daisy hesitated. "No one mentioned the Bennetts, at number ten."

"Number ten was last on Sergeant Mackinnon's list, so he probably hasn't got there yet. Why?"

"I can't help thinking that anyone who had talked to them would have had plenty to say on the subject."

"As you do?"

"Just that you shouldn't believe a word they say. They're the worst kind of gossips, avid for any breath of scandal even if they have to make it up themselves. If they have no meat for outright rumourmongering, they're expert insinuators."

"I shall so advise Mr. Mackinnon," Tom said gravely. "Thank you, Mrs. Fletcher. Now we'd better go on up to the nursery before the others start wondering where we've got to."

At New Scotland Yard, with the Assistant Commissioner and Superintendent Crane pacified at least for the present, Alec returned to his office. An internal message form lay on his desk. Dr. Popkin had telephoned to say he'd be delighted to pop round and take a dekko at anything the chief inspector wished to set before him—the message Alec had left for him at the British Museum switchboard had been a model of discreet nonspecificity.

Regarding the piles of paper still awaiting his attention, Alec decided he could, if forced to do so, justify going to the museum, rather than inviting the expert to come to him.

Beside the message was a large manilla envelope with the photography department's stamp in the corner. Inside were a dozen enlargements of the dead man's passport photo, four of the entire passport, and the passport itself.

Alec studied the photo with interest. They had blown it up to the point that it was just barely beginning to blur. While agreeing with Shakespeare that "There is no art to find the mind's construction in the face," he judged the subject of the portrait to be a tough man. His eyes were hard beneath dark slicked-back hair, and his thin-lipped mouth was a straight line with no sign of softness or humour. Not that that made him a criminal, of course. Besides, as well as the unreliability of features as a guide to character, passport photos were notoriously uncomplimentary.

And regardless of the victim's character, his murderer must be punished.

He made arrangements for copies of the passport to be sent to the FBI and the New York police, to follow up his cables. He couldn't expect a response for at least five days, probably longer. With any luck, he wouldn't have to wait that long to find out the man's name. If Dr. Popkin managed to read it, perhaps he'd have wrapped up the case by then. Slipping the passport into his pocket, he set off for Bloomsbury.

Hunger overtook him en route, and he popped into an Express Dairy milk bar in Oxford Street for a quick lunch.

When he reached the British Museum, he showed his warrant card and asked for Dr. Popkin, saying he was expected. A messenger led him at a great rate into the labyrinth of corridors hidden away behind the equally labyrinthine public halls, galleries, and libraries.

"Do you ever lose visitors in here?" Alec enquired.

"Hardly ever," the man replied in a lugubrious tone that suggested he wished the answer was "Frequently."

At last they stopped in front of a door labelled DR. N. POPKIN. The guide knocked.

"Come in!"

Opening the door, the guide announced, "It's the police, Dr. Popkin." Now his tone implied that he expected Dr. Popkin to be hauled off to prison on the instant.

"Police? Ah, Mr. Fletcher." The tall, lean man wore a white coat and white gloves. He had the permanently disappointed look of a basset hound.

"I'm afraid I'm interrupting you, Dr. Popkin," Alec said, entering and closing the door firmly on his guide. They shook hands.

"Not at all. After all," Popkin pointed out, gesturing at a sloping glass table with a bright light underneath and a couple of ancient manuscripts on top, their curling corners held down by broken clay tablets incised with strange markings, "these have been lying around for a millenium or two. A few minutes longer won't hurt them. I beg your pardon if I seemed unwelcoming. The truth is, I was looking forward to escaping this mausoleum for a visit to Scotland Yard."

"I'm sorry to have deprived you of the outing, sir. I hoped to disturb your work as little as possible. Though if we're telling the truth, my desire to escape from my office was probably as strong as yours."

The basset hound grinned disarmingly. "Oh, by all means, let's have the truth. It's rare enough here, where practically everything I produce is a matter of inference and interpretation. What have you got for me?"

Alec handed him the passport. "Water has seeped between the pages, and the name is unreadable. I don't know if there's any chance you might be able to suggest what it might be."

"No bloodstains," Dr. Popkin noted, disappointed again. "No bullet hole."

"I'm afraid not."

"Ah well, we must work with what we have." He opened the booklet. "Odd, I'd have expected India ink in an official document of this nature."

"So would we. What do you think?"

"Oh, I expect I can give you something. This may take a few minutes. Do sit down."

"I'd like to watch, if I may."

"Certainly, though there won't be much to see. It's a matter of training the eye to read shadows. I dare say it's not unlike police work in some ways, eh?"

"Very like. Only our shadows tend to come in larger sizes. Man-size, for the most part."

Popkin laughed. He took the passport to his glass table, which had brilliant lights above as well as below, and picked up a magnifying glass. He studied the open page closely, first looking straight down, then squinting sideways. Then he set down the magnifying glass, turned off the underneath lights, and stuck a jeweller's loupe in one eye. Picking up the passport, he examined it at an angle.

"Easy. They used an inferior pen nib as well as inferior ink. It has scratched the paper. If you wouldn't mind passing me that notebook on the desk there—"

"I'll write it in my own, sir, if you'll dictate the letters to me."

"*M I C H E L E*, capital *C, A S T E*, double *L, A N O*. Michele Castellano. Italian, wouldn't you say?"

"Yes, I would," Alec said thoughtfully. "Thank you, sir. I never dreamt you'd be able to give me so definite an answer, let alone so quickly."

"We aim to please."

"Needless to say, the matter is confidential."

"Of course," Popkin agreed cordially. "Dare I hope to learn what it's all about when you have bagged your villain?"

"I'd say of course, sir, if it weren't for the possibility of international ramifications. . . . Oh, what the hell, after what you did in the War, you know all there is to know about international ramifications! I'll be glad to send you a report."

Popkin beamed. "Thank you, Chief Inspector. I'll look forward to it."

Rather than ring for a messenger, he himself escorted his guest out to the great portico, so not until Alec was descending the steps to Great Russell Street was he able to consider what he had learnt.

Michele Castellano. Italian American. His mind went back to that evening a couple of months ago, in St. John's Wood, when the Pearsons had come to dinner and an unexpected American had turned up.

Pearson had spoken of reading about Irish, *Italian*, and Jewish bootleggers in America organising into increasingly violent gangs. Scotland Yard were naturally most concerned about the Irish aspect. In spite of the Irish Free State, the Irish were in general anti-British, yet fugitives from the American police were quite likely to have relatives living in Britain.

Despite a growing number of Italian restaurants in London, the community of Italian expatriates was minuscule in comparison.

The subject of American gangs had arisen because of Lambert's advent, and, lo and behold, Lambert had turned out to be a Prohibition agent. The young idiot had babbled about following gangsters to England, but Alec hadn't paid much attention. In his opinion, Lambert's superiors had probably sent him across the Atlantic to get him out of their hair.

What was it he had claimed to be his purpose in England? All Alec could recall was that he had tried to bring a gun into the country—which implied a willingness to use it.

Lacking the firearm, could he have resorted to other methods with one of the villains he purported to be chasing? Had the apparently ingenuous Lambert hit Michele Castellano over the head and then, with his thumbs, compressed both carotid arteries until the man lay dead? *Lambert*, who would lose his head if it weren't firmly attached to his body? He would never have found the right spots to compress.

Lambert, who was still to be seen out and about in Hampstead, even after leaving the Fletchers'.

Still, the only reason to connect Lambert with Castellano was that they were both Americans. Except that Castellano had been found murdered in Constable Circle, where Lambert had spent considerable time . . . What had Daisy said about Lambert and their next-door neighbours, and about the Jessups' mysterious American visitor?

Once again, it seemed he ought to have paid more attention to Daisy's guesswork, or intuition, or whatever it was that made her so often and so infuriatingly right. His sigh was so heartfelt that the woman sitting next to him on the number 24 bus he had unthinkingly boarded gave him a look of sympathy and said, "Never you mind, ducky. The night is darkest before the dawn."

He nodded an acknowledgement, but as the bus negotiated Trafalgar Square, with Nelson's Column in the middle, he found himself dwelling on the admiral's death in battle. Then the Charing Cross statue of Charles I brought to mind the king's execution.

The bus trundled down Whitehall, with all the panoply of government on either side and the Houses of Parliament ahead. Alec reminded himself that Nelson's fleet had won a glorious victory at Trafalgar, and that Cromwell's grim rule had ended with the restoration of Charles's son to the throne in a constitutional monarchy with no claims of "divine right."

Alec swung down from the bus at the Cenotaph stop and hurried into the Yard. Things were really not going too badly. He had far more information than when Daisy had broken the news of the body in the garden to him, just a few hours ago. More important, he had a good idea of where to look for more answers. The most frustrating moment in any police investigation came when one didn't know where to turn next.

This time, he knew. First, he had to cable Michele Castellano's name to Washington and New York. And then he needed to talk to Daisy.

FOURTEEN

"Daisy?"

"Darling! You've rung just in time. Tom wants to interrogate me."

"So do I. Tell him to hold off with the thumbscrews until I arrive."

"Right-oh. Are you at the Yard still? I'll give him a cup of tea in the meantime. And all the others, too, I suppose. Mrs. Dobson's getting a trifle fed up."

"What are they all doing there? No, don't tell me! Doubtless I shall find out in due course. I'm on my way."

Daisy hung up. If he was coming home, surely he wouldn't then take Tom and Mackinnon back to the Yard, or even to the local station, to give their reports. With any luck at all, she would manage to listen in.

Instead of trying to guess from Tom's questions what the Jessups had told him, she would hear it from his own mouth. It wasn't that she intended to lie on their behalf, but nor would she disclose everything unless she was convinced that the police needed to know. In her experience, they were all too apt to read a sinister significance into the most innocent actions.

Tom and Ernie had arrived first. When Elsie announced them, Daisy had told her to show them into the dining room. No sooner had she joined them there than Mackinnon and Warren turned up, looking for Tom. Before Tom had made up his mind whether Daisy ought to leave while he and Mackinnon discussed the results of questioning the Jessups and the Bennetts, the telephone rang.

But Alec's call had been very brief. Returning to the dining room, Daisy hoped she hadn't missed anything.

As she pushed open the door, Ernie Piper was saying in an incredulous voice, "Shopping? The biggest gossip in the neighbourhood, with a murder on her doorstep, and she goes *shopping*? You're having us on."

Daisy slipped in and sat down as quietly as possible. Tom and Ernie were staring at Mackinnon, Ernie looking quite indignant.

"Simmer down, lad," said Tom calmly. "Mr. Bennett told you his sister went shopping, Mr. Mackinnon?"

"So did the servants."

"Ah. Well, that'd be what they were told."

"It's not as odd as it sounds," Mackinnon protested. "It seems she has a school friend living in the country who comes up to town once a month. The ladies go out to a show and supper, and then, rather than come home late—I gather Bennett objects to being disturbed after midnight—his sister stays at the friend's hotel. And next day, they go shopping together. Sometimes, if they manage to get tickets for something good, they'll stay over another night."

"Sounds to me like a load of codswallop," said Warren.

Though Daisy would have used a less vulgar term, that was exactly what it sounded like to her. Why on earth had the Bennetts—or Mr. Bennett—invented such a farrago? Surely not to give Miss Bennett time to escape the police? It just wasn't possible that she had murdered the man in the garden. She wasn't capable of killing anything but reputations.

"He claims he doesn't know what hotel she stayed at last

night," Mackinnon went on. "Nor whether she intends to come home today."

Tom glanced at Daisy. She should have known her return had not escaped his eagle eye. She shook her head. She'd never heard of Miss Bennett's monthly outing, or her school friend, come to that, and she hadn't had time to develop any theories.

"Tell it to the Chief," Tom said. "I take it no one in the house saw or heard anything last night?"

"The servants didn't. Mr. Bennett was . . . What would you say, Warren? Evasive, perhaps."

"Kept on and on about how they hadn't thought anything of it at the time and he wouldn't want to say anything that might get someone into trouble when he wasn't absolutely sure—"

"Ha!" escaped Daisy inadvertently.

They all looked at her. She was afraid they'd stop talking about the Bennetts, though they'd find it difficult to ask her to leave her own dining room.

However, Tom turned back to Mackinnon, produced an *ah* laden with meaning, and asked, "Anything else?"

"It's what he refused to say that seems to me significant, Mr. Tring," said Mackinnon. "He refused to tell us anything more until he talks to his sister to see if she remembers the same."

"Never heard that one before, Mr. Mackinnon! Now, Mrs. Fletcher knows the Bennetts. What do you think he meant by it, Mrs. Fletcher?"

"I wouldn't say I know them. In fact, I've gone out of my way to avoid them. But if you ask me, neither of them saw anything and they're waiting to see which way the wind blows before they invent a story."

"Waiting to find out what happened and who's suspected, you mean?"

"Exactly. I simply can't believe she'd go off to a show and a day's shopping if they had really seen anything. She's keeping out of the way to give him an excuse to postpone telling what they'll claim to have seen, so that when she returns, they can concoct a tale to fit the facts."

"I bet that's it," said Ernie Piper enthusiastically. "I bet you've hit the nail on the head, Mrs. Fletcher."

"Ah," said Tom, his eyes twinkling. "We'll see."

"Nae doot the chief inspector will try to persuade Mr. Bennett to tell his tale before he has a chance to learn the facts from servants and neighbours and pass them on to Miss Bennett."

"Not much hope of that, Sergeant," Warren put in with his accustomed gloom. "We've talked to every servant in the Circle, and you can bet they're all comparing notes by now. However careful we've been, they'll have a good idea of what it's all about."

"In any case," said Daisy, "I should think Alec's more likely to send you to do it, Tom. He doesn't like the Bennetts any better than I do, and I expect they know it. Not that he'd let his dislike get in the way of the truth, but if he disbelieves them, they might make a fuss and start spreading nasty rumours about prejudice."

"Sounds to me like they'll do that anyway," said Warren.

"Probably, but there's no point adding fuel to the flames. One thing's certain: Whatever they claim to have seen will be aimed at making trouble for someone. That's what they live for. Don't you think you should have a go at him, Tom?"

"It's for the Chief to decide. In the meantime, now that I've talked to the Jessup household, I've a few questions for you, Mrs. Fletcher, before we go back to the Yard to report to him."

"That was Alec I talked to on the phone just now, and he said he's on his way here." Daisy sighed. "*He* wants to ask me questions, too. So, since I'm so popular at the moment, why don't we just wait till he arrives? We can have a cup of tea while we wait."

She was pouring second cups all round when the front doorbell rang again. Elsie ushered in DC Ardmore. He looked somewhat nonplussed at finding himself in the middle of a tea party.

"Do sit down, Mr. Ardmore," Daisy invited.

"Another cup, madam?" asked the parlour maid resignedly.

"Yes, please, Elsie, and some more hot water."

"I telephoned in, Sarge," Ardmore told Mackinnon, "and they told me the chief inspector left a message to meet him here."

"That's right. Any luck?"

"Depends how you look at it. No one at the Hampstead station recognised the passport photo. Me and a couple of the uniformed lads covered Well Walk, Flask Walk, and the High Street and we found four people who thought they might have seen him. Only not a one of 'em would swear to it, and they didn't know anything about him anyway, just seen him about. We went to a couple of hotels and lodging houses, but no luck there. It'll take more time or more men to check everywhere in the area."

"And he could be staying anywhere," said Tom. "Doesn't have to be Hampstead. I expect we'll have to circulate the picture to all stations. Go on."

"The other American, your friend Lambert, Mrs. Fletcher—lots of people recognised the description, and the woman at the newsagent's told me where he lodges. So I went along there and had a chat with the landlady—it's a widow who lets out a couple of rooms. Hodge is the name."

"He wasn't there?" Mackinnon asked.

"No, nor he didn't come in last night," Ardmore said with heavy significance.

"She doesn't know where he went?"

"No, but she does say he's often away for a night or two," the detective constable conceded, "so she wasn't worried. She says she doesn't usually let to foreigners, but he speaks English quite well, and he's a nice young chap. Keeps his room tidy and very helpful about the place when he's home."

"That sounds like Lambert all right," said Daisy. "Did he tell Mrs. Hodge why he's here? In England?"

"It seems he said he's in the import business and looking for suppliers."

Daisy laughed. "It's true, in a way." She didn't know how much of Lambert's clandestine mission Alec had entrusted to the others, so she didn't explain that he was in the business of preventing imports and looking for the suppliers of bootleggers.

The coincidences really were too much to swallow: A Prohibition agent who was interested in a wine merchant who was visited by a mysterious American who turned up dead a hundred yards from his house. Although Daisy couldn't see Lambert as a cold-blooded killer, she couldn't forget the irresponsible way he had waved his gun around at their first meeting, when she and Alec were in the States. Yet if anyone was going to get bumped off, an agent of the law seemed the most likely victim.

Into the middle of a discussion of which she hadn't heard a word, Daisy dropped the question: "What if Lambert has been murdered, too?"

Everyone stared at her in silence.

Tom was first to recover. "Have you any reason to think he might be?"

"Alec didn't tell you why he came to England?"

"Not just to visit you and see the sights, I take it."

"No. Oh dear, if Alec didn't, I'd better not. I can tell you that Lambert seemed to think it was a dangerous business. He even tried to smuggle a gun into the country. Well, not exactly smuggle, because he apparently didn't know he wasn't supposed to have one, and he was quite upset when Customs took it away. Admittedly, he's given to exaggeration for the sake of excitement, but still, it does seem to me possible that he could be another victim."

As she spoke the last few words, the dining room door opened and Alec came in, with DC Ross on his heels.

"Who could be another victim?" Alec asked sharply.

"Lambert. He's disappeared, darling!"

"Not exactly disappeared," Ardmore protested. "We found his lodgings, sir, and it's true he didn't come home last night, but his landlady said he often goes away for a few days."

Alec sat down at the table and motioned to Ross to do likewise. "Lodgings?" he said. "A private house, not a flat or a hotel?"

"A furnished room, sir, let by the week. He's paid up to the end of next week."

"What's the landlady like?"

"Uh, fiftyish, grey hair—"

With an impatient gesture, Alec said, "Her character, Constable! Is she likely to allow you to search Lambert's room without a fuss? And preferably without telling all her neighbours."

"Yes to the search, sir. She was quite friendly and helpful. About the neighbours, I dunno. She didn't seem like the gossipy sort, but you never can tell with women. Oh, she did say she was glad I wasn't in uniform, because she wouldn't want people to know she'd had the police in the house."

"Right-oh. Do your best to impress upon her that it's best to keep quiet, and also that we have no reason to suspect Lambert of any wrongdoing. We're just concerned for his safety."

"Oh, darling, do you really think—?"

"You're the one who started this hare, Daisy. We have to chase it."

Ardmore stood up. "So you want me to search his room, sir? What'm I looking for? A gun?"

"Great Scott no! At least, I sincerely hope not, but if you find one, you'll confiscate it, of course. No, see if he's taken his toothbrush with him. If he has, we can stop worrying."

"And if he hasn't?" Daisy asked.

"Then we'll start worrying. Ardmore, give Piper the name and address, if you haven't already, then off you— No, come to think of it, a few more minutes won't make much difference. You'd better stay and hear a bit more."

Ardmore sat down again.

"Chief," said Tom, "can you tell us a bit more about Mr. Lambert? Why we may be worried about him? Mrs. Fletcher decided she shouldn't, as you hadn't."

"How uncommonly discreet!"

"Don't be beastly, darling. He did make a point of telling us in confidence. If he's missing, though . . ."

"You probably remember a good deal more of what he said than I do. Why don't you explain."

Daisy gave him a suspicious look. He was actually inviting her to get involved? It was true she knew Lambert much better than he did.

"Right-oh. Shall I start with New York?"

"Great Scott no! All that need be said about New York is that when you met him there, he was an agent of the Federal Bureau of Investigation."

"And a very enthusiastic one, but hopelessly incompetent. When he turned up here—or rather, in St. John's Wood—we weren't a bit surprised to find out he'd lost all his papers and his money. He said he'd transferred from the FBI to the— What was it, darling? Something to do with money."

"Treasury."

"That's it. Though why they should put the Treasury in charge of enforcing their law against drinking is more than I can understand. Still, they did, and Lambert was working for them."

"Over here? Not trying to stop *us* drinking, I hope, Mrs. Fletcher?" asked Mackinnon, only half joking. "The English might stand for it, but the Scots, never."

Four English detective constables glared at him in outrage. Whether they were outraged by the idea that the Americans might try to keep them from their pints, or by the suggestion that they wouldn't fight as hard for those pints as the Scots would for their drams, or both, Daisy didn't wait to discover.

Hastily, she reassured them, "No, they couldn't do that."

"They better not try," muttered Warren.

"Lambert was sent to try to stop the export of alcohol from England—Britain—to America."

"Single-handed?" Tom asked dryly.

"Well, that's the thing. Surely they must have sent more

than one agent. Suppose the dead man was another? What if a bootlegger unmasked both him and Lambert and murdered both of them?"

"What would a bootlegger be doing over here, Mrs. Fletcher?" asked Piper.

"It was something about codes, wasn't it, Alec? I don't remember exactly what Lambert said. Something about the Prohibition people intercepting the rumrunners' radio messages, so the gangs are sending men here to arrange codes with their suppliers."

"Gangs!" Ardmore exclaimed. "Don't say they're exporting their gangs now!"

"Not wholesale, and just visiting, I gathered."

"And the enthusiastic but incompetent Lambert is supposed to stop them?" Tom enquired in a tone of deep interest. "By shooting them?"

"Heavens no! He's supposed to identify them and follow them to see which English wholesalers they get in touch with. Oh, and try to find out what ships they use to deliver the stuff. You can imagine he was quite thrilled when we moved in next door to a wine merchant."

"The Jessups," said Tom.

"The Jessups," Daisy confirmed. "He used to watch them through binoculars, believe it or not. Then, after he moved out, I'd see him lurking in the undergrowth, presumably still spying on them."

"You never told me that, Daisy!"

"You were so relieved when he left. Besides, I couldn't swear it was him. I never came face-to-face with him. But he's such a rotten lurker, I'd catch glimpses now and then. It reminded me of the old days in New York."

"We'll have to find out if he's been seen 'lurking' around the homes or business premises of any other large-scale licensed victuallers. Piper, that's a job for you. Get a list of all the major wine merchants in London for a start, and call on them."

"Right now, Chief?"

"Yes, let's get cracking on this. Lambert's been lurking in the bushes, Castellano's body was found—"

"Castellano?" said three or four voices simultaneously.

"Michele Castellano," said Alec, trying to be nonchalant but looking smug. "The chap at the British Museum read the name in the passport without the slightest difficulty." He spelt it out and all the detectives wrote it down in their notebooks. "You'd better take his photo, Ernie, and make enquiries about him, too. He may have nothing to do with the booze trade, but we might as well kill two birds with one stone."

"Right, Chief."

"Ring up now and then to see if there have been any developments you need to know about."

"Uh . . . where?"

Leaning back in his chair, Alec ran his fingers through his hair. Dark, thick and springy, it showed no signs of depredation. "Uh, Daisy," he said reluctantly, "would it be very disruptive if we used this room as our headquarters, just until we finish our enquiries in the immediate area?"

Daisy quickly changed a burgeoning grin into a frown. "I haven't planned any dinner parties for the next few days," she said—she seldom did, never knowing when Alec would be home. "We could eat in the office or the kitchen, I suppose. It'll mean extra work for the servants, though. They're sure to kick up a dust."

"I suppose it wouldn't work—"

"But I expect I can talk them round," Daisy interrupted before he could dismiss the idea out of hand, the last thing she wanted. "In fact, with half a dozen policemen in the house, perhaps Nurse Gilpin will stop declaring that the murderer will have to climb over her dead body to get at the babies. If she carries on much longer, she'll end up giving them a complex. All right, darling, I should think we can manage."

And just let them try to keep her out of her own dining room!

FIFTEEN

Ernie Piper and Ardmore departed, the latter with instructions to search Lambert's room for anything that might connect him with Castellano, as well as for his toothbrush and other overnight necessities.

Alec turned back to Daisy. "Any more revelations about Lambert?" he asked.

"Not that I can think of."

"Can you, by any chance, remember how he found out that the Jessups are in the wine trade?"

"It was when they invited us, him and me, for cocktails. I'm sure I told you. He was helping me go over the house and decide what to do. It was an awful mess when Alec inherited it," she informed Tom and the others in an aside. "Mrs. Jessup sent her maid to ask us over for a drink, under the impression that Lambert was my husband."

"The Jessups knew Castellano, too, Chief," said Tom, his voice carefully neutral. "Mrs. Fletcher recognised him."

"What? Great Scott, Daisy—"

"I *told* you they had an American visitor, an unwelcome visitor. You just said so did we, and that it's not against the law."

"And forgot about it," Alec admitted ruefully.

"No one showed me Castellano's passport, not until Tom showed me a copy of the photo after lunch. How was I supposed to know it was the same man?"

"You're sure of that?"

"Not absolutely. I didn't get a really good look at his face. I wouldn't swear to it in court, but if I wasn't pretty certain, I wouldn't have mentioned it." Or rather, she wouldn't have let Tom wring it out of her.

"How do you know he was unwelcome? Did they tell you so?"

"No, I overheard him trying to bully Mrs. Jessup. I wasn't eavesdropping. I happened to be leaving and couldn't help passing the door of the room where they were."

Alec gave her a sceptical look but didn't comment. "What was he bullying her about?"

"I didn't hear much. I gathered he wanted to see Mr. Jessup, who was travelling on the Continent. He seemed not to believe that Mrs. Jessup didn't know exactly where he was or when he was due to come home. He gave up while I was still in the entrance hall, and I caught a glimpse as he left, but he'd already put on his hat and turned up his collar. He didn't look at me, so, as I said, I didn't get a good look at his face."

"Tom?"

"You want the lot, Chief, or just the Jessups? Not that there's much else."

"Apparently we're going to be concentrating on the Jessups, so let's get the rest over with first. Mackinnon, did you get anything of interest?"

"Not a bite till I got to the Bennetts, sir. And then nothing actually useful, just a hint that they might have seen something."

"You couldn't get it out of them? They're usually only too ready to spread stories."

Mackinnon explained about Miss Bennett's absence and Mr. Bennett's evasions.

"I'd better have a word with him myself," Alec said with a sigh.

"Darling, you're not going to believe anything they say, are you? They'll concoct a story just to make trouble. They're utterly poisonous!"

"I know, Daisy, and I promise I'll take their claims with a pinch of salt, but the fact is, they have the best view of the garden of anyone but us and the Jessups, and they're notorious for keeping an eye on what's going on. It's just conceivable they actually did see something."

"Then why wouldn't he tell? Why did she go off with her mythical school friend?"

"Is the school friend mythical?"

"I don't know," Daisy conceded. "I've never heard of her before, but I don't exactly go out of my way to chat with Miss Bennett."

"Mackinnon?"

"I talked to the servants first, sir, before I talked to him. They told me she had gone to meet an old friend. When he told the same story, it never dawned on me that the friend might not exist."

"No, why should it?"

"Well, sir, Mrs. Fletcher had warned us about the Bennetts not being entirely reliable."

"She did, did she?" He glared at Daisy.

"Be reasonable, darling. I couldn't let him walk into their lair assuming they were nice, normal people."

"All the same, I should have—"

"Never mind, Mackinnon. It was natural to believe them, and it may even be true. But someone in the Circle may know if she exists. Ross, I'll leave that to you. Ask the Bennett servants first whether they have heard of her before, or seen her. If not, go round the Circle, asking the ladies of the house whether Miss Bennett's ever mentioned her. We may not get an answer, but it'll give them all something to think about."

And distract attention from the Jessups, Daisy hoped. The situation was beginning to look pretty black for them.

"I've got it, sir," said Ross. "Right away?"

"Yes. It's probably just a distraction, so let's clear it out of the way. You can skip the Jessups, at number five. Report back here."

Ross went out. Alec gazed thoughtfully at the remaining DC, Warren, whose cheeks were still fiery red from the flaming umbrella. He had had a hard day. His shoulders were slumped, and if it weren't for the scorching, his eyebrowless face would probably be pale and wan, Daisy thought. He straightened under Alec's gaze.

"How are you feeling, Warren?"

"A bit sore, sir, but I can carry on all right."

"Good man. Go to the kitchen and ask Mrs. Dobson to give you some more ointment for that burn; then I want you to ring up the Yard and tell them to transfer calls to this number. Stay by the phone—there's a chair beside it—ready to answer if anyone rings. We don't want the parlour maid going on strike."

Alec, Tom, and Mackinnon remained—and Daisy, who wondered if she was about to be ejected.

Alec subjected her to the same thoughtful gaze he had turned on Warren. She, too, felt the urge to straighten her shoulders. She resisted it.

"You know the Jessups quite well, don't you?" he said.

She nodded. "As well as one can after being next-door neighbours for a few weeks."

"You'd better stay. But you are not to pass on to them a single word of anything that's said here."

"Of course not, darling."

"Tom, Mackinnon, as I'm sure you realise, I'm caught between the devil and the deep blue sea. The Jessups are my neighbours, and I've no desire to have to move out. The connection with the victim is not proof that any of the family had any hand in his death, even if he was here because of that connection. I'm not saying we will in any way compromise the investigation. I'm saying tread gently, and above all, don't talk about the case to anyone outside this room."

"Right, Chief."

"Yes, sir."

"All right, Tom. Your turn."

"Nothing of interest at numbers one to four. No one recognised Castellano's photograph; no one had seen or heard anything. Three of the men had gone to work, and one housekeeper was out at the shops, so we'll have to go back, but I doubt we'll have any luck there."

"All the ladies were at home?"

"Every one of 'em, Chief, and dying to know what's happened. Miss Bennett leaving like that, it's not natural."

"Alec, you don't suppose Miss Bennett could have killed Castellano?" Daisy asked.

"Highly unlikely. It must have taken considerable strength to move the body."

"But if he helped her—"

"Then why didn't he scarper too?" asked Tom.

"He's verra arthritic and not a big man," Mackinnon commented.

"We'll keep them in mind, of course, Daisy, but don't get your hopes up."

Daisy was afraid he guessed that not only would she be happy to dispense with the Bennetts as neighbours but she was also doing her best to provide an alternative to the Jessups as chief suspects. Whenever she "interfered" (as he put it) in one of his cases, he accused her of trying to protect someone she was fond of, even to the extent of ignoring evidence against them. It wasn't true. She never ignored real evidence, and he himself was always telling her hearsay and speculation were not evidence. It wasn't her fault if sometimes it was not clear which was which.

Tom was continuing his report. "Before I reached number five, Mrs. Fletcher had a look at the photograph and recognised the victim, so I already knew he had visited the Jessups.

Their parlour maid, Miss Enid Bristow, identified him at once. She didn't know his name—she said he had terrible manners and never gave it to her—but she'd admitted him to the house twice, before she was ordered not to. A smart girl, that."

"Our maid's sister," said Daisy.

"Ah. I thought I detected a resemblance."

"So you should. You're a detective."

Impatiently, Alec asked, "Did she know Castellano's business?"

"Not much more than what Mrs. Fletcher happened to hear. He wanted to see Mr. Jessup and got pretty shirty when Mrs. Jessup wouldn't tell him where her husband was."

"I wonder why he didn't go to the shop and talk to Aidan?" Daisy muttered. Then she wished she hadn't.

Suppose Castellano had known Aidan—or, more likely, had known something about Aidan that he was going to report to Mr. Jessup. What was it Alec had mentioned as a possible reason for the Jessups and Mr. Irwin to be nervous of a policeman moving in next door? Evasion of duty on wine and spirits, that was it. Aidan was in charge of the financial side of the business. Suppose he had been paying the tax money to himself instead of the government? Aidan was Mr. Irwin's daughter's husband, so if the solicitor knew, he'd have every reason to be worried sick.

What a gift to a blackmailer! He could threaten Aidan with telling his father and threaten Mr. Jessup with telling Customs and Excise, which would probably ruin the business.

But how on earth could Castellano possibly have found out?

Not merely groundless speculation, but a wild flight of fancy, Alec would say if she told him. Much better not to.

"What did you say, Daisy?" he enquired, his tone of voice suggesting it was not the first time of asking.

"Oh, nothing."

He raised his eyes to heaven in exasperation but did not press her. "Go on," he said to Tom.

"The housekeeper only knew what Enid Bristow had told her, but at least she confirmed the girl wasn't making it up on the spot for my benefit. There's no lady's maid. The nanny's away, and the daily help 'don't know nothin' about nothin',' and doesn't want to. The others don't take her into their confidence."

"What time does she leave?"

"Four o'clock. She has children coming home from school and her husband wanting his tea at six. She walks down through the garden, but she would have been too early to see anything yesterday evening. That's assuming nothing happened before dusk. Mrs. Innes—that's the cook-housekeeper—and Enid Bristow were busy from five to eight clearing up tea things and preparing dinner. I'm pretty sure neither could have got away without the other knowing about it."

"And what about the family?"

"Ah, now that's another story, Chief. Comings and goings like a merry-go-round." Tom put on the wire-rimmed glasses he had recently taken to wearing for reading and took out his notebook. "Let me get this straight. I'll start with what the servants told me."

Alec nodded.

"First—being neighbours you'll know this, I expect—the younger son, Patrick Jessup, has been abroad for some time, on his own. He's always gone with his father before on these buying trips to the vineyards on the Continent."

Daisy knew all that, and she was fairly certain she had told Alec. She couldn't tell from his expression, though, whether he had actually been listening at the time, and remembered.

Tom moved on to the events of the previous night. "Patrick Jessup came home last night. They're not sure exactly what time, just that it was after dark. He came in through the kitchen—said he wanted to surprise his parents, and besides he was starving and could do with a bite before dinner. He gave 'em each a kiss, and they agree he had beer on his breath. He said he'd stopped in at the Flask public house for old times' sake."

"We might be able to get a check on the time from the pub, but he was certainly out and about between five and eight."

"Only thing is, Chief, he'd left the country before the first time the American turned up. Miss Bristow—Miss Enid Bristow's sure of that."

Alec frowned. "That does rather— No, it doesn't. They could have met abroad. Possibly their meeting set the whole peculiar business in motion." He scribbled a note to himself. "We'll consider it later. Go on."

"Patrick Jessup goes on up the back stairs. Next thing they know in the kitchen, before the maid's had time to lay a place at table for him, is Mrs. Jessup coming down to say not to bother. With Patrick home, Aidan was going to catch the night express to the North."

"Great Scott! Were they on such bad terms?"

"On the contrary, according to what I was told. Not to say there wasn't an occasional spat. Like, f'rinstance, Aidan didn't approve of this trip of Patrick's. Mostly, they got on about as well as brothers can. No, it seems Aidan had been on the fidget for a couple of weeks on account of some urgent business needed doing up north, but his mother—their mother—didn't want him to go while his brother was abroad."

"They'd known about this for a couple of weeks, or they were told last night he'd been fretting to get away?"

"They knew, though it was a bit of a surprise that he up and left so quick. A cab pulled up and he was off and away before the others sat down to dinner. He was going to get a bite to eat at the station, so as to be sure of not missing the train."

"He was in a tearing hurry, wasn't he! Did you get any further explanation? What his urgent business was?"

"Yes, Chief." Tom started to thumb through his notebook.

"Never mind; when you get to it. Go on with what the servants had to say."

"Let's see, now. Enid Bristow doesn't serve at dinner. She takes the dishes in and they help themselves, so she only heard bits and pieces when she fetched plates and took in the next course. Mr. Patrick seemed happy to be home, and Mrs. Jessup was happy he was home safe, and Mr. Jessup was pleased with some business he'd done. They all seemed cheerful, 'cepting Mrs. Aidan, who was in the dumps because of her husband leaving. Leastways, that's what Miss Bristow assumed was wrong with her."

"She didn't actually hear it said?"

"Not in so many words. But after dinner, when she took coffee to the drawing room, Mrs. Aidan asked her to help Nanny pack, because she was going to take the children to visit her sister while he was away. And this morning, off they went, with Patrick along to lend a hand."

"Don't tell me Patrick Jessup's left town, too?" Alec demanded in dismay.

SIXTEEN

"*Hold on,* Chief!" said Tom. "Patrick didn't go off with Mrs. Aidan. He just went to the station to see her and the children onto the train. Mrs. Fletcher telephoned the shop, or showroom, or whatever they call it. . . ." He looked at Daisy.

"I was afraid you might think I ought to have stopped Audrey leaving," she admitted, "though I really don't see how I could have. But it seemed to me at least I could find out for you whether Patrick had hopped it, too. I rang up Jessup and Sons and asked for Aidan—"

"For Aidan!"

"Because I knew he wasn't there."

"For pity's sake, Daisy!"

"Patience is a virtue," she reminded him severely. "It worked just as I intended. The receptionist said he wasn't available but either Mr. Jessup or Mr. Patrick could help me. I told her I really needed to speak to Mr. Aidan and asked when was he expected back. She said he was travelling on business and the date of his return was uncertain. So there you are. One flown, one in the bag."

"I hope you didn't leave your name," Alec said acidly.

"Of course not, darling. And I put on Mother's *grande dame* voice."

"Thank heaven for small mercies!"

"Heaven had nothing to do with it. It was entirely my own notion."

"And I suppose the notion didn't dawn on you to warn me that Mr. and Mrs. Aidan were flitting?"

"Be reasonable! Last night, not only did I not know Aidan was going; I didn't even know there was a body in the bushes. This morning, Mrs. Jessup told me only a few minutes before Audrey left that she was departing, and that Aidan had already gone. But I still didn't know the victim was an American, let alone that he was the Jessups' mysterious visitor. I had no idea they were any more involved than any of the neighbours. If you'd shown me the passport right away, I could have chained myself to the bumper bar of Audrey's taxi, like a suffragette. Not that I think for a moment that she had anything to do with whatsisname's death."

"Castellano," Mackinnon put in, checking his notebook. Both he and Tom seemed to be enjoying the skirmish between Daisy and Alec. "Michele Castellano."

"Italian-American," Daisy exclaimed. "I knew it!"

"Knew what? What else haven't you mentioned? And what the deuce do you mean, Mrs. Jessup told you about Aidan leaving? I wish for once you'd start at the beginning instead of dropping bits and pieces here and there."

"It all goes back to Lambert's arrival. And all I have are bits and pieces, like a jigsaw puzzle, half of them *pure speculation* you wouldn't have wanted to hear. But the picture is beginning to come together."

"Let's have it."

"Only it's more like a jigsaw than a consecutive story, so starting at the beginning isn't going to—"

"Great Scott, Daisy, start where you want, but let's have the whole of it! Or as many damn bits and pieces as you have."

"On the other hand, perhaps Lambert *is* the best place to

start," Daisy said reflectively. Alec looked about to explode, so she hurried on. "No, actually, it was Tommy, not Lambert. Tommy Pearson. Do you remember, he said something about gangs of criminals in America being Irish, Italian, and Jewish? We were worried about the Irish because of their habit of blowing up policemen, but even though Mrs. Jessup is Irish, it looks as if it's one of the Italians who's ended up dead on our doorstep."

"There are plenty of law-abiding Italians in America. Castellano may even be another Prohibition agent, sent to check up on Lambert."

"I *said* a lot of my picture is speculation. The next bit is Lambert, of course, who came to England to find out who are the wicked Englishmen whose shipments of alcoholic beverages are corrupting the morals of America."

"Excuse me a moment, Mrs. Fletcher," said Tom. "I assume Lambert's on the up-and-up, Chief? You checked his credentials? He couldn't be a non-Irish, non-Italian, non-Jewish crook?"

"No," Alec said regretfully. "It would have given me great pleasure to extradite him to America."

"He lost his papers," Daisy reminded Tom, "and it took forever to get them replaced, but he did. Which makes me wonder: You didn't find similar papers in Castellano's pockets, presumably. If he was an agent, he would have had them, and if his passport wasn't stolen, it seems unlikely his credentials would have been."

"Good point, Daisy. It doesn't prove he was a gang member, however."

"Don't forget the shoulder holster, sir," said Mackinnon.

"A shoulder holster!" said Daisy. "What else haven't you told me?"

"You're supposed to be telling us," Alec reminded her. "You're right, though, Mackinnon. With or without a gun in it, it's significant. We'll take it as a working hypothesis that Castellano was up to no good. Go on, please, Daisy."

"Right-oh. Next was finding out we were moving in next to a wine merchant. Lambert was instantly on the qui vive. Asinine, because there must be hundreds of wine merchants in the country who have nothing to do with bootlegging, but these were convenient for him to keep a watch over. And—let me see—after that, I discovered the younger Jessup son was abroad, not with his father as always before, but on his own. I can't remember what made me suspect he'd gone to America. No reason at all, really, just being mixed up with Lambert and his obsession."

"Do you know now for a fact that Patrick was in the USA?"

"No, actually. That's one thing that made me wonder: the way no one ever mentioned where he'd gone for such a long time. That and Mr. Irwin's jitters at the prospect of a policeman moving in next door to the Jessups. Mr. Irwin is Audrey's father, and a solicitor," she explained to Tom and Mackinnon, "so it seemed probable something a bit fishy was going on."

"Tom, did you by any chance ask Mrs. Jessup where Patrick had come home from?"

" 'Fraid not, Chief."

"What I canna understand," said Mackinnon, "is what Castellano was here in England for, assuming he was a gangster, if Mr. Patrick had gone over there on that verra same business of codes and such. It doesna make sense to me."

"No, it's odd," Daisy agreed.

"We'll be able to tell from Patrick's passport if he was in the States," Alec pointed out. "Daisy, let's get back to your jigsaw puzzle."

"Where were we?"

Mackinnon consulted his notebook. "Mr. Irwin," he said.

"Oh yes, his having the wind up was a small piece. So was Mrs. Jessup's anxiety. In general, she seems such a calm, practical person, but she worried about Patrick, and why should she if he was just across the Channel, where he'd been often before with his father? Then we have a murder in our quiet, secluded garden, followed by the news that Patrick came home and Aidan went off the very evening it took place. And then"—she glowered at the three men—"*much* later, I'm shown a photograph of the victim and recognize him as . . . Well, you know that bit. There's definitely a picture emerging, but it has too many holes left to make out what it is."

"The one part that's clear as a bell," said Tom, "is that square in the middle of your picture are the Jessups."

"However," said Alec, "we've no proof that Daisy's picture bears much relationship to reality. It's made up of a few facts and a lot of inference and sheer guesswork. Tom, did Mrs. Jessup tell you anything you didn't already get from the servants?"

"She explained Aidan's rush to leave. Seems he usually visits some of their customers up north at this time of year. The customers expect him. In particular, one gentleman, a Mr. Dalton, rang up to say his shooting party had depleted his cellar. He wanted to place a big order but wouldn't do it without the personal guidance of Aidan, on the spot. He telephoned several times and they were afraid he'd take his business elsewhere if Aidan didn't get there pretty quick."

"At least we know exactly where he went today, then."

"Mrs. Jessup didn't know the address. We'll have to get the details from the shop."

Alec looked at Daisy. "I don't suppose . . . ?"

"Of course I didn't ask, darling. I didn't want them to know who was calling, remember? Or that I had any connection with the police. In fact, I didn't even know Mrs. Jessup hadn't given Tom the information."

Tom gave his rare rumbling laugh. "You see, Chief, it doesn't pay to keep Mrs. Fletcher in the dark!"

"Mackinnon, go and ring the shop. This is official. You're a police detective and you want to know the whereabouts of Mr. Aidan Jessup today and his planned itinerary. Make sure you speak to Mr. Jessup himself, though. There's no need for his staff to know what's up. While you're about it, tell him I want—no, make that 'would like'—to speak to him and to Mr.

Patrick at home." Alec checked his wristwatch. "Half past six this evening. Got it?"

"Yes, sir. A command disguised as a polite request."

"Exactly."

Mackinnon went out.

"Tom, anything else from Mrs. Jessup?"

"I asked what time the gentlemen generally came home from work. She said it varies. The shop closes at eight. The Jessups generally leave at five-thirty or six, but quite a few of their better customers like a private appointment later on. Whichever of the Jessups stays on to deal with them sometimes goes in late or comes home early the next day, depending on how busy they are. Yesterday, though, both Mr. Jessup and Aidan came home earlier than usual because they were expecting young Patrick. Mr. Jessup went in early this morning to make up."

So much for that hurrying figure that had so alarmed Daisy! She wasn't going to tell them about that.

"They knew what time Patrick was coming home?" Alec asked.

"Not exactly. He sent a cable from the steamer as it approached the Liverpool docks—"

"Liverpool!" Daisy exclaimed. "So he *was* in America."

"Or Ireland, Mrs. Fletcher. You said Mrs. Jessup was Irish. Patrick could have been visiting relatives, or maybe calling on breweries and distilleries."

"Or talking to Irish Republicans about bombs," she said darkly.

"Not impossible," said Alec, "and I'll keep it in mind, but I'm inclined to believe your original notion was right, Daisy." He grinned at her look of triumph. "I think Patrick was in America, on business concerned with outwitting their forces of law and order. Tom, if he was still on board when he cabled, the Jessups didn't know what train he'd catch?"

"No. The men came home about four o'clock, she said, which agrees with what the servants told me. Just in case Patrick disembarked and got through Customs quickly, to be there to welcome him."

"Or—I wonder—to meet Castellano? I'm assuming Castellano refused to go to the shop because he knew Prohibition agents were over here on the watch. Suppose Jessup had at last agreed to talk to him at home, to find out what he wanted? And when they found out, they didn't like it."

"But they wouldn't *kill* him," Daisy protested, "not deliberately."

"Pending the autopsy report, I'm afraid we're virtually certain he was killed deliberately. I'm not yet prepared to swear he was killed by one of the Jessups, but with the information we have, I have no choice but to work on that basis. I realise it's no earthly use trying to tell you what to do, but I hope you'll steer clear of the family, all of them, until we have this sorted out. And while we're on the subject, how did you happen to be chatting to Mrs. Jessup this morning?"

Tom, who in the middle of this peroration had gazed up at the ceiling as if trying to pretend his considerable bulk was elsewhere, returned his attention to the proceedings.

"She came round," said Daisy, feeling somewhat subdued but on the whole heartened that Alec seemed at last to have grasped that he couldn't order her about. "She told me Audrey was just leaving to visit her sister, and before she went, she wanted to know what was going on in the garden."

"What did you tell her?"

"That I couldn't enlighten her because you never tell me anything."

A muffled snort emerged from the depths of Tom's moustache.

Alec visibly relaxed. "Good. What did you make of her manner?"

Daisy thought back. "As far as I remember, she seemed perfectly relaxed. Or at least as relaxed as one can be with hordes of policemen quartering the neighbourhood. But don't forget, darling, she was an actress."

"Ah, was she now?" said Tom. "Then it's no good reading anything into her reactions."

"How did she seem to you, Tom?"

"Just the right amount of concern if there's hordes of policemen quartering the neighbourhood and you don't know what's going on and one of them comes to ask you nosy questions about your family's movements. And you can't give satisfactory answers, and you have to admit you recognise the victim. I wish I'd seen her on the stage. She must have been pretty good."

"Or else she doesn't know what's going on," Daisy suggested.

"That's always a possibility," Alec agreed, "but I think I have enough to apply for search warrants for the house and shop. He looked around as Mackinnon came in. "Did you find out where Aidan is?" he asked.

"No such luck, sir. Apparently this chap Dalton lives in some godforsaken part of the country. Aidan's the only member of the firm who's ever been there. He has the address and telephone number in his address book—"

"Which he took with him."

"Which he took with him. What's more, he took the only list of the customers he has to call on, all of whose names and addresses are only to be found in his address book. All they know is that they're scattered all over the North, including Scotland. He takes the train up and then hires a car and driver. Mr. Jessup said he could probably come up with a few names if he put his mind to it, but he can't recall any with unusual names we might be able to run to earth."

"They must have an order book with the names and addresses of people they ship stuff to."

"Yes, but a lot of them just write with their orders; they dinna insist on a visit from a knowledgeable representative."

"There should be letters in their files, Chief," said Tom. "It may take a bit of digging, but we should be able to sort it out. Course, that won't tell us where he'll be on any particular day."

"Search warrants," said Alec crisply. "Tom, I'm leaving you to find a friendly magistrate. Mackinnon, you come with me to take notes. It's about time I had a word with Mrs. Jessup for myself."

Not five minutes after Alec went over to the Jessups, the doorbell rang. Daisy was still sitting in the dining room, writing down everything she had heard, which she hadn't dared to do with Alec present. She ignored the bell, thanking heaven that Elsie had proved quite capable of dealing with nosy reporters. However, the parlour maid showed in DC Ross, who had returned from his errand.

"You've been quick," said Daisy. "If I remember your instructions correctly, that means the Bennetts' servants confirmed the existence of Miss Bennett's old school chum. What a pity."

"Is it?" Ross asked. "To tell the truth, Mrs. Fletcher, I don't feel I've really got the hang of this case, coming in on it late, so to speak. I don't s'pose you'd be kind enough to explain what's going on?"

"I'd be glad to. It would help get it straight in my own head." About to add that she didn't actually know everything, as Alec refused to tell her, she realised just in time that nothing could so effectively cut off future confidences from Ross. She told him all she had already told the others, as well as what she had learnt from them, adding to her notes as she spoke.

He had his notebook out, too, but unlike Ernie Piper, he didn't have an endless supply of well-sharpened pencils. She had to wait while he shaved one into the fireplace. He did know shorthand, though, like Ernie, and unlike Daisy's version of Pitman's, his was probably legible to anyone who had studied the subject.

"Thanks," he said when she finished her exposition. "That was very clear. I see what you mean about the Bennetts. I wish I could report no one had ever heard of Miss Lagerquist."

"Lagerquist—is that the friend's name? They could never have invented that, alas. Pity her name's not Smith. Of course, even if she's real, she's just an excuse, giving the Bennetts time to make up a credible story. But if Miss Lagerquist were a figment of their imaginations, then the police could dismiss the Bennetts' story as another figment. Now they'll have to take it seriously, whatever they come up with."

"With a pinch of salt, Mrs. Fletcher, seeing they didn't see fit to come to us right away."

"Oh, the Chief will take anything they say with a pinch of salt. He knows them. It's because he knows them that he'll have to act on what they'll say they saw."

Ross looked somewhat confused. Daisy was about to elucidate when the doorbell rang again. Poor Elsie was going to be run off her feet, Daisy thought, but it was DC Warren who ushered in DC Ardmore.

"Hope it's all right, madam," Warren said, "if I answer the door. Miss Bristow passed a remark when Ross here arrived and I offered to do it for her."

"Thank you," Daisy said warmly. "With all of you coming and going, I was beginning to worry about Elsie. What about the telephone? No one has rung up yet?"

"Not yet. D'you mind if I leave this door open a bit? Then I'll be able to hear it ring from here, and the front doorbell, too. I'd like to know what's been found out."

"Of course, leave it ajar. Mr. Ross found out that Miss Bennett's school friend is real."

"And Miss Bennett spends a day with her in town every month, and sometimes doesn't come home for the night."

"What about you, Mr. Ardmore?" Daisy enquired.

"Bad news, I'm sorry to say, Mrs. Fletcher, him being a friend of yours. Mr. Lambert didn't take his toothbrush with him, nor his hairbrushes or anything else he'd need for a night away. Any way you look at it, it don't look good."

"Oh dear, I wonder what can have happened to him! He's so helpless and hopeless and hapless, I can't help feeling a bit responsible for him. Surely Castellano's murderer can't have got him, too."

The three men exchanged glances.

"We've no reason to think so," Ross said soothingly.

Warren inevitably looked on the gloomy side. "'Cepting he was int'rested in the Jessups, same as Castellano."

Ross frowned at him. "Mr. Lambert was . . . is a sort of policeman, and it looks like Castellano might've been a crook."

His slip of the tongue didn't make Daisy feel any better. Clearly he, too, had a feeling Lambert was dead. Equally obviously, he assumed the Jessups were responsible. Daisy refused to believe any of them was a cold-blooded killer.

She had to remind herself that she had never met Patrick Jessup. He had been described to her as "adventurous," often a euphemism for *reckless*, or even for *aggressive*. Was it possible that he had come home from America to find his family being persecuted by Castellano, and decided to do something drastic about it?

Yet Aidan, not Patrick, had done a moonlight flit. Staid, sober, sensible Aidan, father of two small children—and adept of the rugger field. Rugby football was above all a game invariably associated with physical aggression.

Daisy felt she was going round in circles again. Then suddenly a new idea struck her. Whichever brother was a murderer, if either was, she would expect the family to rally round to protect him. Could Aidan have left to draw suspicion away from Patrick?

There were too many unanswered questions. She wished she knew how Castellano had been killed, not in too much gruesome detail, of course. And she wished she knew what he had been doing in England.

"It's all very well saying Castellano may have been one of a bootlegging gang," she interrupted the subdued discussion of the others, "and that they've started sending people to England to coordinate codes with their suppliers. It doesn't explain why the Jessups didn't want anything to do with him, does it?"

"It would if they're not selling booze to America," Ross

pointed out, "and he's been trying to persuade them to join the trade, and they don't want to."

"Oh. Yes." Daisy had been assuming Jessup & Sons were rumrunners, if the word could be applied to British wholesalers. It fitted so well with her theory that Patrick had been in America. Or had she first guessed that they were shipping to America and from that deduced Patrick's whereabouts? She couldn't remember. And then there was Mr. Irwin's nervousness, suggesting some sort of illegal carrying-on. Perhaps evasion of duty owed was behind that after all. How dull!

Whichever, it didn't make sense for Patrick to be sent over to arrange the deal while the bootleggers sent an envoy in the opposite direction on the same business.

She badly wanted to meet Patrick. Normally, she would expect to have him introduced to her shortly after his return from abroad, but circumstances were anything but normal. After this, innocent or guilty, the Jessups might never again want to have anything to do with the Fletchers.

"Tea," she said, and rang the bell.

SEVENTEEN

Opening the Jessups' front door to Alec and Mackinnon, Elsie's sister Enid bristled. He hoped her obvious disapproval would not be transferred to his own parlour maid.

"The mistress is resting, sir," she announced forcefully. "She's already talked to them other policemen and she's wore-out."

"I know. I'm afraid I have a few more questions to ask her."

"It's not right to keep on at her like this!"

"It can't be helped. We have a job to do. Mrs. Jessup may be able to help us catch a murderer. You wouldn't want to leave him running around, would you?"

"No-o. Long as you don't think the poor lady did it." Enid changed her tack. "I hope as my sister's giving satisfaction, sir?"

"Absolutely." He assumed he'd have heard from Daisy if she wasn't.

"She didn't tell me nothing about this dead body she found," the maid said resentfully, "her and the little dog. Not till after the police came here and I knew anyway, she didn't."

"I'm glad to hear it." From a police point of view, Elsie was definitely giving satisfaction if she'd managed to hold her tongue in such circumstances. "She had strict instructions not to talk about it and would have been in serious trouble if she had. Did Mrs. Jessup instruct you not to let us in?"

"Oh no, sir, it just doesn't seem right."

"Then be a good girl and tell her we're here to see her."

"Beg pardon, I'm sure." The girl allowed them across the threshold and went off up the stairs.

His gaze following her, Alec saw at the top of the first flight a most attractive painting of a vineyard, a grape-harvest scene, in the French Impressionist style. Hanging there, it was at the perfect distance for proper appreciation, and he allowed himself to be distracted for a moment.

He tore himself away. He needed to put his thoughts in order and he didn't know how quickly Mrs. Jessup would put in an appearance.

"D'ye know Mrs. Jessup well, Chief?" Mackinnon asked.

"I've met her three or four times, but always in passing or in a social setting."

Where, he thought, it was impossible to gauge anything but her social proficiency, and that she had aplenty: charming, good-looking (well preserved, one might say, but he disliked the phrase, with its suggestion of mummification), well dressed and groomed, and an excellent hostess.

"Best face forward, as you might say," Mackinnon suggested.

"She's always seemed very pleasant. Bear in mind the fact that she was a serious actress." The ability to project unreal emotions was a skill like riding a bicycle—once learnt, never wholly forgotten. "Mrs. Fletcher likes her," Alec continued, "and she knows her much better than I do. However, she's been acquainted with her for only a few weeks, and I gather she spent more time with the daughter-in-law, Audrey, than with Mrs. Jessup herself."

True, Daisy always expected to like people. At the same time, she was a fairly shrewd judge of character. She would disregard minor flaws and quirks, but face her with people like the Bennetts . . .

After that first meeting on the Heath, Daisy had looked for an excuse for Mr. Bennett's rudeness. After the party, she had written him and his sister off as irredeemable. Though he didn't suspect them of murder, Alec had a nasty feeling they were going to cause problems.

Mrs. Jessup, on the other hand, was likable. The trouble was, the most likable and otherwise-admirable people frequently had—or imagined they had—reasons for trying to bamboozle the police. On present evidence, Mrs. Jessup's reasons might be sound.

Enid came down. "If you'll come this way, sir, madam will be with you in a minute." She turned towards the back of the house.

Alec had been shown the Versailles room on the occasion of the Jessups' party for the neighbours. He remembered well its startling, bewildering effect. He wondered whether Mrs. Jessup had chosen to see Tom therein. Tom hadn't mentioned it, but with Daisy constantly interrupting his report, that was hardly surprising. Bedazzlement might explain why he had extracted less information from the interview than Alec expected of his right-hand man. The endless mirrored reflections were confusing and distracting. How could one concentrate on a person's expression when she was repeated ad infinitum in all directions? Alec did not intend to be lured into a similar situation.

Instead of following the girl, he opened the door to the drawing room and said firmly, "We'll see Mrs. Jessup in here."

She turned back. "Oh, but—"

"I don't mind if you haven't dusted yet."

"Of course I've dusted!" she said, bridling. "Hours ago."

"Then we needn't worry." He went on into the room, Mackinnon at his heels.

Another painting caught his eye, a bar scene in the style of Renoir. In the crush of people at the party, he hadn't noticed the pictures on the walls. This one was quite small, so he went closer to have a good look. He didn't know much about art, and most of what he did know was about the artists of the period he had studied, Gainsborough (of the Gardens) and Constable (of the Circle) among them. He had no idea what Impressionists sold for in these days of Cubism, Surrealism, Expressionism, or whatever the latest fad might be, but he recalled a terrific fuss when a couple had been stolen. Presumably they were valuable.

"The real thing, d'ye reckon, Chief?"

"It's not a print. It could be a good copy, or 'after the school of Renoir,' but I'm inclined to think it genuine. The wine business must be much more lucrative than I had imagined."

Or Jessup & Sons had made a huge profit on a cargo or two to America.

"Could be Mr. Jessup's father or grandfather picked it up for a song before the Impressionists became popular, on one of their business trips."

"You know a lot about art?"

"Nay, not me. I'm one of those people the connoisseurs despise: I know what I like."

Alec laughed. "That's about my level. I like this, and the subject might well appeal to a wine merchant!"

When Mrs. Jessup joined them, she showed no sign of being ruffled by his change of venue. She didn't even mention it, as would have been natural, which made him suspect that she was, in fact, disturbed. If so, she hid it well.

"More questions, Mr. Fletcher? Do sit down, both of you," she said, taking a chair by the fireplace. She held out her hands to the flames as if chilled, though a pair of radiators made the room quite warm.

"This is Detective Sergeant Mackinnon, Mrs. Jessup. He's here just to take notes, so that there can no misunderstanding later about what was said." Also to dispel any suggestion that this was a friendly chat between neighbours.

She nodded to the sergeant and turned back to Alec. "This is a dreadful business!"

"Murder is always dreadful."

"It's . . . You're quite sure it was murder? Yes, of course; the other sergeant said you're certain it was not an accident."

"So it would appear."

"And not random. Not a robbery, that is, or a madman."

"We can never rule out a madman, Mrs. Jessup, but in this case, it seems highly unlikely."

"So we needn't be afraid to leave the house, for fear of meeting a like fate?" she asked, wide-eyed.

Alec was taken by surprise. If he were not already fairly sure that one or more members of her family were involved, the question would tend to disarm suspicion. In the actual circumstances, it made him wonder whether whatever had happened had somehow been kept from her.

Or was it a calculated, subtle plan to throw him off balance, and if so, was the subtlety hers, her husband's, or that of one of her sons? The best way to find out, he decided, was not to ask questions but to get her talking.

"You're more likely to be run down in the street by a careless motorist than attacked by a madman," he assured her. "I gather you had a busy evening yesterday. Tell me about it."

Her face lit up. Alec could see her as Nerissa, reunited with Gratiano, as Hero, exonerated and reunited with Claudio, but it was no young lover she had awaited; it was her son. "Patrick came home!" she said joyfully. No hint of unease marred her delight. "My younger son—no doubt you've heard he was travelling?"

She paused. Alec looked at her attentively but did not speak. For the first time, a shadow of anxiety crossed her face. Silence must be peculiarly difficult for actors to bear, he thought. In the theatre, it usually meant someone had fluffed his lines.

At any rate, only a few seconds passed before Mrs. Jessup resumed. "I was rather worried about him. Silly, really. He's not a boy anymore. But I must admit I was quite annoyed, when at last he came home, to find he'd stopped in at a public house on the way from Euston. As though we didn't have here any drink he could possibly want! Young men can be very thoughtless, can't they?"

She stopped again, and again Alec provided no answer.

"And then, to top it all, instead of all the family under one roof for a change, Aidan decided he couldn't postpone his business up north any longer. He dashed off to catch the night express from St. Pancras."

St. Pancras was a terminus for trains to the North, but also for boat trains to Tilbury. If Aidan had run for the Continent, he'd have been well on his way across the Channel by the time Castellano's body was found. The family had plenty of acquaintances on the other side to give him shelter.

Or was Mrs. Jessup's mention of St. Pancras a bit of "corroborative detail intended to lend verisimilitude to an otherwise bald and unconvincing narrative," à la *Mikado*? The whole exposition was beginning to sound like a well-rehearsed speech, and who better to memorise and deliver it than the ex-actress! The Jessups couldn't rely on Audrey to be word-perfect, so Audrey went to her sister's—assuming that was really where she had fled—as Mrs. Jessup was now relating.

She hadn't told him anything she had not already told Tom. In this case, perhaps direct questioning was the better way to go.

"What is the sister's name and address?" he asked, glancing at Mackinnon to make sure he was ready to take down the information in black and white.

"Her name is Vivien . . . Oh dear, I simply can't remember her surname." She gave a faint smile. "I suppose I'll have to pronounce those hateful words, 'I'm not as young as I was.' I refuse to believe one's memory fails. It just gets so cluttered, one can't find the needed fact. Enid shall fetch my address book."

She rang the bell and sent the parlour maid to find the address book in the bureau in her bedroom.

While they waited, Alec asked, "Does your daughter-in-law often visit her sister?"

"Every autumn, when Aidan has to travel on business. Audrey and Vivien are quite close, as their mother died young, but Aidan has nothing in common with Vivien's husband, so it works out very well."

The regularity and timing of the visits would be easy to check with the servants, so that was probably true. "Why did Aidan leave so abruptly, when his brother had just returned after a lengthy absence? Did they quarrel?"

For the first time, she looked disconcerted. She hadn't expected the question. Tom had asked the servants and been satisfied with their answer.

"Patrick and Aidan quarrel with each other?" She frowned. She not only hadn't expected the question, she didn't like it one little bit. "No, they've been good friends since childhood. Just the occasional squabble. You know how siblings are."

"I was an only child," Alec said woodenly, further disconcerting her.

"Oh, I'm sorry. And your two aren't old enough . . ." She remembered Mackinnon's presence and veered away from a cosy chat about the twins. "My sons do have the odd disagreement, inevitably. I find it hard to believe they had a . . . fight in the short time they were both here. But I wasn't with them every second, of course."

Apparently, she had decided on the spur of the moment that it might be advantageous to leave open the possibility that Aidan and Patrick had quarrelled, even come to blows. The obvious inference was that Aidan had sustained some presumably minor injury in his encounter with Castellano and had fled because the marks could not be hidden. But in that case, his mother must surely have noticed when she said good-bye, even if she had not witnessed her sons' putative battle. Alec wondered how long it would take her to realise that her red herring would not fly, to coin a phrase.

He had to assume Aidan was still in England and track him down before the bruises faded. A hired car and driver might be traceable, with the driver possibly ringing up to report daily. All they had to do was find the car-hire firm.

"Sergeant Tring tells me Aidan has the only list of customers he's gone to call on, but no doubt he mentioned where he intended to start out, which city he took a railway ticket to."

A mantle of vagueness settled over her. Like Tom, Alec wished he had seen her on the stage.

"Oh . . . No, I don't believe he told me. As he was not going to stay, there wouldn't have been any point, would there?"

"I dare say not, but I'm sure his father or brother must know. I'll ask when I see them here this evening."

There was nothing stagy about her passionate plea. "No, not here! If the Bennetts see you haunting the house, they'll make up some horrible story, and half the neighbours will believe it!"

"You have a point," Alec acknowledged wryly. "I'll make arrangements to see them at their place of business, after hours."

"Mr. Fletcher, why are you hounding us? Why are you hunting down Aidan? He hasn't done anything wrong. None of us has."

"Then you have nothing to worry about. Except the Bennetts. But a man has been murdered, and that man is known to have associated with your family, however briefly or unwillingly on your part. Would you have the police ignore it? I can ask to be relieved of the job, but whoever might take my place will follow the same trail."

"No. No, I'd rather have you, I suppose."

"What was Michele Castellano's business with your husband?"

"I don't know. I only know that Maurice didn't want anything to do with him." She turned with relief to Enid, who came in carrying a small green leather-bound book.

"Sorry I've been so long, madam. It wasn't where you said, in the cubbyhole. I found it in the top drawer."

"That's all right, Enid. Thank you." She took the address book and started to riffle through it as the maid went out. "The one thing I'm certain of is that Vivien lives in Lincolnshire, in or near some small village. Funny, I can't find a single Lincs address. *X Y Z*. Nothing." She turned back to the beginning.

"Allow me." Alec rose to take the book, and continued to stand, examining each page swiftly but with care. Most of Mrs. Jessup's friends and acquaintances lived in London and the Home Counties, with a few, very likely relatives, in Ireland. Almost all of the latter were in the Six Counties, he noted, rather than the Free State. Not that Northern Ireland lacked disaffected citizens.

He found no addresses in Lincolnshire, no one named Vivien or listed with the initial *V*, and no sign of a page torn out. Closing the book, he handed it back. "That's a pity."

"I suppose I've always been able to ask Audrey for the address if I needed it, though, to tell the truth, I can't remember ever having written to Vivien, nor can I imagine why I ever should. Sending kind regards via Audrey has always been perfectly adequate."

Alec felt he was wasting his time with her. "One last question, for the present," he said. "Where—"

"Not another word!" Mr. Irwin burst into the room. "My dear Moira, I hope you haven't been answering questions. You cannot be required to do so. Mr. Fletcher, I am shocked to find you questioning Mrs. Jessup without her solicitor present. It's against all the rules."

"On the contrary, sir. As I have absolutely no intention of arresting Mrs. Jessup, it's her duty as a citizen to aid the police in a murder enquiry."

"In any case, Jonathan, I'm afraid I've been most unhelpful to Mr. Fletcher. I don't seem to know anything he wants to know."

Irwin regarded Alec with suspicion. "What have you been asking, Chief Inspector? I'm sure it's most irregular."

"I was about to ask one last question. May I proceed?"

"I suppose so," he said grudgingly. "Now that I'm here."

"Mrs. Jessup, where has your younger son been these past weeks, and on what business?"

The solicitor turned apoplectic red and his mouth opened and closed several times, but no words emerged.

"Patrick's been in America," said Mrs. Jessup with the utmost calm. "Something to do with exporting 'the demon rum' to the deprived citizens of that country. I'm assured that no English laws have been broken in the process. Jonathan, you look as if you'd better sit down at once. Let me get you a whisky."

"My dear Moira! Law is Law! And these are policemen!"

She guided the horrified man to a chair and went to the drinks cabinet.

"I'm sure you'll feel better for a whisky, sir," Alec said soothingly. "In the meantime, I'd be grateful for your daughter Vivien's surname and address."

It was Mrs. Jessup's turn to look appalled. She froze with the decanter in her hand. Her reaction suggested Audrey really had gone to her sister's, not abroad. Alec breathed a silent sigh of relief.

Irwin looked merely astonished. "What can Vivien possibly have to do with a murder in London? She married a farmer called Bessemer. West Dyke Farm, Butterwick, near Boston." Noticing Mackinnon writing down the name and address, he clarified: "That's the Lincolnshire Boston, not the American one. Vivien has no connection with America whatsoever. Nor does her husband."

"I'm glad to hear it, sir. Do you happen to remember the telephone number?"

"They're not on the telephone."

"Thank you." Alec glanced at Mrs. Jessup. She had regained her self-possession and was pouring whisky with a steady hand, though Irwin no longer appeared to be in need of fortification. Perhaps she intended to drink it herself. "May I ask what brought you here?"

"An impertinent telephone call from one of the neighbours,"

Irwin said angrily. "He advised me that the entire family was about to be arrested for murder. Naturally, I hurried to my daughter's assistance."

Alec and Mrs. Jessup exchanged a look. Simultaneously they said, "Mr. Bennett."

EIGHTEEN

Returning home, Alec arrived with Mackinnon just in time to follow the parlour maid into the dining room.

"Tea, please, Elsie," said Daisy.

"How many for, madam?" the parlour maid enquired pointedly.

Daisy looked at Alec.

"Six," he said. "Tom may not be back for a while, and Piper certainly won't."

"I'll come and help you carry the tray, miss," offered Warren. "If that's all right, sir?"

Elsie looked mollified. Daisy gave Warren a grateful smile. His assistance might serve to avert mutiny in the kitchen.

Alec waved his permission and the two went out.

"Ross?"

"Miss Bennett's friend exists, sir. I talked to all the servants. None of 'em's been there more than a few months, and none of 'em's planning to stay more'n a few months, but as long as they've been there, she's spent a day or two each month with a Miss Lagerquist. They saw the lady a couple of months ago, in the summer, when she came in a hired car to pick up Miss Bennett for a jaunt in the country. There was some argument as to was it July or August, but they all agreed it happened."

"I don't suppose you asked whether this is the usual time of the month?"

"I did, and it is, and she told 'em yesterday she wouldn't be in for lunch or dinner today."

"Good work," said Alec, "even if it's not the answer I'd hoped for. Ardmore?"

"No trouble with Mr. Lambert's landlady, sir. She went up to his room with me and pointed out all the stuff he usually takes with him when he goes away for a night or two. She cleans a couple of times a week, so she's had a good nose around and knows exactly how many pairs of socks he owns, and how many pairs of under— Begging your pardon, Mrs. Fletcher! And what's at the laundry, too."

"All right, we don't need a list of every item of clothing he possesses! The conclusion is that he didn't plan his departure."

"That's right, sir. He's never gone off without warning like this before, seemingly. Proper worried about him is Mrs. Hodge."

"Daisy, you know him best. What do you think would make him dash off without his traps?"

"The slightest hope of getting mixed up in some sort of havey-cavey business where he could use what he fondly imagines to be his undercover skills. I'm worried about him, too, Alec. If the Jessups' connection with bootlegging isn't utter piffle, then Lambert was on the scent."

"It's not utter piffle," said Alec. "Mrs. Jessup admitted it."

"She didn't!"

"It's not illegal here, as she pointed out."

"Then Patrick was in America?"

"He was. She must have realised we had only to ask to see his passport to find that out. Of more immediate use to us, Mr. Irwin gave me Audrey's sister's address. Mackinnon, I'm going to send you to take a statement from her—from Mrs. Aidan, that is. The children's nurse, as well. What we need most is

Aidan's whereabouts. But who knows, it's always possible one of them will provide some revelation about what happened last night."

"Aye, sir."

"Ring up the Boston police and request a car and driver to take you to the farm. You'd better get going. Goodness only knows how you get to Boston."

"Mrs. Jessup said it's two changes. There's a *Bradshaw's* in the drawer of the little table beside the phone," Daisy told Mackinnon.

The detective sergeant met Elsie and Warren in the doorway and stood back to let them through. He cast a longing glance at the tea trays as he disappeared.

No biscuits, Daisy noticed sadly. She poured a cup and said to Elsie, "Take this to Mr. Mackinnon, at the telephone, please."

"Yes'm." Elsie took the cup and saucer and added with a touch of belligerence, "If you please, madam, Mrs. Dobson wants to know how many for dinner."

"Alec?"

"Just the two of us. Or possibly just Mrs. Fletcher, Elsie. I'll try to get back in time. I'm going to see Jessup and Patrick at the shop after all. Mrs. Jessup pointed out that to keep going in and out of their house will just add grist to the Bennetts' mill. Though there will be enough coming and going if Tom gets those warrants. . . ."

"Couldn't you just have asked her to let you search?" Daisy handed cups of tea to each of the men.

"Not once Irwin turned up. To ask and be refused would just give warning, give them the opportunity to clear everything up thoroughly."

"They had time to do that before the body was even found, sir," said Ardmore.

"True, but in the flurry and scurry of getting Aidan away, they may not have thought of it, and they could hardly do much today, under the eyes of the servants."

"On the contrary," said Daisy, "the absence of both Audrey

and Aidan and the children would give them the opportunity for a grand turnout of their rooms and the nursery. And what more natural than that Mrs. Jessup should take a look around first to make sure any valuables are safe, and to see what needs doing?"

"Dash it, Daisy, you're right. We'll just have to hope they don't get to it till tomorrow. Now. Ross, you'll come with me to Jessup and Sons. Ardmore, it's a late night for you. You'll help Sergeant Tring search next door, and then, if you don't find out where Aidan took a ticket to, you can be off to St. Pancras to see if we can trace him there. Mrs. Jessup gave me a photograph of him." He handed it over. "Mr. Irwin simply couldn't think of a reason why she shouldn't."

"He's about as ordinary-looking as a bloke can get," said Ardmore in dismay.

"Just do your best. I don't want to have to ask every big-city force in the North to make enquiries at every car-hire firm near their main stations. We may get his destination at the shop, but I don't want to wait."

"Can't trust 'em to tell the truth anyways," Warren pointed out.

"What are you going to do about Lambert's disappearance?" Daisy demanded.

"Circulate a description. Why don't you write one out for me?"

"Right-oh." Daisy turned to a fresh page of her notebook, glad that being a journalist meant she always had one available when needed for police business.

It was a pity Lambert had been in England long enough for his very American haircut to have grown out. He still kept his fair hair cropped very short, but in an English way. Horn-rimmed glasses, American-cut clothes, and an American accent were pretty distinctive, though. Unfortunately, the face behind the spectacles was about as ordinary as Aidan's. "Never mole, hare-lip, nor scar, nor mark prodigious" to make him either "despised in nativity" or instantly recognisable.

Concentrating, Daisy missed Alec's instructions to Warren. As she tore off the sheet and slid it across the table to him, Mackinnon came in.

"There's a train I can catch if I leave right away, Chief, but I willna get to Boston till after nine. They're booking a room for me and they'll take me out to the farm. Should I go this evening or wait till tomorrow morning?"

"Farm people generally retire early. Better wait till the morning. It won't make much odds. When you get to Boston, ring up for the latest developments here."

"Right, sir." He turned towards the door, then swung back. "I'll be forgetting my own head next. Mr. Tring rang up while I was looking up the trains. He says he has the warrants and he's on his way here."

"Excellent. I hope he's springing for a taxi, as you may if you need to. Go catch your train." As Mackinnon went out, Alec consulted his wristwatch. "Five o'clock. I want to go and see what visibility is like in the garden."

"The sky's cleared," said Daisy. "It's lighter today than yesterday. By the way, what time did Mr. Whitcomb walk up through the garden yesterday on his way home from work?"

"Who went to the Whitcombs? Number seven."

"Number seven?" Warren thumbed unhappily through his notebook. "DS Mackinnon and me, sir. Mr. Whitcomb wasn't there, and we only asked did he mention seeing anything out of the ordinary. We knew we'd have to try again this evening to talk to all the gentlemen as was off at work."

"I'd forgotten that," Alec said ruefully. "I need more men! You're right, Daisy. Even if Whitcomb saw nothing, the time he didn't see it may help pin things down. Let's see. . . . Tom had better—"

The telephone bell rang in the hall.

"Warren." Alec jerked his thumb towards the door and the eyebrowless detective constable hurried out. "Ardmore, Ross, come outside and we'll check what can be seen from where."

They followed Warren out to the hall. Daisy sat on for a

moment, wondering why Alec was being so obliging about letting her join their conclaves. True, she knew the Jessups better than he did, but such was usually the case when she found herself enmeshed in one of his investigations. In fact, that was almost always why she was involved in the first place. Yet usually he strove to exclude her. Though she felt she had made one or two helpful suggestions, she found it hard to believe he had suddenly realised the inestimable value of her assistance.

There was no understanding it. With a shrug, she went after the men.

She was just in time to hear Warren call Alec back from the front steps. He stood at the rear of the hall, holding the telephone receiver at the full length of the wire and his arm.

"Sir, it's DC Piper. He's talked to three booze sellers, two wholesale, one retail on a large scale. They all recognised Castellano's photo and Lambert's name, though one of 'em tried to deny it. Castellano came to their houses, not their business places, trying to coerce them into shipping to the U.S. Then Lambert came along to the business, claiming to represent the U.S. government and warning them of dire consequences if they did. Half a mo— What's that?" he said, stepping back to the telephone under the stairs.

"So Castellano *was* a bootlegger!" Alec exclaimed. He sent Ross and Ardmore out, shutting the front door after them against an icy draught. As he turned back, Warren reappeared, receiver at arm's length.

"Do you want him to go on, sir? Seems there's a list as long as your arm."

"Not now. Tell him to meet me at Jessup and Sons at quarter past six."

Warren retreated again. After a brief muffled colloquy, he once again reappeared, without the receiver this time.

"Get this, sir: Piper says one of the blokes is already exporting to America. At least, he admits he's sent one smallish shipment. Castellano tried to bully him into selling to a diff'rent gang over there. He says he told Mr. Lambert he didn't want to get mixed up in a battle between gangs and he was getting out of the transatlantic trade."

"Good heavens," said Daisy, "Lambert won one. If only by default!"

Daisy went off upstairs to visit the twins.

Leaving Warren to man the phone, Alec went out. As Daisy had said, the clouds had cleared. In the west, the sky was still pale blue; a cold wind blustered, already drying out and scattering the neatly raked piles of fallen leaves. He wished he had put on his overcoat. He nearly went back for it, but his men were waiting. It had been a long day and the end was not in sight.

Far from clarifying matters, Ernie Piper's report amounted to confusion worse confounded. It meant Castellano had had a motive for killing Lambert, yet Castellano was the one who had ended up dead.

Self-defence? The bootleggers' emissary had been done in with cool deliberation. Pending the autopsy report, Alec reminded himself. Ridgeway had been pretty certain, though.

Alec was utterly unable to see Lambert as a cold-blooded murderer, or even a hot-blooded one, except by mistake.

And where did the Jessups come into all this?

Time enough to puzzle over that when Tom arrived. For the moment, Alec was glad of something practical to do.

Ross and Ardmore were down by the fountain, in the centre of the garden. He could see them quite clearly from his own front steps. There was a lamp standard opposite the house, at the top of the path, and another at the bottom, but none in the middle. He was pretty sure he wouldn't recognise the men from here if he didn't know who they were. The glow of their cigarettes was not visible, though he could tell from their gestures that both were smoking.

The Bennetts had field glasses, of course. Alec wondered whether they had really seen anything.

He waved. The motion caught the eye of Ross, the taller of the two. He waved back. They went round to the far side of the fountain, nearer to the trail where the body had been dragged across the lawn. There followed an ambiguous melée. Alec had told them to do whatever came to mind, as they didn't know what had really happened. He could make out that they were involved in a struggle, but not exactly what was going on. Then one dropped to the ground. The other followed suit.

The first was supposed to lie on his back, the second to kneel over him, hands to throat. What with the twilight, the marble maiden with her urn, and the eighteen-inch-high rim of the pool, Alec could only assume they were sticking to his orders.

By the time he reached them, both were standing again, Ardmore brushing himself off.

"Get down again. I want to take another look from below."

"Have a heart, sir," protested Ardmore. "It's bloody freezing lying on the flagstones."

"It's Ross's turn. You can just freeze your knees. Wait till I get down to the lamppost."

From the bottom of the slope, though Alec made allowances for the deepening dusk, the scene was even less intelligible. He could see the kneeling figure silhouetted against the pale marble and the paving beyond, but Ross, lying on the flat at just about his eye level, was virtually invisible.

Alec looked back at the Bennetts' house. Their ground floor was only a couple of steps above street level. The view from their first floor, however, would be considerably better than his own from down here.

The best he could do was to take anything they said with a pinch of salt. Perhaps they'd decide they didn't have anything to say after all.

He walked back up.

"Any help, sir?" asked Ross.

"Not really. Certainly not enough to narrow the time frame.

I take it you could see each other well enough to proceed with whatever nefarious business took your respective fancies?"

"Easy," Ardmore averred.

"It'll have to be tried again in full darkness, when the only light comes from the streetlamps. Does either of you know whether there's a moon tonight?"

"Quarter moon," said Ross promptly, "rises after midnight."

"Perfect. How do you know?"

"I'm a sort of amateur astronomer, sir," Ross explained as they walked up the hill. "Very amateur. My great-uncle left me his telescope. Trouble is, you can't see much in London skies, what with smoke and fog and clouds, but I keep a track of the moon's phases, in case there's a good viewing night. You'd be surprised how often knowing comes in handy."

"Good for you. I hope that's Sergeant Tring," Alec said, lengthening his stride as a taxi pulled up in front of number 6.

The cab rose perceptibly on its springs as its passenger climbed out. Definitely Tom.

When they reached the pavement, he had just paid off the cabbie. "Hope that'll go down on expenses, Chief."

"Certainly. I ought to have told you to take a taxi if you were successful."

"Right here in my pocket, Chief." Tom patted the relevant part of his extensive anatomy. "Signed, sealed, and delivered."

They went into the house. Warren's scarlet face peered out from his telephone cubby.

"Any phone calls?"

"Not a whisper, sir."

"Did my wife come down yet?"

"No, sir."

Heavy Teutonic thoughts of *Kinder, Küche, Kirche* crossed Alec's mind. But much as she loved the babies, Daisy could barely boil an egg and was by no means a regular churchgoer. Besides, she was occasionally helpful in his work, and he was a modern husband, content to allow her hers. Still, he didn't send someone up to invite her to join them.

"All right, Warren, you'd better come and listen to this. Leave the door open in case the telephone rings."

They went into the dining room. Tom extricated the search warrants from an inner pocket and spread them on the table. "I managed to get hold of old Fanshawe," he said. "He'd give you a warrant to search Buckingham Palace if you asked him nicely."

Alec looked them over. "Very good. Tom, you'll take Ardmore next door. Ross will go with me, and Piper's meeting us in New Bond Street at six-fifteen. I have to interview the Jessups, *père et fils*. The search there will concentrate on their papers, so Ernie's the best one for that. We have a Yard car, but we'll have to leave in a minute, so let's fill you in quickly on what you've missed. Discussion will have to wait until tomorrow."

He gave a succinct exposition of the results of their enquiries to date. Ross, Ardmore, and Warren also listened closely, he was pleased to see. "Have I missed anything?" he asked them.

Ross spoke up. "About Sergeant Mackinnon going to Lincolnshire after the young lady, sir?"

"Thank you. Yes, he's on his way. It's not to be mentioned to any of the rest of the family. Apparently, there's no telephone at the farm, but I don't want to risk their somehow getting a message to Audrey Jessup. Tom, just run through what you'll be looking for next door."

"Most important, I reckon, Chief, is clues to just what happened last night, though what they might be is anyone's guess. Also, any indication of where Mr. Aidan went. Some sort of weapon Castellano could've been hit with——that'll be difficult till we get a better description from the pathologist."

"And Castellano's gun," put in Ardmore.

"Ah!" said Tom. "That'd put the cat among the pigeons, right enough!"

"Wait till half past six," said Alec, ignoring the ring of the telephone, which Warren dashed to answer. "Ask permission to search before you start waving the warrant. If I'm not back when you're finished, go round the Circle and see if you can catch those who were out this morning. And have another go at the visibility question—Ardmore, you can explain that to Mr. Tring. Warren's to stick to the telephone. When you get home tonight, Tom, you'll have to present my apologies to Mrs. Tring! Come along, Ross; we'd better get a move on."

They went out to the hall. Daisy was coming down the stairs. She waved and called, "Are you leaving? Toodle-oo, darling. See you—"

"Sir!" Warren popped out of the cubby. "Sir, it's Superintendent Crane, and he doesn't sound too happy!"

NINETEEN

"*Oh Lord!* I can't talk to the Super now," Alec groaned. "Daisy, tell him I've left, will you, and see what he wants now."

"Me!" said Daisy in ungrammatical outrage.

But her outrage was wasted on the closing front door. With a sigh, she went to the telephone.

"Spitting fire!" Warren warned her, disappearing into the safe haven of the dining room.

She picked up the phone, held the receiver at what she hoped was a safe distance from her ear, and raised the transmitter to her mouth. "Mr. Crane?" she said cautiously.

"Who the . . . ?" Even at arm's length, his bellow was deafening. "Mrs. Fletcher?" The voice moderated, and Daisy ventured to move the receiver towards her ear. "This is Crane. I must speak to your husband."

"I'm afraid he isn't here, Superintendent. I believe he's gone to interview some suspects. Can I help you?"

"I'm not sure anyone can," he said bitterly. "But you can transmit a message to Fletcher, if you would be so kind."

"Of course, Mr. Crane. Just let me get something to write on." She had left her notebook in the dining room, but there was always a pad in the drawer of the telephone table, and usually a sharpened pencil. Yes, here they were. She sat down, so that she could set the daffodil phone on the table and have a hand free to write. "Right-oh, go ahead."

"I have just had an extremely uncomfortable interview with the Assistant Commissioner. He, in turn, had just received an extremely uncomfortable telephone call from the Home Secretary. You are aware, I dare say, Mrs. Fletcher, that the Home Secretary oversees all of this country's police forces?"

"Yes." Daisy might not know much of politics, but she could hardly help knowing that, being married to a fairly senior policeman. She stopped trying to scribble down every word, realising that Crane was blowing off steam as much as trying to convey important information.

"The Home Secretary," he continued, "had just spoken—or perhaps I should say 'been spoken to'—by the Foreign Secretary."

"This is beginning to sound like *The House That Jack Built*," Daisy said unwisely, and went on to compound her error. "It's Oliver's favourite book at the moment."

There was an ominous silence at the other end of the line. Then: "This, Mrs. Fletcher, is *nothing* like *The House That Jack Built*, which, as I recall, has a happy ending. If I may continue . . . The Foreign Secretary had just received a telephone call from His Excellency, the Ambassador of the United States of America."

Daisy managed just in time to stop herself saying brightly, "I expect they talk to each other quite often." For some reason, Superintendent Crane's grimness was making her feel more frivolous than she had felt since Nana found the body that morning. Who, she wondered, had told the ambassador what? No doubt she was about to be informed. "U.S. Amb.," she wrote down.

"The embassy," Crane continued relentlessly, "had received a cable from the State Department, which, I gather, is their equivalent of our Foreign Office. The State Department had received an enquiry from the Federal Bureau of Investigation—to be precise, from your husband's friends at the Federal Bureau of Investigation—regarding a certain American passport."

"Castellano's. Michele Castellano's."

"Oh, so there's a name attached, is there?" The superintendent's gloom seemed to have lifted a little. At least he had some information to pass back along the chain. "Would you mind spelling that? You see, the FBI had only a number, and it happens to be the number of a passport that was stolen, along with several more blanks."

"It was faked?" said Daisy. "That would explain the ink."

"*Ink!*" exploded from the receiver. "No, don't tell me. I don't want to know. Or rather, Fletcher can explain when he reports at eight o'clock tomorrow morning. On the dot."

"I'll make sure to set the alarm clock. But Mr. Crane, why—"

"The Americans take as serious a view as we do of the sacrosanct nature of passports. Naturally, the State Department wanted to know why Scotland Yard had asked the FBI about a stolen passport. They asked the embassy, and the embassy wanted to know why they had not been notified that the police had found an American passport. How it reached the ambassador's august ears, I have no idea, but he, naturally, approached the Foreign Office and—"

"Please, let's not go back through the whole rigmarole! I'm sure Alec had very good reasons not to get in touch with the embassy right away, which no doubt he'll explain to you tomorrow."

"He'd better! I authorised the damn—dashed cable he sent to the FBI. I could swear he told me the U.S. embassy would have to be notified. Surely he didn't expect *me* to do so, with no information! I ought to have my head examined. I want to know what it's all about."

"He's been rushed off his feet all day, and he's still working," she reminded him. "I'll give him your message."

"Is he getting anywhere?"

"You'll have to ask him, Mr. Crane," Daisy said demurely. "You know he doesn't like me to get involved."

"*Pah!*"

Daisy was sure only the courtesy due to the offspring of a viscount enabled the superintendent to say a choked good-bye before he hung up. She wondered whether she ought to have told him Lambert was missing. But no, it would only mean more fuss if he felt obliged to notify the AC and the AC notified . . . et cetera.

She had scarcely replaced the receiver on its hook when the bell rang again. Sighing, she picked it up again and said, "Hampstead three nine one three."

"This is the Scotland Yard exchange," said an impersonal female voice. "May I speak to DCI Fletcher, please?"

"He's not here, I'm afraid. May I take a message? This is Mrs. Fletcher."

"Mrs. Fletcher!" The change in tone was obvious. Daisy was famous at the Yard—or infamous, depending on how high up the hierarchy one went—as the wife who kept falling over bodies. Sometimes her fame was useful, sometimes the reverse. "I have a cable for the chief inspector, from New York. He left a message to let him know at once. Shall I read it out?"

"Yes, please." Daisy tore the top sheet off the pad. "Not too fast."

" 'Mitcheel'—spelt *M I C H E L E*—'Castellano,' open quotes, 'enforcer,' close quotes, 'for Luckcheese'—spelt *L U C C H E S E*—'family bootlegger gang,' stop, 'delighted news Rosenblatt NYDA.' Got that, Mrs. Fletcher?"

"Got it. Thanks."

District Attorney Rosenblatt. She and Alec had saved him from making a serious mistake a couple of years ago. Now, apparently, he was pleased to learn that they had found a New York gangster dead in London.

What was an "enforcer"? American gangs must be alarmingly well organised if they had rules to be enforced.

Daisy decided she didn't really want to know how they did their enforcing. "Tough guys," she recalled Lambert mentioning when regretting the loss of his gun. "Guys"—plural. Could there be others of Castellano's ilk in England?

Alec ought to have the information as soon as possible. She glanced at the long-case clock. He would still be on the way to New Bond Street. If she waited till he reached the shop to ring up, she'd probably interrupt his interrogation of the Jessups. He hated having interviews interrupted. Too bad, the news would have to wait till he came home.

"What happened to Castellano's gun?" Alec pondered aloud as Ross drove down the hill.

"I don't know, sir. I think maybe I missed a bit, coming in later than the others like I did. He was wearing a shoulder holster?"

"With no gun in it. Suppose Castellano drew the gun, either to threaten his assailant or in self-defence. Why did the murderer not simply put it back in the holster, thus eliminating a link between him and his victim?"

There was silence while Ross negotiated the tricky five-way intersection in Camden Town, competing with four omnibuses and half a dozen taxis. Safely buzzing down Albany Street, he said, "Prob'ly he wasn't thinking too clearly, sir."

"He was thinking very clearly when he pressed his thumbs on exactly the right spots in Castellano's throat. He knew what he was doing all right. Let's say the gun got lost in a struggle and the darkness prevented his finding the damn thing. Why didn't we find it next morning in broad daylight, in the course of an intensive search?"

Again, Ross had the excuse of traffic and the even more complicated multiple intersection of streets at the southeast corner of Regent's Park. Having made it safely into Great Portland Street, he ventured, "I s'pose they looked in that pond thing?"

"Raked it out thoroughly. Can you think of any conceivable reason why Castellano might have gone out wearing the holster, an uncomfortable contraption, without his gun?"

"No, sir."

Nor could Alec. Customs might have confiscated Castellano's gun when he entered the country—did Customs keep records of such things?—but unless he'd managed to acquire another, he'd have packed away the holster. And if he'd managed to acquire a gun, the question remained: Where was it?

Customs had confiscated Lambert's gun, to that young idiot's disgust. Lambert had disappeared. Castellano's gun had disappeared. Had Alec completely misread Lambert's character?

He shook his head. Lambert was a young idiot, but no cold-blooded killer. Which left the Jessups.

Oxford Street, left into New Bond Street, and then Ross pulled alongside the kerb just beyond Jessup & Sons, Purveyors of Fine Wines and Spirits. The fashionable shops were still open, though most of their clientele would be people of leisure, able to shop earlier in the day. The biting wind whistling down the street was icy enough to deter pedestrians, and passersby were few.

The nearest plate-glass shop window, next door to the Jessups', displayed five skeletally thin celluloid mannequins elegantly posed in jewel-toned, elaborately beaded silk with jagged hemlines. They looked to Alec as if sharks had been at them. Not for the first time, he thanked heaven that Daisy didn't care two hoots about the latest modes.

In the Jessups' window stood a rustic pergola with artificial vines climbing it. The bunches of purple grapes peeping coyly from among the vine leaves looked like trimmings for an Edwardian hat. Under the pergola stood an equally rustic wooden table and three chairs, and on the table were three wineglasses and two bottles. It was a most inviting scene, though probably the bottles were empty, with the corks forced back in. A shop window was not exactly an ideal storage place for wine, and

Alec felt sure the Jessups' vintage wines were stored under ideal conditions.

He wondered what their markup was. Pretty hefty, certainly. New Bond Street leases must cost a fortune, and the sort of people who shopped there didn't cavil at high prices. Pity it was quite impossible to accept Jessup's offer of wholesale prices, especially now he was investigating the family for murder!

Still, since inheriting his great-uncle's fortune, he could afford a bottle of good wine now and then. The difficulty was finding time to sit down and enjoy it.

"There's Piper, sir," said Ross, nodding towards a 125 bus just coming to a halt nearby.

Ernie Piper swung down and came hurrying over to them. "Hope I'm not late, Chief. I was in the City."

"Did you notify the City force? You know how touchy they are."

"Had a word with a mate of mine. All I did was ask a few questions. It's not like I was looking to arrest someone on their patch. They'll prob'ly never know, and if they find out, he'll cover for me."

"I hope so. Right, you're going to be doing the search."

"Single-handed!"

"I want you to start with their papers."

Piper was extraordinarily good at noting and remembering details and picking up discrepancies, though it wouldn't do to tell him so too often. Alec was guiltily aware that he didn't give the young detective as much credit in that line as he deserved, because he didn't want to lose him to Fraud. He justified himself with the certainty that Ernie would hate working in Fraud.

He made sure Ernie knew what he was looking for, adding, "Of course, if you happen to notice a gun among the files, you can abandon them temporarily to let me know. Discreetly."

"You think they'd be that careless, Chief? Knowing we're coming?"

"They don't know about the search warrant. If you're still at it when we're finished asking questions, we'll lend a hand."

Alec saw a sarcastic "Cor, ta, Chief!" on Piper's lips. He'd say it aloud if Ross were not there, but Ross, though they had often worked together, was not one of Alec's usual team.

The glass shop door displayed a CLOSED sign, but it opened to Alec's push. The clock on the tower of St. George's, Hanover Square, struck the half hour as the three detectives stepped over the threshold. Alec noted an inner security door, standing open.

It was immediately obvious that this was no ordinary off-licence. The floor was paved with flagstones. The long narrow room had brick arches along each wall, framing trompe l'oeil vistas of more arches and rack after rack of bottles, row after row of wine tuns stretching into the illusory distance. A few real racks of bottles added to the illusion.

"Blimey!" said Piper. "Reminds you of that mirror room at the house, don't it, Chief?"

"Mr. Jessup certainly has an exotic taste in interior decor." Alec could imagine the younger Jessups at once embarrassed and proud of their father's exuberant imagination.

Spaced along the walls were several desks disguised as rustic tables, like the one in the window, each with a bottle and a couple of glasses. No one was there, but opening the door must have rung a bell in the back premises. Beneath a pergola against the rear wall, the twin of the one in the window, a door opened. Mr. Jessup came through, and with him his long-absent younger son.

Patrick was taller than his father, and very much slimmer, his leanness not willowy, but fit and athletic. He looked as Irish as his name, with black hair, blue eyes, and a scatter of freckles. He had not, however, inherited his mother's acting talent: His face was troubled and wary.

So was his father's, the expression sitting uneasily on Jessup's genial features.

"Thank you for agreeing to see me here," said Alec. "I'm sorry you had to close early. Your wife—"

"Moira rang up to explain. It's we who should thank you.

The Bennetts . . ." He grimaced. "Let me introduce my son Patrick. Our next-door neighbour, Detective Chief Inspector Fletcher."

"How do you do, sir?" Patrick didn't hold out his hand, relieving Alec of the eternal quandary of whether shaking hands with a suspect was appropriate.

"I'm sorry to make your acquaintance in such circumstances."

"Believe me, so am I. It's not exactly the homecoming I was looking forward to."

"These are my assistants, DCs Piper and Ross. Mr. Jessup, I'd like to have a word with you first. Is there somewhere we can go—"

"Can't you 'have a word' with both of us at once, and save time?" Jessup asked, the first sign of annoyance or impatience he had shown.

"I'd prefer to see you one at a time," Alec said firmly.

"Oh, very well. We'll go upstairs. We each have an office up there. Patrick, lock the street door before you come up. This way."

He led the way through the door at the back. It opened into a room furnished like a gentleman's den, with comfortable leather chairs and an antique writing table, but with wine racks where one might expect bookcases. On the desk, the usual blotter and a brass inkstand were supplemented with a tantalus and a tray of gleaming glasses of various shapes and sizes. On the right-hand wall hung a Cézanne still life featuring a bottle, a glass, and a bunch of grapes. Straight ahead, a solid-looking door with bar and bolt as well as a lock probably led to a yard or alley. The left wall had stairs going up and a door that, no doubt, opened on steps down to the cellar.

This must be where favoured customers were invited to consult the Jessups about the replenishment of their cellars, or the provision of drinks for wedding breakfasts and other parties.

"This will do very well," Alec said, stepping behind the desk, to Mr. Jessup's obvious displeasure. He turned to Patrick. "Would you be so kind as to take DC Piper up to the offices? Do you have keys to any locked desks, cabinets, or cupboards?"

"Yes, but . . ." The young man looked to his father.

"And the safe?" Alec cut in before Jessup could respond. "I assume you have a safe?"

"What the deuce is this?" Jessup demanded. "What business do you have going through our papers? This is a private partnership!"

"Have you something to hide?"

"Of course not, but—"

"Then I may assure you that anything DC Piper may see will remain entirely confidential. Your son may stay with him and make sure everything not pertaining to our enquiries is left just as it was found. Until he comes down to see me, at which point you can go up."

"Oh, very well!" Exasperation changed to gloom as Jessup added to Patrick, "Your mother's already told Mr. Fletcher about our sales to America."

"Which, as you need not remind me," Alec said tartly, "are not against English law." In one way, it was a relief not to have to serve the warrant. It would undoubtedly have engendered ill feeling—*more* ill feeling. On the other hand, Jessup's acquiescence to the search after a brief and natural protest suggested they would find nothing useful here.

Alec nodded to Piper, who preceded Patrick up the stairs.

Alec sat down behind the desk. Jessup hesitated, then reluctantly subsided into one of the armchairs facing him. Ross had unobtrusively brought in a straight chair from the main shop. He set it near the door, behind Jessup, where he could take notes without being observed.

"Tell me about Castellano," Alec invited.

"Castellano? That's the man you say has been murdered?"

"Mrs. Jessup didn't tell you his name?"

"She didn't catch it when you mentioned it to her. She told

me she recognised the photograph you showed her as an American who came to the house and was extremely unpleasant to her. He didn't give his name at that time, or subsequently."

"He returned, then. To the house, or here?"

"To the house. In view of his rudeness, I had given orders that he was not to be admitted. If he wanted to do business with the firm, he went the wrong way about it. Had he been an emissary of my American customer, I'd have been notified in advance of his intention to visit us. As it was, I did not meet him, nor had I any intention of doing so."

"Tell me about your transactions with America, and why you sent your son there."

"There's really nothing in it. The firm has been dealing for many years with a chap in Boston, the owner of a drinking establishment. Not our usual sort of customer, admittedly, but we simply continued the relationship with his son. The fact that it's now against the laws of his country is his lookout. I see no harm in supplying superior products to the wealthy elite of America when their alternative, I gather, is what they call 'moonshine.' I'm sure you're aware that improperly distilled alcohol can be deadly."

"Yes, indeed. I can see that, regarded in the proper light, you're a public benefactor," Alec said with only the merest hint of irony.

Unexpectedly, Jessup grinned. "That's a good line. I must remember it."

"You're welcome to it. So, everything was running along smoothly, I take it. Why Patrick's travels?"

"Everything ran smoothly because the American government wasn't putting enough money into enforcement. It stands to reason, as half of them probably enjoy a good whisky as much as anyone. Then last year, President Coolidge talked them into voting more money for the Prohibition people and more ships for the Coast Guard. Perhaps you've heard of the Anglo-American Liquor Treaty?"

"Yes."

"That made things more difficult, too, especially as they'll impound British ships outside the new twelve-mile limit. Even before the change, when it was three miles, they took the *Tomoka* five miles offshore. Well, to cut a long story short, they started intercepting our ship-to-shore messages. I approached a certain brilliant cryptographer of my acquaintance—being very familiar with certain parts of the Continent, I was able to be of some assistance to our government during the War—and he provided me with a suitable code—"

"Not Dr. Popkin, by any chance?"

Jessup looked at him suspiciously. "What my friend did was not against the law, even in America, I believe."

"No, no, it's just that I've had cause in the past to ask for his help."

"As a matter of fact, it was Dr. Popkin. He gave me what I needed. My customer didn't want the information sent in the post, for fear of its being intercepted. My son, having missed the War, was eager for adventure. *Et voilà.*"

"Patrick went ashore in America to deliver the code in person?"

"Since that was the point of the whole exercise . . . He met an agent of our customer, not the man himself. He's a banker with political ambitions and steers clear of personal involvement."

"Will you give me his name?"

"I will not."

Alec nodded. "Or that of his agent?"

"No. In any case, Patrick is fairly sure all the names he was given while in America were aliases, so they would be useless to you."

For the moment, Alec let the question lie. He doubted the principal's name would be helpful, but any others, real or aliases, though meaningless to him, would be worth trying on the New York police.

"I assume the business is profitable."

"Very. Enough to risk losing a cargo now and then, though we've been lucky in that respect."

"Yet you were not interested in hearing whatever business proposition Castellano had to set before you," Alec said sceptically.

Jessup was clearly perturbed by the return to the subject of the murder, but he quickly recovered. "After his behaviour to Moira, it was out of the question. But if you want a more businesslike reason, we are a small family firm. Taking on more American business would seriously stretch our resources."

"I'd have thought with such an unpleasant character hanging about, you'd at least want to know what he was after. You could have arranged to meet him in the garden, so that there was no chance of his encountering your wife again."

"I dare say I could have. I didn't."

"Or perhaps you sent Aidan in your place."

"Certainly not."

"Why did Aidan leave so suddenly last night?"

Shaken, Jessup said, "He . . . It wasn't sudden. He'd been planning the trip for some time. He always goes about this time of year."

"And it was so urgent, he left within an hour of his brother's return?"

"He . . . I don't know. I wasn't watching the clock."

Alec let a moment's silence point out the irrelevance of this statement. Then he snapped out, "Where did he go?"

"North!" Jessup took out a silk handkerchief and wiped his forehead. "To see customers in the North."

"Which city? Where did he take the train to?"

"What does it matter? He wasn't going to stay there. He has to travel all over the place."

"Which city?"

"I don't know. York, I think. I'm not sure."

Anywhere but York, then, Alec thought. He had been hoping he wouldn't have to arrest any of his next-door neighbours,

217

but if he didn't, after this interrogation, he'd never be able to face them again. Momentarily, his mind wandered. How long did he have to live in his great-uncle Walsall's house to satisfy the terms of the will? He couldn't remember Pearson specifying a term.

Alarmed by his silence, Jessup said, "Perhaps it was Newcastle."

Alec wondered whether, if he maintained a ominous silence, Jessup would gradually run through all the major northern cities he could think of except Aidan's destination. It wouldn't do to underestimate him, though. He wasn't so rattled that he wouldn't catch on quickly and throw the actual place into the list.

"Give me the names of customers he has to visit."

"Aidan took the records of their names and addresses with him."

"Mr. Jessup, I find it quite impossible to believe that you don't remember the names, at least, of customers sufficiently valuable to warrant one of the firm's principals travelling hundreds of miles to call on them at their homes."

"That's Aidan's side of the business. I deal mostly with our suppliers. I dare say I can remember one or two names if I put my mind to it."

"Please do so."

He came up with four surnames, all of such banality that they probably encompassed several thousand families in the northern counties alone. Besides the Dalton already mentioned by Mrs. Jessup, there were a Fisher, a Richardson, and a Parsons. Alec thought he was telling the truth, if not the whole truth, but it wasn't much help. He could only hope Ernie Piper's search of the files would be more fruitful.

"Why are you so anxious to keep Aidan's whereabouts from me?"

"I'm not!" Jessup blustered defensively. "Why should I?"

"That's what I'd like to know. Anyone would think you didn't care whether we caught a vicious murderer who killed as close to your home and family as to mine."

"Aidan is not a vicious murderer!"

"In that case, he may have vital information that will lead us to the right man—if we get it in time."

"I don't know where he is."

"All right, you don't know where he is. Let's see if he mentioned where he was going to his brother as they passed in the doorway. Ross, escort Mr. Jessup upstairs, please, and bring Mr. Patrick down."

TWENTY

Ten minutes after Tom Tring and DC Ardmore left the house, Elsie came into the office and told Daisy that Mrs. Jessup was asking for her, "and in such a state she is, madam, she don't seem to know whether she's coming or going. She's waiting in the hall. . . . I wasn't sure . . . considering . . ."

"Oh dear! I'll come right away. Show her into the sitting room, please, Elsie. You'd better bring in the sherry. And brandy, perhaps."

She rolled the paper out of the typewriter. It was a nuisance stopping in the middle of a page. Either one left the paper in and afterwards it curled up and never quite flattened or one took it out and could never put it back in exactly the right spot. Fortunately, this wasn't part of an article, just her notes on Alec's investigation, so there were no messy carbons to cope with and it didn't matter if the lines didn't match up properly.

Before she went to join her unexpected visitor, she powdered her nose. Mrs. Jessup was always so immaculately made up.

Considering . . . ? she thought as she crossed the passage to the sitting room. What exactly had Elsie meant by that? Had her sister told her the Jessups were under siege, or were the abominable Bennetts already at work with the rumour mill? Their binoculars had probably been trained on the Fletcher and Jessup front doors for hours. Daisy wondered whether Miss Bennett had come home by now, and whether they had decided on their story.

In the sitting room, Elsie was lighting the fire. Mrs. Jessup stood at the window, the curtains parted slightly with one hand, staring out, though she surely could see only her own reflection.

"Mrs. Jessup?"

Moira Jessup turned. She looked quite composed. Either she had pulled herself together or the parlour maid had been wildly exaggerating. "Good evening," she said. Was there a tremor in her voice?

The fire flared up. Elsie departed. Mrs. Jessup came over to the fireplace and held out her hands to the flames.

"It's a chilly night," she said. "I'm so sorry to intrude at such an awkward hour."

"Not at all. Is there something I can do to help?"

The smile was definitely shaky. "I'm seeking sanctuary. I find it quite intolerable to stand by while those policemen rummage through all our belongings."

"I'm not exactly the best person—"

"On the contrary. You make me feel there must be some sanity in all this. You remind me that it's not a whim, not sheer persecution, that the police have some reason, however inscrutable, for what they're doing to my family. I don't know what they're looking for, or why, but if *your* husband is in charge, it must make sense, somehow."

Daisy was at a loss for words. All she could say, weakly, was, "Won't you sit down?"

Elsie came in with a tray of drinks. Mrs. Jessup gratefully accepted a b and s. Daisy, who didn't like sherry and didn't feel the need of brandy, was impressed that Elsie—she really was a jewel of a parlour maid—had thought to bring her own favourite aperitif, Cinzano. She poured herself a drop of vermouth with lots of soda water and then sat down opposite Mrs. Jessup.

"The police can't just search wherever they feel like it," she said tentatively. "It's against Magna Carta or something. They have to persuade a magistrate that they have enough evidence to justify a warrant."

"But what evidence can they possibly have against my boys? What makes your husband so sure it was . . . murder?"

"He won't tell me. Did they show you the warrant?"

"Oh yes."

"Knowing Sergeant Tring, I'm sure he was perfectly polite."

"Yes, he asked my permission first. I'd have given it for my own room, and perhaps Patrick's, but I couldn't let them poke around in Aidan and Audrey's, when they aren't even in town."

"I do understand." Daisy sipped her drink, wishing she had made it stronger. What on earth could she say to bring comfort when everything she knew confirmed Alec's belief that the Jessups were involved in Castellano's death?

"I'm sorry, I shouldn't have come." Mrs. Jessup put her brandy down, almost untasted. "It was thoughtless of me. I'd better—"

"No, don't go. You're very welcome to stay here until . . . until they're finished in your house. Just think, the Bennetts are bound to be glued to their field glasses, and if they saw you leave so soon, they'd be convinced I'd thrown you out. You can't want to give me such a reputation for inhospitability!"

Mrs. Jessup summoned up a smile. "No, it's bad enough that they'll be shredding our reputation." She leant back wearily in her chair.

"Do you think anyone credits anything they say? Among people who know them, I mean."

"Those who want to. And there are those who wouldn't dream of inventing nasty stories about people but can't resist passing them on. At least, so far, I haven't had neighbours dropping in to ask nosy questions."

"What about reporters? They haven't discovered you yet?"

"No." She looked aghast. "I hadn't thought of that possibility. I suppose they're bound to come?"

"We had one earlier, but Elsie got rid of him very quickly. She's simply marvellous. I dare say he told the rest there was nothing doing. I'll tell her to explain the technique to your Enid. I'm so glad Enid mentioned her sister needing a position when we first came here."

"I'm glad you're happy with her. So many people never stop complaining about their servants. We're very lucky in ours."

"Luck's a big part of it, but in my opinion, how you treat them makes a huge difference." Daisy had started simply ages ago doing research for a serious article on domestic service, concentrating on the contrasts between the way servants were regarded by the middle class and by the aristocracy. Though she hadn't made much progress, having been diverted by other matters, she was still interested in the subject. Discussing it with Mrs. Jessup not only gave her further material but distracted Mrs. Jessup from her woes for quite forty minutes.

When they started to run down, Daisy said with a laugh, "I told Belinda she'd better prepare for a day when there are no more nannies."

"How is Belinda doing at school?" Mrs. Jessup asked.

"Very well. She's learning science, and Latin, and all sorts of things girls weren't supposed to be capable of in my day."

And there was another fruitful topic, that lasted another quarter of an hour. Unfortunately, in the end it reminded Mrs. Jessup that her grandchildren were far away.

"I hope they arrived safely," she fretted.

"Haven't you heard from Audrey?"

"They have no telephone. It's . . . not primitive, but very *rural*. The village is several miles away. I'm sure she'll write as soon as they get settled."

"I'd like to write to her. I know Alec has the address—"

"That fool Jonathan Irwin!"

"But I'd rather get it from you than from him." *Pour la politesse*, and because he might refuse to give it to her.

Listlessly, Mrs. Jessup told her. "You won't mention that the police are looking for Aidan, will you? In her condition . . . That's why we didn't want to tell your husband where she is, of course."

"Of course," Daisy agreed, but hadn't the refusal—or rather, claim of ignorance—come before the hunt was apparent?

"Though I suppose she'll find out soon enough from the police."

"I'm afraid so. You haven't heard from Aidan since he left?"

"No." She frowned. "No, not a word. I hope . . . But he'll have been on the road all day. Sometimes the people he calls on offer him a bed for the night, but usually he just stops at the nearest inn. Even in this day and age, not all wayside inns have telephones."

"Does he usually ring up when he stops for the night, if there's a phone nearby?"

"If Audrey were at home, he would. As she's not . . . I can see it looks odd, both of them leaving at such a moment, but they honestly had been planning their trips for ages. How could they guess there had been a murder, let alone that the victim was someone I'd met? I didn't know myself until they showed me the photograph, didn't even know his name until they told me. Neither Aidan nor Patrick had ever seen him before. I suppose Enid had to say she recognised the man in the photo." She sighed.

"She really had no choice, and no reason not to. She couldn't have guessed it would cause so much trouble for you," Daisy assured her.

"Nor could I, or I might have insisted she was mistaken. I'd better be getting home. I only hope the servants don't all depart when they see the mess the police leave behind."

"Tom Tring—Sergeant Tring—won't leave a mess. You'll find everything just as it should be."

Mrs. Jessup looked sceptical. "Thank you for lending a sympathetic ear," she said. "And for the brandy. I didn't notice it going, but I see I've finished it! Good night, Mrs. Fletcher."

Daisy saw her out. The wind had died and the sky was clear, as bright with stars as ever a London night could be. There would be a frost tonight.

No reluctance to face the police was apparent in Patrick's jaunty step as he came down the stairs. He sat down opposite Alec without waiting for an invitation, and started talking before Ross was ready with notebook and pencil.

"To think I was afraid I'd be bored coming home to the business! No fear of that with a 'tec moving in next door in my absence."

"You had an exciting time in America?"

Patrick considered. "Not so much once I was ashore. The voyage had its moments."

"You seem to have brought a spot of excitement home with you. A curious coincidence, don't you think?"

"Oh, I don't know. The world is full of coincidences."

"But it was no coincidence that your brother left within an hour of your return. Did you quarrel with him?"

"With Aidan? Lord no! None of that prodigal son stuff, with the disgruntled older brother. I was on business, remember, even if it involved a spot of fun. Besides, old Aidan and I get on quite happily together. He's a bit of a stodgy sort of chap. I tease him about it, and he reads me the odd lecture when I'm not stodgy enough, but that's about it."

"Then why did he leave in such a hurry?"

"Aren't you bored with the story, Mr. Fletcher? I'm sure my parents have both told you, and likely the servants, as well."

"Detective work is often boring, believe it or not. I'd like to hear your version."

"Duty called! It's not a call Aidan is capable of disregarding. Some old geezers up north have to have their hands held when it comes to choosing their booze, and Aidan's elected. He's very good at it, I understand."

"Tell me whose hands he's gone to hold."

"Their names? You forget, I've been out of things for a couple of months. I haven't the foggiest."

"And did he happen to mention, in the brief hour you had together after a two-month parting, where he intended to begin his peregrination of the northern reaches of the kingdom?"

"He did not. We had other things to talk about."

"Such as?"

"Why, the success of my mission, of course."

"Of course. And was it successful?"

"It was indeed. Sold all the goods, brought home the shekels, and paved the way for the next venture. If this chappy getting done in doesn't put paid to the whole thing."

"Why should it?"

"Well, if you were an American . . . let us say 'businessman,' and you heard that an American had been murdered just outside the house of the people you were doing business with, how keen would you be to continue the association? Especially as he happened to be an Italian American. I don't know if you're aware that the Italians are rapidly taking over the bootlegging business? At any rate, it's certainly not going to help the firm, so it hardly makes sense to suspect us of having a hand in his death."

"I'll bear it in mind. Did you ever hear the name Michele Castellano while you were in America?"

"Not that I recall. I don't think so. I wasn't actually there very long, you know. That kind of voyage is apt to be a lengthy affair. As a matter of fact, the people I was with didn't go in for introductions on the whole, and those names I did get, I'm not at all sure they were their real ones."

"Fair enough. Come to that, we can't be sure Castellano is the real name of the deceased. Tell me about coming home. Where did you land?"

"Liverpool. We ran into a squall in the Irish Sea that slowed us down, so I was glad I'd sent a wireless cable telling the parents not to try to meet the boat train. And as they weren't expecting me at any particular time, I simply couldn't resist popping into the Flask—"

"The pub just off the High Street?"

"That's the place. Not that I'd been deprived of alcohol for two months. I came home on a British ship, and over there, there was no shortage of 'hooch,' as they call it. But speakeasies and ships' bars just don't measure up to the local pub."

"I suppose they know you there?"

"Oh yes. Ask the proprietor or any of the regulars. I was there from—oh, I don't know—about six till half past or there-abouts. Just time enough for a pint and a chat. Then I went on home."

"You walked up through the garden?"

"Well, yes. It doesn't make sense to go round by the street, does it? Not to our house, or yours. I didn't see any bodies, nor anyone hanging about."

"Was it raining?"

"Coming down cats and dogs."

Alec nodded. He thought he heard the merest breath of a sigh of relief. He was pretty sure nine-tenths of what Patrick had said was true. The other tenth was hogwash. He suppressed a sigh of his own. No hope of getting home for dinner.

In the offices above, a telephone bell rang. Piper would answer it.

Alec took out his fountain pen and wrote down reminders to himself: The pub must be checked, and the time it had started raining, and the time of arrival of the delayed boat train.

"What ship did you sail back on?"

"The—"

"Chief!" Piper came running down the stairs. "Sorry to interrupt. It's the Manchester Royal Infirmary on the line, the head almoner. Aidan Jessup was taken ill at his hotel and he's in hospital."

TWENTY-ONE

After showing Mrs. Jessup out, Daisy decided not to change for dinner. If Alec came home in time, which she rather doubted, he wouldn't want to change, and a man should be allowed to be comfortable in his own home, when there are no guests.

She went back to the sitting room, kicked off her shoes, and curled up in a chair, sipping the remaining half of her vermouth and soda. She had a feeling Mrs. Jessup had said something important, but she simply could not pin it down. She went back over their conversation. As far as she could recall, no new information had emerged.

The doorbell rang.

"Again!" she groaned aloud. "Who now, for pity's sake?" It was too early for dinner guests, even if she had expected any, and much too late for anyone else.

She heard Elsie come through the baize door and tap-tap along the hall. The fire flickered in the draught under the sitting room door as the front door was opened.

Elsie's voice came to her loud and clear, and firm. "Madam is not receiving."

A murmur of voices. Reporters?

"No, there's not a policeman in the house, neither. Not at the moment, there isn't."

Although the voices were slightly raised, Daisy couldn't quite make out the words, nor recognise the voices.

"Well, really!" Elsie sounded thoroughly put out. "You can just wait right here and we'll see what madam has to say about this!" The front door closed with a thud.

What on earth had ruffled the polite, well-trained parlour maid to the point of being rude? As Elsie's footsteps approached, Daisy stood up and started to go to meet her. Then she changed her mind: Discretion was the better part of knowledge—or rather, vice versa. Better to wait and find out what she was going to face before she went to face it.

"Oh, madam!" Elsie closed the door behind her. "It's them Bennetts. I said you're not at home, but they up and pushed right past me. Worse than that reporter they are, and that's saying something. They want to see the master. I told 'em he's not here, but they won't take no for an answer. I'm that sorry, madam."

"Oh, BH! if you'll pardon my language. I'll go."

"I left 'em in the hall, madam, but I wouldn't put it past them to go into the drawing room without an invitation."

This measure of the Bennetts' iniquity proved all too accurate. Daisy found them in the drawing room. They had turned on the electric light. Miss Bennett was sitting by the unlit fire, and her brother stood with his back to it. As Daisy entered, Miss Bennett said in a voice meant to be overheard, "Too penny-pinching for a fire in every room, I dare say."

Since the room had not been in use—and, in any case, the radiators made it quite warm enough for comfort—the remark was quite uncalled-for. Daisy ignored it.

"I understand you hoped to see my husband," she said. "I'm afraid he is not here and I don't know when he'll return."

"Some men are so inconsiderate about letting their households know when they're going to be late."

That was a bit of cheek, in view of Mr. Bennett's claim that she hadn't told him when, or even whether, she'd be home tonight! Daisy nearly pointed out that it was inevitable in Alec's job, but once again she decided not to rise to the bait.

"I presume you wish to see him in his professional capacity," she said sweetly—was there such a word as *saccharinely*? "If you have a statement to make, may I suggest you either ring up the local police or go directly to Scotland Yard?"

"It's not the local bobbies we want," snapped Mr. Bennett, "and I should have thought you could see I can't possibly be dragging myself down to Whitehall with my arthritis. We'll tell you what we saw and you can pass it on to your husband."

It dawned on Daisy that this was exactly what they had intended all along. Doubtless they had watched through their binoculars until they were sure she was alone before they came. Quite a few people found it more comfortable to avoid the official commitment of reporting to the police, by telling Daisy what they wanted the police to know. Usually she was in sympathy with their concerns, but not this time.

Warren was still on duty by the telephone. She could call him in, but a mere detective constable, and one, moreover, without eyebrows, would neither appease the Bennetts nor be able to cope with them.

What would Alec want her to do? It was all very well thinking she ought to put the Bennetts off until he could talk to them, but suppose they refused to see him? On the other hand, did she really want to hear whatever slander they chose to promulgate?

Daisy decided she had better hear them out. She didn't have to pass on to Alec anything she considered gratuitous twaddle.

"You won't mind if I write down what you tell me," she said, with an inward smile at their obvious dismay. "It wouldn't do to get it wrong when I report to Alec."

Without waiting for a response, she went off—not hurrying—to fetch her notebook from the office.

Returning through the hall, she met Elsie, breathless and

chilled. "Oh madam, I hope as I haven't done wrong. I dashed over to my sister and told her to go right away and tell that Sergeant Tring the Bennetts are here pestering you. I know he's a friend of yours, 'sides being a policeman."

Bother! thought Daisy. If she didn't get a move on, there would be an official witness to their mischief making, if Tom Tring's arrival didn't shut them up altogether.

"That was very thoughtful of you, Elsie. If he comes, show him right in, won't you?"

"I'm sure he'll come, madam," said the parlour maid, shocked. "He wouldn't leave you alone with the likes of them. Why, it wouldn't surprise me a bit if it was them as done that American in. Nasty, they are. Me and Enid don't believe it was the Jessups, not if it was ever so. I'll wait right here to let Mr. Tring in quick as can be, madam, so if you need me, just call out."

"Thank you, Elsie." Daisy was touched by the Bristow sisters' loyalty.

She hurried into the drawing room. Mr. Bennett had taken his seat opposite his sister. He made no attempt to rise when Daisy came in, tapping his knee as if to remind her of his rheumatics. She was not impressed. She knew plenty of elderly gentlemen far more rickety who would die rather than not stand up when a lady entered the room.

She sat down, notebook and pencil at the ready. "All right, let's have your statement. Then I'll type it up and you can sign it."

They exchanged a glance. "We're not signing anything," said Miss Bennett belligerently.

"That's for you to decide. Of course, the police won't take anything you say very seriously if you're not willing to put your names to it." Daisy hoped to make them think twice before letting their unpleasant imaginations run riot. "Go ahead."

"We saw him!" Miss Bennett was eager now.

"Who? When? Where?"

"Patrick Jessup, of course."

"Everyone knows he came home yesterday," Daisy said dampeningly.

"We were the first to see him," Mr. Bennett claimed. "He came out of the passage, right beside our house, a few minutes after half past five."

"That's right!"

That's torn it! Daisy thought. "How can you be sure it was Patrick? It was dusk on a gloomy evening. He must have been wearing a hat, and very likely a muffler."

"No muffler. Patrick Jessup has always claimed he doesn't feel the cold. He goes around without an overcoat in midwinter. Just wait till he starts getting arthritis; that'll put a stop to him."

"He had a hat on, one of those newfangled soft felts, a trilby or a homburg, or whatever they're called. What's wrong with a bowler, I say. But he always wears his hat on the back of his head."

"Makes him look like a racecourse tout."

"Lowers the tone of the neighbourhood."

"But one can see his face."

"And he turned his head towards us, speaking to the man with him. It looked as if he was pointing out the Jessups' house."

"There was someone with him?" Daisy asked sharply. Did Alec know Patrick had a companion?

"*He* was wearing an overcoat, and had his hat pulled down over his ears. One of those soft felts, like Patrick's. If he'd been wearing a nice hard bowler, it wouldn't have been so easy to knock him out, would it?"

"You saw Patrick hit him over the head?"

"Well, not to say 'saw.' I had to go and pack for a night away from home, to be ready to meet my friend Emmeline Lagerquist for the theatre. My brother's eyesight is not as keen as mine."

"I had the glasses. I watched them walk up the path. They stopped near the fountain. Aidan—" He stopped, glancing resentfully at Daisy's pencil and pad. She allowed herself a smug feeling that she had stymied the worst of his venom—if that was what one did to venom. "There ought to be a lamp-post by the fountain. It's much too dark for safety in the middle of the garden. Someone else came down the slope to meet them. I can't be sure who it was."

"Fortunately, I hadn't quite got around to writing down any name," Daisy said in that saccharine tone. Then a dismaying memory struck her: Mrs. Jessup saying that neither Patrick nor Aidan had seen Castellano *before*. Before what? She couldn't think about it now. She had the Bennetts to be put in their place. Firmly, she went on: "I believe juries are awarding quite tremendous damages for slander these days."

Mr. Bennett blenched and repeated hurriedly, "I can't be sure who it was."

Miss Bennett gave him a scornful look but didn't actually contradict him. "You saw what happened next, though."

"Not clearly, not clearly at all. It's shockingly dark in the middle of the garden, and then, my eyes are not what they were. That vulgar statue—"

"Barely half-clothed!"

"It complicates things, too. One can't be sure how many people one is seeing, when they're moving about in front of it, and one keeps catching glimpses—"

"You should have called me! I would have gone upstairs and had a much better view."

"It was over very quickly."

"What was?" Daisy demanded.

"I saw . . . what appeared to be . . . what might have been a struggle. Someone fell down. I'm fairly certain someone fell down. Then suddenly there was no one standing, no one at all."

"What!" Daisy frowned at him. She couldn't begin to guess what the police, let alone a coroner, prosecutor, or jury, would make of this farrago. It didn't make sense.

"It started to rain," Mr. Bennett said querulously. "I really couldn't see much at all after that."

"That's not what you told me!" his sister snapped.

"You weren't writing down every word to throw up against me in a court of law. Besides, with you badgering him, how is a man to think straight? What I saw isn't necessarily what you'd have liked me to see."

What he had seen was bad enough, Daisy thought. She was glad she had taken notes, and not only because of the dampening effect. If she could quote to Alec their exact words, then any tall story Miss Bennett might persuade her brother to tell, or come up with on her own account, would be belied before uttered.

"Detective Sergeant Tring, madam."

The Bennetts' quarrel had covered the sound of Tom's arrival. Daisy jumped up and went to meet him. Brown eyes twinkling, he raised his eyebrows questioningly at her, with an effect like a pair of woolly bear caterpillars crawling up an egg.

"Mr. Tring! How lucky that you happened to drop in." She waved her notebook at him and turned back towards the couple by the fireplace. "I believe you haven't met Mr. and Miss Bennett?"

"I have not had the pleasure."

Daisy wished she were not far too well brought up to inform him that it was no pleasure. "They came looking for the police. Since you'd all left, they've been telling me how the disgracefully bad lighting in the garden prevented their seeing anything much last night. You'll be glad to hear I wrote down their statements verbatim, so there can't be any disagreement about what they've said."

His moustache twitched. "Very good, Mrs. Fletcher," he said gravely. "If you would be so good as to type your notes, the lady and gentleman can sign them immediately and we shan't have to trouble them again this evening."

Miss Bennett gave him an affronted glare. "We cannot possibly wait."

"It won't take me more than a few minutes."

"We dine precisely at eight. It is now twelve minutes before the hour."

"We have to go round by the street," Mr. Bennett explained, levering himself out of his seat, "what with the steps and my arthritis, and the lighting so poor in the garden."

"We wouldn't have come out at all, but unpleasant as it is to have anything to do with the police, we know our duty as citizens, I hope."

"Very obliging of you," said Tom as Daisy rang for Elsie, who must have been listening at the door, since she arrived instantly to show the Bennetts out.

They departed, noses in the air.

"Paint themselves into a corner, did they?" Tom enquired.

"Not at all. I painted them into a corner."

"You didn't go putting words into their mouths, Mrs. Fletcher."

"Of course not! I just made pointed remarks about slander and *huge* damages, and made sure they realised I was taking down every word they said. Oh Tom, aren't they awful? And the worst is, the one unshakable thing they agree on is that they both saw Patrick Jessup coming into the Circle at half past five with a companion who sounds just like Castellano."

TWENTY-TWO

Alec's first call was to Superintendent Crane.

"You again!" moaned the Super. "What the devil is it now? We're just sitting down to dinner. I trust your wife has passed on my message?"

"No, sir," Alec said cautiously. "I'm still at the wine shop. I haven't spoken to Daisy since I left to come here. Is it urgent?"

"I suppose not, unless you consider a complaint from the Home Secretary urgent. Nothing to be done tonight, at any rate. I haven't my notes with me, so ask her when you get home."

"I'm not going home, sir."

"What! Here, I say, Fletcher, don't go off the deep end! She means well, you know. She can't help falling into these scrapes, and you have to admit she's pulled your irons out of the fire once or—"

"I mean, sir, I'm asking your permission to go to Manchester."

"Manchester! Filthy dump. What the devil do you want to go there for, eh?"

"The man we've been looking for has turned up there—in hospital."

"He has, has he?" The policeman alter ego took over from the diner interrupted in the middle of his soup. "Don't suppose you could send that sergeant of yours? No," he answered his own question, "touchy business questioning a sick man."

"I really think I should do it myself, sir."

"Right-oh. Leaving at once, are you?"

"Yes, I'll just stop by my office to pick up the autopsy report—it should have come in by now—and my bag, and catch the same train Aidan Jessup presumably caught last night. I may find out something from the train staff on the way."

"You'll telephone Mrs. Fletcher to tell her you're off," Crane said severely.

"Of course, sir. And ask her for your message about the Home Secretary."

"Don't worry about him. I'll deal with him," the Super promised. "I'll ring up the Manchester force for you, too. And now, if you have no objection, I'm going to finish my soup before it's stone-cold." He hung up.

Alec rang home. Warren answered.

"How is your face?" Alec asked.

"It feels sort of tight, sir, like I was wearing a rubber mask. And hot. But Miss Bristow brought me some more ointment from Mrs. Dobson, and that helps, so could be worse."

"Good. Anything to report?"

"Mrs. Jessup came round, sir, and had a long talk with Mrs. Fletcher. And then those Bennetts—Miss Bristow fetched DS Tring to give Mrs. Fletcher a hand with them. I dunno what they said. Mr. Tring's still here."

"All right, put Mr. Tring on the line, and then you can go home. There's not likely to be anything else this evening. You can go to your own station tomorrow morning, and you needn't turn up till noon, unless you're called in earlier. I'll make that all right with— Oh, your sergeant's on his way to the wilds of Lincolnshire."

"Yes, sir. He was going to ring up when he gets there to find out what's up here."

"That's right. My wife can tell him." Which meant telling her more than Alec had intended to, but she seemed to know a good deal more than he did of some matters, so he supposed it all came out even. "Off you go, Warren. I suggest you see a doctor in the morning if your face is still uncomfortable."

A moment later, he heard Tom Tring's deep rumble. "Chief?"

"Tom, I have to catch a train to Manchester, so let's keep this as brief as possible. Have you found anything in the Jessups' house?"

"Nowt, like they say in Manchester. We were nearly done, me and Ardmore, when I was called over here to repel boarders."

"The Bennetts. Warren told me."

"Not that Mrs. Fletcher needed help. She'd routed 'em, foot, horse, and artillery, before I got here."

"She didn't—"

"Not to worry, Chief. She got their story out of 'em first, and wrote it all down. She's typing it up now. The bit you need to know is, they're ready to swear Patrick Jessup reached the Circle at half five."

Alec whistled. "Did he, now! Six-thirty, he says."

"And there was a bloke with him, with his hat pulled low."

"Indeed! The Bennetts are sure they were together?"

"I don't know about that, Chief. I haven't read their statement, and you know how Mrs. Fletcher does her best to avoid leading questions."

"Insofar as she understands the term," Alec said dryly. "If you have nothing more to report, put her on, would you, please?"

"Have a heart, Chief! At least tell me why you're off to Manchester."

"Aidan's there. In hospital."

Tom whistled. Alec could imagine his moustache puffing out. "Right, Chief, I won't ask any more. For now. What do you want me to do tomorrow?"

"Let's see . . . The Bennetts first; Whitcomb— We still haven't much to go on in the way of times, but maybe the post-mortem report will help—you'd better have a look at it. And see if you can get any news of Lambert. That should keep you busy for a bit."

"Right, Chief."

"Ardmore can help you. He won't need to catch up on his beauty sleep, as he needn't bother with St. Pancras tonight after all."

"Right, Chief. Here's Mrs. Fletcher."

"Darling! Manchester?"

" 'Fraid so. I'm going to have to rush to catch the train, so tell me the absolute minimum. I'll ring from Manchester tomorrow to get the rest."

"Right-oh, darling. The Home Sec—"

"Crane's dealing with him."

"Thank heaven! Did he tell you Castellano's passport was stolen and faked?"

"No, he didn't go into detail. That would explain the ink."

"That's exactly what I said, at which point Mr. Crane exploded. Did you get the telegram from Rosenblatt in New York?"

"Rosenblatt? The district attorney?"

"That's the man. He says Castellano was an 'enforcer' for a crime gang."

"Great Scott!"

"Rosenblatt's pleased as punch to hear he's dead. I think that's all the essentials, darling. I hope you get something decent to eat on the train."

" 'Bye, love. I'll talk to you tomorrow."

"Toodle-oo."

Alec hung up. Too pressed for time to consider the implications of what Tom and Daisy had told him, he strode to the door of the office where he had taken the call. Opening it, he found himself looking at DC Ross's back. Beyond this solid and effective barrier, Mr. Jessup confronted him, with Patrick at his shoulder. Both looked more distressed than belligerent.

Hearing the click of the latch opening, Ross spoke without turning. "Mr. Jessup wants a word with you, sir."

"Thank you, Ross, that's all right now. I'm finished on the telephone." As Ross moved aside, Alec said, "I can spare you two minutes, Mr. Jessup." Not "sir," not yet. There was still a possibility, though it seemed more and more remote, that one day they would once again be amicable neighbours.

"Patrick says Aidan is in hospital in Manchester. Do you know what's wrong with him?"

"It appears to be the aftereffects of a severe concussion."

Aidan's father and brother looked worried but not surprised, Alec noted.

"I'm sending Patrick up there to make sure he gets the best possible care." Jessup sounded determined not to take an expected no for an answer.

But nothing could have suited Alec better. "He can travel with me. I have to stop in at the Yard on the way to the station. Ross will drive you both back to Hampstead and then bring Patrick to St. Pancras to meet me. Pack lightly," he told Patrick, "and quickly. We'll catch the express your brother took last night"

"I'll go to Scotland Yard with you," Patrick said eagerly, apparently regarding a visit to the headquarters of the Metropolitan Police as a thrill, not a possible prelude to arrest. "I don't need any bags. I was travelling pretty rough for weeks, remember?"

"Nonsense," said his father. "If you're to organise Aidan's care, you'll need to look your best. Come along. You'll make sure the place is locked when you leave, won't you, Fletcher?"

"Of course."

As Ross and the Jessups hurried down the stairs, Ernie

Piper came out of the next office, switching off the electric light. "I'm done here, Chief. Could've told you Manchester. There's a note to their secretary to send a cable booking him into the London Road Station Hotel."

"So the trip really was planned in advance, as they claim," Alec said in a low voice, following the others down, Piper at his heels.

"For tonight."

"He intended to travel today! Anything else of interest?"

"Not a thing. You talked to Mr. Tring? Did he find the gun?"

"No."

"Aidan probably took it and threw it out of the window of the train."

"Why? Why the devil should he do anything so stupid? The gun must have been Castellano's." Alec checked that the inner shop door had latched securely behind him. The lock was one of Chubb's best, set in a door that had the heft of steel. The outer glass door had no lock. "If he, or they, hadn't moved the body and had left the gun beside it, they'd have had a good chance of getting off with self-defence."

"If it was just a bash over the head." Piper waved down a taxi. "Not if Dr. Ridgeway's right about the way he was killed."

"No." Alec sighed. "That's the sticking point."

The taxi whirled them to Scotland Yard. Alec found the autopsy report on his desk. Amid a great deal of obscure medical verbiage, the plain fact stood out: Castellano had first been knocked out by the impact of an unidentifiable blunt instrument on the skull. Subsequently, he had been murdered by compression of the carotid arteries. It would have taken no more than a couple of minutes.

Alec sent Piper home and took a taxi to St. Pancras Station. Ross and Patrick were waiting for him, anxiously scanning the arriving cabs. Not until he saw them did Alec realise he had been metaphorically holding his breath, worrying that Patrick might give Ross the slip and run for cover.

Though nothing like it was during rush hour, the station was still busy. Passengers and porters streamed in and out of the brick archways. Alec had cut it fine, so he was relieved when Patrick said, "I've got your ticket. Platform seven. We'd better hurry."

"Thanks. Ross, you'll be giving DS Tring a hand tomorrow."

He and Patrick joined the swarms beneath the cavernous iron-vaulted glass roof. The cries of boys hawking food baskets augmented the voices of anxious travellers, the rumble of luggage trolleys, and the din of steam engines.

"I'm ravenous," said Patrick as they made haste towards Platform 7, dodging old ladies with umbrellas and lapdogs and young ladies wielding careless cigarette holders. "I don't know whether the dining car will serve supper this late, so I bought us a couple of baskets. Rather infra dig in first class, but it can't be helped. A porter's taken them and my bag to nab seats for us."

First class! Alec had intended to travel third, as was appropriate to a lowly policeman who had to explain his expenses to a clerk intent on saving the taxpayers money. However, the scion of a wealthy wine merchant would be accustomed to better things. Thanks to his great-uncle Walsall, Alec could reimburse him without wincing.

"Over here, guv!" A porter waved vigorously from an open door. "Gotcha two window seats." His waiting hand was appropriately filled by Patrick. He took Alec's bag, led them a little way down the corridor, and ushered them into a compartment. Chucking the bag up onto the rack, he wished them "Bong voyidge," and departed.

Both the corner seats by the corridor were occupied. Dismayed, Alec recognised the gentleman facing forward as a distinguished King's Counsel with whom he had more than once clashed in court.

The KC frowned at Alec, as if he felt he ought to know him but couldn't quite place him. One thing was certain: He would not have chosen to travel in this compartment if he could have found an empty one. He was not going to approve of his unwanted companions' impromptu meal.

Alec had hoped for privacy on the journey in order to continue his interview with Patrick in light of what he had learnt. It was not to be.

With the usual whistle, clanging and clashing, and the hiss of escaping steam, the train pulled out of the station.

TWENTY-THREE

Daisy dined alone, an occurrence too frequent to be bothersome. It allowed her to read while she ate, though, naturally, she'd rather have been talking to Alec. After a delicious apple snow, light and frothy and sweetened just enough, she took her demitasse of coffee up to the nursery.

Miranda was fast asleep in her crib, but Oliver was teething yet again and inclined to be fretful. Daisy rocked him in her arms, crooning a lullaby, while Nurse Gilpin and Bertha went down to the kitchen to have supper with Mrs. Dobson and Elsie.

Oliver soon settled down, sucking his thumb. Mrs. Gilpin would have strongly disapproved. Daisy let him suck. Pulling it out of his mouth would only get him upset again. She debated whether to lay him down in his crib, but she was very comfortable in the rocking chair by the fire, and it was difficult to get out of it holding a large baby, so she stayed put. It was a cosy comfort, not at all conducive to thoughts of murder, yet she couldn't help her mind turning that way.

Aidan was in hospital in Manchester, suffering from the effects of a concussion. Perhaps he had fallen getting in or out of the train. Perhaps something had fallen on his head from the overhead rack.

Unfortunately, it seemed more likely that he was feeling the delayed aftermath of a fight with Castellano. Had he attacked because Castellano had threatened him or Patrick? What had become of the mysterious vanishing gun, or had Castellano not carried one? And why—the question always recurred—*why* was Alec convinced Castellano's death was cold-blooded murder? Not knowing made it very difficult to see either Aidan or Patrick as a cold-blooded murderer. And she must not forget Lambert, though he seemed still more unlikely.

Elsie came in. "Oh madam," she said in a hushed voice, "Enid just brought a note from them next door."

"Whatever can they want now?"

"I'm sure I don't know, madam. It's sealed. Not that me or Enid would stoop to reading someone else's letter!" She came over, holding out a blue envelope. "Ooh, who's a sweetie pie, then!"

"Do you think you could take him and lay him down in his crib without waking him?"

"Sure enough, madam. I've got little brothers and sisters, I have." She picked up Oliver and bore him away.

The envelope was addressed to "Mrs. A. Fletcher" in a hand she didn't recognise. Opening it, she glanced first at the signature—"Maurice Jessup." What on earth . . . ?

He apologised for troubling her. Moira was greatly distressed by the latest development in this horrible business and begged for Mrs. Fletcher's advice. Would she be so very kind as to call at her earliest convenience, tonight if possible?

"Little lamb," cooed Elsie, leaning over Oliver's crib. She turned to the other crib. "And I haven't forgot you, Miss Miranda. Such a good quiet mite." She tucked a blanket in more securely.

Daisy hardly noticed. Her advice? About what? Did Mrs. Jessup still, after Daisy's denials, believe she knew everything in Alec's mind and would be willing to share it?

Alec would undoubtedly say she shouldn't go. Luckily, he wasn't here to say it. She knew she'd never sleep tonight with curiosity gnawing at her. If she could satisfy it while bringing some comfort to Mrs. Jessup . . .

"Elsie, I'm going to pop next door for a few minutes. Did you finish your supper?"

"All but the pudding, madam. Mrs. Dobson will save me some if you want me to stay with the babies."

"Would you, please, until Nurse comes back? I'd hate her to find Oliver crying and no one here. I shan't be long."

Daisy dispensed with hat and gloves, but she did don a coat for the brief venture out into the frosty air, down the steps and up the steps. Enid opened the Jessups' front door promptly.

"I'm ever so glad you've come, madam," she said. "We're all that worried about poor Mr. Aidan in the hospital."

Hospitals were still regarded by many as a place where you were taken to die. "It's the best place for him," said Daisy. "He'll get proper care there."

"I'm sure I hope so. If you'll please to come this way, madam." She showed Daisy into the drawing room.

Mrs. Jessup, as immaculate as ever, came to meet her and took both her hands. "How kind you are!"

"I don't know if I can help." Daisy's voice was full of doubt.

"Come and sit down and let us explain our quandary."

Daisy had expected to see Mr. Jessup, but somewhat to her surprise, Mr. Irwin was still there, as well. As Aidan's father-in-law, she wondered, or as a lawyer, or a bit of each? He had freely given Alec the address of Audrey's sister. Daisy wouldn't give much for his legal advice in a criminal matter.

He was the first of the two men to speak. "Good evening, Mrs. Fletcher. We are approaching you as a friend of my daughter, the only friend we feel able to bring into this shocking affair, as you are already conversant with its details."

"Yes?" Daisy said cautiously.

"Audrey *must* be told that Aidan is in hospital," said Mrs. Jessup. "I simply can't countenance keeping it from her."

"She ought to know," Daisy agreed, reflexively accepting a tiny liqueur glass Mr. Jessup pressed into her hand. She tasted—Drambuie.

"The trouble is, Vivien isn't on the telephone. Jonathan—Mr. Irwin—was going to send a telegram, but I can't help thinking how I'd hate to get such news in a wire, not knowing what to do or—"

"I've *said* I'll go to her." Irwin sounded goaded.

"And take her to Manchester."

"*And* take her to Manchester, if that's what she wants. I'll hire a motor, leave at once, and drive through the night. But it's my opinion that the police will consider our arrival unwarranted interference. I repeat," he added doggedly, "I am not conversant with criminal law."

"Mrs. Fletcher," Mrs. Jessup appealed to her, "do you think your husband would consider it—what's the phrase?—'obstructing the police in the execution of their duties' if Jonathan took Audrey to Manchester? Heaven knows, Aidan and Patrick seem to be in trouble enough already. The last thing they need is any further complications."

Daisy's sympathies were entirely with Audrey. How much comfort her father would be to her was uncertain, but he was indubitably better than a telegram announcing her husband's having been rushed into hospital. On the other hand, Alec might reasonably be annoyed if Mr. Irwin reached Audrey and whisked her away before Mackinnon had spoken to her.

"I can't see that Alec can possibly object to a wife hurrying to her husband's sickbed," she said, thinking fast. "And I don't believe he's allowed to object to the presence of a lawyer, at least in certain circumstances. Couldn't you go with them, Mrs. Jessup? A worried mother as well as a worried wife would be awfully hard to take exception to."

Mrs. Jessup shuddered. "There's nothing I'd like better, but I simply can't travel by motor-car. I'd be no use to either Aidan or Audrey if they had to tuck me up in the bed next to his."

"*Mal de voiture*," said Daisy understandingly, "or it ought to be. I don't know if the French have a word for it. You ought to learn to drive, you know. A friend of mine gets frightfully sick when she's driven, but she's perfectly all right driving herself."

"Oh, I'm much too old to learn."

"Rubbish! But that's beside the point. The more I think about it, the more I think Audrey needs a woman to go with her to hold her hand. Wouldn't you agree?"

"Oh yes!"

"We can't bring anyone else into this," Jessup said grimly.

All three looked at Daisy.

"Well . . ."

"My dear Mrs. Fletcher," said Irwin, "I'd be exceedingly grateful if you could see your way to coming with me. I'm certain your support would mean a great deal to my daughter. Women are so much better on such occasions—'When pain and anguish wring the brow, a ministering angel thou!' "

The solicitor's lapse into poetry startled Daisy. She didn't mind that couplet, but she took serious isssue with the first part of the verse. "Uncertain, coy, and hard to please" was not a description any modern young woman would put up with. Not that she couldn't think of a few to whom it applied neatly, but in her opinion, not a one of them would ever turn into a ministering angel under any foreseeable circs.

"It's a lot to ask," said Jessup, refilling Daisy's glass.

His wife just projected hopefulness that would have easily reached the balcony in a theatre.

"I think it's quite a good idea, actually," said Daisy. "If Alec's furious, it'll be with me, not with you, and I'm used to it. However, I can't possibly be ready to leave before the morning. Reasonably early in the morning, but not tonight."

Mrs. Jessup agreed that the support Daisy could offer her daughter-in-law was more important than speed in announcing the bad news. Mr. Irwin agreed to have his hired car pick her up at eight o'clock the next morning.

Returning home, Daisy breathed a sigh of relief. They might think they had persuaded her into going, but it was just what she wanted. By the time she and Irwin arrived at the farm, Mackinnon would have had his talk with Audrey. When she explained that to Alec, he'd have to agree she'd acted for the best. On top of that, she would not only be a comfort to Audrey; she'd be back in the thick of things, instead of languishing in London while the action was in Manchester.

As she entered the house, the telephone bell was ringing. She reached the instrument just as Elsie pushed through the baize door. "You get it," she requested, stepping back. "I'm not sure I can cope with any more excitement this evening."

"It's that Mr. Mackinnon," Elsie announced a moment later. "The Scotch detective. It's a trunk call."

"Oh dear! Right-oh, I'll talk to him." Daisy took the receiver and put her hand over the transmitter. "Elsie, I have to go out of town for a couple of days. Would you get started on packing? I'll wear country clothes tomorrow—the heather tweed costume and a motoring coat—and then— Whatever do you suppose one wears in Manchester?"

"A dirty place, by what I've heard, madam. You'll want something dark."

"Right-oh. I'll be up in a minute." She uncovered the transmitter. "Hello, Mr. Mackinnon, this is Mrs. Fletcher. What can I do for you?"

The line was terrible, with a crackling noise interrupted by periodic pops.

"Mrs. Fletcher?" Mackinnon shouted.

"Yes!" Daisy shouted back.

"I'm in Lincolnshire, at the Boston police station. The Chief told me to ring up to find out whit's going on, but they told me at the Yard he's on his way to Manchester, and Mr. Tring's gone hame." He always sounded more Scottish than ever when harassed. "Can ye no gie me an inkling whit's happened sin' I left?"

Using initials for those involved, in case the exchange girl was listening in—country operators usually having more time to spare than those in town—Daisy passed on all she knew.

Her exposition was punctuated at regular intervals by the operator's "Your time is up, caller. Would you like another three minutes?" The really irritating thing was that the line always cleared miraculously for these announcements, then reverted to hissing and spitting like an angry cat for Mackinnon's reply.

"So you don't have to try to find out from Mrs. A.J. where her husband is. And that's about the lot," Daisy said at last, "or at least all I can remember. Alec doesn't tell me everything, of course. But if I may venture a suggestion, I wouldn't mention Mr. A.J. being in hospital, if I were you. It'd only upset Mrs. A.J. and make it more difficult for you to get answers out of her. She'll find out soon enough."

"Yon's no the Chief's notion, Mrs. Fletcher?"

"No, just my opinion."

"I s'll have to consider—"

"Your time is up, caller. Would you like another three minutes?"

"No, thank you, operator. Thank you, Mrs. Fletch—"

The line went silent.

Oh well, Daisy thought, she had done her best for Audrey. She could only hope Mackinnon would see the sense in her suggestion. She went upstairs to pack.

TWENTY-FOUR

Alec and Patrick arrived in Manchester in the small hours of the morning. It was raining. Patrick wanted to go at once to the Royal Infirmary. Alec, not entirely disingenuously, persuaded him that his brother would be sleeping and ought not to be disturbed. Indeed, the hospital would certainly not allow a visit to the ward, and moving Aidan to a private room—let alone to a nursing home—in the middle of the night was not a good idea, was, in fact, a rotten idea. Rest and peace were what a concussion victim needed most.

He felt only slightly guilty. The truth of his words was not altered by his own intention of disturbing the patient at the earliest feasible hour of the morning. He was not about to permit the brothers to meet before he had taken Aidan's statement.

They went to the London Road Station Hotel. Patrick went straight to his room. Alec's day was by no means yet ended.

First, he rang up the Manchester police headquarters. True to his word, Superintendent Crane had paved the way. The duty sergeant promised him a car and a detective constable to pick him up at the hotel at quarter past six. Hospitals were notorious for starting their day ridiculously early. Alec reckoned that by the time he had worked his way through the bureaucracy and spoken to the almoner and the doctor, Aidan Jessup should be washed, shaved, fed, and as ready for interrogation as he was likely to be. Assuming he was not inconveniently still unconscious.

This arranged, Alec returned to the reception desk. No one was there, but a sleepy-eyed porter limped over from his post by the door and advised him to ring the bell.

"Thank you, in a minute. Were you on duty last night?"

"Oh aye, that I were."

"You saw the man who was taken away to hospital?"

"Oh aye. Coom in here lookin' like death, he did, 'bout this time last night. Cou'n't stand up straight and wobbling abaht like a one-legged parrot. I thought he were drunk as an oyster, but he were dressed like a gent, an' 'e gave the porter what brought his bags from the station an 'alf crown. Gave me another when I lent him a hand. He'd wired ahead to book a room, so Mr. Greaves didn't—"

"What I did or didn't do cannot possibly interest this gentleman, Wetherby." The voice of authority emanated from a very small man, not much more than a midget, slim and dapper, with only crow's-feet and greying temples to distinguish him from a boy. He had appeared through the door behind the reception counter, which hid all but his head until he stepped up onto a stool.

"But it *does* interest me," said Alec, producing his warrant card. "Detective Chief Inspector Fletcher of Scotland Yard. You're the night manager, I take it, Mr. Greaves? May I have a word with you?"

Greaves raised his eyebrows. "A police matter, is it? You'd better come back into the office."

"Thanks, Mr. Wetherby," Alec said to the porter, and followed the manager through the door.

An electric fire, occupying a stingy Victorian grate, made the office considerably cosier than the lobby outside. There was a utilitarian desk, a safe, and a filing cabinet, but two armchairs flanked the fireplace and the fragrance of coffee filled the air. A pot steamed gently over a spirit lamp on a small table.

"Take a seat. Coffee?"

"That would be very welcome. It's been a long day."

As he poured, Greaves said, "The man who was taken ill was a Jessup. The man who arrived with you was a Jessup. I hope the family hasn't called in Scotland Yard because of any suspicion of skulduggery in this hotel having caused Mr. Jessup's collapse."

"Scotland Yard is not so easily called in, I assure you. Does your recollection of his arrival agree with the porter's?"

"I didn't hear everything he said, but I'd be surprised if it differed by much. As you can imagine, there's been a good deal of talk among the staff."

"Well, then, tell me how you saw it."

Greaves shrugged. "I'm always at the desk at that time, as when you arrived, because of the express from London. Mostly businessmen take that train. It's not unknown for one or two to arrive slightly squiffy, and I can tell you, it's a delicate balancing act whether to give them a room or not. We've the reputation of the hotel to consider, both the reputation for hospitality and as being a quiet, respectable place. If they're not at a noisy stage of inebriation, and if they've booked in advance, we let 'em stay, especially if we know them."

"You know Aidan Jessup?"

"He's stayed here for a few days every autumn since I've worked here. Nice gentleman, sober and steady as they come, I'd've said, but . . ."

"But last night?"

"Last night, he couldn't walk or talk straight, seemed sort of dazed, looked alarmingly as if he might be sick at any moment. You know that greenish look? He complained of a splitting headache. I did ask if he was ill, but he denied it. Said he just needed a few hours in bed. He had a hired car and driver organised for nine the next—that's *this* morning. That's as far as my personal knowledge goes."

"Thank you. You'll be asked to sign a statement later. Now, off the record, will you tell me what you were told about subsequent events when you came to work this evening? As far as we're concerned, this is hearsay, which cannot be used in evidence, but it may help me decide whom else I need to interview."

"Can't you tell me what this is all about? If the hotel is going to be mentioned in the papers in the context of a police enquiry, I'll probably be blamed for letting him stay, and jobs are few and far between. Forewarned is forearmed."

Alec wondered if the poor devil, intelligent and well-spoken as he was, had trouble finding jobs because of his diminutive stature. "It's highly unlikely the hotel will play much of a part, if any," he assured him. "It's a London affair I'm investigating. I can't tell you more, I'm afraid. Go on, please."

"There's not much to tell. I gather the motor-car and chauffeur turned up as expected. Mr. Jessup had got himself down to the lobby somehow and was sitting huddled up in a chair in his coat and hat, still looking deathly ill. The driver took one look at him and said he wouldn't be responsible. He was afraid he'd find himself out in the country somewhere with a corpse in the backseat. And the poor gentleman wasn't even well enough to sit up straight and argue. So Mr. Hatcher, the day manager, called a doctor and Mr. Jessup was whisked off to hospital, a hotel being no place to care for a sick man."

"You didn't hear what the doctor said was wrong with him?"

"No. Oh, I believe he had a bandaged head. A sticking plaster or some such. No one had seen him without his hat before the doctor examined him."

Though Alec was no medical man, he'd dealt with the aftermath of enough assault and batteries and grievous bodily harms to know that the worst effects of a blow to the head are often delayed. The symptoms sounded appropriate. But what on earth had happened the previous afternoon in Constable Circle? Castellano and Aidan Jessup had hit each other over the head with one or more blunt instruments? It sounded ridiculous.

Had Aidan, at the time, remained sufficiently compos mentis to murder his assailant? Or had he been knocked out, leaving vengeance to his brother?

There was still the remote possibility that Aidan had been injured after leaving home, or, even less likely, after reaching Manchester. Tracing him among the hordes at St. Pancras was a long shot, but Manchester's London Road Station after midnight was a brighter prospect. Aidan's railway porter must be found and questioned, Alec decided. Sipping his coffee, he wished it could be postponed till the morning, but the night staff would go off duty and memories would fade.

He swallowed the last drop of coffee, regretfully declined another cup, thanked Greaves, and went to see if the hotel porter happened to know the name of the railway porter.

"Fred Banks," said Wetherby promptly. "We was in the Manchester Regiment together."

Alec trudged back into the station. Knowing the name, finding the porter was easy, and he was as willing to talk as his regimental mate.

"Course I remember the gent," he said, his Manchester accent thick as the industrial city's soot-laden air. "When the train pulled in, I seen him standing at a door. Waved me over and pointed out his luggage."

"Was he talking normally?"

"Yes, sir, normal as any Londoner do. Didn't seem nowt the matter with him, barring he looked tired, which all the passengers do comin' orf that train. He stepped down to the platform as I went over to him, and he missed his footing seemingly. He didn't fall acos I caught him, but he landed on his feet with a bit of a jar. He were a mite shook-up, like, that's all. It's only a few inches. Then when I come down with his bags, he were leaning against my barrow, looking sick as a dog."

"Did you suspect he might be drunk?"

"No, sir, acos he were all right before. I did wonder was it shell shock. It takes some people funny, and a jar like that might bring it on. Any road, I arst was he all right, and he said, sort of slurred, like, yes, he just wanted to get on to the hotel. So I took him, and I can tell you, I didn't think he'd make it, for all it's hardly a step. But I got him there and turned him over to Jim Wetherby, as is porter at the hotel. He give me half a crown. A nice gent, and I'm sure I hope he'll be all right. It's a funny thing, shell shock."

Alec did not need another complication such as shell shock. He wondered what Aidan had done during the War. He'd have to find out, but he didn't seriously consider the porter's theory. A jarring of the spine such as he had described would be quite enough to set off the aftereffects of a concussion.

That, however, brought him no nearer to understanding the crime.

After scarcely three hours' sleep, Alec was picked up at the hotel by the police car and the detective constable he had requested. In a wet, grey dawn, they drove to the Royal Infirmary.

The hospital smelt of disinfectant. Alec supposed it was better than the other smells it undoubtedly disguised. He tried to breathe shallowly.

A long wait ensued before Alec was at last permitted to speak to a doctor. The young man who then appeared looked as somnolent as Alec felt, and nowhere near old enough to have earned his white coat and stethoscope. Dr. Gibson was old enough and awake enough, however, to be adamant that on no account was Aidan Jessup to be disturbed.

"Not even by the police."

"His brother?"

"No one will be allowed to visit him." After many hours of two eminent consultants disagreeing as to whether the patient needed an operation to relieve pressure on the brain, he had at

257

last fallen into natural sleep. "Left to sleep until he rouses naturally, he has an excellent chance of waking as his normal self. He's even been given a private room to reduce the risk of premature awakening. And," said Dr. Gibson with a tired grimace, "his clothes and his hotel suggested he'd be able to pay for it."

"He can. Excellent," said Alec. "I'll be able to leave DC Peters in his room without exciting undue interest or inviting questions."

"Can he sit still and silent for as long as need be?" the doctor asked sceptically.

From the corner of his eye, Alec saw Peters about to burst a blood vessel. Smoothly, he forestalled an outburst that would have seriously undermined their credibility. "It's a skill every detective has to master. He can sit outside the door if you insist, but you must see that people will wonder what's going on."

Not to mention that he wanted Aidan's very first words captured, and wanted to be informed at once when he came round. He hated to badger a sick man, but it would be best to catch him before he had time to come up with an explanation of his plight, and, with luck, before Patrick tried to see him. The story the brothers had agreed upon had very likely been wiped out by Aidan's concussion, always supposing he had taken it in in the first place.

Dr. Gibson capitulated. "Oh, very well."

DC Peters had already been given his instructions. He melted away unobtrusively to take up his post.

"Thank you. I have one more question. Is it possible to tell when the patient received the injury to his head?"

"You'll have to ask the consultant."

"You didn't hear him offer an opinion? I'm not asking you to give evidence, just to give me an indication."

"I wasn't on duty yesterday morning. According to the patient's chart, at the time when Mr. Jessup was brought in, Dr. Penstone considered the degree of healing of the external injury suggested that twelve to eighteen hours had passed since it was inflicted. Now, if you can possibly spare me, I *do* have other patients to take care of."

Alec thanked him absently. Here was unwelcome, though anticipated, confirmation of his guess. Aidan Jessup had been injured the very evening that Castellano had died; another strand in the rope that might hang his next-door neighbour's son.

He went to find a telephone. No doubt he ought to report to Superintendent Crane, but three hours' sleep was not sufficient to enable him to tackle his irascible superior. Whatever the Home Secretary's complaint involved, he'd rather not know.

He asked the operator for Whitehall 1212 all the same. It was still early and Tom Tring might have gone in to the Yard before setting about the various enquiries left for him—the Bennetts' tale, Lambert's whereabouts, Whitcomb's evidence. One might suppose that Whitcomb would have come forward already if he had seen anything. In Alec's experience, however, businessmen were prone to negligence in matters where no profit was to be made. At the very least, finding out the time he had walked through the garden might be helpful.

The connection to London took forever, and when at last Alec got through to the Yard, he was told DS Tring had not come in. Quickly, before the operator lost the London connection, he asked for his own home number. Daisy might have news of Tom. If not, there was a good chance she would see him at some point during the day, and she could pass on the doctor's report on Aidan Jessup. Besides, as always when he was out of town, he just wanted to hear her voice.

Elsie answered the phone. "Oh dear, sir, I'm ever so sorry. She's already gone."

"Gone where?"

"To Lincolnshire, sir. Mr. Irwin picked her up in a motor-car. I think they went to see Mrs. Aidan."

So he just wanted to hear her voice, did he? Now he realised that what he had really wanted was to make sure she wasn't meddling in the investigation.

And he didn't like the answer.

TWENTY-FIVE

By the time they left the Great North Road at Norman Cross, Daisy was heartily wishing she hadn't come. A couple of hours confined with Mr. Irwin, even in the luxurious comfort of a chauffeured Lanchester, was enough to convince her that her first impressions, gained when he showed her around Alec's great-uncle Walsall's house, were accurate. He was a fussbox, and an incredibly boring one.

After she had assured him four or five times that she was perfectly comfortable and quite warm enough, he started fretting about the unfortunate state of affairs that was taking them to Lincolnshire. His concern was natural. Daisy had no quarrel with that. But she felt he should be more worried about his daughter and grandchildren than about the effect on his standing with the Law Society of having a son-in-law arrested for murder.

Nor did she see why she should be forced to listen to a lengthy diatribe on his advice to Maurice Jessup not to engage in shipping alcoholic beverages to America. He went into great detail about the laws and treaties involved, all of which passed over Daisy's head.

She had been trying for some time to shut out his droning voice when it dawned on her that his words were addressed not to her but to Alec, through her. Though she was accustomed to people giving her information they wanted to convey to the police without actually having to speak to the police, she considered it most improper in a lawyer.

He didn't even have the excuse of being a suspect. She listened with increasing indignation as he explained how he couldn't possibly be held to blame for the consequences if his clients chose to disregard his advice.

"I'm sorry, I must have missed something," she said. "Are you saying you advised the Jessups not to bump off Castellano? Because if so, surely it was your duty, not just as a lawyer but as a citizen, to warn the police that they were contemplating murder?"

Irwin stared at her aghast. "Oh, no, no, no!" He took out a linen handkerchief and mopped his forehead. "Oh no, my dear Mrs. Fletcher, you misunderstand me entirely! I knew nothing of their plans in advance, I assure you."

"They didn't tell you till afterwards?"

"No, no, they never breathed a word to me, neither before nor after."

"Then why do you think you could be held responsible?"

"Well, I did know about the . . . er . . . the 'bootlegging,' and since that led to the murder—"

"So you believe they did it, do you? Aidan or Patrick, or the two together?"

"Not Aidan! No!" he said violently. "Aidan is a very steady and responsible young man, or I should never have let Audrey marry him. But who knows what sort of criminals Patrick consorted with in America? The . . . victim was American, I gather."

"Did you know Patrick had gone to America?"

"I was not told. I guessed. Had I been consulted, I should have advised very strongly against it, and with reason. Look what has come of it!"

Mr. Irwin had clearly persuaded himself that Patrick was guilty. Daisy could only be glad he was not her solicitor.

Did he have a reason for that belief, beyond his determination not to suspect Aidan? Did he know something Daisy did not? And if Patrick was the murderer, why had Aidan fled?

As an afterthought, what had happened to Lambert?

Beyond Peterborough, the land was dead flat, crisscrossed by ditches draining the fens. There were pastures dotted with cattle, but much of it was rich arable land. Here and there, a windmill loomed, great sails slowly turning. Daisy's thoughts turned to Audrey's sister's farm.

Audrey had talked about her sister occasionally, saying Vivien had married a farmer. Daisy had no idea what to expect—it could be anything from a cottage to a mansion. The inhabitant of either might be described as a farmer, from a cowman to a gentleman who never went nearer the fields than his bailiff's office. On the other hand, she couldn't imagine Mr. Irwin permitting a daughter of his to meet a cowman, let alone marry one; and if she had married into the aristocracy, or even the gentry, the family wouldn't refer to him as a farmer.

No doubt he was something in between. Daisy realised she didn't know his name, either, but she decided not to ask Mr. Irwin, who had mercifully fallen silent at last. She didn't want to incite another peroration. Sooner or later, she would find out.

The driver stopped in Boston to ask the way to Butterwick, and in Butterwick to ask the way to West Dyke Farm. The end of the long trek was in sight.

Farm turned out to be a modest term for a substantial house. Architecture was not Daisy's strong point, but she thought the original brick farmhouse must have been enlarged as long ago as the eighteenth century to make a pleasant manor. The green-and-brown-striped fields extended right up to the gardens, with no extravagant park intervening. Perhaps a park had been ploughed under during the War. Or perhaps the family— what was their name?—that continued to call their home "Farm" when it might have aspired to a grander title, had seen no sense in wasting valuable cropland.

As the chauffeur pulled up the Lanchester in front of the house, Daisy realised that for all his talk, Irwin had said nothing constructive about the purpose of their trip.

"Are you going to tell Audrey about Aidan privately?" she asked him. "I mean, are you going to try to keep it from her sister?"

"I?" he exclaimed. "But that's what you came for, Mrs. Fletcher, to break the news to Audrey."

"No, I most certainly did not," Daisy said crossly. "I came to support her, to hold her hand, and to accompany her to Manchester if she decides to go."

"But *I* can't tell her. She'll very likely cry!"

"It wouldn't surprise me. That's why I'll be there to hold her hand and make soothing noises."

"You know much more than I do about what's happened. You'll be far better able to reassure her."

"Nothing I know is in the least likely to be reassuring," said Daisy, her tone uncompromising.

"Oh dear! I thought I'd keep Vivien occupied while you—"

"So you don't want her and her husband to be told?"

"That is entirely up to Audrey," Irwin said with some dignity. "But even if she's willing for her sister to hear the whole, she may well not want Bessemer in the picture."

Bessemer—at least Daisy had a name now. She recognised that she was losing the argument, though. What chance had she against a lawyer, trained to keep a dispute running for years? Just look at *Bleak House*!

"All right," she said crossly, "but you'll have to explain why I want to speak to Audrey privately. You can't expect me to barge into the house of people I've never met and drag their guest away from whatever she's doing."

Even a lawyer could scarcely argue with that.

Daisy hadn't realised how stiff she was till she stepped out of the car, nor how cold and hungry she was until she stepped into the warm house and smelled lunch. The Bessemers and Audrey were, in fact, in the middle of their midday meal. The newcomers were welcomed without overt curiosity, and places were quickly set for them.

Vivien Bessemer and her husband indeed seemed genuinely incurious about the reason for the unexpected arrival of her father and her sister's friend. Audrey, however, was very much on edge, and she pushed her food around her plate without, as far as Daisy could see, eating more than the odd morsel. Daisy ate well, not so much to postpone the distasteful task she'd landed herself with as to fortify herself for it.

At last, she and Audrey were settled in a small parlour with their coffee.

"What's wrong?" Audrey asked at once, leaning forward, her hands clasped in her lap. "What's happened?"

At least Daisy didn't have to announce the fact of bad news. Audrey was obviously expecting it.

"I'm afraid Aidan has been injured—"

"I know that much. I thought he was all right, though, just a bit of a headache. The policeman who came this morning, that Scotsman, didn't mention anything else."

"There have been some aftereffects," Daisy said vaguely. "He's being properly taken care of. Don't worry. Why don't you tell me about that evening, the evening before you left, so that I don't go repeating what you already know."

"I already told the policeman."

"It's not for the police I want to know, Audrey. I came as your friend, to try to help. It'll be easier if I have a better idea of what happened, and DS Mackinnon's not likely to tell me."

"Oh, right-oh. Everyone was excited about Patrick coming home. They're a very close family, you see. Usually, I feel very much a part of it. I wouldn't want you to think they shut me out in any way. No one could have a dearer mother-in-law than Mama Moira. But . . . I suppose—I'm afraid, looking back, I was a little jealous. I didn't tell Mr. Mackinnon that. I'm so ashamed of it."

"It seems to me perfectly understandable, and none of the police's business."

"It's not that I don't like Patrick, but they were making such a fuss about his return."

"Mrs. Jessup had been pretty worried about him, hadn't she?"

"Yes. It was stupid of me to feel that way. Anyway, Aidan and his father came home early the day Patrick was expected. Aidan said he was going to go out to walk about and get a spot of fresh air and see if he could spot Patrick's taxi arriving. It wasn't even a pleasant evening! I went up to the nursery. I don't know how long I was there—you know how time passes when you're playing with the children."

"Like a flash," Daisy agreed.

"Then Mama Moira came in—all the servants would have been busy with preparations for dinner—and she asked me to go down. She didn't say why. I assumed Patrick must have come in, but I didn't ask because she seemed . . . well, rather upset. We didn't go down to the drawing room as I expected. She took me to our bedroom—Aidan's and mine—and there was Aidan with a plaster on his head, right on top. He said he'd had an accident and bumped it."

"Didn't you ask how?"

"He just said he'd been careless and slipped. I didn't ask for details because then he told me he'd decided he couldn't put off his trip to the North any longer and he was going to wait to welcome Patrick home and then catch a train. And Mama Moira said she was sure I'd want to make the best of my time and leave in the morning to come here, to stay with Vivien. I felt as if I was being rushed, but they both seemed a bit peculiar, so I didn't like to make a fuss. It was all . . . strange. I did wonder if perhaps Aidan had met Patrick and they'd quarrelled . . . ?"

Her voice rose in a question. Daisy said, "I'm pretty sure you needn't worry about that."

"I didn't really believe it. They've always been such good friends. Anyway, Mama Moira helped me pack for Aidan and start to organise my own packing. Nurse wasn't to be told till after the children were asleep, for fear of them getting over-excited."

"Miranda and Oliver aren't old enough yet to be excited about things that haven't happened yet."

Audrey smiled at that. "They will be, all too soon!"

"No doubt. You started to pack. . . ."

"Then Patrick arrived and we all had Champagne to celebrate, in the mirror room. But it was all frightfully artificial somehow. It's hard to explain. You know Mama Moira was an actress. It was as if everyone was acting, including me. I was desperate to know what was wrong, but I just didn't quite dare to ask. Then it was time to change for dinner. That's when Aidan left. He kissed me, just as if he was going off to work on an ordinary day, and he told me not to worry, but how can I help it? And now my father's come all this way, and you . . ." Her voice failed.

"Only because Mrs. Jessup decided a telegram would be too upsetting. She'd have come herself—"

"Thank heaven she didn't! Travelling in a car makes her frightfully sick. She'd have been half dead and in need of nursing. You said Aidan's getting proper care. What's wrong, and where is he?"

"I don't know very much. We tried to ring up the hospital—"

"Hospital!"

"He was taken ill at his hotel, and they couldn't keep him there. You know what hotel people are like, always worrying about what the other guests might think. Aidan just needs rest and absolute quiet and someone to keep an eye on him. It was too early to speak to anyone at the hospital when we rang up this morning, but I dare say he's perfectly all right after a good night's sleep."

"I must go to him, of course. Vivien won't mind keeping the children."

"Your father intends to take you."

"You'll come, too, won't you, Daisy? I love Father dearly, but . . ."

"If you really want me," said Daisy, but what she thought was, *Try to stop me!* For one thing, she had no desire to attempt what sounded like a wretched train journey back to London. Luckily, Audrey didn't seem interested in why she had come in the first place. It would be hard to explain that she'd let herself be dragooned into doing something she really wanted to do.

"Oh, I do!" Audrey hesitated. "Daisy, is all this something to do with . . . all those policemen in the garden?"

"You saw them?"

"They were hard to miss! The morning after Aidan was hurt—but Aidan couldn't have anything to do with that. It's just a coincidence. It must be."

"The most extraordinary coincidences do happen."

Audrey took a deep breath and visibly braced herself. "Daisy, I don't know what they were looking for, and I don't think I want to know, but your husband isn't going to arrest my husband as soon as he's well enough, is he?"

"As far as I'm aware," Daisy said with careful precision, "Alec hasn't yet worked out exactly what happened in the garden. He's hoping Aidan may have some information that will help him find out."

Which was the truth, as far as it went. Daisy had no desire whatsoever to be the one to enlighten Audrey about the murder in the garden and the indisputable connections between the Jessups and the murdered man.

TWENTY-SIX

Before going to Aidan Jessup's room, Alec had a word with the matron herself. That formidable figure, once convinced of the necessity, assured him that Patrick would not be allowed access to his brother until Alec had finished with him. Hospital visiting hours, though stringent for ordinary patients, were usually relaxed for private patients, but it would be easy to delay the young man. Fortunately, he had slept late and was still breakfasting when Alec received word that Aidan was awake and coherent.

As an added precaution, Alec beckoned the Manchester DC out of the room and posted him outside the door.

"How is he?" he asked in a low voice.

"Fair addled," said Peters succinctly.

Alec raised an eyebrow.

"In his right mind," the young man elaborated, "but no lawyer worth his salt 'd agree he's fit to make a statement."

"Thank you. I won't take a statement, then, just try to get enough out of him to know what questions to put to his brother. Who is not on any account to be allowed to interrupt."

"Got it, sir."

"I take it he hasn't said anything of interest?"

"Nowt but asking for a drink o' water, sir, which I gave him. He seemed to think I were a hospital orderly, and I didn't set him straight."

With a nod of approval, Alec went on into the room. It was Spartan but very clean and neat, a haven from the public wards for those who could pay a little for privacy but could not afford a private nursing home. Aidan lay flat on his back, his arms at his sides on top of the tightly tucked-in covers, a model patient. A nurse must have tidied him back to hospital standards since Peters gave him a drink, Alec assumed.

Aidan turned his head on the pillow as Alec entered. His eyes appeared to focus with difficulty, but he recognised his visitor.

"Mr. Fletcher." His voice was slightly slurred. He didn't seem surprised to see Alec, whether because he was as yet incapable of experiencing surprise or because he had half-expected him.

"Good morning, Mr. Jessup. How are you feeling?"

"*Much* better. My God, it was awful! I've had a concussion before—playing rugger, you know—but nothing like this. It was like being drunk as a lord and having a frightful hangover at the same time."

Alec moved the room's one chair to the bedside and set it so that he could see Aidan's face. "I'm afraid I have to ask you some questions."

"I know. I can't remember much, though."

If he pleaded amnesia, no one would be able to prove otherwise. It was a common symptom of severe concussion. He might be tricked, though, if he were lying about it.

"I'm not taking a formal statement at this time," Alec said, "but if you want a lawyer—"

"My father-in-law? No thanks!"

"Or someone else."

"No, thank you."

"All right, then, tell me what you remember of the evening you left London."

"I've been lying here thinking about it—I'd sit up, but my head still gets a bit swimmy. As I say, I've been thinking about it, and I still don't see what else I could have done. We were expecting Patrick home, as I'm sure you know by now. We weren't sure exactly when he'd arrive, but Father and I left work early so as to be there when he came. I got fed up sitting there waiting, and it had stopped raining, so I decided to stroll down to the corner. If I didn't meet him, at least I'd have had a breath of fresh air and stretched my legs."

"You were very keen to see him."

"Well, he'd been away a long time, and on his own for the first time. And there were business reasons why we were eager to hear his news."

Also, thought Alec, there was a good deal of brotherly affection between them. Though Aidan was no public school boy, he had absorbed enough of the ethos not to mention it, but Alec had a hunch that their mutual fondness played a considerable part in the whole affair.

"You went out of the house. . . ."

"And crossed the street. I expected Pat to come by taxi. The quickest way from our house to the street exit from the Circle is across the garden—though, come to think of it, he could have been driving round the Circle while I cut across. Anyway, it was getting dark and I was nearly at the fountain before I realised that the chap coming up towards me was Pat. And a moment later, that damn Yankee popped out of nowhere—"

"Out of nowhere?"

"I don't know if he'd been hiding behind a tree or if he just happened to come around the Circle and see me walking down, and followed me. He suddenly appeared beside me and started the same old jabber. He had a business proposition for the firm, it would be worth our while, we'd regret it if we didn't listen to him, and so on. Father wasn't interested. I brushed the fellow off, as per usual. Next thing I knew, he was pointing a gun at Patrick!"

"You're sure of that?" Alec snapped.

"Sure as you're a copper," Aidan said wryly. "I didn't get into combat during the War—they put me to running an officers' mess, because of my experience in the trade—but I saw plenty of firearms. Well, I reacted without thinking. I'm still a pretty useful rugger wing forward, you know, or was until this." He touched the top of his head. "I tackled him, as if it were the ball he was holding. I hit him pretty hard and we both went down. The paving was wet, slick, so we started to slide. I don't remember the next bit. I was out. Pat says we both hit the rim of the fountain head-on."

"The missing weapon!" The *other* missing weapon. What the hell had become of the gun? The Jessups would have had no conceivable reason to dispose of it.

Aidan smiled crookedly. "Were you looking for the traditional blunt instrument? It's there, in plain sight, though I presume any blood Pat failed to clean up has been washed away by the rain. I was out for nearly five minutes, Pat reckoned. He was beginning to get really worried. He started splashing water from the fountain in my face—ugh!—to try to bring me round. Maybe it worked, who knows. At any rate, I started to show signs of life. Then it dawned on Pat that he'd better check on the other chap. He turned—"

"Could you explain your relative positions?"

"It's all a bit vague. . . ." Aidan frowned in concentration. "Pat was kneeling between us, so somehow the American and I got separated. Perhaps we rolled apart when we hit the fountain. I suppose I let go of him when I was knocked out."

"More than likely."

"Pat turned away from me to— What's his name? I can't go on calling him 'the American.'"

"He never introduced himself?"

"Neither Father nor I ever let him get that far. We have a long-standing and satisfactory arrangement with our American customer and we just weren't interested in changing."

"Castellano. Michele Castellano. Though there's some question about whether that's his real name, as his passport was faked."

"He looked Italian. He was a thoroughly objectionable type, but I didn't mean to kill him. I couldn't let him shoot my brother in cold blood, could I?"

Silently, Alec cursed. A confession, and he couldn't use it! But having spoken the words, Aidan would find them difficult to retract in circumstances more useful from a police point of view. He was no hardened criminal.

"Tell me exactly what happened," Alec urged.

"Pat said something like 'Oh hell, he's still out. He can't have as thick a skull as yours.' And then he said—he sounded a bit panicky—'He's not breathing. I don't think he's breathing!' I said, 'Feel his pulse,' or perhaps Pat said, 'I'll feel his pulse'— I'm not awfully clear which. I was still a bit groggy. Does it matter? What it comes down to is that there was no pulse. Castellano was dead."

So much for the confession. If Aidan was telling the truth, he was implicating his brother, unaware that the blow to the victim's head was not the cause of death. While Aidan lay unconscious, or semiconscious, Patrick had compressed Castellano's arteries until, starved of oxygen, the brain stopped sending signals to the lungs to breathe, the heart to beat.

"I still don't see what I could have done differently," Aidan said dully, "except not to let the others hustle me away. I wasn't thinking straight. I should have stayed to take my medicine. It wasn't exactly *self*-defence, but I was defending my brother."

"What reasons did they give for your leaving in such a hurry? You're speaking of your parents and your brother? Your wife?"

"Not Audrey! She was in the nursery, thank heaven, when I came in bloody-headed. Before she came down, Mother had patched me up and we'd decided I should go. Why? It's all a bit of a blur, but there seemed to be a dozen reasons. Patrick swore he'd hidden the body so that it wouldn't be found for days."

"When did he do that?"

"While I was sitting holding my head, wondering whether I could make it back to the house. If I'd been able to think, I wouldn't have let him, but he always was impetuous, and once it was done, it was done. He said if I stayed away until my head healed, there be no reason for anyone to suppose I had anything to do with it. Then he buzzed off to create an alibi for himself."

"At the Flask."

"Yes, he really did go there. Luckily, the servants hadn't seen him arrive. If it was luck."

"That remains to be seen. So far, your only reason for having left is that your brother hoped to get away with it."

"He was, naturally, grateful that I'd prevented Castellano's shooting him," Aidan said vehemently, "and he didn't see why I should suffer for protecting him."

"What other reasons?"

"Mother was terrified that I'd go to prison. You've got to remember that she's Irish and an actress, and she has enough temperament for both, though she hides it well most of the time. Father, naturally, was concerned about the effect on the business. And there were Audrey and the children to consider. I suppose I'm bound to go to prison now? It's going to be a terrible shock for Audrey, and awfully hard on all of them."

Alec wondered how much Daisy would reveal to Audrey. She was perfectly capable of being discreet if it suited her ideas of what was right. However, he had never quite fathomed how her mind worked in that regard. In fact, he wasn't at all sure she'd be able to explain it if she tried.

"My job is to find out what happened," he said. "What the public prosecutor and the courts decide to do about it is not for me to decide."

"No." Aidan closed his eyes, looking exhausted and defenceless. "Go easy on Pat, Fletcher, if you can. He's just a boy still. I wish Audrey were here."

She might well be at her husband's bedside soon, if Daisy had her way. Irwin might dissuade her, though. He wouldn't be too happy about having a gaolbird in the family.

As for Patrick, Alec had more than enough to pull him in on a charge of interfering with a corpse, if nothing worse.

Before he sent DC Peters to find Patrick, Alec arranged for the use of a room where they could be undisturbed. It was little more than a cupboard, badly lit, but adequate for his purpose, with a small table and three hard wooden chairs.

While Peters went to fetch Patrick, he moved the chairs into his preferred arrangement, himself facing the suspect across the table, with the DC to sit against the wall, slightly behind Patrick, to take notes. On the whole, people were more willing to talk if they didn't actually watch their words being written down. On the other hand, some found it easier to lie if they forgot their lies could be quoted back to them word for word.

Patrick burst into the room. "He's not . . . Aidan . . . He hasn't died?"

"Great Scott no! He's very much improved."

He slumped onto the chair. "Thank God," he said fervently. "I was afraid . . . I was afraid you were going to break it to me gently. . . . But you're being a detective here, aren't you? Not a friend of the family, I mean."

"Yes. Your brother has been telling me what actually happened the night Castellano died. I'm now going to ask you if you'd like to revise your previous statement. You do not have to say anything, but anything you choose to say will be taken down and may be used in evidence in a court of law. You're entitled to have a lawyer present—"

"A lawyer? I don't need a law— Oh hell, I suppose I shouldn't have hidden the body."

"Why did you?"

"I hoped it wouldn't be found for a while. That Aidan could go away until his head healed and no one would connect him with it. It seemed like a good idea at the time. There wasn't time to discuss it, and Aidan was still pretty woozy anyway. You can't blame him for that."

"All right. Now, suppose we start at the beginning. You took the boat train from Liverpool?"

"Yes, and the tube from the station."

"At what time?"

"The Flask was just opening, so it must have been half past five."

"But you didn't go in." Alec hadn't read the report of whoever had questioned the people at the Flask, but if Aidan's story was true, his brother hadn't had time for a drink on his way home.

He flushed. "No, not then."

"You walked on to Constable Circle." That was for the record. "You took the path up through the garden in the centre."

"Yes."

"Tell me what happened."

"I saw Aidan coming down the hill. He told you about the man with the gun?"

"You tell me."

"I know now it was this fellow Castellano, but I wouldn't have recognised him even if it hadn't been getting dark. I'd never seen him before in my life."

"You hadn't come across him in America?"

"No. I gather he'd been in England for ages, long before I actually reached America. I was at sea for most of the time I was away, as I told you."

"Castellano was with your brother? He introduced him to you?"

"Lord no! The man was pestering Aidan. Aidan was trying to ignore him. My father told me he'd been making a nuisance of himself on and off for weeks. Nothing serious, just irritating. I mean, nothing that would give anyone a reason to . . . to kill him, let alone Aidan, who's the most peaceable man on the planet. He doesn't even have a temper, far less lose it! And why Castellano should want to shoot me— Well, it's beyond the bounds of credibility." Patrick shook his head in disbelief.

"Describe the sequence of events, please."

"Aidan saw me and waved. I think he started walking a bit faster, though it's hard to be sure. Castellano kept up with him, anyway. They came on down the slope until they reached the fountain. As they came round it, Castellano took one look at me and pulled out a gun!"

"Did he say anything?"

"Say anything? He could have sung the 'Hallelujah Chorus' and I wouldn't have noticed. I was too stunned to move. He was pointing the damn thing at me! If it had happened on the other side of the Atlantic, I might have been halfway prepared, but I'd just come home safe. I tell you, I froze. This can't be happening, I thought, not here! But big brother came to the rescue once again."

"Again?"

"He's eight years older than me, you see, and he's always considered it sort of his mission in life to keep me out of trouble. He tackled the brute round the knees, brought him to the ground. Only the ground wasn't a nice muddy rugger field; it was slippery paving surrounding a fountain. They slid into the rim of the pool and both got knocked out."

"*What happened to the gun?*" Alec couldn't keep the urgency from his voice. Without the gun as evidence of a threat from Castellano, the Jessups hadn't a leg to stand on. Not that one of them did anyway, he reminded himself, considering the pathologist's damning evidence.

Patrick looked surprised. "Gosh, I'd forgotten. It flew out of Castellano's hand when Aidan hit him, and I caught it. Aidan may be the rugger star, but I'm a fair hand with a cricket ball."

"And?"

"'And'?"

"What did you do with it?"

"I can't rem— Yes, I can!" he said triumphantly. "I chucked it away. When you get your hands on a ball in cricket, you hardly ever hang on to it unless you've caught the batsman out. You bung it to the wicket-keeper or the bowler. Besides, I didn't know when I caught it that Castellano was unconscious, and I didn't want him getting hold of it again. I don't know much about guns, but I reckoned if it landed in the pool, it wouldn't be much use to him if he did find it."

"You threw it towards the pool?"

"Yes, and on the whole I'm a pretty accurate shot. With a cricket ball, that is. The shape and weight and balance of a pistol are quite different, of course, so I might have missed."

"It has not been found in the pool, nor anywhere near it."

"You mean you haven't found it at all? Damn it, I couldn't have tossed it out of the garden!"

"Never mind that, for the moment. Go on. Your brother and Castellano were lying unconscious by the pool."

"Well, naturally, I went to make sure Aidan was all right. Only he wasn't. When someone gets hit on the head and knocked out, you expect them to open their eyes in a minute or so, don't you? He just wouldn't come round. He seemed to be breathing all right, though. I tried dipping my handkerchief in the pool and bathing his face."

"How long do you estimate he was unconscious?"

"Gosh, I don't know. It seemed like forever. I suppose it can't have been more than about five minutes. It can't have been that much darker when he blinked at me at last, or I wouldn't have seen him blink. I'm telling you, I nearly sang the 'Hallelujah Chorus' myself."

"Explain to me, please, your relative positions while you were trying to bring him round."

Patrick gave him an odd look. "Right-oh. They'd rolled apart, Aidan and Castellano, when they hit. There was just room to kneel between them. Oh! I suppose it was pretty stupid to turn my back on him like that. I never gave it a thought at the time. I was too worried about Aidan to worry about anything else. And then, when I did remember him, it turned out the crack on the head had killed him." He was silent for a long moment. "It was an accident. Or at least pure chance. Aidan attacked him, but he didn't intend to hurt him, just to stop him shooting me. You must see that!"

If it weren't for those two telltale bruises on either side of his throat, and the internal evidence that confirmed their meaning . . .

The rest of Patrick's tale matched Aidan's closely. After hiding the body, he had helped his brother home, quickly explained to his parents what had happened, and then gone to the pub to establish an alibi. When he returned home, Aidan was ready to leave. He seemed perfectly all right except for a bit of a headache.

Alec found the brothers' story damnably convincing. He couldn't see either of them as a cold-blooded killer, yet everything suggested one of them, probably Patrick, was just that.

Could the pathologist be wrong? Or had they both inherited their mother's thespian talent?

He wasn't quite ready for an arrest. First, he'd get them both to Scotland Yard and see whether they had a different song to sing in those austere premises.

One thing was certain, it wouldn't be the "Hallelujah Chorus."

TWENTY-SEVEN

By the time Daisy, Audrey, and Mr. Irwin reached the Manchester Royal Infirmary, Aidan had been pronounced out of danger. He would have to forswear Rugby football for at least a year, preferably forever. But if, after another night in hospital, there was no relapse, he might go home.

The consultant was not happy to learn that home was two hundred miles away. A train journey was out of the question. But he conceded that a private automobile driven with the greatest care at a moderate rate of speed could do his patient no harm.

Mr. Irwin's hired car could not accommodate everyone in comfort if Aidan was to have room to lie down on one of the seats. Alec announced very firmly that he and Patrick would take the train. Daisy expected to go with them, but Audrey announced equally firmly that she wanted Daisy to travel with her and Aidan. She knew, she said, her father wouldn't mind going by train, so as not to crowd the invalid.

Her father did mind, but he gave in after a little grumbling. Audrey explained to Daisy later that Aidan would go mad shut up hour after hour with his father-in-law, unable to escape his homilies.

In the meanwhile, the only time Daisy saw Alec alone was back in their bedroom at the Station Hotel. By then he was so exhausted, he hadn't the energy to rag her for going to Lincolnshire and then proceeding to Manchester. He did ask whether she had learnt anything useful from Audrey or Irwin, but when she said, "No, nothing," he promptly fell fast asleep.

She was glad to be able to tell the truth. She didn't know what she'd have done if Audrey had told her, as a friend, something she really ought to pass on to the police. But Audrey *did* know she was married to a policeman, she reminded herself drowsily. She wasn't—wouldn't have been—hearing confidences under false pretences. . . . She, too, fell asleep.

The next day was a different matter. As the Lanchester purred southward, the strictly admonished chauffeur doing an excellent job of avoiding bumps, swerves, and sudden stops, Aidan told his wife what had happened on that fatal night.

Daisy couldn't help but hear. When he started talking, she pointed out that she was, to some degree at least, the ear of the Law. Aidan said it didn't matter.

"I've already told your husband everything," he said wearily.

Audrey listened in increasing distress, Daisy with interest that turned to puzzlement. Something was missing, though she couldn't quite put her finger on it. She didn't mention it. Audrey would only assume she was accusing Aidan of deliberately concealing the worst.

The story was bad enough. Aidan expected to be prosecuted for involuntary manslaughter, or something of the sort, and Patrick was in trouble for moving the body and concealing a crime.

"But they won't send you to prison, darling?" Audrey asked in anguish. "You didn't mean to kill him! And he would have shot Patrick."

"They can't find the gun," Aidan told her sombrely. "I don't know whether they believe Castellano really threatened Patrick's life. If they can persuade a jury I attacked him without immediate cause, even not meaning to kill him . . ."

Audrey got a bit weepy. Daisy pretended not to notice Aidan comforting her and not to hear her promising to wait for him forever.

The missing gun—was that what was bothering her? More crucial was Alec's certainty that Castellano had been murdered with cool deliberation. Was Aidan protecting Patrick still, with lies now, rather than with action? Was Patrick protecting Aidan, similarly, by lying about the cause of death, as he had previously hidden the body and rushed his brother out of town? Did neither of them know the police had evidence of purposeful murder?

Would Alec have let her travel with Aidan and Audrey if he believed Aidan to be a cold-blooded murderer?

With a brave attempt at normalcy, Audrey started to talk about how much the children were enjoying her sister's farm. They had helped feed chickens and collect eggs, watched the milking from a safe distance, and even taken brief rides on the broad backs of the cart horses. Her description of the last, with Marilyn hanging on like grim death and Percy blithely waving with both arms, made Aidan smile. But his eyelids soon drooped and he slipped into sleep.

Daisy and Audrey stared silently out of the windows at the endless drab industrial towns of the Midlands. At least it wasn't raining. Daisy was still plagued with a feeling that she had forgotten some vital fact. As so often happened, the harder she tried to pin it down, the less certain she was that she hadn't imagined the whole thing.

It was late when they reached Hampstead. They were all exhausted. Brief good nights were said on the pavement, then Daisy plodded up the steps to her front door, followed by the driver with her suitcase. At the top, he set it down. She tipped him, and as he ran back down to help the others, she rang the bell rather than dig for the key in her bag.

Elsie opened the door. "Oh madam, I'm ever so glad you're back."

"So am I," said Daisy fervently, hurrying into the warmth of the hall.

"There's messages," announced the parlour maid, lugging the suitcase in and closing the door. "The master rang up, and he may be very late tonight. And that Mr. Lambert called twice, and I know it was him, even if he did have his collar up and his hat down and wouldn't give his name."

"Oh no!"

"Yes'm, it was him for sure."

"What did he want?"

"He wouldn't tell me, 'm. Said he needed to speak to you or the master, so I told him you was in the North and if he wanted the master, he'd better go to Scotland Yard, and he said he wasn't going there, thank you very much, the way they treated him last time. He said to tell you it was urgent, but he wouldn't leave an address or telephone number."

"Oh dear, I wonder what's wrong!"

"Not to worry, madam. He said he'd keep coming back till he got hold of you. And there's one more."

"One more what?" Daisy asked blankly, her mind on Lambert's gyrations.

"Message, 'm." She went to the hall table. "My sister brought round this note. They're in a terrible state over there, she said, but she wouldn't tell me what about, and I reckon she don't really know."

Daisy's heart sank. On the whole, she would have preferred to remain in ignorance. Trying to hide a sigh, she said, "Thank you, Elsie. Take my suitcase up, would you, please."

She opened the note. It was from Mrs. Jessup. Patrick had been asked to go to Scotland Yard to "assist the police with their enquiries." What did it mean? Mr. Irwin was no help at all, since all he did was reiterate that he "took the gravest view" of the situation, which she and her husband were quite capable of doing for themselves. Would Daisy please come—when she had recovered from the journey, of course—and explain the significance of those ominous words.

There was a blotch that looked alarmingly like a tearstain. Daisy couldn't imagine Mrs. Jessup crying. Had the note sounded even remotely accusatory, she would have sent a refusal, wrapped decently in mentions of fatigue and the lateness of the hour. But nothing suggested Daisy or her policeman husband was responsible for the Jessups' plight.

She decided she'd better go right away. If she took off her coat and sat down, or went to see the babies, she might never get moving again. With a sigh she made no effort to conceal, she called up the stairs to Elsie. "I'm going next door!"

"The only question I want you to ask him," Alec said to Tom Tring, "is, 'And then?' I want you to hear his story just as he chooses to tell it. With any luck, we might learn something from comparing it with what he told me in Manchester. I want it word for word, Ernie."

"Don't I always, Chief?" Piper asked, injured.

Alec grinned. "On the whole, unless my wife is present." Ernie Piper was expert at omitting from his notes the bits of Daisy's interventions that were best omitted.

On this occasion, close similarity of wording would suggest Patrick was reciting a tale he had learnt by heart. On the other hand, if minor details varied, odds and ends he'd surely remember if they'd actually happened, the presumption would be that he was making it up and had forgotten exactly what he had said before.

Tom and Ernie went out. Alec turned to the pile of reports on his desk. On top were those compiled during his absence.

Mackinnon had returned from Lincolnshire. According to his official typed report, Mrs. Aidan Jessup appeared to have been kept in ignorance of her husband's and brother-in-law's activities. A paper clip appended a single pencilled sheet: He had not tried to find out from her the whereabouts of her husband because Mrs. Fletcher had assured him that was already known.

Alec crumpled the paper into a ball and chucked it in the wastepaper basket. Mackinnon was getting as good as Ernie Piper at covering up Daisy's meddling.

Tom had talked to Whitcomb, who had returned home from the City at about twenty to seven, by taxi because of the rain. He had seen nothing and no one in the garden. It had been dark and wet and he had not been looking.

No one knew where Lambert was, but his landlady, going into his room to dust (so she claimed), thought he had come back while she was out shopping and taken his razor, toothbrush and hairbrush, and some clothes. Alec was relieved that he had shown signs of life. The man was an incompetent, frequently irritating idiot, but one wouldn't want any harm to come to him, not least because of repercussions from the Americans. Daisy would be glad.

And speaking—or rather, thinking—of the Americans, next in Alec's pile was a lengthy tirade from Superintendent Crane explaining exactly what the U.S. State Department had said to the U.S. embassy had said to the Foreign Secretary had said to the Home Secretary had said to the Assistant Commissioner (Crime). . . . Alec skimmed through it. They were all unhappy.

He sent for a cup of tea.

The last of the new reports was Tom's interview with the Bennetts. They had not changed their story in any material way. They had seen Patrick Jessup, accompanied by—

"Bloody hell!" Alec swore aloud. The constable just entering with his tea slopped it in the saucer. "How could I have forgotten?"

TWENTY-EIGHT

Daisy had done her best to convince the Jessups that, though probably more conversant with police procedure than the average law-abiding citizen, she was not an expert on the subject. Nonetheless, they hung on her words.

She didn't want to give false hope, nor to crush all hope. It was very difficult.

"It's true that the police don't usually ask a person to go to the Yard, or the nearest police station, to answer questions unless they have strong grounds for suspicion," she said. "But sometimes it's just for convenience' sake or to avoid interruptions, or something like that."

"Then it doesn't mean Patrick has been arrested?" Mrs. Jessup asked, hands clasped in supplication.

"No, though it quite often precedes an arrest," Daisy admitted. "But he did move Castellano's body, didn't he? That's an offence, I believe. I don't know if it's a felony or a misdemeanour, but surely it can't be terribly serious." She looked at Irwin, who sat with lips pursed, saying nothing. No help there. "They can hold him for twenty-four hours without charging him, I think."

"If that's all they're asking Patrick about," said Audrey, clinging to her husband, who looked pretty much all in, "does it mean they still might arrest Aidan for killing him? When he's recovered?"

"I really can't—"

"Please, madam . . ." The parlour maid turned pink as everyone looked at her.

"A message from Mr. Patrick?" Mr. Jessup asked eagerly.

"No, sir. It's my sister, sir, from next door. There's a gentleman come to call and Mrs. Dobson—that's Mrs. Fletcher's housekeeper—said Elsie better come over right away 'cause the gentleman's already come by twice when no one's home and he says it's urgent. If you please, madam," she added with a bob towards Daisy.

"Mr. Lambert?" Daisy asked, resigned, and quite glad of an excuse to escape the unhappy Jessups, if only temporarily.

"Yes'm."

"I'd better go, Mrs. Jessup. I'll come back if I can, if you'd like me to."

As she rose, Mr. Jessup followed suit, saying, "We mustn't trespass on your kindness any longer this evening, Mrs. Fletcher. We all greatly appreciate your willingness to give us the benefit of your experience in . . . in such matters."

To a general murmur of thanks, he escorted her to the door of the room. The whole debacle was essentially his fault, Daisy thought. He might have nothing to do with Castellano's death, but he was responsible for the illegal trade with America that had brought his family into the orbit of the bootleggers.

Enid showed her out. In spite of a biting wind, she paused on the Jessups' porch, gazing down across the garden. Where could Castellano's gun be, if a thorough search had not discovered it? Finding it was vital to the Jessup brothers' defence. She had to persuade Alec to search again.

The Greek maiden in the fountain was silhouetted against a light in the Bennetts' front room, a light not obscured by a curtain. They must be watching through their binoculars, gloating over their neighbours' misfortune.

They couldn't spend all their time spying. What rotten luck that they happened to see Patrick coming home. . . . Patrick and . . . That's what she'd been forgetting! Patrick and a man with his hat pulled down . . .

Oh Lord, she thought, not Lambert!

Had Lambert somehow found out Patrick was on his way home, from a trip involving precisely the business it was *his* business to prevent? Had he accosted him, or simply followed him? Had he recognised Castellano as a bootlegger, even as a thug belonging to the "Luckcheese" gang? Could he have . . . ?

No, Lambert was no more capable of cold-blooded murder than Patrick was, or Aidan. He wouldn't know how to set about it, in the first place, and if he did, he couldn't carry it out effectively. The pathologist had to be mistaken!

Daisy hurried down the Jessups' steps and up her own.

Alec strode into the room, leant with both fists on the desk, and loomed threateningly over Patrick Jessup. "You blazing fool!" he snarled. "Why the devil didn't you tell me there was someone with you?"

Patrick blinked up at him. "What . . . ? Oh, Callaghan. D'you know, I'd almost forgotten about him."

Alec dropped into the chair behind the desk, hastily vacated—without comment—by Tom Tring, who in turn dispossessed Ernie Piper. Ernie leant against the wall and selected a fresh, well-sharpened pencil from his endless supply.

"Callaghan," Alec said sarcastically. "We progress. Why did you not tell me about your friend Callaghan?"

"He's no friend of mine," Patrick protested. Alec just looked at him. He wriggled under that hard, cold gaze. "Actually, there were several reasons." Alec let him wriggle. "Well, he wasn't a friend, but he looked after me in America. Sort of like a guide, but he called himself my 'protector.' He worked for the man I was dealing with."

"Name?"

"I'm not supposed to . . . Well, all right, he calls himself Frank Costello, but I think he's Italian, not Irish. He's not our customer. He runs the bootlegging for him. Callaghan—Mickie Callaghan, but that may not be his real name—he is Irish, though—he came to England with me. I don't think Michael Callaghan was the name in his passport, actually. Customs took away his gun. I didn't know he'd brought it, or I'd have told him they wouldn't allow it into the country."

In which case, Alec thought, forewarned he'd have taken precautions and smuggled it in. One must thank heaven for small mercies. He waited.

"It didn't seem fair to get him mixed up in our troubles when . . . when Aidan accidentally killed that man."

"Lord preserve me from chivalrous fools!"

Patrick flushed. "Anyway, he skedaddled pretty quick."

"You saw him go?" Alec asked sharply.

"Well, no. But when I looked for him to ask him to help me get Aidan into the house, he wasn't there."

Alec exchanged a glance with Tom, who nodded with a look of enlightenment.

"I was quite glad, as a matter of fact," Patrick went on. "I didn't really want to take him home."

"Not the sort you'd want to introduce to your mother?"

"No. That was another reason for not mentioning him, keeping him out of things altogether."

"And? You had other reasons?"

"Well, once I'd not told you about him, it seemed best not to complicate matters. There didn't seem to be any point, and I thought you probably wouldn't believe me anyway."

"It didn't cross your mind . . . No, why should it? You believed your brother had killed Castellano."

"Accidentally!"

"Accidentally. As it happens, Castellano did not die from the crack on the head. He was murdered, deliberately, probably while he lay unconscious."

"And you think . . . You thought . . . No wonder . . ." Patrick's mouth dropped open as realisation dawned. "Oh Lord, you think Callaghan did it? While I was taking care of Aidan?"

"And then scarpered. You're not off the hook yet, but it seems likely. If you had informed us right away of his existence, we might have had a chance to catch him. Still, however long the odds, we'll have to give it a shot. Let's have all the details."

Elsie had left Lambert standing in the hall, a mark of disapprobation with which Daisy heartily concurred. It was quite the wrong time to drop in without an invitation.

Lambert seemed uncharacteristically pleased with himself, as Daisy could see, because he had hung his hat on the coat tree and his coat collar was for once turned down. Nana fawned adoringly about his ankles, obviously remembering all those wonderful walks she had taken him on.

"Good evening, Mrs. Fletcher. I thought I'd never catch you home."

"Good evening." She hoped he hadn't had his wallet pinched again and come looking for a bed. Then she remembered that he had rescued her from a sticky wicket next door, albeit inadvertently. "Do come in, Mr. Lambert, and tell me what I can do for you."

She led the way to the small sitting room and waved him to a chair. "May I get you a . . . Oh, no, of course, you don't drink. I'll ring for coffee."

"Never mind that." He was too excited to sit down. "I've collared him!" he announced triumphantly, striding back and forth.

Daisy was not too excited to sit down. She slumped into a chair and enquired, "Collared whom?"

He looked at her in surprise. "The murderer, of course."

Daisy sat up. "The murderer?" she asked incredulously. "You mean the man who killed Castellano?"

"The guy in the park out there. That's his name?" His eyes gleamed behind the horn-rimmed glasses. Daisy noticed a bruise on his cheek. "Oh wowee! That's one of the guys I was sent to find. I've seen him about, but I never could discover his name. Oh wowee!"

"Mr. Lambert, you didn't kill him yourself, did you?"

"Gosh, no, Mrs. Fletcher." He gave her a look of reproach. "I wouldn't do a thing like that, not even for the Government. I saw Callaghan strangle him and I've been tailing him ever since. Didn't you wonder where I was the last couple of days?"

"No. Who the blazes is Callaghan?"

"He's a heavy for the Luciano family."

Daisy thought of the Lucchese family. "Is that the same as an enforcer?"

"More or less."

"You *saw* him kill Castellano? Why on earth didn't you come straight to Alec? What do you mean, you 'collared' him?"

Lambert went for the first question first. "I saw Castellano pull a gat and the Jessup guy tackled him—boy, that was some neat tackle—and both of them went down."

"What happened to the gat? The gun?"

"Geeze, I don't know. It flew up in the air, but I didn't see where it landed. Does it matter?"

"Yes, but never mind now. Go on."

"The other two, Callaghan and the guy with him, they knelt down. I didn't know what was going on, and I couldn't properly see what they were doing, so I worked my way around. When I got to where I had a better view, Callaghan had his hands around Castellano's neck. I was trying to figure out what to do, when up he jumped and ran off, so I followed. Geez, Mrs. Fletcher, d'you think I should've stayed?"

"Yes. No. *I* don't know. No, I suppose you did the right thing. Especially if you've really caught him."

"I have!" Lambert sat down at last. "See, I tailed him for two days. He never stopped moving except to get a meal in cheap cafés. I couldn't collar him in public, so—"

"You could have stopped a policeman."

Lambert looked sulky. "These British bobbies, they didn't take me seriously when I got here. I know Mr. Fletcher doesn't have much of an opinion of me. I wanted to show them I could do the job."

Daisy had been brushed off by police officers—American as well as English—often enough to sympathise, to a degree. "Right-oh. But now you've caught him, you should have gone to Scotland Yard. Where is he?"

"And get sent home with a pat on the head and a dime for bus fare? Sure!"

"Where is he?" Daisy repeated.

"He took a room at a hotel in a lousy part of town, the sort of place where you pay up front and they don't ask too many questions. I slipped the porter a pound to give me his room number and I went up there and knocked on the door. I put on a limey accent and I said I was the manager and he'd been overcharged. Told him I had some change for him."

"Brilliant! Who wouldn't open the door for that?"

"I thought it was kind of cute," Lambert said modestly. "We had a bit of a roughhouse. He got in a lick or two." He touched his cheekbone and winced.

"So I see."

"But I floored him and tied him up with an electrical cord and a ripped-up towel. It had a tear in it already," he assured her. "I know I'm not allowed to arrest anyone here, so I locked him in the closet. Wardrobe. I stuck a sign on the door saying 'Do Not Disturb.' I've been back a couple of times to check and tighten the knots, and he was still there, quiet as a mouse. I don't figure he'll be making a lot of noise that might make the hotel people call in the cops."

"Well done!" said Daisy warmly. "And now it's time *we* called in the cops."

Piper answered the knock on the door. There was a murmur of voices; then he turned back. "It's Mrs. Fletcher on the telephone, Chief."

"I said *no* interruptions!"

"Seems it's about the case and it's desp'rately urgent. I bet she's worked out who did it, Chief."

Alec gave in and went to the phone.

"Darling," said Daisy, "you'll never in a million years guess what . . ."

The Jessups' dinner party in honour of Lambert was a small affair. They didn't want to broadcast their troubles to their friends and acquaintances, even now Patrick and Aidan were cleared of all but minor offences. The Fletchers were invited, of course, and, at Daisy's request, Mrs. Jessup kindly included the Pearsons.

"They're frightfully discreet," Daisy promised. "He's a lawyer, after all. As they saw poor Lambert's disastrous arrival, it's only fair that they should witness his triumph."

Over the meal, Patrick, Aidan, and Lambert told their stories. Alec finished up with the extrication of Callaghan from the wardrobe and his arrest.

Madge was thrilled. "What an adventure!" she exclaimed. "What a terrible time you had, Mrs. Jessup, and Audrey."

"I know you don't need to specify motive in court, Fletcher," Tommy Pearson objected, "but what I don't see is why Callaghan killed Castellano. And come to that, why Castellano aimed the gun at Patrick in the first place."

"He didn't, sir," Lambert blurted out. He blushed as everyone looked at him, but he continued gamely, "He was aiming at Callaghan."

"You may remember, Pearson," said Alec, "when Mr. Lambert appeared among us, we were talking about the bootleggers organising themselves into gangs? It would appear to have come to open warfare among them."

"Castellano belonged to the Lucchese family," said Lambert, "and Callaghan to the Luciano mob."

"Castellano was poaching—or attempting to poach—on Luciano territory," Alec explained. To Mr. Jessup, he added, "That's you, sir. Callaghan was actually sent here to rectify the situation—that is, to deal with Castellano. He nearly got potted first, but thanks to Aidan's tackle, he was presented with the opportunity to turn the tables."

"I have a question, too," said Madge. "What happened to the gun?"

"Oh, I forgot," said Daisy. "I think I've guessed—"

"Great Scott, Daisy!" Alec exploded.

"Well, Mr. Lambert says it flew up into the air. No one's been able to find it. Don't you think it might have landed in the fountain's urn?"

Patrick stared at her. "Gosh, Mrs. Fletcher, what a pity I wasn't aiming at it. That would have been the throw of a lifetime!"

Alec said repressively that he'd send a man to check in the morning.

Champagne came out with dessert. At the head of the table, Mr. Jessup rose to propose a toast to Lambert. After an effusive expression of gratitude, he continued: "And I may add that I've come to a decision. Jessup and Sons will no longer be shipping to America. There's just too much risk involved. Mind you, we shan't refuse to deal with any customers who come along, no matter their country of origin, but what they do with their purchases is up to them. So there's another success for you, Mr. Lambert."

He raised his glass and everyone drank to the blushing American.

"Speech!" cried Tommy Pearson.

"Speech!" Patrick seconded him.

"Who, me?" Lambert spluttered.

"Yes, do please say a word, Mr. Lambert," said Mrs. Jessup.

Lambert stood up. His mouth opened, and closed again. Then he leant forward and picked up the unused Champagne glass that Enid had set at his place.

"The heck with seltzer!" he said recklessly. "Pour me Champagne!"